WHAT HAPPENS AFTER

portia moore

What Happens After

This is a work of fiction. Names, characters, businesses, places, events, and incidents are either the products of the author's imagination or used in a fictitious manner. Any resemblance to actual persons, living or dead, or actual events is purely coincidental.

Cover Design:
Murphy Rae, Indie Solutions

Cover Photography:
MHP Photography

Editing and Proofreading:
Cassie Cox, Joy Editing and Chelsea Kuhel, Madison Seilder

Interior Design and Formatting:
Christine Borgford, Perfectly Publishable

prologue

HOW CAN YOU love someone when you know they will never truly love you back because they can't ever love you back? Your brain should stop you from loving them. There should be a defense mechanism embedded deep within you to stop your soul from allowing you to give your heart to someone who doesn't deserve it, who doesn't even want it, someone who *couldn't* have it even if they did want it.

Unfortunately, there's no fail-safe for love, no brake to stop you from throwing your life—and the lives of those around you—completely out of balance. There are no warning lights or flashing danger signs. There's nothing to stop the planted seeds from growing and taking root. And once they grow, there's nothing you can do about it. Your desire to water those wretched seeds only increases. Once you realize those seeds weren't supposed to grow, it's already too late. At seventeen, you haven't got a clue . . .

gwen

HE LIED TO me. What's worse than him lying to me as my husband and the father of my child, my so-called soul mate, is that he lied to me as my friend. Our history, our bond, our love, didn't stop my best friend from lying to me all these years. He kept secrets from me, and it hurts. It hurts so badly—the half-truths, the deception, the words I never ever thought I'd use . . . it all hurts.

I never thought that anything associated with love could be so painful, but love betrayed definitely is. This unfathomable heartache snuffs out all of my urges toward forgiveness because now I know the truth. At least what I *imagine* the truth to be—those images run continuously through my mind.

The love that once was so sure has been replaced by anguish . A pain that erases the joy and closeness we shared, pushing it further and further away, like a mirage—unreal. Our history seems more like an illusion. Only vague images of our love and life together remain, but those spectral images are tainted.

While my own memories are like a half-forgotten dream, those moments I *imagine* are all too vivid. Everywhere I look, I see betrayal, and I can't get his duplicitousness out of my head. My faith has been shaken to the core. Those thoughts become an unbearable weight, a sickening fog that suffocates me, a stench so bad it chokes all the beauty and joy out of life. All that remains is blinding rage, anger, bitterness, and hatred. These thoughts turn my consciousness into an abyss that I can't escape. I secretly pray for the moment I'll feel nothing because anything is better than this.

Adultery.

Affair.

Betrayal.

Words I try to escape from as the hours tick by. It feels like time has slowed down, but in reality it is moving so fast it sneaks up on me—like a thief in the night. I look in the mirror at the fine lines that have formed around my mouth and eyes, things I overlooked before but are like flashing lights now. I wonder when this happened. When was my youth stolen? Did it happen when Christopher turned ten, or did it happen when I first saw my grandchild? Is today just the first day I noticed them? This morning when I looked in the mirror, I didn't see them, but they were there. Right? I just never noticed until now. I wasn't even alarmed by the increasing number of grey hairs I've accumulated over the years. Why should I worry over trivial things like that anyway when there's so much more to regret?

I always knew life was precious. You realize it when you find out you'll never be able to produce it. When you find out that you're unable to do the one thing you believe you were put on the planet to do—your God-given right as a woman to bear children. I have come to appreciate that fertility is a gift, not a right, even though I'm slightly resentful. The realization of just how precious the gift of life is became even more evident once I heard the words, "You have stage-three breast cancer." Aging, living is a blessing, not something to worry about. When I was able to say, "I beat cancer," I quit worrying about the small things. If I could survive cancer, I could survive anything. To wake up in the morning and take a breath became so much more of a welcome event than one would ever think.

So it isn't a wonder why today, of all days, I notice the things I didn't use to care about but *today* mean everything.

I wish I were just being dramatic, but without hesitation, I can say being alive doesn't seem as important as it once was. These badges of maturity feel less like an honor and more like a punishment, a cruel inside joke I'm not in on.

What else could I think of it as?

My husband, my dear husband, the man I love more than anything in the entire world, has always made me feel beautiful. When I said wrinkles, he said laugh lines, and not only that, he said they made me more beautiful than the day he first met me. I believed him.

I believed him because he's my best friend, my confidant, my own personal superhero . . . or at least he was yesterday. Today, he's my personally-crafted villain. One who knows my weaknesses and knows me better than anyone else in the world. I've shared my deepest secrets with him. He's been my glue when my world was on the cusp of falling apart several times over—at least I thought he was. Maybe he wasn't, or maybe he was for a while, or maybe it was all a façade.

Maybe I was just a fool. I must have been a fool, an arrogant one. Because until today, I never understood why the women I grew up with felt self-conscious about their appearances as each birthday passed. Because I knew it all, I had it all figured out—they'd married the wrong man. I thought that if you married your soul's true mate, a life partner, they should appreciate who *you* are *now*, who you've grown to become. My husband, my best friend, told me that, and like a fool in love, I never once questioned it—until today.

Because today is the day I found out that my husband—my best friend, the man I turned my world upside down for, whom I gave my youth to, my best days, my joy, my entire self—has not only been screwing my son's best friend but also has a child with her. Before today, I considered her—the twenty-seven-year-old without a single laugh line who grew up before my very eyes—like a daughter. But now I know her as my husband's *lover.*

So today, I look in this mirror and see every single thing that makes me different from the girl he fell in love with *and* the girl he betrayed me with. Today, I question all the times I stood in front of this mirror, pulling myself together to greet each day with a smile while I fought the flesh-eating monster living inside me, to make life easier for him. Today it all seems pointless, worthless! If I'd just given in when death came for me, I wouldn't be experiencing the pain I'm in now, a fate that seems worse than death. I hate thinking like this! I hate these thoughts, but they're honest and feel more real than anything else today. Truer than love, more honest than forgiveness, and more authentic than the last twenty-five years of what I thought was an unbreakable marriage.

I want to cry and vomit at the same time. Maybe I could just crawl into myself as if I didn't exist. Here I stand, forty-nine years old, a woman and mother who beat the odds of advanced cancer. Yesterday morning, I felt invincible. Now I feel as fragile as a seventeen-year-old whose heart has been broken, crushed, demolished.

A grown woman decimated and paralyzed.

It's hard to remember how to move. Not so much in the literal sense, even though my limbs feel heavy, but how do I get out of this space I'm in? How do I escape from what feels like a prison? My husband has cheated, broken my trust, and produced a child with my *son's* best friend.

When I think about Christopher, all of this feels so much worse. He had to be the one to tell me. The words that came from his mouth crashed all around me. They were the worst words I've ever heard, words so jarring, so life-altering, so unbelievable my psyche couldn't comprehend them. My soul sang out to God, *Please, please let what he just said, what was just released into the universe, be a mistake.* Somewhere in my mind, I believed it could be changed, that there was an error that could be easily fixed. That it could be taken back. But it couldn't. It couldn't ever be taken back.

I'd give anything just to have found out first so my son wouldn't have had the burden of delivering the message from hell. To say things that had to have been almost harder for him to say than for me to hear . . . my baby . . . their baby. My son has a sister, a half-sister.

My husband has a child, a biological one. One I could never give him, no matter how much I wanted to, but she could. A twenty-seven-year-old who can barely remember where her keys are was able to give my husband a child.

"Mom?" Christopher's voice comes from the other side of the bathroom door, where I've been for I don't know how long. A half hour, or has it been two hours? "Mom, can I come in?"

His voice is low and laced with sorrow, like when he was a little boy who'd done something bad and was coming to tell on himself.

I try to muster up sound from my dry, constricted throat. "Umm, one minute, honey."

I move quickly and turn on the sink to splash water on my face. I try but fail miserably to mask my pain, the dull, throbbing ache coursing through me that has my breath tightened and my head heavy. I attempt to break out of the catatonic state I've been trapped in and conjure up any amount of strength to hold myself up, to keep my emotions from pouring out of me. My son . . . my son needs to see that I'm not a complete blubbering mess even if I have to fake it. I take one more breath before opening the door.

I open it and look at the man I've raised since he was five years old. He used to be so small. Now he's a foot taller than me, broad-shouldered, and can appear intimidating but wouldn't hurt a fly. When I look into his eyes, I never know who I'll see: the mild-mannered gentleman with a heart of gold or the person who's built a wall around himself to protect himself from being hurt. I should've taken notes on how to build that wall.

His big green eyes find mine. They shift from my face to his feet several times before I force myself to give him a smile and hug him the way I did when he was a little boy.

"I'm so sorry, Mom." His voice quivers.

I rub his back and open my mouth to tell him everything will be okay, that this all will work out, but I can't bring myself to do it. I can't lie to him, because I know how it feels to be lied to, betrayed, and treated like a child who can't handle life's realities.

"I shouldn't have told you like that. I-I—"

His voice gives in, and I pray for him to have the strength he needs—that he doesn't fall apart. He has his own daughter he has to be strong for now. My and his father's problems should be just that—ours. But I know life doesn't work like that; love doesn't allow you to just shift burdens that you want to help carry.

"You have nothing to be sorry about," I say, commanding my voice to steady.

"How could they do that to you, to us? How could he do that, Mom?"

I can see his distress as I continue to rub his back, hoping to calm him down. "I don't know."

I've been trying to figure out how he could lie and betray me and his son, how he could do so without guilt, how he could continue to live as if nothing had changed, and I can't come up with anything. Christopher lets me go and turns his back toward me, grabbing a towel and wiping his face. I walk past him out of the bathroom and sit on the settee in my bedroom.

"Is your dad still out there?" I ask quietly, gesturing to my bedroom door where his father has been camped out.

"Yeah, he fell asleep." He's cross, his jaw tight and his hands clenched into fists.

As angry as I am with William, I loathe what I've just seen, the look of hatred and bitterness that flashed across his son's face at the mention of him.

"You should come back to Chicago with me and Lauren. You can't stay here with him."

My thoughts haven't even gone beyond what I heard tonight, but he's right. I can't stay in this house with him. I don't know if I can stay in this house at all, where they . . . where he and Lisa . . .

"This is my fault. If I wasn't friends with her . . ." he mutters.

I gently grip his chin and make him look at me. "This is *not* your fault. You had nothing to do with this." My voice is stern, but he shakes his head. I see his anger intensify.

"That's the thing. He didn't think about me. He didn't think about you! I can't forgive him for this. There's no way we can get past this."

I put my face in my hands and try to think of life without William. A day without William. To think that the William I believed in is no more. He's a lie, a distant memory. No longer my protector, my confidant, my best friend. I squeeze my eyes shut and rub my temples. How do we get past this? How do I save my family when the damage is beyond repair? I fought cancer with all I had to save my family. I knew the family would crumble without me. At the time, William and Chris had been at odds because of Cal, and without me as their buffer and mediator, I knew they'd be lost. Now at least Chris has his own family, a beautiful little girl and a wife who loves him the way I loved William.

Loved William?

I wish after all of this I could truly use past tense with confidence. At least whatever happens, Christopher will be fine. He has to be.

"Do you want to leave in the morning?"

His question interrupts my thoughts.

"I just want to sleep right now, I think. We'll figure everything out tomorrow," I tell him, squeezing his hands.

He looks at me with worry and concern, and a moment later, his face is hard and his expression has gone cold. "Do you want me to make him leave?"

His voice is low and bitter, which makes my stomach drop. I can't take more fighting, more confrontation, confusion, and anger. Is this all that's left of my family? No. It can't be. I want to fix it, but how do I fix it when I'm broken? How do you fix yourself *after* you break?

chapter two

IT'S SEVEN IN the morning. I've been sitting in the chair by my window since five. I've been dressed and ready to go since before then, but I can't seem to bring myself to walk out the door. I watched the sun rise, leaving the darkness of the previous night behind, and living on a farm, early mornings are normal. If only I had a miracle to do the same with my life. I dread the idea of leaving my room. I haven't seen William working outside, so there's a good chance he's still outside my door—camped out, wanting to talk, wanting to apologize, wanting to explain. There's no way to explain sleeping with your son's best friend.

There's no explanation that can make this better, nowhere to move forward. I barely know any details about the how or when. Then again, anything that increases my knowledge isn't going to help either; it's only going to hurt. I can't take any more hurt than I already have.

I still have a son and a family. A family that needs me, that I can't run away from. My faith teaches forgiveness, but how can I forgive this? How can I forgive *him* and mean it? How can I forgive him for having a child outside of our marriage? How can I forgive betrayal, lies, and secrets? I should have had Chris ask him to leave last night. How can I face him without wanting to rip off his head or bursting into tears?

I open the door and sigh with relief when I see that William isn't sitting next to it. I'm relieved, but I also feel disgusted with myself because I'm disappointed by his absence. I haven't felt this conflicted since I was a teenager. I close the bedroom door and cautiously make my way down the stairs to the kitchen. I usually cook breakfast every morning no matter what. This is the first time I haven't since I was sick. No, that's not right. There was also that time when Chris went missing and I left Lisa to wait on him while Will and I went looking for him, and . . . I feel sick.

I try to push her name out of my mind because whenever I think of it, I feel rage boil up from the pit of my stomach. I'm angry at her, at him, at myself. How could I not see it? How could I not have a clue that something was going on between them? How could I not notice my husband was having an affair right under my nose? I have to be the biggest idiot on the planet. Before I step over the kitchen threshold, the smell hits me. As I step in, I see a plate already fixed with waffles, grits, fresh fruit, and sausage.

"Good morning."

I look up and see Will step into the kitchen from the pantry. He looks a mess. He looks how I feel. I try to speak, but no words come out of my mouth.

"I-I made breakfast. I tried to make it healthy. You've been talking a lot about that lately, and I've listened," he says, his blue eyes encapsulated by puffy eyelids. His hair is completely disheveled, as if he's run his hands through it a thousand times. His five o'clock shadow is pronounced and his dimples absent because his lips are pressed so firmly together.

This is the first time I've looked at him since I found out. The first time I've ever looked at the man I married and felt anything but love, hope, and strength. It's funny how a few hours have changed everything for us.

Seeing him makes my emotions crash against each other. Each second I stand here, I become more enraged. How could he do something so stupid, so selfish, and so . . . unforgivable? And he stands here like nothing has happened, as if we're going to eat breakfast together and everything will be okay?! Nothing will be okay. I realize this as I stand in my kitchen in front of him, the same place he and his whore ate with me and sat with our family.

"I can't believe you did this to us." The words are automatic, as if triggered by his presence. They hurt to speak but hurt even more to hold in.

"Gwen."

His voice breaks as he tries to approach me, but I step back and push my arms out to let him know to stay back.

"Please, just let me explain," he begs. His voice sounds pained, and my heart aches for him—for me

"I can't. I can't. I don't want to hear it, and there's nothing that you can explain. Anything you say will only make things worse!" I'm frantic. It's a lie; I want to know everything, but I don't think I can survive hearing it.

"Gwen, you're my best friend," he says with tears in his eyes.

I have to turn away. I grab a chair to keep my balance. To see him like this hurts, but I can't hurt for him. He didn't hurt for me. I don't even know if he hurts for me now. I'm sure he hurts for himself.

"I never meant to hurt you. I know how that sounds, but if I could take it back—"

"You did hurt me! Worse than anything I've ever experienced, and you cannot take it back." My voice is loud and unrecognizable.

His gaze isn't on me but set on the floor instead.

"In our home, William. How could you? With Lisa of all people!" I'm close to screaming at the top of my lungs.

"There's no excuse for what I did," he whispers.

His words make me want to throw something. To see him broken . . . I haven't seen him like this since I was sick. A chill shoots down my spine.

"Were you seeing her when I was sick?" I ask cautiously. I don't know if I can take hearing the answer. His eyes widen, and he approaches me; I retreat again.

"No. I stopped before I found out you lost our child," he promises.

The pain of that memory shoots through me. I know he thinks what he said should give me some consolation, but it doesn't. It tears open a wound I've tried to forget, a wound that has become purulent. "You stopped out of pity. You stopped out of a sense of duty, guilt, and a mournful promise but not out of love. Do you love her?"

He shakes his head. "It's always been you, Gwen—"

My eyes narrow on his. "Except when you were screwing her."

He looks defeated, as though he's given up and realized there's absolutely nothing he can say to fix this. I feel as though my soul is beginning to crumble. I can't talk to him about this. I can't think about this.

"I need you to leave."

"Gwen, please. I'll give you time. I owe you that, but we can get past this." His voice deepens with each word to the more familiar, authoritative tone I'm used to from him instead of the sad, broken one.

"How dare you!" I scream. "You have a daughter, William! A daughter! How can we get past that? Tell me?!"

He covers his face. "I didn't know." He attempts to touch me again, and I swat him away.

"You didn't know? You think that makes it better?" My whole body shakes as I shed angry tears.

Tears are falling down his face now too. He gets on his knees and grabs my waist. "What can I do? Tell me—what can I do? I'll do anything. Please!"

I try to get out of his grasp, but he holds me tighter.

"We can get through this. I promise you we can," he cries against my stomach.

I realize getting him to let me go will be futile unless I hit him on the head with one of the table utensils, so I gently grasp his face and make him look up at me. "*We* don't have to do anything, and *you* don't get to decide that. *You* decided to ruin us—everything we had, our family, our history, *you* decided that. *I* get to decide whether I can even consider the possibility of looking at you without seeing you as the person who hurt me more than anyone in my entire life.

"You have no idea how this feels, how badly I hurt. You can't, because if you got it, if you understood, you would leave me alone. You'd know how much it hurts me to see you, to hear your voice as I look around our home and think about how you desecrated and disrespected the place where we built our family. And the very worst part of it all is that I was completely oblivious. I thought we were fine, that we were okay. I've been happy!"

"I've been happy too! I haven't been involved with Lisa in years!" he shouts, and hearing him say her name makes my stomach churn.

I cover my face, trying to catch my breath.

"Is everything okay?" my son's wife, Lauren, says from behind me.

"William was just leaving."

His face falls, his expression crushed. "We have to talk about this."

"I need you to go now! Right now, William." My screeching makes even me flinch.

He glances behind me at Lauren, then he nods. "If that's what you want."

He wipes the tears from his face. I've only seen William cry once in his life besides today, and that was when his mother passed away. Now I have to squelch the instinct to go to him and hug him and tell him everything will be okay. A task made easier as my urge to lash out at him consumes me.

"I'm just going to get a few things, and I'll go. If that's what you want," he says quietly, his eyes on mine.

After taking a deep breath, I say, "There isn't any other choice."

His eyes fall to the floor, and he walks past me. As I hear him leave the room, I feel my spirit shatter. The wail I release is embarrassing. I cover my face with my palms, immediately soaking them with tears. I feel two arms wrap around me.

"Is there anything I can do?" Lauren asks.

I can't speak because I can't stop crying.

"HERE YOU GO," Lauren hands me a cup of chamomile tea. She cautiously sits across the table from me.

In the short time we've known each other, we've grown close. She has my granddaughter, so that automatically puts her near the top of the list of my favorite people, and she makes my son happy, happier than I've seen in such a long time. Things had been going so well until yesterday. When everything came to a head—no, that explanation is too mild. When the volcano erupted and destroyed everything near it.

"Thank you," I say, breaking myself from my thoughts. I can't imagine how awkward it is for her to be here right now. I know that she and Lisa had grown to like one another. Now to be in the middle of all of this . . ."I'm sorry you're here for all of this. We're usually quite the normal family."

My pathetic attempt at levity falls flat. Her eyes widen, and she shakes her head.

"No need for apologies. I-I can't imagine what it's like to be in your shoes right now," she says earnestly.

"It's not the greatest place to be right now," I say, successfully coming off a little lighter.

She nods again and lets out a deep breath. "Chris and I talked, and we would love to have you come back to Chicago with us if that's something you would like." She sounds hopeful.

"Thank you for the invitation. As much as I'd love to have more time with my Caylen, I just don't think it's the right time," I say before taking a sip of tea.

She nods understandingly.

"I hate to run from my own home, you know?" I swallow as hard as I can to keep my voice from breaking. "But how can I stay here? Everywhere I look . . ." I lift my hands off the table in disgust. "I don't know where they . . ." I'm too exhausted to complete my thought.

"Maybe it wasn't as bad as you think," Lauren says lightly, and her face scrunches up immediately. "That was a stupid thing to say. I just think sometimes our imagination, the unknown, is so much worse than what actually happened." She gives a small shrug.

"It's almost funny. Yesterday we sat here and ate breakfast, and everything was fine. All was well. Now today—" I stop as my voice breaks. I hate who I've become, a sobbing pitiful mess. I push the tea away as I rest my head in my hands on the table. "I shouldn't have told William to leave. I can't stay in this house."

"Where are you going to go?" she asks.

That's the question. I don't want to intrude on my son and his family just as they're settling into their life together. I surely don't want to be around my granddaughter in the state I'm in now—hating her grandfather. She's only one, but I'm sure she'll still pick up my feelings rather than my words. I don't want to be the cloud over them. They've had enough gloom to last a lifetime.

"I have a sister. I can stay there until I get my bearings," I murmur. "Gia's great. She'll be able to put up with my moping."

Lauren stands and walks over to me. "I think you're allowed to sulk." She gives me a warm smile and a big hug. I can tell her smile is an attempt to cover her worry. "And it's great that you have someone who can be there for you. I always wished I had a sister or brother."

"It's funny, I always wanted Chris to have a sibling. Now he does," I say, unable to mask my bitterness.

"Do you want me to help you pack or drive you to your sister's?"

"No. The drive will clear my head. I know I look like a mess, but I'm fine. I've been through worse." Before I leave the kitchen, my feet stop, unable to move, and I feel embarrassed about what I'm about to ask. "Lauren, did you—was there anything you noticed between them since you've been here?" I feel more pathetic than ever.

Lauren walks closer to me and looks me directly in the eye. "No, not once."

I laugh at myself. She isn't his wife. Whether she noticed anything or not isn't important. I was the fool. I was blind, and what bothers me the most is the little voice in my head that tells me I had this coming . . .

lisa

LOVE IS LIKE a parasite rooting within you. It affects every part of you that matters, tainting it. A virus that spreads so quickly that by the time you realize you've caught it, there's no stopping it from gaining ground. It's a drug that changes how you feel, how much you eat, what you hear, and the decisions you make. A good day on love is better than any high imaginable; a bad day on love immobilizes you. Love unrequited is even worse than love unspoken. Love—something that you've tried to forget about, a door that had been shut though not locked. Yesterday I blew that door wide open, and every foul thing it hid became visible for all to see.

It's my worst nightmare. My deepest, darkest secret revealed. My worst fear confirmed. I had to tell the one person who has been one of the only real friends I've ever had. A person who never judged me, who loved me like a sister, and I told him something that would destroy him. That did destroy him. I thought that since telling him was the right thing, it would at least make me feel better, my conscience satisfied for the first time in years. But it didn't.

It didn't make him feel better, and with the way he looked at me, I know he'll never ever forgive me. Time won't heal the hatred he had in his eyes. The thing I feel worst about is the small glimpse of disappointment he showed before pure malice consumed him. That hurt more than anything, the thought that all the things everyone has said about me and my family—the rumors, everything he refused to believe about me—were true. I didn't live up to his expectations. Turns out I'm nothing but a whore's daughter who grew up to be just like her mother. I'm worse actually because to my knowledge, my mom never slept with her best friend's married father. She never did something so careless to someone she called a friend.

When you're young, you don't think; you just feel. You crave, you want, and you take. I wish I could just blame that on my age, on being a stupid hormonal teenager, but I can't. Because I'm still like that. As much as I don't want to, I think of myself first, and as much as I wish I could convince myself that I told Chris the truth because it was the noble, right thing to do, I didn't tell him because of that. I told him because it was eating away at me. The secret, knowing what I caused to happen, and I was afraid—afraid of being responsible for raising a little girl alone and even more afraid that she'll turn out like me.

That scares me more than anything as I look at her sleeping. The same long blond hair as mine, the blood running through her veins that was passed down from my mother and her mother. I want her to stay peaceful, sweet, and innocent. I want her to hold on to the lie that she isn't a Garrett. I wish more than anything that the lie she knows were real, that her real mother was a sweetheart, that her real mother was selfless and would do anything in the world to make her happy. I wish more than anything to trade places with the woman who deserves to be her mom. I don't even want to call myself her mother. I don't deserve that title.

I gave my daughter away before she was even born. I abandoned her before she was even thought of. I wish more than anything I could trade places with the woman who deserves to be her mom so that she could raise her to be the woman she's capable of, but I can't. She's stuck with me, and my punishment is telling her that the world she knew was a dream, a lie. My daughter's reality is that she has a mother with no clue how to be responsible for anyone besides herself and a father who didn't even know she existed.

I fight back tears because I know out of everyone involved in this, I deserve tears the least. I never meant to hurt anyone, but I guess that's what every fucked-up person says after they hurt so many people. You don't mean it though. In that moment, you don't think about someone else's hurt—you think about pleasure, your own pleasure. Something that feels so good can't be that bad, right? That's what you tell yourself at least, and when you're young, you believe it.

"Hey." My friend, or anti-friend, Aidan stands in the doorway. His expression's unreadable, and I'm grateful for that. "I've got to head out."

He looks tired. I'm sure he didn't get much sleep last night with all my crying and him coddling me. Aidan isn't a coddler. He's the friend you call when you want someone's ass kicked. He's the doer, not the one who stops and thinks. Aidan is anything but the person you call to sulk with.

"Are you going to be okay?" he asks, looking at me, but his eyes don't reach mine.

I can't blame him for being unable to look me in the eye. Chris is his real best friend, not the anti-friend he and I are. Enemies who have been friends with the same person for so long we had no choice but to become friends in the most unfriendly way possible. We argue, we tease, but the reason we even tolerate the other is Chris—was Chris. Now that Chris wants nothing to do with me, I wonder how much longer Aidan will be around.

"I'll be fine. I have to be, right?" I ask with a fake laugh.

He frowns at me. "I'll come back and check on you after I get some sleep. Your couch has fucked up my back. I need to sleep in my own bed." He massages his shoulder.

"Thank you for everything, A," I say, getting off the bed and walking over to him.

A small smile creeps across his face, showing two dimples. His blue eyes are soft and comforting, unlike the wide grin he usually flashes me after an insult. "You're good. Well, *you're* not good, but no thanks necessary." He nudges me playfully in the shoulder.

It's comforting, our banter. Our petty arguments are the only things I'll have to remind me of my best friend.

"C-can you let me know how he is once you talk to him?" I say, sounding desperate even to myself.

"I-I don't know," he says hesitantly.

"Please, Aidan. I just want to know he's okay."

His eyes fall from my face to the floor, then he puts his hands on my shoulders. "He'll survive this." He gives me a reassuring squeeze, and I nod. He opens the door to leave, sweeping his hand over the blond hair that's grown out from the buzz cut he had during the tour he just finished. "I don't know a lot of people who can forgive what you did, but if there's anyone who can, it's Chris."

I nod.

"I'll see you later, okay?" he says before heading down the stairs of my porch.

I shut the door and rest on it once it's closed. I take a deep breath and wish for my head to stop pounding and for the thousand-pound weight on my chest to give me just a little bit of a break. I sink into my couch and pull a pillow onto my lap. My thoughts are going in slow motion. Everything that happened yesterday consumes me. My mind tries to drift to before yesterday, to a time I've done my best to block out.

I'm thankful when my doorbell rings. Aidan must have left something. I push myself off the couch, open the door, and my heart clenches when I see him standing on my porch. His usually bright blue eyes are dim and squinted at me. His golden brown hair, which is so much longer than the days I used to run my hands through it, looks as if he hasn't touched it all day. His facial hair has grown since I saw him a couple of days ago, a far cry from the five o'clock shadow covering his rigid face. His presence is overwhelming. Anger and sadness radiate off him, his emotions so strong that if they were a physical being, I'd be knocked down. It's been so long since we were this close, since we were alone. I don't know why I haven't prepared myself for this moment, but I'm completely vulnerable.

"I thought you understood, Lisa," he says, his voice not matching his heated gaze. His voice is quiet, somber, and broken.

"I don't know what to say to you, Will," I force the words from my throat.

He pushes the door open and stalks past me to the center of the living room. I shut the door and cross my arms.

"I didn't have a choice," I say, cautiously approaching him.

"We all have a choice!" he roars.

I don't say anything. I know that he's not done, and I don't want his yelling to wake up Willa. With how he is now, they'd have an awful first meeting.

"You could have talked to me first. Given me some type of warning. I was blindsided! Chris will never forgive me for this!" he says frantically, walking closer to me so we're only inches apart.

"We haven't talked in a very long time. You wanted it that way, remember?" I say harshly.

His eyes widen. "So this is your way of getting back at me? Years later and at the worst possible time?"

"This isn't about getting back at you. How could you think that? This is about doing the right thing. I thought that it would help Chris!" I yell back.

"Help him? You think destroying his family is the way to help him?" He laughs condescendingly.

"I thought that—I just thought that maybe if he knew the truth, about us and what he saw before he started to act differently, that it would help his treatment." Tears start to fall from my eyes. Not for William, not for me, but for Chris.

"Him not remembering what happened between us was the best thing that ever happened. Not just for you and me but for him! You broke him. That was something that never had to be brought up. He was doing fine. You saw it!" His tone is desperate and I don't know if he's trying to convince me or himself.

We are both guilty. We relished in the secret that was gratefully forgotten. It was almost like a do-over with Chris. When I came back home after college and realized that not only had he forgiven me but, it was like it had never happened, it was a gift. Or so I thought then. I let out a deep breath.

"Chris hasn't been fine since he saw us that night. He's been seeing a therapist on and off for years. Him not remembering seeing us together wasn't a blessing, it's *his* curse, a repressed memory that has been tearing him apart. We always knew it. No one just simply forgets seeing his father fucking his best friend!" I yell back at him. He lowers his head and shakes it.

"I thought that maybe he had really forgiven us. That he chose to not ever bring it up because he didn't want to hurt his mom. I didn't literally think that he repressed seeing us together," I say pleadingly. He looks up at me with a scowl.

"Well, let me just say, Dr. Lisa, that he is still not fine. None of us are after your confession," he says with a forced laugh, and tears slip from his eyes. He wipes them away quickly.

"Is he okay?" I ask desperately.

"What do you think?" he asks.

"Lisa, I can't sleep with all the yelling," Willa says quietly, standing in the doorway.

"I'm sorry, honey. My friend is just upset. Go back to bed and watch some cartoons, okay?" I say before ushering her back to the bedroom.

When I return to the living room, Will's face is expressionless. His wide blue eyes glisten. "Is that her?"

I feel butterflies in my stomach. I've imagined this moment so many times, but it was never like this. In my imagination, the daydreams of a nineteen-year-old girl, I would call him right before I went into labor. He would rush to my side and tell me everything would be okay, and I would have my family. Then it didn't matter if I had to share him with the other one. When you're young, you don't see life for what it is. You disregard its harsh realities. You think if you just wish hard enough and say your wishes aloud, believe in them long enough, you can give them life and they can be granted. Life doesn't necessarily turn out like that.

"Yes," I say quietly.

He nods, makes his way slowly to the couch, and sits. I look at the man I had my first crush on, whom I gave myself to, whom I wanted to not just love me but be in love with me more than anything. After he ended us, he ended me for a while. I was heartbroken, I was lovesick, and I went into mourning.

"Why didn't you tell me?" he says, his eyes finding mine.

For the first time in years, I'm drawn in once more. I remember everything between us, everything I've pretended for eight years never happened, and I close my eyes to break the spell. "I thought I was doing the right thing."

I sit next to him, keeping the requisite inches between us. He puts his head in his hands and lets out a deep sigh.

"For who?" he mutters.

"For all of you. For Chris, for Gwen," I say, feeling guilty even saying her name. As much as I grew to love Will, my love didn't stop the guilt growing inside me, knowing what I was doing to her. A woman who had only shown me kindness. She never looked at me as anything other than Chris's friend. She didn't judge me based on who my mother was or what she did, and knowing that I was what everyone said I would be hurt more than anything.

"Does she know that I'm her—her father?"

I sigh. "She doesn't even know that I'm her mother." I chuckle sadly.

He looks at me questioningly. "How is that possible?"

I roll my eyes. It's funny that he thinks I could balance a life as a preschool teacher and bartender and secretly be a mom. "She hasn't been with me, Will."

"Where has she been?" he asks, his eyes zeroed in on his hands.

"With Aunt Dani. I went to live with her after I found out I was pregnant. I knew she'd make a better mother than me," I say honestly.

His head snaps up. I now have his full attention.

"And what about her father?" he asks angrily.

"What father? The father who was married and had a family? The father she'd have been a bastard to?" I say, tears falling from my eyes.

"That's not fair. If anyone knew how much a child would mean to me, it would've been you," he says.

I ignore the stab of guilt. "Tell me, if I had come to you and told you that I was pregnant—or better yet, after she was born—what would you have done? Would you have accepted her with open arms, or would she have been a secret love child? Is that what you would have wanted for our daughter?"

"And now? Now what life do you want for her?" he asks, his eyes boring into mine.

I look away as memories of touches trying to fight their way to the forefront of my consciousness, feelings that I've fought to keep down for so long. "I want her to have a better life than I did," is all I can say.

"Gwen kicked me out of the house. Chris is furious with me. I don't know how he's going to handle all of this." His deep sigh contains palpable anguish as he runs his hand through his hair. "I've got to figure out a way to fix this. I can't lose my family."

I feel anger rising in me. This man whom I loved and gave my youth to, whose child I brought into the world, is talking about how he has to save his family as if the little girl in the next room isn't his family. I try to calm my anger—I'm being selfish and unreasonable. I have to stop myself from lashing out at him.

"I'd like to meet her when I'm not like this," he says, standing from the sofa. I immediately stand as well.

"Where are you going?" I ask him as I follow him toward the door.

"Right now, I don't think I'd be a good father to anyone. I need to—I just need a little time. I'll be back. I promise."

When he leaves, I do something I haven't done in years. I cry over him and hope this isn't the beginning of a trend.

chapter three

gwen

IF THERE WAS ever a complicated relationship between sisters, it would be Gia and me. My mother called us summer and winter; she not only called us that but named us that. Gwen Summer and Gia Winter are what's on our birth certificates accompanied by our last name.

We're different in almost every way. Gia has dark, almost coal-black, long hair with hazel eyes, taking after my mother. I'm my father's child, with light brown hair—almost red in the light—green eyes, and pale skin. She was the perfect child: beautiful, well-mannered, eager to please, and enjoyed the things mothers want their little girls to do. I was born on the hottest day of summer, so my father said I was born to be temperamental. My mother had to practically fight me to get me into a dress, and I hid my homework under the ugly frilly things she tried to make me wear. I grated on my mother's last nerve, but my father was always my knight in shining armor, swooping in to save me when things got rocky. My father was my best friend. He understood me. We were alike, different from my mother in every way. The old saying that opposites attract definitely applied to them.

My mother was raised to be the wife of someone prestigious. She came from New Orleans, her parents were very old money, and she was groomed to be the wife of a senator, governor, or a CEO—someone proper, important, and wealthy. My father was a musician passing through after a canceled gig in Texas. He was a free spirit who blew my mother away from all that she knew. Looking at my mother was like looking at Gia, and mother said I'd always been my father's child.

Looking back, I admit I was jealous of Gia. I envied the relationship she had with my mother, how she so easily lived up to the image my mother had of her daughters, how it was never forced, how naturally elegant and beautiful she was. Beautiful in a classic way. Gia's features are entirely symmetrical, her voice the perfect hint of feminine, and not only that, she's smart and dainty but always a little cold.

Most people took her coldness as mysteriousness—at least boys did. If we hadn't been born into the same family, in the same house, we would probably have never been friends. But since we were sisters, we were best friends. She was my secret-keeper, and I think she found my rambunctious, rebellious nature entertaining. Since my antics highlighted her attributes, I'm sure she didn't mind them as much as an older sister normally would. When I was punished and my dad wasn't around to save me from my mother's iron will, I'd run to Gia and jump in her arms for protection. Gia always had a way of reasoning with my mother that calmed her and even calmed me—for a while, that is.

I haven't seen Gia in almost seven months, a timeframe I couldn't have imagined as a little girl. I'd like to say we grew apart, but the reality is a coincidence, a force of nature so to speak, almost tore us apart. It didn't, but it had certainly left holes in what used to be a solid relationship. As I walk up the stairs to her home, the circumstance that damaged our relationship is no longer content to lay dormant. It has moved to the forefront of my mind, taunting me, teasing me, wrapping threads of the past all around me.

When I was younger, I imagined Gia in two scenarios: married to someone important and intellectual, like a professor or scientist, or the first woman president. Opposite sides of the coin but both easily conceivable for her. She was like that, able to be submissive or completely in control. Better said, she could appear to be submissive while always in control.

Her house is large and immaculate. White columns in the front, perfectly manicured lawn, and two luxury vehicles parked in the garage. Space in Madison doesn't mean much, but in this Chicagoland suburb of Burr Ridge, space equals status. The bigger the house, the more money spent, and Gia's house represents a lot of money well spent.

My fingers tingle after I ring her doorbell. She should be home because Gia surprised everyone by not becoming a governor or marrying a CEO but by becoming a bestselling novelist. She's sold enough books that she wouldn't have to write a sentence again in her life unless she wanted to and could still live well. It's the novelist part that surprised me, not the bestselling part, because whatever Gia does, she does to absolute perfection. Even her editor thought so, swept off his feet by the brilliant mind of Gia Dwyer. Her editor, now her beloved husband.

"Gwen!" Her green eyes widen as they land on me, a small smile on her face. She's surprised, but at least she's happy to see me.

She looks great, her thick dark hair falling in waves down her back. She's fully dressed, wearing a cream-colored blazer covering a black shirt and jeans. That doesn't mean that she's headed out. Gia wouldn't be caught dead with a hair out of place at any time of day. I think she sleeps looking perfect.

"I'm so glad to see you," she says, pulling me into a tight hug.

I let out a sigh of relief as I hug her back. She steps back and takes in my appearance, frowning. Today isn't a day when I particularly take pride in my appearance. My eyes have bags under them that could carry ten pounds of luggage. My hair hasn't been washed in two days, and my oversized Packers sweatshirt isn't doing anything for my figure. It's funny I only think about things like that around my sister.

"What are you doing here? Not that I'm not glad to have you," she says, flashing a wide pageant-girl smile.

On the drive here, I'd practiced managing my emotions, or at least containing them so as not to fall apart on her doorstep. I run my hand through my hair.

"Can I come in?" I say jokingly, and she laughs.

"Of course. I'm sorry. I'm just so shocked. When was the last time you landed on my doorstep unannounced?" She giggles, taking me by the hand and pulling me into the house. In less than a moment, we're seated at her large kitchen table, and she's making coffee. "So are you going to fill me in on what brings my little sister all the way from Podunk, Michigan?"

I can't help but laugh. Gia has only been to my house three times in her whole life, for many reasons, but one is that she hates the country. Since I'm pretty much smack dab in the middle of Small Town Country, USA, my house isn't very alluring to her.

"I missed you. I needed to see my sister," I admit with a tight smile.

When she turns around, her eyes run over me. Her wide smile disappears into a concerned frown. She pulls up a chair next to me and angles her body toward mine. "What's the matter?" Her tone is more serious, more concerned, and she focuses on me.

This change in her demeanor makes my tightly wound emotions want to unravel and reveal themselves. I take a deep breath and try to think of exactly what I want to say because once said, there's no going back. Once I reveal what's happened to my marriage, it will be a wound that will never close, a loose thread that can be pulled on to unravel my existence. Sometimes it's a lot easier for you to move forward and possibly forgive the one who has done you wrong than it is for your family and friends. They can't forgive and they never let you forget, and secrets like that can be ammunition used to destroy you when they see fit. She notices my hesitancy, which is ridiculous since I drove almost four hours to get here. I'm sitting in front of her as a ball of energy that's so hard to contain I just want to release it all.

"Gwen, you can tell me anything. I'm your sister."

The thing is I can't tell her anything, because some things, no matter how badly you want to say them, can open doors that should remain locked, can create cracks in things that took years and years to rebuild. I feel my eyes well up, and I try to smile away my tears.

"Gwen, are you sick again?" Her eyes tighten as she grabs my hand and squeezes it.

"No. No, it's nothing like that," I tell her, and her arms wrap around me.

"Thank God," she says, squeezing me tightly. "Then what is it? Is Christopher okay?" She pulls away, surveying my face.

"Not really," I answer honestly.

"Is he having episodes again?" she asks urgently.

"No, it's nothing like that," I say, stifling my broken voice. "Not yet at least." I shrug and laugh to cover my cry, but it's unsuccessful.

Gia takes my hand again and lifts my chin. "You're scaring me. Tell me what's wrong."

I stand up from the table and turn away from her. "You know. We don't really talk about what happened."

I don't want to face her, but after a long stretch of silence, I do. Her face has gone dead, her eyes wide like she's seen a ghost, and that tells me she knows exactly what I'm talking about. She looks away from me.

"Some things are better not discussed," she says quietly, but there's an edge to her voice.

"I know." Tears are streaming down my cheeks. I walk back to the table and sit across from her so she can see my face. "But I have to know now. Do you really . . . have you really forgiven me? Or have you just chosen to act like it didn't happen?"

Her gaze doesn't leave the table. "What does this have to do with anything?" Her frustration is evident in her voice.

"It has to do with everything for me. I need to know. Because right now, I have this hatred, this rage, this desire for vengeance coursing through me, and I have to know that it goes away, that I can let it go," I beg.

Her eyes cut through me, and there's a look on her face I haven't seen in a long time. "You're my sister. I *had* to let it go . . . and what does that have to do with anything?"

"Everything."

She looks at me closely, as if she's trying to read my mind. She folds her hands in front of her and stares at them as if she's frozen in place. "It still hurts sometimes."

I feel a stab of pain. "Even after all of these years?"

"That type of pain doesn't go away. It only dulls." Then she shakes her head and smiles, returning to the woman she was earlier. "You were young. You always only thought about yourself. What does *that* have to do with why you're here now? What's going on?" She pours me a cup of coffee, and something in me makes me stand up from the table.

"Coming here was mistake," I say, feeling my nerves colliding against one another.

She looks at me with confusion evident on her face.

"I'm sorry. I love you, but I shouldn't have come," I say, grabbing my purse and heading toward the living room door.

"Look, this is why we don't talk about what happened. It doesn't matter. Everything that happened in the past isn't important. What's important is that we made it past that. We didn't let it destroy us. It could have, but it didn't." I have to get away from her before I burst into tears.

"And whatever happened, it doesn't have to destroy you!" she yells, and I stop in my tracks. "I know how it feels to hurt more than you ever thought possible. To feel betrayed, duped. I understand what's that's like. I know something's happened. That look on your face, you can't hide it with a smile. I know that you came here for a reason, so just let me in."

Before today, there had never been a single thing I did that I wanted to take back, to rewind time and make a different choice. Never once had I thought it. But looking at my sister now, after what's happened over these past few days, I almost wish I could. If I could go back and change one thing, if I could tell the girl I was then, and even the woman I was up until yesterday, that every choice you make has a price, I would. But then again, the girl I was wouldn't listen. The girl I was then was just a girl who fell in love with a boy.

The wrong boy.

before

gwen
. . . seventeen

I DON'T UNDERSTAND what the big deal is. There're so many worse things I could be doing. They're mad. Well, a little beyond mad—they're furious—and for what? I smoked a little pot and got caught making out with Zach behind the bleachers. I mean, it wasn't like I was having sex and doing blow, but as red as Martin's face is right now and as tight as my mom's wringing her hands together, you'd think I'd just assassinated the freakin' President.

"Do you understand what we're saying to you, young lady? If I can even call you that," Martin bellows at me as he paces the dining room.

"Mom, you're going to let him say that to me? He's acting like I'm some type of tramp." I laugh, still a little buzzed from the joint that caused all of this ridiculous hysteria.

"Well, Gwendolyn, you aren't acting like a lady. I can't believe you," my mother adds predictably.

"Your actions reflect on this entire family. These ridiculous antics you pull not only make you look bad but make all of us look bad," he continues.

I focus on the ceiling fan turning above us. It's a lot more interesting than anything he has to say. I know how this is going to end—me being grounded, him and mom talking about how much of a mess I am when, in fact, I'm fine.

"Look, you guys are blowing a gasket over nothing. I was just having a little fun. This whole campaign thing may be fun for you guys, but it's stressing me the hell out," I say, folding my arms across my chest.

"Watch your language, young lady!" my mom says, her eyes squaring in on me.

"I'm sorry—it's stressing me the fuck out." I giggle, and their eyes widen. Okay, maybe that *wasn't* as funny as it seemed in my head. I wish they'd just waited until my buzz was done to have this conversation. It would have gone a lot better for all of us.

Martin's plump face is beet-red, and he runs his hand over his thick orange hair. When Dad first introduced him to us, I'd figured he was what Opie Taylor would look like if he was a late-fifty-something car salesman with a chronic case of cornball. I start to imagine cheese balls, and I burst out laughing.

"Oh, this is funny? You think it's a joke, huh? Well, you wouldn't think it was so funny if we took away the car you don't deserve to drive and those records you listen to that are probably killing the brain cells you have anyway," he says, folding his arms in his polyester suit.

"You can't take my car, Martin. It was a gift from my *actual* dad," I remind him, starting to find this conversation more annoying than entertaining.

"I can take the car," my mother asserts. "I can take the car and your clothes and everything else that belongs to you because we provide it. You are a child, and you are proving it more and more as each day passes. You are being selfish and completely self-centered, but you are not stupid. If I didn't know any better, I'd think that you were doing this on purpose, but I have to banish that thought because I'd hate to think the daughter I birthed could be so callous and immature."

I feel a burning in my chest. "It's not that big a deal! I wasn't trying to sabotage anything! I just wanted to have a little fun. You knew what that was when Dad was alive!"

"You lower your voice, young lady," she says warningly, with a glint in her eye that makes me want to cry.

"I just don't get it. What did I do to you, Gwen? What did I do to make you act so disdainfully toward me?" Martin asks in a tone that would make someone think he actually cares what I think of him. When, really, he couldn't give two shits. He's crossing his fingers I just get on a bus one day and never come back. "I know I'm not your dad. He was a good man—if anyone knows that, it's me . . ." He's oh so sincere, such a good actor. That works great for tricking people into buying the cars off his lot and getting poor saps to drive off with cars they know they can't afford.

I smile at him. "Of course you'd know. You were his best friend and didn't wait six months after he was in the ground to move in on his wife." I shrug.

I hadn't known it was possible, but Martin's already pale face goes whiter, and my mother's naturally tanned skin even turns a little pale. Martin nods slowly and leaves the room. My mom stands and walks over to me.

"Look at me, Gwen," she says, her tone warm but stern.

I glance up at her.

"We all miss your father," she says quietly.

I scoff. You couldn't tell. They never talk about him. All the pictures of us suddenly "went missing" a few weeks after she married Martin as if my father never existed.

"I miss your father," she says adamantly.

"Yeah, okay," I say, rolling my eyes.

"You don't think I miss him? You're his spitting image. Every time I look at you, I see his face," she says sadly. "You're beautiful, intelligent, and you're wasting it. You know your father wouldn't want you behaving like this."

"Don't bring Dad into this. If Dad was here, things would be different." My throat burns, but I refuse to let her see me cry.

"Are you being this way because you miss him? Do you need to see a counselor, to talk to someone again?" she asks sweetly. Her Southern belle charm coming out, as my father used to say. It used to work on him, and it works on almost everyone around her. It doesn't work on me.

"I don't need to see anyone. I just want to be left alone. I don't want to be in any pictures or pretend like we're a happy family for any interviews. I don't give a shit about Martin being the mayor. I just want to be left alone!" I sound a lot angrier than I intend to.

She nods. "Well, alone you shall be." My mom calmly walks away from me toward the door. "You're grounded. Three weeks. No TV, no phone, and no car. Give me your keys."

"You're kidding. It's spring break!" I say in disbelief. I'd known she'd be mad. I thought I'd get maybe a week of extra chores, but this is ridiculous.

"No, I am not, Gwendolyn," she says pointedly. "You're running around doing drugs and acting like a little slut, so I am not kidding! You are my seventeen-year-old daughter, and I will not stand for it. You are extremely out of line, and regardless of how you feel about Martin, as of now, he is the reason you get to drive your car and wear those designer jeans you like and have a roof over your head. You will not, and I mean this, Gwendolyn, *ever* disrespect him again, or so help me, you will finish the rest of your senior year at a boarding school in Burma!" She grabs my purse and shuffles through it until she finds my keys and snatches them.

"Great, you think I'm a slut and a drug addict?" I say, trying to laugh, but I can feel myself starting to cry, and I hate it.

"Actions, Gwen, are what people go by. You're smoking pot and kissing boys who aren't even your boyfriend. What do you think people believe about you?" she says sharply.

"I don't care about people! What do *you* think? Do you think I'm a slut? Do you think smoking a little pot, which I know you and Dad have done, makes me a druggie?"

"I don't know what to think. I never had these types of issues with Gia. I don't know how to help you if you don't even see what you're becoming," she says before leaving my room and shutting the door.

I stomp across my room then throw myself on my bed. She probably does think I'm a step away from being a basehead or prostitute. They act as if they caught me in a drug house having an orgy. I just needed to relax, and Zach helps me to relax. We were only making out, but of course she'd jump to conclusions because I'm Gwen, not Gia. If they caught Gia doing that, she'd of course have the perfect explanation and it'd all be forgiven, not that she'd ever get caught being anything less than perfect.

I walk over to the shelf over my desk and pull out our photo album. A lot of people hate their older sisters, especially their perfect ones, but I never have. Even though Gia does everything right and has things so easy it can make you want to slap her sometimes, things were so much easier when she was here. Then again, she was here when Dad was here. Things changed so much after he passed away. I lost not only my dad but my best friend. If he were here, he'd understand. He'd tell my mom she was overreacting. But then again, if he were here, I wouldn't be so stressed that I needed to smoke and ended up frenching Zach at school.

I grab the pink teddy bear off my bed, the one my dad won for Gia and me at a carnival when we were little, and hug it as tears come down my cheeks. I wipe them away quickly. I know my dad wouldn't want me crying. I remember whenever I did, he'd sing that old song "Big Girls Don't Cry" and tickle me until I had no choice but to stop. If Gia was here, things would be better. She can calm my mom down just how my dad did—that's the one trait I didn't get from him.

I sit on my bed and sigh. Three weeks of basically living in a box with no communication with the outside world. I'll go crazy. I hate it here. Living in this house is so dead. Martin has all of his political people over, and they schmooze and strategize, and my mom floats about, smiling and coddling people. She only talks to me when she's lecturing or yelling. Martin's her focus now. She'll be the wife of someone important if he wins because that's how gullible the people in this town are. Vote for the flashy guy with the wide smile who tells you what you want to hear and lies to you with ease.

Maybe I should lie, wait awhile and tell them I'm sorry and I'll never do it again. They probably wouldn't believe it. I'm not a believable liar in the least—I can't fake sincerity—but to avoid three weeks of sitting in a box and staring at the wall, I can at least attempt it. I get off my bed and suck it up, prepared to come to some type of amends. I head down the stairs and hear my mother speaking in the tone she uses when she's doing business.

"Hello, this is Ava Jenson. I spoke with you last week about my daughter attending your program. I'm hoping I could come out this week and get a tour of your campus. If you can give me a call back when you're able, I can be reached at . . ."

My heart beats a thousand miles a minute. Is this for real? *Program?* What the hell is she talking about? She really wants to send me away? She can't do that. Where would she send me, boarding school? That seems like some jacked-up shit Martin would put her up to.

I turn around as quietly as I can and head back up the stairs, into my bedroom, and close the door. It makes so much sense. They can send me away for the rest of the year, then they won't have any issues with me during the rest of Martin's campaign. I can't believe her. I sit on the bed and try to catch my breath. I think I may hyperventilate. What do I do? I can't go to some boarding school, or worse, military boot camp. My best friend's cousin got sent to a place like that, and she hasn't been the same since. If my mother's going so far as to tour the campus, her mind could already be made up. Only one person can talk her out of this, and she's five hours away. I haven't talked to my sister in weeks. Ugh, all of this over a joint and a stupid hormonal moment of weakness with stupid Zach. I'm going to kill him.

I know what I have to do. I have to talk to Gia and get her to convince Mom not to send me away. I run to my closet and rummage through it to find the letters she sent me. I grab my book bag, dump everything out of it, and stuff a few shirts and pairs of underwear in it. I look at the clock. It's nine thirty. If they follow their routine, they should be in bed by eleven, so my mom will probably come check on me in the next hour.

I take off my top and put on my pajama shirt and climb into bed. Exactly an hour later, like clockwork, I hear my door open. I close my eyes, pretending to be deep in slumber. My mom touches my forehead with a deep sigh and tiptoes back out the room. One more hour, and she'll be asleep.

I get out of bed and throw on my sweatshirt over my pajama top, put on my gym shoes, and grab my backpack. I grab the box at the top of my closet and count the money in it. One hundred and eighty dollars. That should be enough to get me a bus ticket to Chicago. I open my door and listen for noises, making sure it's all clear. I tiptoe down the stairs and grab the phone in the kitchen. I dial the number and cross my fingers he'll pick up.

"Hello?" Zach sounds groggy.

"It's me," I say in a hushed tone.

"Me who?" he asks irritably.

"Me, dumbass," I say sharply.

"Ooohhh. I thought you'd be on lockdown right about now." He chuckles, and I want to smack his face. He's lucky he's the only one I know who has a separate phone line from their parents.

"I need you to pick me up."

"Where we going?" Now he's interested.

"I need you to take me to the bus station."

"That doesn't sound like it'll benefit me at all. Good night," he says.

"Zach, stop being such an ass. I need you to come now, please!"

"Look your stepdad's about to be the mayor, and I don't need those type of problems," he says through a yawn.

"You didn't give a damn about him being my stepdad when you had your tongue in my mouth earlier," I say angrily.

"Well, that was worth it." He sounds smug.

I don't have any time for jokes. "Look, can you for once in your life think of something besides getting laid? My mom might be shipping me off to boarding school, and the only person who can change her mind is my sister, and I have to go talk to her, so can you just please come . . ." I can hear the disinterest in his sigh. "Okay, I'll give you ten bucks."

"I'll be there in fifteen minutes," he says and hangs up.

God, I can't believe I let him feel me up.

ZACH IS OUTSIDE as promised, driving his older brother's beat-up blue pickup truck. I run down the street to where he's parked on the corner and hop in. Zach pulls off before I can even shut the door.

"Well, I would say thanks for coming to help in my time of need, but since you're a jackass, I guess that won't be needed," I say after punching him lightly on the arm.

"Oh, you're so welcome, your highness. I mean, since it's certainly my obligation to get you since I'm your boyfriend or brother, right?" he says condescendingly.

I roll my eyes, pull out the ten bucks I promised him, and toss it on his lap.

"You're lucky I'm kind of into rude women with sucky attitudes," he says, giving me a wink.

I cross my arms and look out the window, hiding my smirk. I don't know what's wrong with me or why I am the way I am, but God if I could literally change my taste in boys, I so would. Zach Riley is every father's worst nightmare. He works at a gas station his uncle owns but *only* when he feels like it—mostly after he's gotten high and wants the free snacks to binge on. It's apparently also a good place to pick up some unsuspecting teenage girls he can feel up while smoking.

He's lazy, self-centered, and thinks he's God's gift to women—not that he isn't. With that thick coal-black hair, mesmerizing hazel eyes, a six-pack, and a bad attitude, he attracts them like moths to a flame. Maybe he's God's gift to women after we've really pissed God off.

I can't really say I don't like him. I do—he's the closest thing I have to a best friend—but unlike other girls, I know he's damaged goods. There will be no changing him or happily ever after for us. We've been hanging out, smoking pot, and making out when the need arises for the past seven months. Sometimes when he's high enough and lets his guard down, I see the cracks in his bad-boy persona. Maybe one day, after a few more birthdays, he'll grow up and decide to do something with his life. He's super smart—he almost had a perfect ACT score—but he hates school and shows up only when he feels like it, if it's some benefit to him. He comes just enough to get his diploma so he won't hear his parents nag him.

We almost had an accident once because he didn't want to hit a confused baby squirrel that ran out in the middle of the street, so I know he has a heart even if he tries to deny it, but this broken man surely won't be mine to fix. I'll let another girl try to break through his smug, conceited—albeit super-hot—exterior.

"So your mom's sending you up the river? Cuffing you to the ball and chain?" He laughs, taking a puff of his cigarette.

"It's not funny. I can't go to some crappy boarding school or fix-your-attitude boot camp," I scoff.

He chuckles. "It's not like your attitude needs fixing or anything."

"You're one to talk," I spit back at him.

"Hey, I know I'm not winning any congeniality awards anytime soon, but I'm a guy. Chicks think it's hot. My mom thinks it's normal at my stage in life, expected even, but you're a *girl*."

I feel my face scrunch up. "What does that mean?"

He laughs again before taking another puff of his cigarette. "It means that you can't be the female version of me." He glances at me with a smirk I used to find sexy but I'm now annoyed with.

"Oh, my lifelong aspiration is crushed," I say sarcastically.

"What I'm trying to say is you can't do what I do, what any guy does. It won't look right. Especially with stepdaddy having the political aspirations he does," he says before drumming on his steering wheel to the solo playing on the radio.

"I don't care about him and his dream of becoming the mayor, governor, or whatever else. I'm not going to change who I am because he's an opportunistic jackass," I say defensively.

"Look, it's not just about that. You can kind of come off . . . like a bitch sometimes, and I mean that in the best way possible," he says with a shrug.

"You can't call someone a bitch in the best way possible."

"Look, I know it's the eighties and women's lib and all of that good stuff, but at the end of the day, girls are expected to be sweet, demure, smart . . . well, since you're cute you don't necessarily have to be smart, but you get what I mean," he says, and I turn the radio up to end this conversation. "Don't touch the radio." He turns it back down.

"I don't want to talk. I just want to listen to music before I get on this bus for God knows how long," I say, frustrated.

"Hey, it's my car,"

"Your brother's car," I correct him.

"I'm driving it, and if I want to talk, we talk," he says simply.

"Did someone lace your pot or something? What prompted you to go all mentor on me?" I scoff at him.

"I'm not trying to be your mentor, but I'm trying to tell you some good stuff so your ass doesn't get packed away to boarding school," he says, his voice rising.

For a moment, I think he's offended. "You're telling me to be someone I'm not, to change who I am, and it's not cool!"

"Is this who you are?" he asks.

"What is that supposed to mean?"

"I just remember this girl named Gwen Dwyer. She was a fourteen-year-old honors student who volunteered at the blood drives and followed her older sister around like she was Jesus. She was nice, sweet, and the type of girl who would be the perfect daughter to any political candidate," he says simply.

I feel my face heat up.

"Something happened that made you say, 'Fuck the world and anyone in the surrounding universe.' You're pissed, and hey, maybe you deserve to be, but deep down, you're still that same sweet little girl who can play by rules and be what they want you to be." Each syllable he speaks makes me madder and madder.

"Stop the car," I say quietly.

"What, you have to pee or something?"

"Stop it!" I scream, and he slams on the brakes.

"Chill. What's your problem?" he says angrily as I swing my door open, pulling on my bag behind me and walking to the side of the road. He's still in the car, looking at me as though I'm a psycho.

"I'm going to catch another ride. You can go. Keep the ten bucks!" I yell.

He looks shocked then laughs. "Get in the car, brat." He says it as if it's a joke, as if I'm a joke. I hate when he calls me that or kid.

"I'm not a brat or a kid. You're only a year older than me, and if you look at me like a kid, that makes you a pedophile since you've been trying to get in my pants for couple of months," I shout.

"What did I do?" he says as if he's clueless.

"You won't shut up. All I want is a ride to the bus station—no long talks, no lectures, no advice, just a ride. I don't know if it's a full moon or something, but you're not acting like the Zach I know. The Zach I know would take my ten bucks, blast the radio, and shut the hell up and expect me to do the same. So can that guy tell me to get back in the car? Because this one is really pissing me off."

He shakes his head and grins at me. "Or I could drive off with your ten bucks and leave you here to get picked up by the police or some serial killer." He shrugs with the indifferent smugness I know him for.

"That's more like it," I say with a small smile.

I hop back in the truck, and as I suggested, he blasts the music occasionally singing when one of his songs come on. I glance at him out the corner of my eye. I occasionally forget that Zach grew up here and knows as much about the people as I do. He's so different, sometimes I forget that I only think that he's from another planet.

When we finally make it to the bus station, he turns the music down. "Your stop, my lady."

"You were being weird tonight. I don't like it," I say before climbing out of his truck and shutting the door.

He leans toward my side. "You like everything about me."

I roll my eyes at him. "Careful, Zach. If I didn't know any better, I'd think that you're starting to like me. Well, for more than just my amazing ass."

"I'd definitely miss it if it got sent to boarding school," he retorts.

"I'm not going to boarding school. I'd just have to run away and shack up with you since I now know you're in love with me and all," I tease.

He rolls his eyes, but I do notice his cheeks turn red, and I get little butterflies. He shakes his head and gives me the middle finger before he pulls off.

The bus ride to Chicago should have been titled the bus ride from hell. When you take forty people, most of whom haven't showered for hours, add screaming kids, and put them all on a bus with little to no air circulation, you're asking for trouble. The only thing I can say was half okay was the two hours I was able to sit by myself, which didn't last long. I got a chatty Cathy on steroids who had the worst breath in the entire world as my neighbor for the rest of my three-hour ride.

After I get off the bus and thank God for the privilege of air that doesn't smell like ten different colognes, BO, and dirty diapers, I immediately realize I'm not in my small town in Michigan anymore. Even the bus station is different from ours. Where ours is just a few benches and elevator music playing in the background with one payphone in the center, this station is bustling. They have arcade games, a dozen restaurant kiosks, and a currency exchange booth. Everyone seems to be in such a hurry that I'm almost knocked down a few times. It's something like out of the movies—people everywhere, all different races, hairstyles, and clothes I've never seen before. It's exciting but a bit intimidating, and for a moment, I'm even scared. Do I look like a little country girl who's never been more than a half hour away from home alone and now I'm in the middle of one of the biggest cities in the US, thirty dollars in my pocket, an address on an envelope, and the clothes on my back? I walk over to a hot dog stand that already has six people waiting in line.

My stomach is growling. It's five thirty in the morning, but I don't see anything that looks as though it's selling breakfast. The funny thing is no one looks tired or like they just woke up, but I feel like a zombie. The line moves fast and I grab my hot dog, eating most of it before I make it outside of the station. Thankfully there's a line of cabs waiting to take you anywhere you want to go. I scan the faces of the drivers standing outside the cars and find a short, chubby Hispanic woman standing next to one. I bypass the other drivers and ask if she's free.

"I sure am, sweetie. Let's get going." She hops in, and I get in the back, fumbling through my bag for the address. I realize I probably should have memorized it.

"Where we headed?" she asks just as I find the envelope.

"Here, please," I say, handing her the envelope.

She chuckles. "Evanston. That's going to be about an hour from here." She glances at me in the mirror.

"Can you take me?" I ask, trying to sound sweet and innocent.

"Honey, I'd drive you to New York City if that's where you wanted to go, but the question is, do you have the fare? It's going to be about twenty five bucks," she says through a chuckle.

"Twenty-five dollars? Are you kidding?" I say in disbelief.

"Yup, and that's only because traffic is pretty light."

I groan. This trip has wiped out my savings from the past two years. Back in Claredon, I could have had a personal driver for the day for twenty-five dollars.

"You're not from here, are you?" The cab driver chuckles.

I feel my stomach knot up. I don't want to make it so obvious, so instead of answering her question, I dig into my bag.

"It's fine. Just get me there, please," I say, handing her a twenty dollar bill.

She smiles widely. "My type of woman."

IN CLAREDON, EVERYTHING looks the same. Of course some houses are a little bigger than others—you can tell which ones cost more and who doesn't bother to keep up with the property upkeep—but here, it's so different. For the first ten minutes, we drive past buildings taller than anything I've ever seen, all lit up as if they have lives of their own. Then we pass smaller buildings only about two and three stories high, clustered together, and after that, the driver tells me we're heading to the suburbs. There, the houses look more like the ones in Claredon—some large, some small, but all pretty similar—but the longer we drive, the more things change. A distinct difference from what I had just seen. Even though some of the houses before were bigger, you can tell the smaller houses here cost more.

"Who are you coming to see here, hon?" the cab driver asks me.

"My sister. She's in her senior year at Northwestern," I reply.

"She must be a smart cookie. Northwestern is a great school," she says, impressed. "We're only a few blocks away from the address you gave me."

"Is this area, I mean, does it cost a lot to stay around here?" I ask.

She chuckles. "Hon, I could work twelve hours a day and couldn't afford a studio apartment here."

How is Gia staying in a place like this? I don't think my dad could have afforded her tuition and board here even if he was alive. Maybe she has a roommate? Is Martin making enough money to write her checks to live here?

We pull up to a house in the center of a block. It's not as large as the homes around it, but it's still beautiful, even more so for a single college student. Last I talked to Gia, she said she'd just started working in some department in her school.

"Are you okay here, little lady?"

"Yeah, thanks," I say, heading out of the cab.

"Have a good one," the cabbie says before pulling off and leaving me on the sidewalk, hopefully in front of my sister's house.

I trudge up the stairs and hope that she's happy to see me. I haven't seen her since Christmas last year, though she writes me letters. I've kind of forgotten to write back after the last couple ones she's sent. I didn't even open them. I'm really regretting that now. I ring the doorbell and bounce my weight from one side to the other.

"Coming," her voice sings from the other side of the door.

It's a little past seven thirty. I'm really lucky she's not headed out for school or work. The door opens, and she's standing there, wearing a white blouse and jeans. Even though it's early, she looks as though she's already showered, put on makeup. She looks at me, a little confused.

"You forgot what your sister looks like," I kid.

"Gwen!" she says, almost knocking me over in a hug.

"You did forget what I look like!"

She steps back and laughs as she pushes my hair off my shoulder. "Well, uh, this is a huge difference."

I'd forgotten I'd dyed it dark brown since she last saw me. "Yeah, no longer the little strawberry shortcake."

"Wow, it's just you look so different," she says, more amazed by the color of my hair than the fact I'm five hours from home and on her doorstep. I'll go with it.

"Can I come in?" I say teasingly.

"Of course!" She pulls me by the hand inside the house. It's beautiful and typical Gia. It's clean, bright, not too cluttered, everything in its place. "Welcome to my home, little sis." She closes the door behind me.

"Thanks," I say, taking off my bag.

"You like it?" She pushes her long dark hair from one shoulder to another.

The house isn't really my thing, but she knows it of course, and Zach's words about me being a bitch still ring in my ears. I've always thought of myself as honest and maybe a little self-centered, but who should your life be centered on if it's not yourself?

"It fits you perfectly," I say with a wide smile.

"Sooo, tell me what you are doing here?" she asks the million-dollar question.

"I wanted to see you. I missed you," I say, avoiding the real answer for now. It's not a lie. I have missed my sister. I didn't realize how much until now. I hug her again.

"I've missed you to. You're the one who hasn't responded to any of my letters," she says with a playful nudge.

"I know. I'm bad with stuff like that."

"You're in high school. People who say that usually have families or jobs or something substantial going on to make them be so absentminded," she says.

"Great. My life isn't substantial," I say sarcastically.

She rolls her eyes at me with a laugh. "You know what I mean. Come on, you, let me get you something to eat and get the real reason why you're here out of you."

I follow her and see I have a choice of Sugar Smacks, Apple Jacks, and Cheerios for breakfast. I feel my face fall.

"Everyone's not Chef Boyardee," she says to my expression, and I laugh.

"I'll cook breakfast tomorrow," I say, choosing the box of Sugar Smacks.

"Tomorrow? Meaning you're staying overnight?" Her eyes narrow in on me.

"If that's okay. You trying to get rid of me already?" I ask playfully.

She folds her arms with a small smirk. "It depends. Is it okay with Mom that you're here?"

Instead of answering, I pour the Sugar Smacks into the bowl she handed me earlier.

"She doesn't know you're here. Of course she wouldn't know," she says anxiously.

"Okay, look, I need your help, Gia. She's trying to send me away to boarding school or something. I'm not sure where, but I can't be in one of those places. You have to get her to change her mind!" I whine.

Gia throws her head back in frustration. "Why would Mom send you to boarding school?"

I take a deep breath and catch Gia up on everything that's happened. She looks at me with frustration as she folds her hands at the table and shakes her head, then she laughs.

"So instead of talking to Mom, telling her you're sorry and that you're going to clean up your act, you sneak out of the house, while you're grounded, catch a bus to a different state, while you're grounded, and think that's the best way to get her to see that you're not completely out of control?" she says sarcastically.

I roll my eyes. "You sound like Zach," I mutter, defeated.

"Who's Zach?"

"He's not important," I tell her with a shrug.

She looks at me knowingly. Ugh, we're getting off track.

"Look, Mom doesn't listen to me, Gia. I know she thinks I'm too far-gone. You know how she is, and with Martin in her ear, it would have been a lost cause. You're my only hope," I plead.

She sighs and shakes her head. "Gwen, you always jump the gun. You eavesdropped on her phone call, so you don't know really what the conversation was in regards to. What if it's something completely different from what you think? Mom hasn't mentioned sending you to boarding school or some bad girls' camp." She says the last part with a chuckle.

"What else would she be talking about when she's touring a facility for me? An asylum?" I say sarcastically.

"You always jump to the absolute worst conclusion. Mom would have told me if she was thinking of doing something like that."

"Maybe she forgot to mention it, or she's so fed up with me that she's going to call and tell you today." I grimace.

"You know our mother is far from absentminded, and she would have told me. Mom tells me everything." She stands, walks over to the phone, and picks it up.

I jump out of my seat and hang up the receiver. "You can't call her!"

"You ran away while you're grounded. Mom's going to wake up and not know where you are," she says as if it's obvious.

"Please, Gia! Can we just finish talking first?" I plead. I give her my best puppy-dog eyes, then I spot the humongous ring on her finger. "Gia, is that what I think it is!"

My eyes get wider as I continue to look at it. She glances at it, and a smile spreads across her face and her cheeks light up like Rudolph's nose. I grab her hand and examine it.

"It's so pretty!" I say enthusiastically. It's a beautiful diamond ring and just my ticket to changing the subject. I nudge her. "You little sneak. You're engaged?"

She takes her hand back and walks into her living room. "It's not an engagement ring," she says bashfully.

"Bullshit, it looks like it to me," I say, flopping onto the sofa beside her.

"Language, Gwen," she says with a small smile. It disappears, and a wide grin spreads across her face.

"Does Mom know? Why haven't you said anything? I can't believe you're getting married!" I say in disbelief.

"Slow down, sis. First off, again, it's not an engagement ring. Mom does know that I have it as a promise ring, and maybe you'd have an inkling if you read my letters or picked up the phone and called me," she says, swatting me playfully.

I instantly feel guilty. "I'm sorry." I guess I have kind of blocked her out since she's been gone.

"Mom's really worried about you." She sighs.

I roll my eyes.

"She is. She cares, and she thinks you've done a personality one-eighty since dad passed away," she says, her voice full of concern.

"Everything else has changed. Dad's gone, Mom's obsessed with Martin, and you're gone. Sometimes you change who you are to adapt," I snap.

She scoots closer to me. "I know a lot has changed, but you can't let it ruin you," she says solemnly, stroking my now-darkened hair. "Like this, this isn't you. Hanging out with trash, being rude, shutting yourself off from the people you care about—"

I scoot away from her. "You believe anything Mom says. It's not like that. My friends aren't trash. I'm not rude, only honest, and I don't hang around places I'm not wanted."

"You can't believe Mom doesn't want you," she says in disbelief.

"I'm sure her and Martin's lives would be easier if I wasn't around. He wants this perfect family with a perfect kid, a Stepford child or something. That's not who I am!" I say angrily.

"Well, I don't know your side of the story because besides today, I haven't talked to you in months," she spits back.

I look down guiltily.

"Look, I know Dad's loss affected you the most. You were the closest to him out of all of us." Her voice is softer now. "But living as if he didn't exist doesn't help anything. We can honor his memory by living as if he's still here, by implementing the lessons he's taught us."

I have to laugh. Gia and her way with words. Hopefully she can use them to get my trip to boarding school canceled.

"I'll talk to Mom for you," she says with a sigh.

My spirits immediately lift. "You will? Oh, thank you, Gia!" I jump on her lap and hug her tightly.

"But you have got to at least work with Mom. I know you're not Martin's biggest fan . . ." she continues as I resume my seat on the sofa.

"I don't get how you both can pretend that he wasn't dad's best friend and Dad would've been okay with his wife screwing him," I say with a laugh.

"It's not like they were having an affair while dad was alive," Gia says.

"As far as we know," I mutter.

"Gwen, really," she asks angrily. "I can't believe you'd think Mom would do that. I know you guys have never gotten along, but that's really low."

"Just forget I said anything," I scoff.

"Mom would never do anything like that. She loved Dad as much as we do. Sometimes things happen in life. Can you imagine what it was like for her, losing the man she'd been with for over thirty years, becoming a single parent in an instant, no time to prepare or adjust? Dad was her best friend. They both miss him and took solace in each other. We could have ended up with a lot worse for a stepdad. Martin isn't a stranger. He's the same man we always knew—funny, kind, and ambitious. He's perfect for Mom, and when you're seventeen, I know you don't think about things like health insurance, mortgage payments, and tuition, but when Dad passed, Mom became responsible for all of that by herself. Dad's life insurance couldn't cover everything for us to survive on. Without Martin, life would be a whole lot harder for all of us."

"I don't care what Mom and Martin do. In a couple of months, I'll be free to live the life I want without anyone on my back or threatening to send me away," I retort.

"And what kind of life will you be living?" she asks condescendingly.

"I don't know, but it'll be better than it is now." I shrug.

"You're seventeen. You only have one semester of school left. You haven't made any plans for higher education, so what are you going to do? Because as of now, you look like you're going to be with Mom and Martin a lot longer than you're planning on."

"I don't care if I have to join the circus. The second I turn eighteen, I'm out of there," I tease.

She smirks and rolls her eyes.

"And back on the subject, this ring," I say, grabbing her hand again.

"Like I said, it's not an engagement ring. It's a promise ring," she says shyly.

"A promise-to-marry-him ring?" I say sarcastically.

"Well, he offered it as an engagement ring, and I accepted it as a promise ring," she says innocently.

I feel my face scrunch up. "He must be ugly then."

She laughs. "Not even a little bit,"

"Boring?" I ask, confused.

"No, he's anything but that," she replies, amused.

"Stupid? Oh, I'm sorry, *intellectually challenged* would be the nicer thing to say, huh?"

"No, Gwen. He's nice, funny, smart, handsome—all the things a girl could want." She sighs.

"Of course, any guy *every* girl wants, you wouldn't want," I say, rolling my eyes.

Gia's the pickiest person I know. Everything has to be a certain way. She's a handful to put up with, and any guy with all the traits she's listed who wants to spend the rest of his life with her, she should hold on to for dear life. In high school, she was a senior during my freshman year, and she was like a legend. No one was good enough for Gia. She turned down football players, class presidents, guys with amazing hair who played guitar. She was untouchable. She believed boys were a waste of time. She became a grand prize, and there were bets on if one would nab her before she graduated, but not one did. Not even her prom date, the super-hot foreign exchange student from France who looked like a model and had the body of an athlete. Gia told my mom he was boring. What French hot guy is *boring?*

"I love him," she says solemnly.

My eyes widen. I've never heard her say that. "Then what's the problem?" I ask with a laugh.

"Marriage is a big deal. Love isn't the only thing that should be considered." She shrugs, and I groan.

"You take the most romantic act on the planet, in the history of humanity, and examine it like a legal brief. You're going to make the perfect lawyer," I tease.

"See, that's why divorce is becoming so prevalent. You can't just get married because of love. You have to consider if your values, beliefs, and goals match," she says, and I pretend to shoot myself. "You're young, Gwen, you wouldn't understand."

"First off, I turn eighteen in just five months, which means you are only four and some odd change years older than me. Secondly, I've probably had more experience with guys than you, hon."

"Let's hope to God that's not true," she teases me, and I hit her with a pillow.

"Just admit it—the sex is bad, isn't it?" I say jokingly.

"I'm going to say yes." Her face has turned completely red.

"The sex is bad?" I ask, shocked at her for divulging something so private.

"No! I mean I'm going to say yes to marrying him . . . eventually," she says quickly.

"Then what are you waiting for? A guy like that won't stay on the market forever," I say, ripping a loose thread from my shirt.

"The right time. After we both graduate, when we see if our lives are going to line up, when I'm absolutely sure."

"Are you ever really going to be absolutely sure about anyone? I know I'm only *seventeen* and all, but as far as I know, marriages don't come with a guarantee. Do they?"

"With a good enough prenup, they do," she says jokingly.

I roll my eyes at her.

"You'll understand when you're older," she says.

I hate when people say that, like I'm a twelve-year-old. To me, that's the go-to answer when you're talking to someone younger than yourself and can't come up with a good retort. I lie across her living room sofa and put my legs on her lap.

"So when do I get to meet the lucky guy?" I say, braiding loose strands of my hair.

"Well, that depends on how fast Mom wants you home when I talk to her."

I sit up. "Can I stay the weekend? I need some time away from them."

"If Mom's okay with it, fine."

As if Mom would be okay with anything I wanted to do. I give her my puppy-dog eyes.

"You know, that's not as cute as when you were ten." She chuckles, and her phone rings. "That's probably Mom now. She calls me every morning." She pushes my legs off her, then she bounces over to the phone and picks it up. "Hello? Hi, Mom!"

I fall back onto the sofa and cover my head with a pillow.

"No, no, Gwen's not missing. She's, uh, she's here actually," Gia says, amused.

I can actually hear my mom's head blow off her body. I get off the couch and bounce over to Gia, trying to hear my mother through the phone.

"I'm not sure how she got here. She was on my doorstep this morning," Gia reveals, giving me a questioning look. "I think she knows she's in a lot of trouble, Mom."

I roll my eyes.

"I know, Mom, you know how Gwen is. The rational thing is the last thing that she does," she says.

I nudge Gia, and she nudges me back, giving me a wink. They talk for a few more minutes. I'm sure my mom is rambling about what a terrible, disobedient child I am and how my punishment will be one for the history books. Gia nods and agrees with her, but at about the five-minute mark, Gia begins to work her magic.

"I completely agree with everything you just said, but obviously what's been going on isn't working. Let her stay the weekend with me. Maybe I can get through to her. I think she just needs to hear your point of view from someone else . . . no, Mom, you know it's not going to be a party here with me. We're going to talk, and I'll show her around campus and introduce her to some of my friends . . ."

No one can settle my mom down like Gia can. I can already hear my mother's voice calming.

"Yep, first thing Sunday morning, she'll be headed back. No, I won't send her back on the bus by herself." She winks at me.

"See, she thinks I'm still a little baby. I can't even ride back by myself even though I came all by my grown-up self," I say.

Gia shoots me a warning look. "I'll see if I can switch shifts with someone. You know my Monday class is in the evening, so I can bring her," she says into the phone, turning her back to me. "Everything'll be fine, I promise. No, I don't think you should talk to her until she's back. Just give things a little air."

I hug her from behind.

"Of course, I get it . . . yup. I love you too, Mom. Tell Martin I said hello. I'll call you tonight. Love you, buh bye," she says and hangs up. She turns around and frowns at me. "You owe me big time."

"Of course I do. I'll start by making you a real breakfast instead of this crap," I say sweetly.

She smiles widely—she never could resist my food. I bounce over to her refrigerator and see that it's mostly crap I can't pull off breakfast with.

"Okay, we've got to go to the store."

"How about this? I have class in about an hour. I'll trade you breakfast for dinner. How about my favorite?" She sounds excited.

"Lasagna, right?" I say.

"Yes," she says with a wide smile. "And since you're staying the weekend, you'll get to meet him."

"Cool, when do I get to meet the Prince Charming who stole Queen

Gia's heart?" I tease.

"No need to call him Prince Charming. William is just fine," she says happily.

chapter four

lisa

. . . seventeen

FOR ANY NORMAL person in a normal world whose mother wasn't named Evangeline Garrett, knocking on your bathroom door would be a normal occurrence. But in our house on 2312 Johnson Street, knocking on our bathroom door is almost like playing a game of roulette. I never know exactly who's going to come waltzing out of it. This morning it's Jack Doe. It's the first time I've seen him, so he's definitely not one of my mother's regulars. He's short, the same height as me, with a beer belly he's obviously proud of since he's not wearing any shirt. It looks like he's worn his jeans for the past few days.

"Who are you?" he says through a grunt.

"Doesn't matter. I have about ten minutes to get ready before school, so if you don't mind, can you speed it up?" I say, exasperated.

His initial confusion is replaced as his eyes roam my body. Situations like this are the sole reason why I wear full-on pajamas in the morning complete with house shoes.

"You look like your mother," Jack Doe says with a grimy smile.

The absolute worst thing he could say to me but the truth. Sometimes I hate looking in the mirror because I see her staring back at me. He walks out of the bathroom, making sure to brush against me, and I dodge past him into the bathroom and shut the door. I immediately regret it when the rancid stench hits my nose. I back out of the bathroom quickly, and Jack Doe is still standing there, obviously aware that I wouldn't stay in there long.

"Sorry about that. Me and Evie had Mexican last night," he says, leaning on the wall.

It's great they ate last night since I didn't. The only things in our fridge are some molding bologna, guacamole, and week-old casserole.

"What's your name, sweetheart?" he says as if he's trying to pick me up from a bar.

"Doesn't matter. I'm sure I won't see you again after today," I say.

"Actually, I think you'll be seeing me around here more than ya think. So I'm going to ask you again—what is your name?" His tone is more stern.

I feel my stomach clench up. It's time for me to carry my mace in the mornings again, but I've faced off with more intimidating guys than this. He's actually one of the smaller ones. My mom usually likes them big and stocky. This one's short, and I'd call him lean, but the meat he actually does have on his bones is loose and like putty.

"Lisa bear, you being mean to my Jacky?" My mom appears from her bedroom wearing a short T-shirt that's barely covering her butt. Her long blond hair is all over her head, and her blue eyes are full of sleep.

How ironic—his name is actually Jack.

"Of course not, Mom. You know I treat all of the *many* guests in our home with the utmost respect," I say with a dazzling smile for Jack. My eyes dart to my mom, who's scowling over the dig our visitor hasn't seemed to pick up.

"How about you make us some breakfast, Evie?" Jacky says, heading over to her.

I can't help but laugh. Jacky's in for a rude awakening since breakfast is never on my mom's itinerary. I almost want to stick around to hear her response, but I'm already running late. I take a deep breath and dive back into our bathroom where I open the window to release Jacky's stench. I shower quickly and scald my toothbrush before brushing my teeth—there've been too many instances of my mom's lovely friends using it. I guess it's a plus that they actually brush their teeth. Luckily I have swimming first period, so I save the time it'd usually take for me to blow-dry my hair.

I grab my backpack out of my room and head to the kitchen to grab my mom's keys off the table so I can take the car to school, but they're not there. I head to her room. The TV's on, so I know she hasn't passed back out again.

"Mom, where are the car keys?" I ask as she stares at the news.

"Oh, Jack's car is having a little bit of an issue, so I let him use mine. He's bringing it back this afternoon," she says.

"You let him take our car?" I ask in disbelief.

My mom has done some pretty dumb things, like letting random guys into our house and lending them money here and there, but letting some redneck douche take our car, the only vehicle that can get us both to work and me to school, is on a whole new level of dumb.

"How could you let that jackass take the car? You don't even know him!" I yell.

"Don't be so dramatic. I do know him. I've known him for about three years now; we've just kind of made it official. He's good people. He'll bring it back, and if he doesn't, I know where he works," she says, waving me off.

Official? What the hell does that mean? It's too early for me to even want to think about the effects of that statement.

"How am I supposed to get to school?" I screech.

"Can't you get a ride from that Scott boy? The cute one who's always hanging around here. What's his name?" she says, unfazed.

"Ugh!" I groan before storming out of the house. I sit on the porch, trying to calm myself down. It's already September, but thank God the weather is still warm out.

"Just one more year, that's it."

I cut my pity party short and trek the few blocks to hopefully catch Chris before he leaves. I should have called him before I left, but it would have ruined my dramatic exit. Hanging out was a lot easier when we lived next door to each other, but after my mom and stepdad got divorced, she sold the house and moved us to where we are now—which is a downgrade to say the least. My old stepdad wasn't one of my favorite people when I was growing up. I'd thought he treated my mom like a child, almost like my sister. Little did I know my mom liked acting like a selfish, impulsive little kid and the normality of my life was strictly because of him. I learned that when, at thirteen, I had to take over paying our bills so stuff didn't get turned off, reminding her to get groceries, and getting her up in time for me to get to school and her to get to work.

The worst habits I couldn't break her of are the drinking and bringing home random guys who make her feel pretty. Only Evie would pick up guys who didn't have their own houses, or better yet, guys who shared their houses with the women they went home to and the children who weren't bastards.

I used to try to pinpoint when my mom became a whore. It's harsh but completely true. The reason we're on the poor side of town, why I had to move from next door to my best friend, is she couldn't keep her legs shut and opened them for my stepdad's younger brother. I don't know which is worse: slut or prostitute. Some would say prostitute, but at least they get paid. My mom gets nothing most of the time—at least nothing that's worth it.

My stomach growls, reminding me to pick up some food today. She's been out almost every night after work, and I've been eating at the Barrow, a little coffee and pastry shop in town. I've been working there as a waitress for five months. I see Chris's mom's car still parked on their lot, so I haven't missed a ride to school. I glance at my watch and see that I'm twenty minutes ahead of schedule. Maybe I've made it in time to get some leftovers from the breakfast Chris's mom makes every single morning. She's like Martha Stewart and Rachael Ray tied into one. I go around the back and knock on the door, a habit I've had since when we lived across from them. Gwen greets me with a warm smile.

"Hi, Lisa. Happy Monday," she says cheerfully as she welcomes me into the kitchen.

I smell bacon and potatoes lingering in the kitchen. "Hi, Mrs. Scott." I try to muster up the same amount of enthusiasm she has.

"Chris is upstairs. Come in and have some breakfast," she says.

I follow her, grateful for the invitation to quiet my grumbling stomach.

"Our hot water tank has been on the fritz, so he's running behind," she explains as she fixes me a plate from the small amount of food remaining. "How is your morning going so far?"

"It's a Monday." I laugh before putting a spoonful of food in my mouth.

"You know, most people hate Mondays, but I always try to think of it as a new start, the ability to wipe last week's slate clean," she says as she sits next to me.

That's one way to look at it. The other is that a whole new set of problems is about to start.

"So Chris hasn't mentioned which school you've decided on yet," she says.

"Anywhere outside of the great state of Michigan would be great actually." I chuckle, and she smiles. "But since the tuition for out-of-state schools is more expensive, it'll probably be somewhere here. My check from the Barrow only goes so far." I feel my tone starting to drain the good vibe from the house, so I try to lighten the mood. "I'm excited though. It'll be good to get out, a place where I can start somewhere new. Where everyone doesn't know me or my parents."

"I'm hoping Chris stays close. I know it's selfish, but I can't imagine him being in a different state for four whole years," she says with a smile, but there's a sadness in her voice.

If I had Chris's parents, I wouldn't need to move across the state. I look around and lean in, and she does the same.

"If it makes you feel a little better, he's really pulling for Michigan State," I tell her, and her smile becomes wide and bright.

"I really hope he chooses there. I know there's so much more to picking a school than being close to Mom and Dad, but I can't help it."

"I think your chances are good. Chris isn't running away from you guys," I tell her.

She smiles widely, then her smile softens. "You know, sometimes running isn't the answer."

My gaze leaves her face and focuses on my food. That's exactly why I hate small towns. Almost everyone knows what's going on in everybody's house. It's not that I don't appreciate Mrs. Scott's advice, but she can't possibly know what it's like to be judged not for who you are but for who your mother is. To feel out of place, like you don't belong.

"When I was younger, I was runner," she says as if she can read my mind.

I look at her in disbelief. What could she possibly have had to run from? She's so put together and nice. Her parents probably loved and doted on her. She's beautiful, and I could see her as a prom or homecoming queen. I know she's concerned about me, but she couldn't understand what it's like to run.

"I wasn't always like this." She chuckles, sounding almost embarrassed. "Time can definitely change you . . . for the better."

I smirk and wonder what Mrs. Scott would consider rebellious. Probably coming back five minutes after curfew. I giggle to myself.

"My mother and I didn't get along at all. We were like oil and water, and it just got worse as I became older," she says quietly.

I feel my eyebrows rise. Now that I can relate to.

"I didn't do much to make things better though. My family relationships already were stressed by the time William and I got together," she says with a small frown.

"They didn't like him?" I ask.

She laughs. "Not for me." With a sigh, she trails her finger around her coffee cup.

That says it all. If she had parents who cared enough about who she was with, they beat Evie in the parent contest. She couldn't care less if I brought a drunk convict home—she'd probably just ask where his dad was.

"Hey, Lisa," Chris says, bounding into the kitchen. He grabs a couple of pieces of bacon off the tray Mrs. Scott has out. I'm sure Chris has already eaten breakfast and the meat he's devouring now is like a before-the-road snack. "You riding with me today?"

"Yup, my mom's car is indisposed thanks to my new stepdad," I say sarcastically.

Chris shakes his head with a chuckle, and Mrs. Scott looks confused but doesn't say anything. She has no idea what my life is like—well, she probably has an idea but not the whole extent.

Chris walks past me and kisses his mom's cheek. "Love you, Mom. See you later."

"Thanks for breakfast, Mrs. Scott," I say, following him out of the house.

On the way to school, I explain the whole story of my morning from hell and "Jacky" and how I think my mom has lost the little bit of sanity I'd believed she had.

"Do you think the guy's okay, that you're okay being there?" Chris asks, his big green eyes on mine.

My best friend's concern for me, even being a hormonal seventeen-year-old boy, is more than I've felt from my mom in the past eight years. I didn't say anything to his mom, but I'm really hoping he goes to Michigan State University too. I can't imagine life without my best friend.

"Yeah, you know, I'm always fine. I think the guy's bark is worse than his bite, and to be honest, I don't consider his word his bond. My mom's touting that they're together, but you know how that goes. Together today, gone tomorrow." I wink at him, and he smiles the smile that has all the girls in school crushing on him.

Chris isn't just gorgeous; he's a sweetheart and honest and responsible. The complete opposite of the third member of our clan, whom we're picking up.

Aidan hops into the backseat with a frown. "What are you doing here?"

Aidan Ryles has been Chris's best friend for eleven years, which means he was Christopher's friend one year earlier than I was. A fact that he throws out whenever we argue. Christopher and Aidan are like the opposite sides of a coin. Chris's hair is dark and grown out while Aidan's alternates between light brown and blond. Chris has green eyes, and Aidan's are stark blue. If they had superpowers, Chris would act for the greater good, and Aidan would use his strictly for himself. It's not that that's such a bad thing. Aidan and I are probably more alike than Chris and I are, but sometimes being similar to someone means clashing, and Aidan and I clash a lot.

"Why, you're in a glorious mood this morning, aren't you, sweetie?" I tease as I pinch his cheek.

He pulls away from me and puts his baseball cap over his face. "Wake me up once we're at school."

"Good morning to you too, Aidan." Chris laughs at us.

SCHOOL GOES BY as normally and drably as it does every day. After first period swimming, Aidan and I have second period science together, where he barely pays attention and flirts with Cassie Adams, a girl I know for a fact has a huge crush on Chris. Aidan is too confident or arrogant to notice, or maybe he doesn't care since Chris seems oblivious to the fact that almost half of the senior class wants to do him. Aidan and I got drunk one time and discussed if Chris was gay, but then we realized if he were gay, he'd probably dress a whole lot better and wouldn't complain so much when I made him watch my favorite TV shows. Aidan summed up his argument by saying that if Chris were gay, he would have for sure made a pass at him by now. While Chris seems oblivious to his looks and the affect they have on the opposite sex, Aidan is absolutely aware of his.

My next period is history, which was my favorite period until I went out on a date with Malcolm Hunter. He's cute and the captain of the lacrosse team but the most boring person in the history of dates. He talked about nothing but lacrosse. I've watched it a couple of times, but I don't know enough about it to write a dissertation on it, which I would have needed to be able to do in order to hold a worthwhile conversation with Malcolm. For some reason, he thought our date went great, maybe because I let him kiss me—okay, we made out so I could get him to shut up, and he was cute and turned out to be a really good kisser, but not good enough to subject myself to that type of torture again. I declined when he asked me out again, and ever since, he's looked at me with these big regretful puppy eyes.

I try not to feel so bad about it since Jessica Sims sits on the other side of the class and she's ready to make him feel better whenever he's ready. And truthfully, like with every other boy I've dated, I didn't feel anything with Malcolm. After reading as many romance novels as I have, I know the feels are so important. That's what I hold on to, how I'll know when I've found the one . . . if there is even such a thing.

As cynical as I can be sometimes, I do believe in love. I believe in lust, but sadly, out of all the boys I've kissed and the one I let go further with me than anyone else has, I've never had the feels. The butterflies, the touch that makes tingles run up your spine, the guy who wins you with his words and coaxes you with his promises. I would swear that sort of thing only happened in books if so many girls I knew didn't swear they felt it every five seconds. Why was love or lust so easy to come by for everyone except me? Sometimes I think because I want it too badly, that I dream about it so much that I know the real versus the fake stuff. These kids have no clue.

My class before lunch is fourth period math, the class I hate the absolute most. Precalculus to be exact, and the one thing in the world that should be stricken from history books and never used to torture students who have no intention of ever using more than addition and subtraction. I've been working my butt off just to hold on to a low C, and as my teacher, Ms. Gregory, hands me my exam with a big D-minus, I feel that low C on the cusp of slipping away.

"Stay a few minutes after class, Lisa," she says before she continues to pass out the tests.

I slink down in my seat.

"What'd you get?" Amanda Hines asks me loudly.

I give her the look of death.

"That bad, huh?" she says, giving me a "that sucks" face.

I wish she could have spared a few of her points. Her test proudly displays a ninety-six percent.

"If I didn't have science club after school and the newspaper, you know I'd tutor you," she says with fake but convincing sincerity.

Amanda has been on a being-a-better-person kick. She saw some movie, *Pay It Forward* or something like that, and has been all about helping people ever since. Well, not really helping people but expressing her wish to help people. Amanda's like that—she really latches on to the things she's exposed to. Our freshman year, she became a vegetarian for six weeks after watching a PETA video. Our sophomore year, she decided to learn Italian because we had a cute foreign exchange student, and then she was on this female empowerment kick, which for some reason she thought meant wearing only pants and fake big-rimmed glasses. Most people find her phases annoying, but living with my mother has given me an extremely high level of patience, and since Amanda and I have been friends since the fourth grade and I don't have a lot of female friends, I put up with it.

"Have you decided if you're coming to Claire's party this weekend?" she asks as we pack up our things since class is almost over.

"It depends on if I can pick up an extra shift at the Barrow or not."

"I hope you come. We haven't done anything fun in a while," she whines, sweeping her blond bangs out of her face. I told her bangs would annoy the crap out of her.

"I'll try, but you know I need all the money I can get if I want a chance in hell of getting out of Evie's house."

Amanda presses her lips together tightly. "I wish you could just come live with me. Our house is huge. We could ride to school together, and we could be sisters—you know, one I actually like."

I laugh at her. The offer would be appealing if Amanda didn't have three sisters I absolutely hated. Amanda is a lot of things, but she's no snob, even though she has the makings of one. Her dad is a lawyer, and her mom owns a little boutique downtown. They have a big house on the ritzier side of town, and Amanda has a two-year-old BMW she inherited from her older sister who had to have the new Mercedes.

"Well, I hope you come and maybe bring Chris and Aidan with you," she says slyly.

I roll my eyes. Amanda isn't sure which one she has a crush on—it changes as often as her new projects—but I know that if she dated either of my best friends, especially Aidan, it would be super awkward. When it went bad—and if it was Aidan, it most definitely would go bad—I'd be stuck in the middle.

"I'll see what I can do," I say and laugh.

The bell rings a few minutes later, and everyone files out of class. I begrudgingly make my way up to Ms. Gregory's desk.

"You wanted to see me," I say quietly.

Ms. Gregory is middle-aged with tan skin, long dark hair, and bright blue eyes. She's one of the teachers Aidan refers to as bangable. She's tough but fair.

"I'm pretty sure you're aware that the last test you've taken has pulled your grade average down considerably," she says, folding her hands together on her desk.

"I'm good enough at math to at least figure that out," I say, and she smirks.

"Lisa, you've got to do better. A D in precalculus is not going to look good to an admissions department," she says seriously.

"I know. I've really been trying, but it's just math and me are like worst enemies," I say honestly.

"I told you that if you came in after school during our tutoring sessions, I believe it would help you greatly. I believe coming twice a week would at least get you to a solid B," she says.

"I wish I could, but I can't make them. I have to work."

"It's the first semester your senior year. If you plan on going to college, this math stuff isn't going to get any easier. It's going to be something you build on, and with a shaky foundation, that will not go well," she says, sincerity evident in her voice.

"I'll figure out something, Ms. Gregory." I sigh. What am I going to do?

"I hope so."

I SLIDE INTO my usual seat in the lunch room across from Chris, his friend Mike, and Devin. Amanda slides in next to me.

"You look like you just fucked your brother," Devin says and gives Mike a high five.

"You're so funny. I think you should quit school and do stand-up," I spit back.

"What's wrong?" Chris asks.

"I got a D on my math test which is sucking the life out of the fledgling C I had, and if I screw up any worse, I'm going to have a big old F in the middle of one of my most important report cards." I sigh.

"I told you I could help you," Chris says.

"That's so sweet of you, Chris," Amanda says, practically swooning.

Chris blushes.

"Your way of helping is actually doing it. And that's great and all, but it doesn't really help when it comes to me taking these tests." I chuckle.

"I offered to help her, but she won't take mine either," Amanda interjects.

I frown at her in disbelief.

"Don't they have afterschool tutoring? I heard if you go, the teacher gives you five points just for showing up," Devin adds.

"She can't go after school. She works," Chris informs him.

"Who's your teacher again?" Mike asks.

"The super-hot Ms. Gregory. I told Lisa to give me a hundred bucks and I'd convince Ms. Gregory to give her an A," Aidan says, pulling a chair up to the table.

"Oh, please, after you were done, she'd probably fail me," I say sarcastically.

"What's up, Amanda?" Aidan says with a wink that makes Amanda smile goofily.

"So are you guys coming to Claire's party this weekend?" Amanda asks.

"Who's Claire?" Mike asks.

"My big sister Claire. Our parents are gone for the weekend, so we're taking advantage," she says.

"Free alcohol and older chicks? I'm down," Devin says enthusiastically, giving Mike and Aidan a high five.

"What about you, Chris? You coming out?" Aidan asks.

"I don't know. My dad's just getting back from out of town, so my mom's probably going to do a dinner for him or something," Chris says with a shrug.

"Come on, man. Quit acting like a grandpa," Aidan whines.

"So you want me to blow off my dad's welcome home dinner to go and watch you get drunk and turned down by a whole new set of women?" Chris smirks, and I beam.

"Nice!" I say and mock the guys' high fives.

Chris winks at me.

"I think it's sweet that you put family first," Amanda says, taking the opportunity to touch Chris's hand.

God, Amanda just pick one already.

"Hey, is this pick-on-Aidan day?" Aidan grabs a french fry off my plate and throws it at Chris.

"Only in a perfect world," I say, slapping Aidan's arm.

"Look, how long does dinner last at your house? You should be done by, at the latest, nine, and then we slide over to Claire's party."

"Pleeeaaase, Chris," Amanda says in a sugary tone.

I look at her, surprised, and before I know it, Aidan, Devin, and Mike have all joined in on her pleading.

"Okay," Chris relents.

They all erupt in cheers.

"What about you, Lisa?" Amanda asks.

"I'll see if I can make it."

I CUT MY last class. It's only an elective, and I have a solid A. Since Chris and Amanda have a student council meeting after school, both of them are out as far as a ride home, so I start my hour-long walk early enough to get home to grab the car and head to work since my boss said I could work an extra shift. As I round the corner to our house and see the car isn't in the driveway, I feel my head pound. I run up the stairs, grab my keys, and open the door. My mom's in the living room and smoking a cigarette, her foot tapping continuously.

"Evie, where's the car?" I ask, already afraid to hear the answer.

Her lips are pressed together, and her worry lines are showing underneath the blond strings falling into her face. "I've been calling Jack all day. He told me he was just going to run to his brother's and he'd be back. I don't know." She shakes her head.

I feel my face fall. "Why would you let him take the car? God, Mom, you can't be that desperate to just hand over the only way you and I get to work for some guy with a beer belly and a dead colon!"

"I don't want to hear it! If it's not back by tonight, I'll call the cops. Just calm down," she says angrily.

Oh yeah, get angry at me, not the guy who's pretty much stolen your car. "Mom, I'm on a final warning at work. If I'm late, that could be it. I asked for this shift!"

"What do you want me to do? I can't do anything right now. Can't you call one of your friends to take you?"

"Yeah, because it's my friends' responsibility to look after your child's well-being!"

I storm past her into my room, put down my book bag, and grab my hat and apron for work. When I leave my room, I hear my mom screaming into the phone—I presume it's Jack. I roll my eyes, head out of the house, and jog over to Chris's. I feel my stomach drop. I absolutely hate asking people for stuff, but if I lose this job, I'm screwed. Evie works just enough to keep a roof over our heads and buy frivolous shit we don't need. I swallow my pride and head up the stairs, going up the front since Chris isn't home, and ring the bell. A few minutes later, Gwen is at the door.

"Hi, Mrs. Scott. I'm sorry to bother you," I say hesitantly.

She immediately looks concerned. "Is everything okay?"

"Sort of. I'm hoping you could drop me off at work. My mom has a friend looking at her car, and I won't make it if I walk. I can get home. I just have to get there, or they'll probably fire me," I say, doing my best to hold in my tears.

"Of course, sweetie. I'll grab my keys. It'll just be a minute."

"Thank you, thank you, thank you!"

THE RIDE TO the Barrow is quiet except for Mrs. Scott humming along to the radio. She's seems to be in a really good mood. I try to calm my nerves and suck up all the angst I'm emitting.

"I really commend you, being in school and working your senior year," she says, and I smile. "When I was your age, I did the bare minimum to get by."

I feel my face scrunch up. It's funny, but I don't get that from her. I would have thought she was a cheerleader, class treasurer, and homecoming queen. Mrs. Scott has always had a way of emanating warmth and good feels. Something I wish Evie had an ounce of.

"Really?" I say with a chuckle.

"Oh yeah," she says, giving me a wide grin. "I hated school and thought I knew everything of course. You're seventeen?"

"Yeah. I turn eighteen in January."

She nods. "I had so much growing up to do." She sighs a little, and I detect a hint of sadness behind her expression.

"Well, you turned out pretty awesome," I say.

She smiles and chuckles. "I did, I guess, huh?"

I can't help feeling confused. How could she not think that? She's, like, Suzie Homemaker. All of Chris's friends love her—she's miles ahead of my mom at least. I've known the Scotts since I was little.

She sings to the music again. I pull out some notes Amanda gave me earlier from precalc, but they might as well be in Japanese.

"What's that?" Gwen asks.

I sigh. "Precalc notes. I'm having the worst time with it. I hate math."

"Oh, I'm glad I get to avoid those classes when I start back."

I raise my eyebrow.

"I'm taking a couple of courses at the community college this fall. Chris sort of inspired me to go back," she says.

"That's cool. I wish I could skip math altogether and choose what to take like they do in other countries. I don't need math. I don't plan on becoming a scientist or anything."

"You never know when you'll need it though. You'd be the surprised how often it comes up. I hated math too. Luckily my math teacher senior year was more interested in being a musician than teaching us and passed us just for showing up." She chuckles. "Chris is pretty good at math. He can't help you?"

"Yeah, Chris is great, but he's more of a doer than a shower if that makes sense," I say, trying to hide the fact that her son does most of my math homework for me. But he struggles with how to show me how to do it. I hope I haven't given too much away.

"Oooh. Doesn't the school offer tutoring or something?" Gwen asks.

"They do, but its right after school, and I'm at work while it's going on."

"Hmm, I think I might have the perfect tutor for you," she says.

"Really, who?"

"My husband, William," she says cheerfully.

"He's good at math?" I haven't really been around Chris's dad in a while. He's always working on their farm or gone somewhere on business for it. I don't think I've even seen him up close in a few years.

"He's great at it. He taught math for a while right after college, and he's really patient."

"Really?" I ask, surprised. Chris's dad was a teacher? How do you go from teacher to farmer?

"Yes. He'd probably get a kick out of helping you. Sometimes I wonder if he regrets not sticking with it . . . I think it'll be great for him."

"You sure he wouldn't be too busy?"

"No, with fall practically here, things will really slow down for us. He's just closed a big deal for a contract for the farm he's been working on, and with me starting night classes, he'll probably be bored. It'd be perfect," she says as we pull up in front of my job. "What do you think?"

"If he could help, that'd be great. He'd probably have to be a miracle worker though. I'm pretty bad," I say, embarrassed.

"Don't worry about it. He used to tutor in college, and you can't be any worse than the kids he worked with then. I'll talk to him about it once I'm home, and I'll have Chris call you with the details."

"O-okay, great. Thank you, Mrs. Scott," I say, getting out of the truck.

"No thanks needed." She watches me walk to the door of the

Barrow. "Have a good workday, Lisa!"

I wave as she leaves and smile before hurrying inside. Today is looking a whole lot better than it started.

gwen

STAYING AT GIA'S house felt like being on vacation from my sucky, boring, micro-managed life. She didn't have much in her fridge, but she had junk food and a lot of it. By eleven in the morning, I was on a complete sugar high. Gummy bears, licorice, potato chips, and soda was my meal of choice. If Mom knew what I was eating and what Gia's cupboard looked like, she'd have a complete meltdown. I always knew my sister loved candy from the packs of M&M's I used to find in her room. While most parents had to worry about their kids hiding porno mags and drugs, Gia hid candy. She ate so much of it I have no idea how she's never had a cavity.

After my sugar binge in front of the TV, I manage to spill Pepsi all over myself while dancing with Madonna and turning her solo into a duet, singing "Like a Virgin" with a bottle of Pepsi in my hand. I take off my shirt and wipe up the brown liquid spreading across her hardwood floor, thanking God Gia doesn't have carpet. I grab a pair of jeans, an oversized shirt, and underwear out my bag, take a towel from Gia's linen closet, and turn on Gia's shower. Gia's stereo helps me finish off my serenade while I clean up.

God, this is the life. Own house away from annoying moms, school with sophisticated people doing sophisticated things, no curfew, no rules—just living. Gia is living the life, and for a day or two, I can pretend I'm living it as well. The only problem is being here alone in Gia's apartment, living a little piece of her life, makes me realize I have no idea how the hell I would get here. Gia's right, as always. I've kind of blown off school. My grades are okay but only because most of my classes are blow-off electives. I haven't done a lot of homework, but since I work when I'm in class and I'm a pretty good test-taker, my grade point average is a low B. I haven't applied to any schools since there's nothing I see myself wanting to spend the rest of my life doing.

Since we were kids, Gia loved playing courtroom. She'd always make me the bad guy while she asked me a bunch of questions and yelled at me like she saw in the movies we watched with Dad when Mom wasn't around to tell him we were too young. Gia's always had a plan, and now she's about to finish her four years of college and start her dream of law school. As boring as it sounds to me, she's doing something about her dream, and I admire that.

Me, I don't have a dream. Well, not a realistic one. I wish I could be one of Madonna's backup dancers, but since my only talents are being able to sway my hips on beat and adding a sexy shimmy, I think the qualifications for that may be out of my league. I start to feel myself becoming too serious and depressed, so I sing even louder to the radio as I rinse out the shampoo in my hair.

"Mind if I join you, babe?"

Then I feel a hand cup my butt. When I turn around and he sees my face, "Oh shit," is as far as he can get before I start screaming my head off and land an elbow in his eye.

"Ouch!" he screams.

I try to think of what to do first—run straight out of the house naked and covered in soap? Since he's blocking my escape, I snatch the shower curtain down and cover myself with it.

"Who the hell are you?" I shout.

"Who are you!" he asks angrily, still holding the eye I elbowed.

I stop a minute and think about why he would be asking who I am if he was a crazy serial rapist.

"I'm sorry! I thought you were someone else!" he says, frantically covering his eyes, probably so he won't see me.

"Get out, get out, get out!" I shout, pushing him out of the bathroom.

I slam the door behind him and try to calm my beating heart. I look around the bathroom which has water everywhere. The radio was knocked down by Mr. Grabby Hands, and I've ripped Gia's shower curtain. Who was the guy, and how did he get in to feel me up in the freakin' shower? Then it hits me—Gia's promise ring guy. It had to have been him. He thought I was Gia. Ugh, I just . . . it doesn't seem like Gia to give a guy a key to her apartment. She must really be into him, and I've elbowed in the eye the man who could be my future brother-in-law. Things like this would only happen to me.

I drop the shower curtain from around me and grab my towel and wrap it tightly around me. I crack the door. "Ugh, William? You out there? " I don't hear a response. "I'm sorry. I didn't know who you were," I say with an embarrassed laugh.

I step out cautiously and look around the house. After I do a sweep through the whole place, I determine William has gotten the hell out of Dodge.

When Gia gets home, she can't help but burst into laughter as I tell her what happened. Turns out she heard the story when William showed up at her class immediately after running out of here.

"I'm sorry, Gwen. I should have told you William has a key. He thought you were me." She continues to laugh.

I'm glad she finds it funny. I hadn't known how she was going to react, so I laugh along with her. "Obviously he did."

"I was going to meet him at work and tell him you were staying here for the weekend, but he came here to take a nap and thought . . . well I'm so glad you didn't give him a concussion," she says.

"Is his eye okay?" I ask sheepishly.

"A little red, but he's a big boy. He'll survive."

"I feel so bad. All he was trying to do was get a little nookie from his girlfriend, and I nearly blinded him," I tease her, and her face turns bright red. "It's nothing to be embarrassed over. You're a grown woman."

"I'm not embarrassed," she says, so obviously embarrassed.

"You're my big sister. You should be able to talk to me about these things, give me advice," I say jokingly.

"Advice? The all-knowing womanly sex guru needs my advice?"

I roll my eyes at her. I'm really all talk. The only guy who has gotten past second base with me yet is Zach, and he's far from rounding home.

"Besides, William knew he wasn't getting any nookie," she says, pulling me up from the couch and pushing me toward the kitchen.

"What, you tell him when you're on your period or something?" I ask.

"No," she says, looking almost more embarrassed of that than when I said nookie. "It's because we haven't had sex yet."

She sits at the table, and my eyes almost bulge out of my head.

"He's proposed to you before you've had sex?" Well, I shouldn't be so surprised. If any woman could get a man to propose before letting him round her playing field, it would be Gia. "He must be ugly," I say, shaking my head.

"You didn't see him?" she asks.

I start to prepare all the things I need to make the lasagna. Gia picked up all the things I needed after her class. "No, I didn't take time to get a good look at the guy I thought was a crazy psycho who'd broken in your house."

"Oh yeah." She giggles.

"I feel kind of bad though," I admit.

"He shouldn't have been sneaking in on me in the shower anyway," she says.

She gets up to try to help, but I wave her away. Gia is a terrible cook—I guess no one is really perfect.

"So what about you? Any special guys in your life?" She leans on the counter near me as I shred the cheeses.

"Not really." I shrug.

"Who's the Zach guy you mentioned earlier?" she says, surprising me. I only mentioned him once, but of course she's incredibly astute.

"I wouldn't call Zach special."

She looks at me in disbelief.

"Well, actually, that's wrong. Zach is a special kind of crazy, so in that way, yes, he's very special to me," I tell her.

"You like him," she says teasingly.

"I don't dislike him." I laugh, and she raises her eyebrows at me. "Fine, I like to make out with him. I like to make fun of him. I like to smoke—"

Gia throws up her hands to stop me, and I giggle at her.

"Mom never mentioned him," she says.

"I'm sure she did since he's the guy who's sort of the reason for all of this."

Her eyes widen. "Oooh, that guy. He must be really cute for you to do something so stupid with him."

I ignore the insult. "He is."

"But you don't have feelings for him?" she asks.

"No. Not really. I mean, if something happened to him, I'd be sad. But I think we're just friends who make out because, well, we don't have anything better to do."

"I'm sure you both could manage to find something better to do, but you choose to do that with each other," she says, her tone right in the middle between optimistic and disapproving. "But I don't think you should waste time being with someone you don't love. Especially in that away. And I wish you could find a guy who would take you on a nice date, who encourages you to be a better person instead of inspiring you to do things that are detrimental."

"Zach doesn't inspire me to do anything I don't want to do," I say defensively. "Why can't you and Mother understand that I can make completely bad decisions entirely on my own?" I stick my tongue out at her.

"So you admit that what you're doing is completely ridiculous and self-destructive," Gia says, and she's got me.

"Go watch TV or something until I finish," I say, waving her out of the kitchen.

I'm halfway done making dinner when the phone rings, and Gia bounces over to it from the living room.

"Hey, babe. I'm not doing anything, just watching TV. Gwen's making lasagna. No, she's not easily embarrassed. We'd love to have you come over. I'm sure she wants to grill your intentions for me." She giggles into the phone.

Oh no, she's inviting him over. God, I was hoping to have some more time between seeing him again after the awkward "You saw me naked and I punched you in the eye" scenario.

"Great, see you in a few." She hangs up the phone. "William will be here soon. Turns out he was able to get off early tonight!"

"Great," I say with fake enthusiasm.

"Come on, I know you're over what happened earlier," she says.

"I was hoping to at least sleep on it, but hey, whatever," I say sarcastically.

"Since when did you become such a delicate flower?" she jokes.

I can't help but laugh. This William guy must really make her happy because she hasn't been this jovial since our dad passed away.

"I'm fine with it, really. I guess it was better me being in the shower than on the toilet." I shrug.

"I can't wait for you to meet him, you know, the normal way this time," she says, giving me a quick hug. "I'm going to go hop in the shower and freshen up."

My sister seems almost giddy. What in the world is going on?

"Okay," I say enthusiastically.

I CHECK ON the lasagna as it's baking—it's almost done, maybe ten more minutes—as its delicious aroma wafts throughout the house. I love cooking. I haven't done it in a while though, and it feels good to be in the kitchen again. My dad taught me how to cook. I remember being five years old, playing with dough in the kitchen as he made up some concoction. I'm good, but compared to my dad, I have a long way to go. With his imagination and creativity, he could have been a five-star chef in any city, but he chose the small town in Michigan where our little family grew and thrived for a while. I'm pulled from my thoughts by the ringing doorbell.

"Gia, your beau's here," I yell jokingly toward her room.

"He has a key. He's only ringing for your benefit. Get it for me? I'll only be a few more minutes," she calls back.

Ugh. I walk toward the door and tell myself that it'd only be awkward if I cared what this guy thought of me. I haven't cared what anyone thought of me for a long time, and he's here to impress me, not the other way around. I'm the first member of Gia's family he's meeting, and I'm sure he wants us to think well of him. I open the door, and he's facing the other way. He's tall, maybe six feet. He has on a jean jacket and matching pants and a baseball cap. I'm a little surprised. I would have assumed Gia's guy would have on a three-piece suit or something.

"Hi," I say.

He turns around with a small smile. "Shower girl?" he says with a laugh. His voice is smooth and easy, not nervous or shaky, which is how I'd expected it to be.

"That'd be me, but I prefer Gwen," I say, resting my hand on my hip.

He takes off his baseball cap, revealing a mop of light brown tendrils. Some fall over his eyes. He sweeps them away, revealing beautiful light blue eyes, one with a noticeably red circle around it. He sticks out his hand, and I stare at it, lost for a second. God, he's hot, and not in the way Gia usually likes: clean-cut, uptight, and bully-able. William has stubble on his cheeks, his hair is naturally messy, and from his stance, he seems laidback. I take his hand, which swallows mine, and shake it. His hand is warm but not sweaty.

"Can I come in, shower girl?"

"Oh, you announce yourself? It would have been nice if you did it the first time," I counter, stepping aside.

"I'm a quick learner," he says, nudging me.

He winks before walking past me, leaving behind a nice aroma. He has on cologne or some type of spray but not a whole gallon like some of the boys at my school pour on before dances.

"What is that smell?" he says, his face scrunched up and not in the good way.

I feel my nerves go on high alert. "Is something wrong with your nose or something?"

"No. What's that terrible smell?" he asks, taking off his jean jacket and revealing a white T-shirt and perfectly toned arms. One has a tattoo peeping from beneath the shirt sleeve, but I can't see enough to know what it is completely.

"Look, buddy, I may not do a lot of things right, but cooking is something I take pride in doing exceptionally well, so if you think my food smells like a toilet, then you're smelling your own shit because you are full of it," I say angrily. A smirk spreads across his face, and I feel embarrassed.

"Is William messing with you? He has a very odd brand of humor," Gia says, appearing in the room behind him.

"Just getting your sister back for punching me in the eye." He winks at her before picking her up and giving her a kiss.

She pushes him away, and I feel so embarrassed, though I'm not entirely sure why.

"William," she says, sounding embarrassed, but she doesn't leave his embrace.

"I didn't punch you. I elbowed you," I correct him.

"Well, since it doesn't seem like you two have properly introduced yourselves, William, this is my sister, Gwen. Gwen, William."

"We actually did, but call me Will. Gia loves calling me by my full name, but please just Will," he says.

"Great, less syllables for me to say." I shrug.

We all stand around a little awkwardly.

"Gwen made lasagna. Doesn't it smell delicious?" Gia says excitedly.

His eyes cut to mine, and we both laugh.

"What's so funny?" she asks.

"We're both jerks." I giggle.

"Gwen!" she chastises me.

"No. She's right," he says with a smile.

WILL'S PERFORMANCE OF not liking the way my food smelled was pretty convincing, but he can't even pretend it doesn't taste good after the way he demolishes the large plate Gia fixes him.

"So it tastes better than it smells?" I tease.

He nods between bites. "Gia, why don't you cook like this?"

"It's just never been my thing. Gwen, Mom, and Dad all are good cooks, so I kind of let that be their thing," she replies.

"You have to show her how to make this," he says, shaking his head.

"Babe, cooking isn't my thing," Gia says with a frown.

"Well, hell, show me how to make it," he says with a laugh.

"Sorry, family recipe." I shrug.

"I'll be family soon. Right, G?" he asks as she grabs his plate and takes it to the sink.

She smirks when she returns to the table.

"I've asked your sister to marry me. She turned me down," he says teasingly.

I pretend she hasn't already told me this. "Aww, Gia, quit playing hard to get."

William shoots me a grateful smile.

"I didn't turn you down," she says with a sigh.

"You didn't say yes," he says adamantly, and suddenly I feel as though I'm part of a conversation I shouldn't be present for.

Their eyes lock in on each other as if they're having a staring contest. Gia breaks away first.

"William doesn't have a filter. You two have that in common, I think," she says, sounding a little irritated.

"I have a filter. It's just not very clean." I shrug.

William's jaw is clenched. I can see he isn't too happy about Gia turning him down.

"So are you going to law school too?" I ask, grabbing a piece of store-bought garlic bread that actually doesn't taste half bad.

He laughs and shakes his head. "No, I hate school. I couldn't imagine going for four more years."

"Which is ironic since William is teacher, isn't it?" she says, shooting me an amused glance.

"How do you hate school if you teach? What are you, a masochist or something?" I ask, confused.

"I hated being taught by other people. I'm a great teacher," he says smugly.

"So you're a hypocrite?" I ask.

"How does teaching make me hypocrite?"

"You're in a profession where you make others suffer the same fate you want to avoid, and you're probably stressing how important education is and how they should appreciate it," I say.

"That doesn't make me a hypocrite. If you want to survive, unless you have a really rich uncle or something, education is important and should be appreciated. Just because I don't want to go to college a minute longer than I have to to accomplish what I want to do doesn't make me a hypocrite," he says, folding his arms.

"He's right, Gwen. It makes him a sadist, not a hypocrite," Gia says, sitting on his lap and giving him a quick peck on the cheek.

"It's not right," I say.

"I let my students know they have a choice. Love it or hate it, education's important. Since I work with high school students, they could drop out if they wanted. School isn't mandatory," he says.

"Who on earth hired you?" I say in disbelief.

"You wouldn't want me to be your math teacher?" he says, his sparklingly blue eyes holding mine. They're beautiful, the kind you can get lost in.

I feel a pull in my stomach and shake it off. "Yeah, you seem like you'd blow off class a lot, and subs are easy." I grab my plate and put it in the sink. "I'm going to head to bed. You crazy kids have fun."

"You tired already?" Gia asks in disbelief.

I fake a yawn. "Yeah, the bus ride took a lot out of me."

"And assault would too, I guess," William jokes, and Gia swats him. "I'm only messing around. All's forgiven. We're going to be best buds, right, Gwen?"

I'm annoyed by the fact my heart is speeding up a bit. "Maybe. Good night, guys."

I head up to Gia's room. I lie across her bed and imagine what my life will be like in four years. If it's half as good as Gia's, I can see myself being a very happy woman.

I WAKE UP to Gia's nudge. She's sitting on the edge of the bed next to me.

"What's up?" I say groggily.

She sets my head on her lap and strokes my hair with a sigh. "Long day."

"What's wrong?" If she woke me up, something has to be wrong.

"You weren't really tired earlier, were you?"

"A little bit, and I thought you guys would want some privacy."

"How'd you like him?" she asks.

"He's really cool. I didn't think he'd be your type," I say.

She smiles and chuckles. "I don't think he is sometimes. We're so different. He reminds me of you actually."

I groan. "Is that a good or a bad thing?"

"It's good. Mostly. And you think he's cute, don't you?"

As if the question is even needed. Of course he's cute. He's hot. I think I have a little crush on him, but I can't tell her that without her spazzing out. I know what most people don't though—crushes don't mean anything. They're just stupid butterflies and meaningless empty emotions. I used to have a crush on the guy who served pizza at our school on Fridays.

"Of course he is. Are you crazy?" I tell her with a laugh, and she beams. "What's the problem? What am I missing in all of this?" I sit up and face her.

She lets out a sigh. "William is great. He's this amazing man, and I know he's going to make someone really happy one day. I just get these moments when I don't think it'll be me."

"What do you mean? He got the ring for *you*. He's proposed to *you*. The only way it won't be you is if you refuse to take it."

She doesn't look convinced. "Have you ever been in love?"

For a moment, I think of a wisecrack, something to get her to laugh, but seeing the sincerity in her expression, I kill my smug grin. "No."

"Before Dad died, he told me you know you're in love with someone when you can see yourself growing old with that person. You can see your life as clear as a movie screen, and when you see it, it feels right," she says.

I hold her hand. For a moment, I'm jealous of the talks she had with dad about boys, the advice he gave. I'll never get that. I'll never get those moments.

"Well, can you see your tomorrow *without* him?" I ask.

She scrunches up her face, then a look of relief washes over her face. She shakes her head with a soft smile.

"Then there's your answer, sis."

THE NEXT MORNING, Gia gets me up bright and early and shows me around the city. Where she lives is about a forty-five minute drive from downtown Chicago, but it's so worth the trip. We go to the field museum, which is her idea. She takes me to the Sears Tower, one of the tallest buildings in the world, and even though it's chilly, we stand on the observation deck and look at the lake front. The cold air doesn't seem to scare anyone else off from looking at it either. For lunch, we go to one of the most famous restaurants in Chicago, called Lou Malnati's, for pizza. It definitely lives up to the hype.

"I can't believe how good this is," I say before putting a long stretch of cheese in my mouth.

"I think the food here is the best part of this city," she says, cutting into the deep dish pizza that's as thick as the lasagna I make. "I talked to Mom this morning while you were sleeping."

"And what did our lovely mother have to say?" I ask sarcastically, dreading her reply.

"She wants you back home tomorrow and not a minute past." She giggles.

"You know I'm entirely capable of getting back by myself. I don't need a guardian."

"I know, but I don't understand why you'd want to endure another four-hour bus ride with a bunch of strangers. I can't imagine that was the best experience."

Now she's right about that.

"I have a late class, but William is off until Tuesday, so he offered to drive you back." She takes a sip of her diet soda.

My face immediately scrunches up. "Aww, Gia, I don't want to be stuck in the car with your boyfriend for that long." I hear myself whine.

"I thought you liked him," she says with a frown.

"He's seems okay, but a six-hour car ride with a practical stranger is going to be weird," I say, folding my arms across my chest.

"I can't believe you're actually pouting."

"I'm not pouting," I say, feeling myself pout.

"Look, it's not going to take six hours. That was because you were on a bus that probably made a dozen stops. And don't you want to get to know your future brother-in-law?" she teases.

I look at her with a smirk. "You don't even know if you want to marry him yet."

She frowns. "That's why this trip will be good. You can get to know him better and let me know what you think."

"You're going to trust me, a hormonal, self-destructive seventeen-year-old, to have a hand in making the biggest decision of your life?" I say sarcastically.

"Mom and Martin will meet him too," she adds, and I groan.

"Ugh, that's a family dinner I'm just dying to attend," I say, already wishing I had another place to run away to.

"Come on, if you can be nice and make sure meeting my parents isn't the worst experience of his life, that would be great," she says, pleading.

"I guess. It's not like I have much of a choice anyway." I groan.

"Do you think Mom is going to like him?" she asks, her smile tight.

I have to cover up my laugh. "Umm, I dunno." She frowns, so I say, "Okay, it's just . . . I don't really know the guy, but he seems a little rougher around the edges than the type you usually have on your arm."

"You'd be surprised. William can clean up well," she says with a smirk. "And his family is really connected."

"You mean, like, they're in the mob?" I joke.

"No, Gwen, but William's dad is a very important man," she says.

Great, another pretentious snob possibly connected to our family tree.

"You know how Mom can be. Just make sure she's not too hard on him," she says with a pleading grin.

Yeah, because mom always listens to my opinion.

"Okay," I relent, putting up my hands.

What is she thinking? I'd never send a prospective husband home to meet my mom and Martin alone. She's lost it. It would be different if he was some pedigreed guy who wore button-ups and had perfectly coiffed hair. I can already say without a doubt that my mom will not like Will. I wonder if Gia's trying to sabotage things. Maybe she really doesn't want to marry him and this will be the final nail in the coffin. Oh well, I have my own problems to deal with. Will better hope Mom's too pissed at me to bother interrogating him because if he hits her with the "I'm a teacherthat hates school," bit he did me last night . . . at the very least, my return home will be entertaining.

chapter five

lisa

"I WANT MY car back right fucking now, Jack!"

I hear Evie scream into the phone as I walk into the house. I can't help but look at her with disgust before I head to my room and slam the door. Luckily I was able to bum a ride home from my manager, Cindy. I bet my mom's regretting that act of kindness to the jerk of the century now. She's so loud I can still hear her. I take off my work clothes that always smell like coffee and sit on my bed. I grab the house phone and call Chris. He doesn't answer. I sigh and call the other member of our weird, disconnected Rat Pack.

"Hey, I need a ride. Can you come pick me up?" I say, sounding bored.

"No. I don't really want you to come to the party. You're a cock-blocker," Aidan says in that blunt way only he can.

"When have I ever been a cock block?"

"You always are. A lot of girls won't come up to me or Chris because they think we're with you," he whines.

"That just helps you weed out the girls who aren't sluts," I counter.

"Yeah, you're right. Okay, I'll be there in ten." He laughs. "Wait," he says before I hang up.

"What?"

"Your friend Amanda. I think I might have some fun with her tonight. Don't screw it up."

I start to protest, but he's already hung up. *Ugh.* No way. Aidan is *not* going to do anything with Amanda. The reason it's hard for me to keep any girlfriends is because they fall for Aidan's jerk-off appeal and Colgate smile. I grab a pair of jeans and a white sweater, the kind that holds everything a little too tightly but looks good. I run my hands through my hair and put on some lip gloss and a little bit of eyeliner. I rub my lips together, grab my jacket, and head to the kitchen.

The yelling has stopped. My mom's on the couch. Her face is pleasant, not tense and scrunched up.

"Jack apologized," she says happily.

"Great. When is Jack bringing our car back?" I ask.

"Tonight. He said he just had a lot of things come up. He didn't mean to inconvenience us."

I roll my eyes as I grab a bottle of water out the fridge. "We need groceries. If you leave me the money, I'll go tomorrow," I say, intentionally changing the topic from Jack.

"Where are you going?" she asks.

"To a party with Chris and Aidan," I say, heading back to my room.

"Hey, come have a seat."

I roll my eyes but do as she says. I sit on the opposite end of the couch from her.

"You know, you're so pretty. You look just like me when I was your age," she says, her eyes looking past me as if she's looking into the past at herself. "Being pretty can get you in trouble sometimes."

I laugh. I know she's not going to attempt to have the sex talk with me. I've learned more than enough from her leaving the door to her room open when she's drunk.

"I know you and those boys used to be just friends, but you're getting older. Your breasts are getting bigger, and their little wieners notice things like that," she says.

I almost want to vomit thinking about Chris and Aidan's wieners. "Mom. God, please stop."

"I'm just saying. We're barely making ends meet with just us two. I can't afford any trips to the clinic, and I am definitely not ready to be grandmother," she says.

I stand. I'll wait for Aidan on the porch. I don't bother to tell her goodbye.

He arrives with Mike and Devin.

"I need to talk to Aidan," I tell Devin, who has claimed the front seat.

"Come on, Lisa, don't start bitching now. We haven't even gotten to the party," Aidan whines.

Devin laughs as he climbs in the back of the car with Mike, and I take his seat in the front.

"Look, Aidan, you and Amanda are not going to happen. I'm sure there'll be a lot of desperate girls at the party. Can't you just ruin one of their lives?" I ask him, annoyed.

"Ruin one of their lives? I don't think I'm that bad," he says, feigning hurt feelings.

"Amanda likes you, yes, but—"

He cranks up the radio. I turn it back down.

"I like Amanda. She's hot, and I like how she's a different person every month. Maybe it'll stop me from being bored." He laughs, and I roll my eyes.

"No, you're not going to do this. Amanda is someone I call a friend. You of all people know me and girls don't typically get along. Can I have this one friend who doesn't reek of testosterone without you messing it up?" I punch his shoulder.

"Okay. Give me fifty bucks," he says with a shrug.

"I'm not giving you fifty dollars. Have you lost it?" I say in disbelief.

"Okay. If this van's a-rocking," Aidan says loudly.

"Don't come a-knocking," Mike and Devin say in unison, and I want to vomit.

"You all are so lame," I say angrily.

I cannot let this happen. I try to think of what I can say to convince Amanda not to fall for Aidan's peculiar charm that every other girl has fallen for, but I know how much she likes him. If he makes his move, I don't have a lot of confidence in her to turn him down. When we pull up to Chris's house, the idea comes to me as clear as day.

"I'll go get him," I say quickly and jump out of the car as soon as it's comes to a stop.

I make my way up to Chris's front door. He's coming out before I even get to knock.

"See you, Mom," he says as he closes it. "You got to go to the bathroom or something?" he asks me with a grin.

"I need you to ask Amanda out tonight," I blurt.

His face scrunches up, then he laughs. "Why?"

"Because Aidan is going to, and you know how Aidan's dates usually go."

"How do you know she wants to go out with me?" he asks, scratching his head.

I knock on his head. "Chris, seriously. Do you not know how hot you are, the effect that shy smile and perfect dimples have on a girl?"

His face immediately turns pink. My poor oblivious best friend.

"Come on, just ask her out!" I plead.

He rubs the back of his neck. "I don't know. Isn't it wrong for me to ask her out if I don't really like her when Aidan does?"

"Come on, you know what way Aidan likes her. Besides, you might like her. Amanda's not that bad."

"She's kind of weird."

"What! Amanda's not weird," I say, trying to keep a straight face.

"It's like she's a different person every week!"

"A week is exaggerating. Maybe every month tops," I say sarcastically.

He folds his arms across his chest.

"Come on, Chris. Amanda's still finding herself, but deep down, she's really sweet. And pretty, right?" I say, hugging his arm. I can see him starting to relent.

"Yeah, she's cute," he admits.

"So you're going to take her out? Please, please, please," I say like a five-year-old.

"Okay, fine, but if she decides to go out with Aidan, I'm not going chase after her or anything," he says.

I hug him and give him a kiss on the cheek. "Thank you, Chrissy."

When we're back at the car, I give Aidan a smug grin before getting in the back with Devin and Mike. He eyes me suspiciously but doesn't say anything

"Are you guys done making out?" Aidan teases, and Chris swats the back of the head.

WHEN WE ARRIVE at the party, tons of cars are parked in Amanda and Claire's driveway, several people are on the porch, and music blares from the house. We all agree to meet back at the car at one thirty or, per Aidan's words, our asses are walking home.

"Hey, Aidan." A girl from our school walks up to us and pulls him into a conversation, which is perfect because it gives Chris and me time to get to Amanda first.

"I'll only be a minute," Aidan says to us, but I pull Chris by the hand.

"We'll catch up with you, Aidan," I say, pulling Chris behind me.

"You want something to drink?" Chris asks over the music.

"What do they have?" I ask.

Chris can see over the crowd as we make our way to the faux bar area, which is really three card tables with a big bowl of punch, beers, and wine coolers.

"Wine cooler?" he guesses.

I smile, taking the strawberry daiquiri from his hand. I quit trying the mystery punch at these parties a few months ago. I'm not much of a drinker, and every punch I've had so far is like drinking gasoline. Chris grabs a beer for himself and takes a swig of it. I look around the place for Amanda. We really need to get to her before Aidan does. If Aidan asks her first, I know Chris won't go behind him and ask her out. Aidan probably still will since he'll know I put Chris up to it, but I have to hope Amanda will be too excited about going out with Chris to agree to a date with Aidan too.

"My mom said Dad's going to tutor you," he says, leaning into my ear.

I nod. "Yeah. She said he used to be a teacher. You never mentioned that."

"Yeah, right after he finished college or something like that." He takes another swig from the beer can before setting it down. Chris isn't much of a drinker either. He always insists on trying it though we both hate the taste of alcohol.

"You don't mind, do you?" I ask playfully.

He scrunches up his face and laughs. "Why would I mind?"

"Your dad's been out of town a lot, right? I want to make sure I'm not cutting into your father-son time or whatever," I say playfully.

He frowns for just a moment before he's back to his same happy Chris.

"What?" I ask.

He shakes his head and runs his hands through his hair, always a sign that something's bothering him. "It's nothing really."

"No, tell me. You know I'm just going to pester you about it until you do," I say, giving him a nudge.

He sighs. "My dad's been weird lately."

"What do you mean?" I'd always thought Chris had the perfect family. He has a cool dad—well, not exactly a cool dad, but a dad who's always around. His mother and father never fight or yell at each other, and Chris's parents are younger than all the other parents, which made them seem cooler when I was little.

"He's just seems different. Not himself I guess." He shrugs.

"What do you think it is?"

He shakes his head. "I don't know. I heard my mom on the phone saying she thinks he's having a midlife crisis or something." He chuckles.

"What has he been doing differently?"

"Nothing really. Well, it's just he's kind of been avoiding us the past few months . . . my dad always liked being at the farm, hands-on. But now he's been handling more of the business side of things, so he has to be gone a lot. He keeps saying he wants us to be prepared for the future."

"So you think it's money problems?" I definitely know what those are like.

He chuckles. "No, that's the thing. You know who my granddad is." Chris finishes off his beer quicker than I ever have. I don't think I've ever seen Chris finish a whole beer. "Granddad and Dad never used to get along, but now they're all buddy-buddy."

I take the empty can and toss it in a nearby garbage can. Yeah, of course Chris's parents wouldn't have money problems. His granddad is the richest guy in town, which is why my mom always says it's odd they live where they do. Not that they live in a dump, but people would expect them to live next door to Amanda in one of the mini-mansions here.

"I don't want to cause any problems or burden anyone. I can tell your mom I found someone else to help me," I offer.

He frowns. "No, it's cool. I think she's just trying to give him something to do, maybe. If my mom wants him to do it, she must think it's a good idea, that it'll help." He gives me a wide, reassuring smile, the type that can ease anyone's worries and erase all their fears. His smiles have helped me a lot. "Guess what?"

"What?"

"I'm thinking of trying out for this band I checked out a few weeks ago," he says.

I feel my eyes get bigger. "Really! When? Where? How did this happen without me knowing?" I think I'm a little offended. Chris has always played the guitar, and he's good at it. That, of course, adds to his appeal.

"I didn't want to say anything until I'd auditioned," he says bashfully.

"Ugh. No, you should want us there during the audition!" I say as if it's obvious, and he frowns. "You don't want us there? Is it, like, private or something?"

"It's not private. It's just that you and Aidan . . . I know you mean well and you both will be excited for me, but you can come off as . . ." he stops, searching for the right words

"A little much. Yeah, Aidan is totally too much." Then I stop. *He said me and Aidan?*

"It's just you'll make me more nervous," he says, quickly realizing he's hurt my feelings.

"I get it."

"You're not mad, are you?"

I huff a little. "My feelings are a little hurt, but I'll get over it. Let's go find Amanda before Aidan gets to her."

I take his hand, and we make our way through the partygoers. We find Amanda upstairs with her sister Deanna, whom I hate less than Claire but still can't stand. Amanda can't even stand her sisters. They're stuck-up prudes. As soon as Deanna sees me, she excuses herself from the crowded hallway but not before rolling her eyes at me.

Amanda's eyes light up as they land on me and Chris. "You came!" She gives me a big hug. "Hey, Chris! I'm glad you're here." She gives him a wide smile and flirty eyes, which he doesn't even notice, so I nudge him.

"I wouldn't have missed it," he says, nodding.

"Amanda, Chris has never seen your house. Why don't you give him a tour?" I suggest.

She eyes me in disbelief at first, and I wink at her.

"Yeah. If you're up for helping me through the sea of drunken people." She giggles.

When Chris smiles, it seems completely genuine, not at all forced. "Cool. Lead the way."

Amanda turns around and gives me a huge smile. Chris glances back too, and I mouth, "Thank you," and blow him a kiss.

"What's that about?"

I turn around and see Deanna staring at me from behind her Prada glasses and long blond bangs.

"What are you talking about, Deanna?"

"My sister isn't a charity. She doesn't need your pity setups. Especially with a guy who's so obviously into you," she says, crossing her arms.

I scoff at her. "You don't know what you're talking about."

I walk away, but she grabs my shoulder. I have to remind myself I'm in her house to stop me from backhanding her. Since Claire's not here right now to be a bitch, I guess Deanna has decided to take up her mantle. They are twins after all, in all the worst ways.

"It's so obvious. If you can't see that, you shouldn't be involved in anyone's love life. Besides that, Amanda doesn't need your help. My sister is beautiful, smart, and *not* the daughter of a whore. She doesn't need you setting her up with anyone."

I take a deep breath and count to ten to avoid knocking those glasses right off her face. When I get to eight and realize it's pointless—I'm going to rip her head off—I feel someone pick me up from behind. I glance back and see Aidan.

"Let me go, Aidan!" I yell.

"Why are you so mad?" Deanna asks sarcastically. "I didn't say you were the daughter of a whore. I said my sister's not. But if you feel like you're the daughter of a whore like everyone else says—"

"Hey, Deanna, shut the hell up before I let her go," Aidan yells back.

"Don't tell me to shut up. This is my house, and both of you can get the hell out," she says.

Aidan ushers me down the stairs, through onlookers and gawkers. I feel hot, like my face is on fire. I'm not sure if it's from anger or embarrassment.

"Go outside and cool off. You know she won't fight you. She'll just call the police, and that stuck-up bitch isn't worth sitting in jail over," Aidan says, his blue eyes boring into mine.

I nod furiously.

"Aaidan, come heeere," a drunk girl from my science class slurs.

"Stacy, one minute," he says, flashing her a wide smile.

"It's okay, Aidan. Go ahead. I'm cool," I tell him as the redhead drapes herself across his back.

"You sure?" he asks again.

"Yeah. I'm fine," I say before heading outside.

I sit on the porch steps and let out a loud groan. I fight away the tears building in my eyes.

"This party's so terrible I want to cry too," an amused deep voice says.

Too bad I'm not in the mood for jokes.

"I'm not crying, but if I were, it wouldn't be any of your business."

I angrily wipe away my tears. The last thing I need is some drunk guy trying to flirt with me, thinking I'm vulnerable and he's going to get laid.

"Well, tell me, why are you *not* crying?"

I channel all my energy into not taking out all of my frustrations on this annoying, nosey stranger—until I look into a warm pair of green eyes. He smiles as if he's used to making girls speechless. He's tall, taller than Aidan and Chris. He looks a bit older than us, with brown stubble around his cheeks and brown hair so light it's on the edge of being blond. His eyes are so light green they look almost blue.

"Are you a friend of Claire and Deanna's?" I ask, steadying my voice. He looks about twenty at least.

"Sort of," he says, taking it upon himself to sit next to me.

"Sort of are or sort of are not?" Anyone who is Claire or Deanna's friend isn't someone I want to be associated with.

"Claire's seeing a friend of mine," he says, resting his arms on his knees.

"Well, if you want to stay in her good graces, I'd say to stay the hell away from me," I warn him.

"I'm not dating Claire, so I don't particularly care what she thinks." He smirks.

"Well, you'd be the first in this town to not care what she thinks," I mutter.

"If you don't like Claire, why are you here?"

"I'm best friends with her sister Amanda," I say as I give him a quick once-over. I notice he's wearing a Michigan State T-shirt.

"You're still in high school?"

"Last year," I tell him as I wipe the remaining tears from my eyes.

"It gets better after this, you know. You'll see the petty rivalries and things you thought were important just aren't."

"Well that's easy to say from where you're sitting," I say, hugging my knees to my chest.

"A few inches away from a beautiful girl?"

I can't help but smile. "I thought they taught better pickup lines in college."

"Well, it made you smile, so I don't think it was too bad," he counters.

"I guess it wasn't."

"So was it good enough for you to tell me your name?"

"Lisa."

"Nice to meet you, Lisa. I'm Brett," he says, extending his hand.

After a second of hesitation, I take it. "Brett." I chuckle.

"What's so funny?"

"Nothing," I say, covering up my laugh.

I can't help remembering a conversation Chris, Aidan, and I had a few weeks ago when we called out the names of douchebags. Brett was one of the first names we'd called out. Brett doesn't seem like a douchebag. At least not yet.

The rest of the night, Brett Stelson and I sit in our own little world on the front porch. It seems like forever but passes like minutes. We talk for a long time, and he never makes a pass or makes me feel as though I should punch him in the face. Talking to him is easy. He doesn't make me feel as if I have to entertain him or let him feel me up to keep his attention. He's smart, a premed major. He grew up in Chicago and is at Michigan State on a track scholarship. He's an only child, like me, and his favorite food is chocolate chip cookies. I make sure to tease him about that not really being a food but more of a snack, and as a premed major, he should know the difference.

Around twelve thirty, I tell him I have to head toward the car so that my friends won't leave me at the party.

"Well, Lisa who has a prejudice against chocolate chip cookies, would you like to go out with me sometime?" he asks, and I feel my cheeks heat up. "If only to prove to you that your bias against chocolate chip cookies is totally unfounded."

I giggle and try to remember the last time I was asked on a date that I felt really excited about. It's been a while. I like Brett Stelson. He's older and seems to have the right sophistication that's so lacking around here, and he made me forget about wanting to bash in Deanna's head, so maybe he is something special.

"Good to see you haven't been taken away in handcuffs."

I turn around to see Aidan and his girl of the night standing behind us.

"Not yet at least," I retort as Brett and I stand. I see Aidan eying Brett curiously. "Brett, this is my friend Aidan. Aidan, this is Brett."

In only a second, Aidan's eyes meet mine, and he snickers. He's so immature. Brett looks a little confused.

"Don't worry about him. Aidan's six," I tell Brett, and he smirks.

"Me and Kimberly are making a beer run. You okay?" he asks, side-stepping my insult.

"Beer run? They ran out of—" I stop when Brett nudges me, and I realize it's a ploy to get Kimberly alone. "Ooohh. Well, hopefully your beer run won't take long since you're everybody's ride."

They both walk past us. That's the one thing I hate about riding with Aidan. If he decides to go off somewhere and hook up, we're stuck waiting until he's finished. I hear a buzzing noise coming from Brett's pocket. He pulls out a cell phone. Only about ten people in our class have them so far.

"That's your best friend?" he asks.

I recall telling him I was here with my best friends. "Aidan?" I laugh. "No. Far from it. We're more friends of convenience."

"Good, I think I'd be jealous if the girl I had a crush on was best friends with a guy," he teases, and I feel myself blush.

"Well, I actually do have a guy best friend. Chris, who I haven't seen the entire night . . ." I say, just realizing it. Chris and I usually check in on each other a couple of times when we're out together. "I should probably go find him."

His phone buzzes again. "It's Claire and Daniel. They have a flat tire. I have to go save the day." His expression is regretful when he looks up.

"Well, this is where our night ends then. Not bad." My eyes lock on his. It's been a long time since I wanted a boy to kiss me, and today is not the day . . . not yet. But one day soon, I can see myself wanting Brett Stelson to kiss me.

"Well, Lisa who doesn't like cookies," he teases.

"Chocolate chip cookies," I correct.

"I'll be seeing you very soon," he says, heading down the steps.

"I hope so, Brett Stelson." I give him a little wave before I head back into the house.

I push through the partygoers, nearly all drunk now, while trying to avoid Deanna so I can keep my promise to Aidan of not getting taken away in handcuffs. I ask several classmates if they've seen Chris, and finally one girl says she saw him and Amanda upstairs, which isn't super helpful. Amanda's house is huge.

When I get to Amanda's room, her door is closed. I knock but don't get an answer. They probably can't hear me over the music anyway. When I open the door, my eyes bulge out of my head. I see my friend Amanda topless and kissing some guy in her bed.

Eww eww eww!

Amanda and I are close, but that is not something I want to see. I quickly close the door and start down the hallway to continue looking for Chris, but I feel someone grab my arm. I'm relieved when I turn and see Chris, but then I notice his clothes are disheveled, his face is flushed, and his usually perfectly disorderly hair is now just messy. My mouth falls open, and my eyes practically bulge out of my head again.

"Oooh my God," I say in disbelief.

Chris looks down in embarrassment. At first I'm confused. Chris "Goody Two Shoes" Scott wouldn't be rounding second base with my best friend, whom he's appeared indifferent toward for the past couple of years. Then I laugh.

"That wasn't what it looked like," he says, looking completely embarrassed. Only my best friend would think hooking up with a beautiful girl at a party is something to be embarrassed about.

"I'm sure it's exactly what it looked like. I just . . . how? When?" I ask, flabbergasted.

Amanda appears behind him with a wide smile as she takes his arm and clings to it. "Sorry about that, Lisa. You've got to learn to knock though."

Chris looks more than a little uncomfortable at his new appendage, and I feel my stomach sink.

"Lisa was just telling me that she has to get home," Chris says with a tight smile.

Oh no. From the look on Chris' face, I hope I'm not about to have an Aidan problem. Gah!

Amanda's face falls in disappointment. "No, Lisa, just another hour or so. Are you not having fun?"

I don't give her the details of her sister's bitch fit, because it hardly seems the time. My eyes dart to Chris, who has a get-me-out-of-here look on his face.

"No, really. Evie is going to throw a bitch fit if I'm not home before one," I say with exaggerated disappointment.

Amanda frowns. "Evie's going to throw a fit?"

Yeah, I should have thought of a better lie than that. My mom isn't exactly the type to dole out curfews. I suck at lying.

"I'm grounded. Because of the fight we had about the car . . ." I say, trying to think of something that seems semi-believable.

"I drove," Chris jumps in with his own lie.

"Aww. Okay," she says, obviously disappointed. She turns Chris toward her. "You had a good time tonight?" Her voice sounds deeper than I've ever heard, but her eyes are wide, bright, and desperate.

"Great. I had a great time," Chris says quickly.

She beams, seeming satisfied with his answer, and turns to me without leaving Chris's side. I have to stop myself from laughing.

"What about you, hon?" she asks, leaning on Chris. Poor, poor Chris.

"I did, aside from your sister from hell bitching me out," I reveal.

She frowns. "Which one: Claire or Deanna?"

"Deanna, but it all worked out. I met a guy."

She lights up, her excitement contagious. "Really! Who?" She finally lets go of Chris and steps toward me.

"His name's Brett, and he's in college," I say, but Chris's eyes beg me to wrap this up. "But I'll tell you all about it tomorrow. I really have to get home."

"Yes, you have to!" She turns to Chris, stands on her tippy-toes, and plants a kiss on his lips. It looks completely one-sided, but she doesn't seem to notice how uncomfortable Chris looks. "Make sure to call me tomorrow, babe." She might as well be a cartoon with hearts shooting out of her eyes.

"Yeah. Cool," Chris says, slipping from her embrace.

He follows me down the stairs, and I fight the urge to ask Chris a thousand and one questions about what I just saw. Since his face is still flushed a pink I've never seen on him, I decide to wait until we're away from the loud partygoers to get his story. Though I do quickly conclude he's not drunk because I don't notice any signs of inebriation or smell any alcohol on him. The only buzz Amanda appeared to be drunk on was love.

We bump into Devin and Mike, who let us know they've found other ways to get home. Now only Chris and I are left on the porch with the partygoers who seem too drunk to leave. And of course Aidan is nowhere to be seen.

"This is why our parents should get us cell phones, right?" Chris says.

Every time I'd looked at Chris inside the house, I smirked to keep from giggling, and I can't stop myself from laughing now. My best friend is only human.

"Lisa, are you going to keep laughing whenever you look at me?" he asks, exasperated.

"No. I'm sure it'll pass after tonight and after I've grilled every detail out of you."

He grumbles, "I don't want to talk about it," for the fifth time since we've gotten out here.

We wait around for Aidan for a half an hour, and I get tired of being dragged around by Chris. He keeps moving us to inconspicuous spots so as not to run into Amanda since she thinks we left a while ago.

"I don't think Aidan's coming back," I finally huff. "Look, Amanda can give us a ride home. Who knows how long it'll take for Aidan to come back?"

"I'm not riding in the same car with her tonight," Chris says sternly, and I giggle again.

"Did she force herself on you, Chris?" I say jokingly.

He ignores me.

"Because from the brief glimpse I got—which nearly blinded me, I might add—it didn't look like she was holding you against your will."

"This is all your fault," he snaps, and I really start to laugh.

"I'm sorry, but this is not my fault. I am not taking the blame on this one," I say, throwing up my hands.

"Yes, it is . . . I'm going to go call my parents," he says before trotting into the house to search for a phone.

I can't believe he's blaming this on me. Okay, yes, I told him to ask her out and keep her distracted so Aidan wouldn't get his hands on her. I didn't tell him to practically sleep with her. I never actually thought Chris would even kiss her, let alone have a heavy make-out session with her. As hot as Chris is, I kind of just think of him as asexual. He's never really called girls hot without prompting from Aidan, and even then he'd agree or shake his head.

When Chris reappears, he lets me know his mom is on the way, and in less than ten minutes, his mom's big truck has pulled up in front of Amanda's house. We say our good-byes to the few people still sober enough to notice who we are, then we make our way to the truck. I quickly pull out a piece of gum from my purse and stuff it into Chris's hand in case he has any beer left on his breath. His face becomes panicked when he realizes the reason for it. When I head to the back door of the truck, he nudges me to the front. I'm not surprised by that, but I am surprised to see Chris's dad sitting in the driver's seat.

Our small town doesn't offer much, and that's a double-edged sword. The only crime, even on the poorer side of town, is mostly bored kids graffitiing on public property or stealing beer from little mom-and-pop liquor stores for a rush. There aren't a lot of exciting things to do or exciting people to know. So when I get in the car with Mr. Scott, I can't help but laugh at myself for never having realized what a beautiful man Chris's dad is.

Mr. Scott looks amused, and his blue eyes dart between us. The lower part of his face is covered with stubble, about thirty minutes past a five o'clock shadow, and his plump pink lips turn upward. Light from the car door opening displays his deep-set dimples. One strand of his collar-length golden-brown hair falls in his face.

I try to think of the last time I saw Mr. Scott—maybe a couple of months ago? No, almost a year ago. For some reason, he looks different.

I think it's the hair. It's longer now. I remember him always keeping it cut short, and I think the length and the color make his eyes stand out. The way Chris described him, I'd expected a sullen man with frown lines and a permanent scowl, but he looks happy, amused.

"You guys have fun?" he asks, almost as if he's covering up a laugh. Not in the sarcastic, hard way most parents would ask after seeing a dozen teens with plastic cups presumably filled with alcohol at almost two in the morning.

"Yeah," Chris answers quickly.

"Lisa, how are you? It's been a while," he says as we drive away.

"I'm good," I say, making sure my smile matches his upbeat tone.

"I feel like I haven't seen you and Aidan in forever. Where is he anyway?" he asks.

"Aidan is being Aidan," Chris answers.

"You three have always been like the Three Musketeers." Mr. Scott chuckles.

"Yeah, he's always swinging his sword at someone," I say and immediately remember that there's a parental unit sitting next to me.

Instead of a frown, he gives me a hearty laugh.

"Thanks for picking us up, Dad. I thought Mom was coming," Chris says, quickly changing the subject.

"She was tired, and I wasn't doing much of anything. I thought the car ride could help me sleep once we made it home. How's your mom doing, Lisa? I haven't seen her in a while," he asks.

I feel my stomach tighten, but I try to hide how awkward this topic makes me feel. "She's good."

"We used to go to parties like this. Me, your mom, and your dad," he says with a smile.

That makes me perk up. No one ever talks about my dad. He left when I was just two years old, so I guess people think it's a sore subject. As sucky as he may have been to leave my mom and me without as much as a word of good-bye, I can't help yearning to know more about him. I'd known that Mr. Scott and my parents went to school together, but I guess he never had a reason to talk to me about them since the subject never really came up.

"My mom doesn't really talk about my dad," the words slip from my mouth before I can censor them. The emotion in my voice catches me off guard.

Mr. Scott glances at me, and he realizes that maybe he shouldn't have been so free with his words or memories. "When I knew him, he was a great guy."

The rest of the ride goes by quickly and without anyone speaking. Mr. Scott changes the radio station from the eighties hits that Mrs. Scott likes to one Chris and I listen to. I'm a little surprised he even knows what we listen to. I try to distract myself by focusing on the song rather than my lingering thoughts about my dad. I look over my shoulder at Chris, who seems to have fallen asleep. I wonder how many beers he had. He had to have had a few, which is completely out of character for him. That would explain the compromising position he was in with Amanda. I look at Mr. Scott as he drums his hands on the steering wheel along to the beat of the song.

"So what's the problem you're having with math?" he asks, throwing me a quick glance.

I snicker. "I can't think of one problem I don't have with math."

A wide grin spreads across his face. "I've found a lot of people don't have a problem with math. It's more the *idea* of math than anything."

"The idea of math?" I ask.

"Yes. Just think, when did you start having problems with it?"

"Uhm, maybe around seventh grade, I think. When the letters and numbers and equations all started to happen at once."

He nods. "I think you psyched yourself out about it. You became intimidated by it and put up a mental wall. You're making it more difficult for yourself than it actually is."

I can't help but frown a bit. "I don't think that's it."

"Then what do you think it is?"

I stop and think a bit. "I just can't grasp it. It's so unbelievably confusing. It's like my mind just shuts down whenever I try to do it."

"See? That's what I mean. Think about it. Unless you suffer from some type of mental disability, I'm sure your mind doesn't just shut down at the sight of an equation," he jokes. "I think you became intimidated by it. You've already sent cues to your brain that you're not going to get it, which causes you to lose focus, distract yourself, and give up before you've even started. Math isn't something you're incapable of doing unless you've convinced yourself incapable of doing it." He gives me a reassuring smile.

"Maybe you're right."

"I am right," he says with a nod. "I was the same way with English. I hated to read. I hated to write so much that I convinced myself I *couldn't* do it. I didn't want to do it until I really started to believe that I could."

"I guess that makes sense," I say, noticing that we're pulling up to my old house. He must have forgotten I don't live near them anymore. "Uhm, we've moved."

His face scrunches up and realization dawns on his face. "Oh yeah. I remember Gwen telling me something about that."

I try to swallow the embarrassment stuck in my throat and ignore the flicker of sympathy in his expression. I can imagine what was said. Mrs. Scott is nice, and I don't see her being catty or gossipy, but anyone from Madison knows when you move anywhere lower than Fourth Street, the move was strictly a downgrade. After the whole thing with my stepdad divorcing my mom for sleeping with his brother, even if you're a saint, you just can't leave something like that out.

"We home?" Chris asks, awake again.

"No, I forgot Lisa moved," Mr. Scott says.

"Can you let me out then? I really have to go to the bathroom," Chris says urgently.

Mr. Scott pulls up their driveway, and Chris opens the door.

"And, son, next time you have enough beers that you can't hold your urine, you're going to be grounded for a week," Mr. Scott says knowingly.

Chris's face turns bright pink before he hops out of the truck.

"See you later, Chris," I say, covering my snicker.

"Just a piece of advice, if you ever want to cover the fact you've been drinking, make sure your bladder is completely empty before getting a ride home from your parent," Mr. Scott jokes.

He and I don't say much to each other before he pulls up in front of my house. I see my mom's car is back. Jack must have run out of gas money to joyride.

"Are you okay from here?" Mr. Scott asks hesitantly.

I nod and give him a wide smile. "I'm fine. Thank you, Mr. Scott."

"So your homework for the weekend is to open up your mind to the possibility that you can be a math genius who is overjoyed by how unbelievably easy it is," he says with a confident smile.

"I doubt it, but who knows?" I chuckle, then I remember we never set a time or specific date or anything. "Uhh. Is Monday at eight okay?"

"Great. Did you want me to come here, or will you be coming to my house?"

I want to vomit at the thought of Mr. Scott sitting at my kitchen table while my mom flounces around in her skanky shorts with her boobs out, interrupting us by continuously reminiscing about their good ol' days. No thanks!

"Your house is fine," I say, and he nods with a smile.

I get out, shut the door, and make my way up the steps to my house. Once I open the door, I turn around and give him a wave, and he flashes the lights before pulling off. I hear my mom and Jack Doe are in the midst of loudly making up. I roll my eyes, and a shiver crawls down my spine at the thought of the last time I saw him. He implied he'd be here more than a few times.

I wonder what his deal is. Is he homeless, jobless, kicked out of his wife's house? Those are usually the only guys who stick around longer than a few days with my mom. Guys who need help more than they could ever imagine helping. I close the door to my room and move the chair from my desk in front of my door. Just in case he *accidentally* mixes up our rooms, which has happened on more than one occasion with mom's friends.

I take off my jacket, toss it on my desk, grab my CD player, and put on my headphones, blasting Kelly Clarkson's newest single. As I fall on my bed, I think of Brett Stelson and his beautiful eyes and how he saved me from a night of brooding over Deanna's bitch attack. I shoot up in bed. I didn't give him my number. I sigh. How did we forget that? Well, maybe he didn't forget . . . maybe he was just being nice to a sad girl sitting on his friend's girlfriend's steps.

My thoughts drift to Chris and the embarrassing episode from earlier. I wonder how many beers he actually had. At least his dad was cool about it. Mr. Scott seems pretty cool in general actually. I've never really been around him much. I guess there hasn't been much of a reason for me to be. Well, hopefully he's a magician because it's going to take magic to turn my awful grades around.

As I start to relax and my lids get heavy, I giggle—Mr. Scott's eyes are the same color as Brett's.

gwen

"THESE ARE SO cute. Can I have them?" I beg Gia as I try on a pair of her sunglasses. As I look at my profile from each side in the mirror and pose for her, she laughs.

"Sure," she says lightly.

I flash her a wide smile and give her a hug. Today is the morning I head back to prison camp. At least she's sending me away with a souvenir.

"You going to miss me, sis?" I ask as I plop on her bed. My bag's all packed. I'm just waiting for her lover boy to come pick me up.

"Of course I am," she says, taking a seat next to me.

"I wish I didn't have to go back." I let myself fall into the softness of her mattress, and she does the same.

"It will only be as bad as you make it. Mom isn't that hard to please," she says.

"If you pretend to be everything she wants and do everything that she wants."

"You don't have to pretend."

"Of course *you* didn't. You're everything she wants already," I say, sitting up. "She promised she's not going to send me away, right?" Paranoia starts to creep up on me. What if my mom is lying and has a bus waiting to ship me off to some juvie center the moment I get home?

"Mom's not sending you anywhere," Gia says as if she's annoyed by my question.

"Because if she is, I'll never speak to her again," I say, pointedly eyeing Gia.

"You're being such a baby. Come on. William should be here any minute." She pulls me off the bed.

We sit in the living room so that we can hear William when he pulls up even though he has a key.

"What type of music does he like?" I ask, picking at a hangnail on my thumb. I can't go for hours listening to heavy metal or something equally annoying.

She chuckles. "I'm sure you'll survive whatever he plays on the radio."

"Does Mom have everything set for the dinner?"

"Yes, I told Will to wear something appropriate."

I roll my eyes.

"This could be your chance to get back in her good graces too," she advises.

I pretend to vomit.

"See, it's that kind of reaction that makes me wonder whether you're seventeen or seven," she says pointedly.

I let out an exasperated breath. "Fine. I'll smile and act polite and even wear a pretty pink dress," I say sarcastically.

"That would be great actually, and you can tone down the heavy eye makeup or lose it altogether." She tries to smudge off my eyeliner while I swat her away.

"What's wrong with my makeup? This is what's in."

"Yeah, maybe if you were onstage shooting a music video. Not for a seventeen-year-old attending her parents' dinner."

"I'm going to wait on the porch." I pick up my backpack and pull her former sunglasses onto my face.

"Wait, Gwen," she says, grabbing my arm. "We love you. I love you. I know Mom may treat you like a child sometimes—maybe even I do as well—but you're my little sister, and I care about you. The thing is you're not a little girl anymore. In a few months, you'll be an adult and able to do whatever you want. Mom is just scared. She wants you to have a good life."

I sigh. She frowns a bit and lifts my chin to make me look at her. She takes off my glasses, but I keep my eyes on the floor.

"I'll make you a deal," she says, making my curiosity get the best of me. "If you finish the rest of the school year strong, without giving our mother a nervous breakdown, once you graduate, you can come stay with me."

My eyes widen in disbelief. "Really?"

She giggles. "Yes, really!"

I give her a big hug. "Oh my God, it'll be great. I can get a job, and we can hang out all the time and—"

She puts up her hand, and I feel my face fall. "There are some conditions."

"Like what?" I ask skeptically.

"Like I said, you'll have to pick up your grades, at least end with a solid 3.0," she says, and I frown. "Okay, a 2.7, but you have to get two As. They can be in whatever you want."

I shrug and nod. I can do that.

"And you can get a job here, but you have to take some classes too. William teaches a few classes at the community college. They have classes for everything," she says excitedly.

This is starting to not sound as fun as I'd imagined. "Gia, I hate school."

"That's fine, but unless you have an alternative, those are my conditions," she says.

I contemplate her offer. I don't even know if I could survive staying at home with Mom once high school is over. A few classes at a community college can't be that bad. She didn't say how many. Two could count as a few, then I could find a job, get my own place, and live by my own rules.

"Do we have a deal?" she asks, trying to read my expression.

"Yeah, we have a deal," I say.

She hugs me excitedly. "That means being better all the way around, no missing curfew, being nicer to Martin, trying more with Mom."

My eyes almost bulge out of my head. "You didn't mention all of that. You said good grades!"

We hear William blow his horn.

"Oh, well, it's implied," she says quickly, walking me to the door.

I frown at her. The temperature's dropped since I arrived. There's a chill in the air that makes us walk quickly. As Gia wraps her arms around herself, her dark hair blowing in the wind, she walks in front of me. William gets out of the truck and meets us at the bottom of the porch.

"It's cold as shit out here," he says, and Gia shoots him a warning glare. He glances at me and laughs. "Sorry, I forgot she's ten."

He pulls her to him and kisses her. I look away, feeling oddly embarrassed. I've never seen my sister so affectionate with any guy, but that was when she was in high school and had her image to maintain. Once they break their embrace, Gia gives me a long warm hug.

"It was so good seeing you, sis. Even under the circumstances, I'm glad you came," she says into my ear.

I squeeze her a little tighter before letting go. I'll miss my sister. I've missed my sister. I didn't realize how much until just now when I feel tears attempting to well up in my eyes. "I'm glad I came too, Sis."

We squeeze hands before finally releasing each other. I climb in the truck, put my backpack on the floor, and adjust the seat for the long ride. I glance at Will and Gia telling each other good-bye. I turn on the radio and hear a song I'm vaguely familiar with. There's a cassette in the player, but I don't look at it. Sometimes looking at someone's music choices is like looking into their soul, and I do have some boundaries. That's good thing because Will is just opening the car door. As he settles into his seat, Gia leans on his window.

"Take care of him with Mom," she says to me.

"Oh, Mom is going to just love him," I say with fake enthusiasm.

Will laughs, but I detect a hint of nervousness.

"You're going to be fine, sweetie," she says before giving him a quick kiss.

"I guess we better get this show on the road then," he says, and Gia nods. "I'll call you as soon as we make it."

She blows us both kisses as we pull off.

WILL'S TRUCK IS definitely an upgrade from the bus and Zach's rust bucket. It's not brand new or top of the line, but it's surprisingly clean for belonging to a guy his age . . . though I'm not sure how old he is. He looks young. And the truck smells good, nothing like that dead-flower-in-a-spray Zach uses to cover up the stink when he sneaks his mom's car. Then again, this is Gia's boyfriend. I can't imagine her sitting in a car anything like Zach's.

"So you're going to be my map buddy," he says, gesturing toward the glove compartment.

I open it and see that it isn't neat and organized like I'd expected from the condition of the car. There are a bunch of old pamphlets, some candy bars, and restaurant menus. Who keeps restaurant menus in their glove compartment? Then I find the map folded into a square.

"I've already outlined our route. You'll just keep me on track. I'll be good for the next hour or so, but after that, you can kind of direct me. You know how to read a map, right?" he asks, and I nod.

"So whose idea was it for you to meet my parents by yourself?"

He chuckles, running his hand through his light brown hair. "That would be Gia's."

"You're crazy. I'd never meet anyone's parents without them being there. It's already awkward enough. Good luck."

Something that I swear is annoyance flashes over his face. "Well, you do things like that for people you love. You'll understand that when you grow up."

"Are you aiming for the role of annoying big brother or something?"

"No, I just think you're too immature right now to understand," he says matter-of-factly.

"I turn eighteen in just a few months. I'm not too young," I spit back.

"I didn't say you were too young. I said you were immature, meaning you need to grow up. There's a difference," he corrects me.

My anger, which had been on a three, goes up to five. How dare he? "Excuse me? You're calling me immature, and you've known me, what, two days?"

"It doesn't take long to get a feel for who someone is."

Why is he upset? Because I said he was crazy for meeting someone's parents without them? That *is* crazy. I start to ask him who exactly he thinks I am since he's such a psychic when it comes to knowing someone's character, but I won't give him the satisfaction of thinking I even care what *he* thinks of me. I don't even care what my family thinks. I feel my face heating up.

"You know what? I was wrong. My family is going to love you. You'll fit right in: judgmental, egotistical, hypocritical, and completely clueless," I say angrily.

I expect him to get mad or retort, but he just shoots me a dismissive grin. "I think you've used up your allotted adjectives for today."

He chuckles, and I'm so angry I huff—I literally huff—to keep myself from doing something that will jeopardize my move with Gia this summer. I shift my body as dramatically as I can toward the window, letting him know our brief conversation is over, and so begins the long, awkward silent treatment he'll get the rest of the car ride. My sister's possible fiancé is an asshole.

THE NEXT HOUR of our car ride isn't as awkwardly silent as expected. Will seems to like singing along to almost every song on the radio. Even though his voice is surprisingly good, it's still rude to sing with another passenger in the car and to assume that your voice is pleasing to the other party . . . even if it is.

"You don't even know the words to this song," I mutter.

He turns the radio down. "What was that?" he asks playfully.

"You're messing up the words to the song." I huff again, annoyed, especially since he's singing a song by my favorite artist on the planet—Madonna. I do give him points though. Most guys would cover up the fact that they even vaguely know the words to this song.

"I am not messing up the words," he says and starts to sing more loudly and dramatically.

"Yes, you are," I say, unable to cover up my laugh anymore.

"Well by all means, show me how it should be done," he challenges.

I don't take the bait though. Instead I turn the music up, shush him, and tell him to listen. He shakes his head and sings again.

I turn the radio back down to a normal level. "How about we just talk and not sing?"

He looks at me, exaggerating his skepticism. "I would, but the words that come out of my mouth may make me seem like a really big hypocritical, egotistical, judgmental jerk."

I roll my eyes. "Well, I think the mature thing to do is to accept people for who they really are."

He can't help but chuckle.

"Look, I promise not to assume things about you if you promise to do the same for me . . . and we can try to not talk about anything that could make one of us look like a really big jerk," I say.

"Deal." He beams.

It feels good to sense the animosity evaporating between us.

"So I guess since we're going to be in this car for a long time together, we might as well get to know each other."

I fight back a comment about him already knowing me since we're trying to get on a good note and we are going to be in this car a pretty long time.

"Or we can guess what we know of each other, so it's not like a weird first date thing," he kids.

I smirk. That actually sounds fun. "Okay, I think your favorite color is blue."

He frowns. "Red. Yours is purple."

Lucky guess.

"Your favorite food is . . . lasagna," I say, and he nods.

"One point," he admits.

I did kind of cheat since the way he devoured it at dinner the other night was kind of obvious.

"Your favorite singer is Madonna, you love to cook, and you got an A in your self-defense class," he says.

I laugh. "You don't have a favorite singer, you love to eat anything that's not nailed down, and you have a knack for amazing entrances."

"Very good."

"And you love my sister," I say, and he nods.

"That I do."

"Well, we have that in common," I say.

"She loves you too."

I grin. I know she does, even if it's in her annoying "big sister knows best" way.

"You think me meeting your parents is, like, her final test for me to get her to marry me?" For the first time since we've met, his voice isn't full of confidence or amusement.

"I don't think so. At the end of the day, Gia makes her own decisions. I just think it's important to her."

"Yeah, that's what I was thinking," he says more to himself than to me.

For the first time, I feel empathy for him. Regardless of what foot we've gotten off on, one thing I can clearly see is that he loves my sister, and as confident as he is, he may not know that she loves him.

"My parents, or my mom at least, she's not that bad . . ." I nearly cringe at the lie that almost left my mouth. "Wear a nice tie and show her your best manners, and you'll be fine. If my mom likes you, Martin will too."

He nods. "Thanks."

"Make sure to cover up your tattoo though. They're really conservative."

He smirks and glances at me. "How do you know I have a tattoo?"

I can feel my cheeks heat up. "You seem like the type of guy that has a tattoo," I say airily. "My friend Zach has two. I don't have any. You kind of remind me of him."

"He's your boyfriend?"

I shake my head with a laugh. "Not really."

"How is he not really your boyfriend?"

"Well, Zach isn't exactly the type to actually have a girlfriend," I explain.

He cocks his head to the side. "And are you the type of girl who likes guys who don't have actual girlfriends?"

I smile and turn my attention out the window.

"So what do you do when you're not hitchhiking across the country and pissing off your parents?" he asks.

I look back at him, noticing his eyelashes are lighter than his hair, thick and long. "I didn't hitchhike. And exactly how much did Gia tell you about me?" I can only imagine the stories Mom has exaggerated to her over the last year.

"Pissing off your parents isn't that big of a deal. I certainly have pissed off mine more often than not," he says, and I arch an eyebrow.

"Nooo, you don't seem like that type at all," I say sarcastically.

"No one can start an uproar at the Crestfield house like I can," he says with a laugh.

"Crestfield. Your last name is Crestfield?"

"Technically, but I'm in the process of changing it back to my father's name. My biological father's name is Scott."

I note hostility in his tone.

I like Scott a lot better than Crestfield.

"Your mom remarried too?"

"Yeah, I was three when she remarried after my dad passed away," he says quietly.

"That's sucks." After my own dad passed away, I'd learned that hearing people tell you they're sorry is pretty worthless.

"I don't really remember him. That's more messed up than him being dead, I think," he says, and I nod. "Gia said you and your dad were really close?"

"We were. He was my best friend," I say, watching the endless rows of fields stretch out along the road. "Things were so much better when he was around." I sigh. I've never said that to anyone, and I'm not sure why I've said it to him. "He was my ally, you know? He understood me. Now that he's gone, it's like I'm the odd man out. I don't fit anymore."

"My best friend always used to say that when people die, they're still with you. Watching over you, pushing you to be better," he says solemnly. "And the best way you can honor them is to listen to their little pushes."

I feel my eyes watering, and I quickly wipe away my tears. I've successfully gone three straight months without crying over Dad, and I really don't want to break my streak. "What about you? Are your parents proud that you grew up and became a fine educator?" I laugh, but he doesn't smile.

"My parents are probably two of the few in the world who didn't want me to teach. My stepfather wants me to follow in his footsteps and work for his company."

"What about your mom?" I ask in disbelief. His parents must be tough if being a teacher isn't good enough. My parents would throw a parade if I chose that path.

"My mom thinks whatever my stepdad tells her to," he says, and I detect the bitterness in his tone.

"Sounds familiar," I mutter, except I'm not sure if my mom thinks what Martin tells her to or if it's the other way around. Either way, their thinking never suits me.

We grow quiet, and the music continues to play. We're both lost in our thoughts when I see a sign saying "State Carnival in Ten Miles." My eyes widen, and I gasp.

"Oh my God, there's a carnival going on!" I sound way too excited, but the inner kid in me is trying to burst out.

"Yeah." He chuckles.

"Carnival. What else is there to say? We have to stop!" I say authoritatively, and he looks amused. "Come on! Games, corndogs, kettle corn, funnel cake." I feel my mouth water.

"And you say you're not immature." He chuckles.

"I will take your insult if it means I get funnel cake." I display my best sweet pleading girl smile.

He glances at his watch.

"We don't have to stay long. We'll make it to my house early enough for dinner," I say.

He looks at me skeptically.

"Please please, please!" I sound like a six-year-old to my own ears, but I don't care. Carnivals have the best food.

He rolls his eyes and laughs. "Okay, but you're buying."

"Actually, you're buying because I'm sort of out of money, but I'll win you something nice, I promise."

"THERE IS NOTHING better in the world than kettle corn and a cold Coke," Will says before stuffing some in his mouth.

"Yes, there is. It's called funnel cake and a root beer float," I say before swallowing the latter. "When is the last time you've been to a carnival?" I steal a piece of his popcorn.

He looks up as if he's thinking. "Never."

I frown at him, expecting it to be a joke. "Seriously, never? Not even as a little kid?"

"My stepdad thought a lot of things were frivolous. That children should focus on more important things, like their future, and not the triviality of childhood that is a distraction," he says, mimicking what I assume is his stepdad's voice.

"Your stepdad sounds like a major ass-wipe." Then I remember that I should have a filter on my mouth . . . per Gia's suggestion.

William's grin lets me know that slip was okay. "Gia likes him." He shrugs, and my face scrunches up. "More impressive is that he likes her."

"Most people do," I say with a reflective smile.

"My stepdad really doesn't take to anyone. He hasn't with me, and I lived in his house for over fifteen years," he says.

"Does Gia know he's never taken you to a carnival?"

He laughs and shrugs. "Nah. Me and Gia don't really talk about my issues with the family. Her stuff always seems like real problems. I didn't want to seem like a spoiled, grumbling rich kid.

"When I did my student teaching, I did a year in the inner city. It was rough, but it was an eye-opener. Seeing how kids live there . . . some didn't even have a parent to go home to because they had to work two jobs just to make ends meet. It really makes you realize what's important and how lucky you are. A lot of kids were smart and had potential but didn't even consider going to college because they couldn't afford it, because no one else in their family had gone. They didn't consider it an option." He's so passionate the blue in his eyes seems deeper. "Even with a snob of a stepdad, life could have been a whole lot worse." He sips the last of his Coke.

With that statement, I really look at Will. His parents are rich, but he doesn't flaunt it. He wears Levi's and plain T-shirts like he's refusing to be what he is—except being beautiful. He can't refuse that. I can see why Gia fell for him and why she's skeptical. He's playful and sarcastic, but behind his eyes, he looks vulnerable. A piece of him seems broken, and it makes you want to fix it.

"So since you've never been to a carnival before, that means you've never played any carnival games?" I ask sneakily.

"You got me." He laughs.

"Oh, this is going to be so much fun!"

We play almost every single game in the carnival. We start from the entrance and make our way around. I don't remember sucking so much at them, but apparently I have amnesia since I'm pretty bad. Will is actually good at almost everything he plays, winning a prize from each. He doesn't keep them though, with the exception the last game. He wins a cute stuffed bumblebee there, and I think he's keeping it for Gia. I don't to tell him that she hates stuffed animals and that when we were younger, she hid all of mine from me.

We ride the bumper cars and the Tilt-a-Whirl, which Will doesn't do great at. He has to sit down for at least twenty minutes, while I tease him mercilessly, but things have gone really well. Will is cool, and I feel like around him I don't have to watch what I say or think too hard about it. It's funny since we've only known each other a few days and got off on the wrong foot, but we're comfortable together, or at least I'm comfortable with him. Or maybe it's easy to be comfortable with someone in such a fun-filled place.

"We should probably be heading back," he says, glancing at his watch.

"Just one more thing," I say, pointing at the Ferris wheel. "No trip to a carnival is complete without that."

We wait in line for about ten minutes before we make it to the front. The ride worker—an older woman, possibly in her fifties—opens the carriage for us with a smile.

"You guys are handsome couple. You're going to make it for the long haul, I can tell," she says with a wink as we climb in.

"We're not together," I tell her before she closes the gate. I'm not sure if she hears me—a part of me hopes she doesn't.

We sit on the opposite sides of the ride.

"I had so much fun today. I haven't had this much fun in a long time," I tell him.

"I did too. You're pretty cool, Gwen Dwyer," he says, squeezing the little stuffed insect in his arm.

"You're not bad yourself. Gia's really lucky," I say, surprising myself with the hint of sadness in my voice.

He gives me a bright smile, then his expression softens. The moment is broken when the Ferris wheel lurches and makes this horrible grinding sound that makes my heart about jump out of my chest. It's so jarring I end up almost on top of Will, who grips my waist. When the death machine stills, I notice his breath is minty. When did he get gum? I then notice how crystal clear his blue eyes are, how strong and warm his hands are against my skin, how they send a tingling through my entire body. For a moment, just for a moment, I forget he's Gia's boyfriend. I want to close my eyes and take his lips in mine. I want him to pull me close and kiss me softly and for him to make it long.

"Are you okay?" he asks quietly, our faces only inches from one another's.

I nod. Does he feel this? Is it one-sided or maybe just a crazy sugar-induced adrenaline rush that's playing with my mind, giving me crazy thoughts about taking his face between my hands and kissing him? Neither of us moves. I feel a pull toward him. Our lips are magnets. I swear I see him slowly inching toward me, our walls both coming down, until the lights and the music of the ride come back on and we both snap out of the trance. And the very next moment is the most awkward and most heartbreaking moment I've ever experienced. His hands leave my waist, and I push myself to the other side of the ride.

"That was crazy, wasn't it?" he says, his voice higher than it was a few seconds ago.

"Yeah, real crazy." I'm not sure if he's referring to the ride going haywire or if he means the moment that would have been certifiably insane if the ride hadn't started to move again.

Crazy *adj.*—definition: wanting to kiss your sister's boyfriend.

ON THE RIDE back, I try to quit replaying the images of nearly kissing Will in my mind. I ignore the excitement that grows within me each second. But thinking about it also makes me terrified and disgusted. Was it just me? Maybe I imagined it all, but as quiet as Will has been, I assume I didn't.

I stop myself several times from bringing it up in the truck on the way home. It's stupid. It was just a stupid moment—one of the best almost-moments in my life. All the energy surrounding me, the intensity of being so close to a man I know little about and sharing a pull I've never felt with anyone else. Even with all the experimenting I've done with Zach, I never felt the same pull toward him I felt today with Will. I've never wanted to be closer to another person the way I did today. I try to think of the right words to end this awkward silence and remove the images running in my head, the nervousness in my stomach, the guilt that's occupying the space between us like a real person.

What the hell is wrong with me? I have to shake this. This is stupid. I can't have feelings for Will. Not Will. They're not feelings; it's a crush. There isn't any chemistry between us. It was just a tense moment—we both thought we might die on a dilapidated Ferris wheel in the middle of nowhere. I am just psyching myself out.

When I see my hometown's welcome sign, something I'd dreaded earlier, I perk up a bit. At least now I can take my mind off of what it's been focused on for the past three hours. I think of what I'll say to my mother, how pissed she's going to be, if she'll play nice since we'll have company. Maybe she'll send me to my room. Hopefully more attention will be on Will than on me. They'll be grilling him, observing him to see if he's good enough for my perfect sister. The limelight won't be on me tonight. Its seven thirty, and dinner will most likely be served at eight sharp. That'll give us both time to shower and clean up before my mother's guests arrive.

"Are you nervous about seeing your mom?"

His voice jolts me. I haven't heard it for the past few hours other than him asking me about a turn here or there, and even then it was low and distant. Now it sounds more like the one I'd gotten used to earlier.

"No. Are you?" I ask, trying to sound casual.

"A little more than I thought." He glances at me with a weak smile.

"I'm sure all her ill feelings will be directed at me," I say, trying to make him feel better.

We pull up in front of my house. I let out a deep sigh before getting out and walking up our porch, Will not far behind me. My mom opens the door, a frown already on her face.

"It's about time. Where have you two been? Gia said you should have made it hours ago," my mother says, dramatically eyeing me without as much as glancing at Will. She's in full-on dinner-party mode, wearing a white Liz Claiborne dress suit. Her manicured hand taps her gold watch, and her dark hair's swept up in a bun.

"I'm so sorry, Mrs. Garten. It was my fault. We got lost on the way in." Will's voice is smooth, his words more articulate, and they seem odd coming from the man I've been with for the past few hours.

My mom's frown instantly perks up as her eyes survey him, searching for flaws. William has virtually none. I can see my mom envisioning what a great addition he'll be to our family portrait. I should be thankful he's soothed her wrath and taken her scrutiny from me, but I can't help feeling annoyed. I'd somehow thought Will and I were kindred spirits, the rebels of our clans. But I guess this isn't Will; this is William.

"Please forgive my manners," my mother says, her voice warm as she extends her hand.

Will takes it.

"It is so nice to meet you," she says.

"It's nice to meet you as well, Mrs. Garten," he says in *William's voice.*

"Please come in." She moves from in front of the entrance so that Will and I can pass, but before I follow him, she puts her hand on his back so that they can walk in front of me, of course. "Come, come, sit. I can't imagine being in such a cramped space for so long.

She doesn't even glance at me, but I actually prefer her silent treatment.

"It wasn't bad. Gwen was a great road trip companion," he says with a fake laugh.

I think it's fake anyway. I roll my eyes, and my mom shoots me a sharp glare.

"You're so handsome. My Gia certainly has my taste," she says jokingly.

"And she's inherited her beauty from you," he says.

I want to gag.

"Oh stop," she says, lightly hitting his hand. "Martin and I have been so anxious to meet you. You have to tell us everything."

"I'd be glad to. I was hoping to freshen up a bit before dinner if possible though," he says, sounding foreign to me. I'd never thought of him as a guy who would say "freshen up."

"Of course! Let me show you to your room so you can get settled. We'll get acquainted at dinner. I hope you like salmon. Marta's salmon is to die for," my mom exaggerates.

Marta is the housekeeper-slash-cook we inherited when Martin became our stepdad. Having someone cook and clean for us seems so pretentious. When my dad was alive, we shared chores, and he and I cooked. Now Marta controls the kitchen as if it's her own personal kingdom.

"I love salmon," William says enthusiastically.

We follow her upstairs, and she shows him the guest room and points out the extra bathroom he can use. She also tells him there's a phone so he can let Gia know he's made it. He thanks her before we leave him, and as soon as his door shuts, my mother scowls.

"*We* have much to discuss, young lady, but I won't let you ruin this night. I laid out a dress for you on your bed. I expect you to be on your absolute best behavior tonight." With an agitated huff, she walks past me and down the stairs.

I SHOWER AND look at the baby blue dress my mother has laid out on my bed. It's her favorite color and the girliest, primmest dress I've seen in a long time. I wonder if this is a test, if she's trying to break my resolve. Maybe she wants me to crack. I bet she wants to send me away to some bad behavior camp or boarding school so I can be out of their hair. She doesn't trust me to just sit and not cause problems. I guess I've done so well at causing them she thinks I couldn't succeed at anything else.

Well, tonight is the night I prove her wrong. I'll show her I can be well-behaved and as prim and uptight as she could want me to be. She's not going to ruin my chance to get the hell out of here and live with Gia when summer hits. I'll be the perfect Stepford daughter. I blow-dry my hair and pull it onto the top of my head in a Audrey Hepburn-style bun, and I put on the stupid ugly dress. I have to fight the urge to put on my black leather boots with it, not that I really want to. They're not really comfortable, but they would piss her off and annoy Martin. Instead I slip on a pair of stockings, which she always nags me to wear, and white Mary Janes. I glance at myself in the mirror and practice a fake wide smile.

"Dinner was wonderful, Mother. I had the most excellent time with William, Martin. I almost made out with my sister's boyfriend, everyone," I say into the mirror with a pageant smile. Instead of feeling a smug satisfaction with myself, my stomach feels sick. I let out a sigh.

I open the door and head downstairs, the stench of salmon hitting my nose before I round the corner to the kitchen. I wonder if my mom chose salmon since it's my least favorite fish. When I enter the dining room, as if on cue, Martin and Will stand. My heart sinks when I see him. His hair is no longer deliciously untidy but is now combed back. He's wearing a navy dinner jacket, white button-up, khaki slacks, and a tie. He looks like a Ken doll, so different from the rugged, jean-jacketed, tattooed guy with the amazing blue eyes. He looks like William Crestfield, not Will Scott. Then I realize I look like Gwendolyn Garten, not Gwen Dwyer. Once I enter the room and our eyes lock, I think he can read my thoughts because his eyes drift to the table and his face turns red.

"You look beautiful, Gwendolyn," Martin says, his eyes lighting up when he sees the picture-worthy stepdaughter he's always imagined.

"I picked out her dress. It's perfect on her, isn't it?" my mother says with a pleased smile as I stand behind my chair across from Martin and my mother and next to William.

"It is," Martin agrees.

William, which I've decided to call him for the rest of the night, pulls out my chair.

"William was just telling us about how fulfilling his job as a teacher is," my mom says, sounding impressed.

I have to bite my tongue to keep from snickering. Thankfully Marta brings out the appetizer.

"Marta is a fantastic cook. You're in for quite a treat," Martin gushes.

"You're too kind, sir," Marta says in the monotone that never deviates from bored and displeased.

My mom couldn't stand her and complained incessantly to me and Gia when we moved in, but Marta had had a place in this house long before my mother. I think Martin told her Marta wasn't going anywhere in the passive-aggressive way he does when he refuses her something, which doesn't happen much.

"Gwen cooked for Gia and me. She's amazing. I couldn't believe she'd made lasagna from scratch," William says, and I suppress a small smile.

"Gwen hasn't cooked in ages," my mom says, mildly enthused.

"It was really fantastic," he says.

I feel my face heating up.

"You'll have to make us some sometime, Gwen," Martin says.

Marta displays a blatant frown before she leaves us to taste her dish.

"So, William, are wedding bells in your future with Gia?" Mom asks.

"Whenever your daughter says yes," Will says charmingly.

"Oh, how exciting. When are you going to ask her?" She beams at William.

My eyes widen, as do William's. My mom looks genuinely interested, which means Gia hasn't mentioned to my mother that Will has proposed. Will, who has been cool, poised, and collected, looks caught off guard.

Martin notices and tries to step in. "Honey, that's nothing to spring on the boy." He laughs, making light of the situation.

"It's just a question, Martin," my mom says charmingly.

William's face turns beet-red. Gia didn't tell Mom that he proposed. Why wouldn't she tell her? His eyes are downcast now, the charming grin gone. The tension in the room has become downright awkward.

"So, honey, Michael was talking to me about the polls the other day," Martin segues into some political mumbo-jumbo, steering the conversation away from a sore that he doesn't even know exists.

I don't understand why Gia didn't mention the proposal.

"Would you all excuse me a minute?" William says as he rises from the table.

My mom and Martin exchange confused looks.

"What was that about?" my mom whispers to Martin once William leaves the room. "I didn't think the question of the future would throw him off so much. Any boy with my daughter should be considering the future. Gia's a senior. She makes plans, so her future husband needs to as well. Don't you think they would look great together?"

"I don't know. You know kids these days," Martin says, finishing the rest of whatever Marta made.

"May I be excused?" I ask awkwardly.

My mother eyes me suspiciously. "Is there something you'd like to share with us, Gwendolyn?"

"I-I don't know. I just need to go to the bathroom," I say with a shrug.

My mother sighs. "Fine."

I feel her eyes follow me as I leave the room. I head through the kitchen and see the door to the patio cracked. William's sitting next to the pool, hunched over and resting his arms on his knees. He seems deep in thought, so I don't say anything. I just sit next to him. He doesn't say anything but keeps his blue eyes on the water.

"I feel like Cinderella's fairy godmother in this dress," I joke.

"Your mom and Gia are close. That's what I gathered from her. Why wouldn't she tell her I proposed?"

"Maybe she didn't want to tell her until she'd said yes," I say, trying to keep my tone upbeat and scrambling for something to say that will make his situation better.

"Or she didn't tell her because she's not going to say yes," he says, sounding exasperated.

"Let's not jump the gun . . . my mom, she's the type to take something and run with it. There are so many reasons she wouldn't tell my mom. She didn't want to tell her until you'd met her. Or she didn't want my mom to go off into this wedding tangent thing she'll most likely do, or she's smart and wants to elope with you and she'll just spring it on them."

He frowns at me. Okay, maybe the last reason isn't very Gia-like, but the rest makes sense.

"Gia loves you. I know it," I tell him, squeezing his knee. "Cross my heart and hope to die."

He gives me a hint of a smile as he loosens his tie, and his stiff posture relaxes. Just like that, he's back to Will.

"You're in there. It didn't seem like that to me," I say, feeling more comfortable around him again like before the whole Ferris wheel thing.

He smirks and shrugs. "I can turn the charm on when I need to."

I want to tell him he's charming without trying, but that wouldn't be appropriate, and tonight is all about being appropriate. "While you were in there, I could definitely see you being Gia's husband."

His wide smile diminishes a bit. "Yeah."

"Not that Gia doesn't like you when you're not like that. I'm sure she likes you for who you are," I say quickly. Whoever that is.

"And who do you think I am, Gwen Dwyer?" His voice is low and husky, soulful and rhythmic, like he's playing an instrument.

He's turned toward me, so his eyes meet mine, and I feel that pull from earlier. The way he says my name makes my heart speed up.

"A guy who's really good at carnival games," I say quietly.

He grins and turns back to the glowing water in our pool. I turn around and see Marta peeping through the cracked door. I wave at her enthusiastically, and she goes back into the house.

"It's so weird having someone do the things we used to do." I sigh.

Will chuckles. "At least there's only one of her."

I look at him questioningly. "You grew up with a housekeeper?"

"Several, not including the gardener, nanny, tutor, chef, and butler," he says with a sigh.

My eyebrows shoot up. I'd forgotten Gia said his family is loaded. "Wow!"

"It's something you get used to," he says with a shrug.

I imagine Gia as the lady of the house, directing several servants scurrying around and wearing those cute little black-and-white outfits, saying, "Welcome to my home." Will—no, William—is by her side, and he's wearing a nice blue suit like Martin's.

"Would you want to live like that?" he asks as if the answer isn't obvious.

I scrunch up my face. "No."

He looks surprised.

"I mean, it would be pretty cool to be waited on. Marta doesn't wait on me here. My mom still makes me clean my room and do my own laundry." I laugh, and he grins. "But one day when I'm really old and I have a family, I wouldn't want strangers in my house. I'd want to be really cozy, a house full kids. I'd cook every day and help them with their homework and read to them at bedtime. I'd teach my daughter how to sew, and my husband would teach my son how to change a tire, and we'd be really old school. And happy. And we can come over to your and Gia's house when we want to live it up with the rich people." I elbow him playfully.

"Teachers aren't notoriously rich," he says.

"Gia will be rich. Don't worry about that. She's going to be the best damn trial lawyer you've ever heard of. Whatever Gia does, she's the best at it," I say, playing with a loose thread on the hem of my dress.

"How many nieces or nephews am I going to have?" he asks.

I close my eyes and squint. "Seven maybe?"

He lets out a glorious laugh, one I want to put in my pocket and keep for later.

"Just kidding. Maybe three or four. Ideally two boys and two girls," I say with a shrug.

"You are a puzzle," he says, looking at me as if he's confused but amused.

"What?"

"I thought you were going to say you wanted to be a dancer and travel the world and never get married or something," he says with a chuckle.

I shake my head and say sarcastically, "Well, who wouldn't want to be Madonna's backup dancer and go on a world tour with her?" I add, "But besides that, I just want what my mom and dad had. They were happy. It doesn't take much to make me happy, contrary to what you may have heard."

"You think Gia would live on a farm?" he asks.

It's my turn to laugh, so hard I feel my body shaking. "Um . . . you mean like with cows and pigs and stuff?" I try to catch my breath, and he nods. "I don't see Gia being a farmer's wife." I notice the seriousness on his face. "What made you ask that?"

"No reason."

"There you two are."

We turn around to see my mother approaching.

"Come in. Marta's bringing out the main course," she says urgently.

THE REMAINDER OF the dinner goes smoothly, and the topics of marriage and his and Gia's plans don't come up. They mostly ask about his family and work. They are very impressed with him being a Crestfield apparently. Martin fills up the rest of the conversation with how his political campaign is going.

Will tells us he's decided to drive back tonight instead of staying the night. Mom and Martin encourage him to stay, but he says that he prefers to drive at night and he's pretty rested up. He obliges them by agreeing to take a short nap before hitting the road, but he says there's no need to wait up for him since he'll leave after his nap.

We all say our good nights. I sort of wish I could say good night to him without the audience. My mom is in a good mood after dinner and a few glasses of wine. She seems pleased with my behavior at dinner and tells me we'll talk tomorrow while giving me a quick hug. She and Martin disappear into their bedroom.

I don't get much sleep. I toss and turn, thinking of everything that's happened today and over the past few days. My gaze falls on the horrid blue dress my mom picked out then moves to the leather boots she hates, and I hear a knock at my door. I step out of bed, wearing my oversized black T-shirt, and open the door to find Will—messy hair, jeans, and denim jacket. I can't help but beam.

"I'm about to head out," he says.

I suddenly feel a tinge of sadness. "I'll walk you out."

We walk silently down the stairs and through the front door.

"You're sure you're going to be okay making the drive back?" I ask him when we're on the porch.

"Yeah, I've stayed up longer grading papers," he says with a laugh.

"Thank you for driving me back. It was much better than sitting next to some stranger with body odor who talks too much," I say.

He chuckles. "Not a problem. I'll be seeing you soon." He walks to the truck and throws his bag inside. He starts to get in but stops halfway in. "Oh wait, I forgot."

He reaches in the back and pulls out the little stuffed bee he won earlier.

"This is for you," he says, handing it to me, and I can't help but smile.

"I thought you got this for Gia," I ask skeptically before taking it.

"No, she hates stuffed animals. I saw you staring at it the whole time I played that game," he says.

I take it from him and give it a little squeeze. "Thank you."

He nods before giving me a buddy-pat on the arm, and it agitates me for some reason, but I manage a smile. He gets in the truck, turns it on, and starts to back out.

"Will?" I say before he backs all the way out, praying he can hear me.

He stops and rolls the window all the way down.

"She's going to say yes," I tell him, and he looks at me skeptically.

"How do you know?"

"Because she'd be crazy if she didn't."

We stare at each other for what seems like forever but is only a second, and I wonder if he's thinking what I'm thinking about, all the what ifs: what if he lived here, what if I'd met him first, what if I could act on what I felt earlier if it was anything at all. He breaks away from our stare down first, and a moment later, he's blasting Madonna, and I can't help but laugh. He honks the horn, giving me a boyish grin before pulling off, and I think if anything, maybe I've made a friend.

chapter six

lisa

"IT WAS THE most magical night of my life," Amanda gushes before throwing herself back-first onto my bed as she finishes her story about what happened between her and Chris. She showed up holding lattes and wearing a super cheesy smile.

"So let me get this straight," I say, trying to not sound condescending or doubtful. What she's saying is just so weird—the stuff about Chris, that is. "So you guys were talking, and you talked for an hour?"

She nods.

"And after that, you guys had some beers," I say, and she sits up.

"Yeah, like I said, he became so much more easygoing after that. He told me about his music and how he's going to try out for a band next week, and I asked him if I could come, and he was like, 'That'd be cool,'" she says.

I feel a tightness in my chest. Amanda gets to watch him try out, but Aidan and I can't? He gave me the impression last night that the thing with Amanda wasn't anything.

"And he told me how his dad had been weird lately, and I told him how my dad was acting the same way, this midlife crisis sort of thing, and how my dad cheated on my mom, and he said his dad would never do anything like that. I told him that he was so cute, being naïve and all." She chuckles.

I'm in complete disbelief that Chris would talk to someone who's practically a stranger—well, she's not a stranger, but they aren't close. They're acquaintances, and she's definitely not his best friend. And Amanda has always been private about her family issues. Her parents believe in keeping up appearances—the perfect family.

"I can't believe you told him about your parents," I say in disbelief.

"He was really easy to talk to. There's something about him that makes you trust him," she says, reflecting on his words. "One thing led to another, and I think it was, you know, us being so honest and open with each other that made it so erotic."

I cringe at the word. "Don't say that, Amanda. You guys just made out. It's not like you had sex."

She pouts. "We might have if you hadn't barged in like someone's parent."

"That wasn't going to happen even if I hadn't. Chris is a virgin." The instant the words leave my mouth, I want to kick myself.

"He's what?" she says, her eyes growing big.

"Just forget I said it."

"No. Oh my God. Are you sure? That super-hot guy with a body like David Beckham is a virgin?" she says in disbelief, her excitement growing with each word.

"You can't tell anyone!"

"Tell anyone? Are you crazy? So that I could have even more competition? Hell no! That is so hot. If he wasn't hot, it'd be kind of weird, but oh my God. No one forgets their first, even if it was sucky and hurt like hell in the back of a Jeep."

I remember how bad she said her first time was with Jeremy Wiley, her second serious boyfriend when she went through her rebel stage.

"Okay, can we get off my best friends' sexual resumes? Both of them," I say, feeling queasy.

She scoots to the edge of the bed. "Are you sure he's a virgin? I mean I know you guys are best friends and all, but he is a dude. Why would he tell you if he hasn't broken anyone's seal yet?"

I look at her, offended. "Because he's my *best* friend."

"I'm your best friend, and there're things about me you don't know," she says, and I roll my eyes.

"Like what?"

She thinks for a moment. "Like I want to be your other best friend's first. Eeek!" She squeals, and I make the universal signal for vomiting. "Won't it be great? Your best friends dating—you'll get to be with both of us all the time. You can help us by gifts for each other, help us when we argue . . ."

I wonder if she trying to make me feel better about this or worse. "Maybe you should slow down a little bit. You guys talked and made out. Did Chris say anything about you dating?"

"No, but why wouldn't we? We're both single, we're the same age, go to the same school, equal on the looks scale, and our chemistry was off the charts," she says enthusiastically, bouncing down next to me. "And of course you'll let him know what a great girlfriend I'd make and give him the little push he needs."

I look down guiltily, thinking of the little push I already gave him, which has turned out to be the dumbest idea I've ever had.

"Are you going to see him today?" she asks, ignoring my complete hesitancy with all of this.

"I should. His dad is tutoring me after work today." I sip what's left of the latte she brought me.

"You know what? You should call Chris right now!" she says, searching the room for my phone.

"Ugh, no!" I laugh even though I'd had every intention of calling him when I woke up—before she showed up at my door to get the 4–1-1.

"Please, please, please," she begs.

"No, but I promise as soon as I talk to him, I'll let you know what he said."

She pouts but accepts my answer. "Do you want to go get breakfast before work? My treat!"

That goes without saying. Amanda always treats. Even though she can be a little kooky sometimes, she's a really great friend. I've never been anywhere near as rich as her parents are, but she stayed my friend even after I fell to the low end of the totem pole when my stepdad kicked us out. That didn't change the way she looks at me one bit, and that's something I can't say about a lot of people.

"Okay. Let me shower, and we can go," I say, grabbing some clothes and heading out the room. Before I do, she stops me.

"And if I turn out to be right and Chris is totally into me, you'll be cool with it?" she asks.

I shut the door and turn around to face her. "Of course, why wouldn't I?"

She shrugs. "I know you've always maintained that you, Chris, and Aidan are best friends, but you know how that can go sometimes."

"There are a lot of reasons I would rather you found another boyfriend, but Chris and I being into each other is not one of them," I tell her honestly, and she smiles.

AMANDA AND I have breakfast at IHOP a couple of blocks from my job so that she can drop me off at work afterward. I tell Amanda about Brett and how handsome, sweet, and mature he was. She says he gets extra points just for being in college and if she wasn't so into Chris, she'd ask if he had a friend. I try not to roll my eyes at that.

She apologizes again for Deanna being a bitch. I tell her I'm used to it and assure her it won't, as it never has, affect our friendship. She says she's going to find out exactly whose friend Brett is and get his number. When Amanda puts her mind to something, nothing can stop her. Still, I tell her I don't want to seem desperate. Brett didn't give me butterflies or the tingling feeling from my toes to every other part of my body, but it was one of the best first conversations I've ever had with anyone. I can see the possibility of butterflies developing, and just the prospect of that makes it worth it.

Amanda and I manage to make it through the rest of our meal without her fawning over Chris, and I catch her up on Evie's recent forays into love and how she wasn't even home when I got back after the party, which was better for everyone. Amanda reminds me that I only have one more year left with Evie before I get into my dream school. I cross my fingers that she's right.

The rest of my morning goes well. When I get to work, the coffee shop isn't bustling as much as it normally is on a Saturday morning, so I'm able to get some studying in, glancing at the notes my boss lets me keep taped up by the register. So it's not surprising when Tara, the supervisor on staff, emerges from the back room with a grim look.

"Hey, Lisa, it's pretty slow today. You can head out," she says dryly.

Tara says everything dryly. It's only four o'clock. My mom won't be home from work until six, and it's pretty nice out—sweater-with-no-jacket weather—so I decide to make the trek home. I'm scanning through my CD player when a honk startles me. I turn to see a silver, newer-looking truck pull up next to me. I don't recognize it, so I keep walking. I'm startled when I hear my name called out. I stop and look back to see Brett Stelson, the blue-eyed dream boy, getting out of the truck and heading my way. Wow, Amanda works fast. I take off my headphones and try to suppress my grin.

"What are you doing here?" I ask, trying to hide my excitement but failing miserably.

"Is that an 'I'm excited to see you' what are you doing here? Or an 'eww' what are you doing here?" he jokes, and I laugh.

"Definitely the first," I say, shifting my bag on my back.

"Claire's sister Amanda called me this morning and said I was a jerk for not getting your number and that she was your best friend and I needed her approval, so I figured showing up here to officially get your number was something I could do to get in good with her." He shrugs with a sarcastic smile. His eyes are even bluer in the sun.

"Well, I'm glad you're here."

"I'm glad to be here," he says, smiling brightly.

This is nice, being with a guy who likes me and doesn't have to pretend that he doesn't like me to make me think he's cool.

"Well, Brett, I changed my mind about earlier. About you showing up here being creepy," I joke.

He nods. "Ah, so you do think I'm creepy," he says sarcastically.

"It would be creepy if you showed up here just to get my number. But it wouldn't be as creepy if you showed up here to ask me out," I say teasingly.

He looks up as if he's pondering. "Well, anything to avoid looking like a creep."

I laugh.

THE RIDE HOME with Brett was much nicer than walking home alone, listening to my scratched up CD. My aunt says that you can tell a lot about a man from his car. Not just if it's new or has all the luxury features—to determine if he has money or is from money—but you can tell how clean he is from how he keeps it. If you touch his radio, you'll know whether he's possessive or not, and if he opens the door for you, you can tell if he was raised right or is a self-absorbed jerk. Based on those theories, Brett is a neat freak, not possessive or selfish at all, and the perfect gentleman.

He apologized again for forgetting my number and asked if there was anything in particular I wanted to do for the date, which was a slight letdown. I'd hoped, with him being older, he'd take charge of things a little more, but he made up for it when I shrugged. He suggested several options, and we ended up settling on dinner and a movie on Thursday night. Though not super exciting, I look forward to seeing him again and getting to know him better.

After he drops me off at home, I hop in the shower, phone Amanda, and let her know that she's one of the best friends in the world for getting Brett to come down and see me—even though I'd deny it if she ever mentioned it. She tells me I can pay her back by finding out what Chris thought of her, and after what she's done, that is the very least I can do. Last night at the party, Chris seemed mortified after their encounter, so I guess what his response will be and prepare myself to tell her to look on the bright side, that there are so many more fish in the sea and Chris isn't as great as he seems.

I have it all worked out as I sit on Chris's bed, flipping through his CD catalog while he plays some stupid war game on his computer.

"Amanda's cooler than I thought she would be. I'm going to ask her out next weekend," he says.

Huh?

When did this happen? What happened between last night and this evening to change his look of complete embarrassment and anger to him seeming to be into her, even if he's nonchalant about it?

"Really?" I ask in disbelief.

He shrugs. "Yeah. She's cute and funny and pretty transparent. I like that."

"But what about last night? You seemed like you were the opposite of into her."

"It wasn't that I wasn't into her. I was just embarrassed having you see us like that. It's like having my sister walk in," he says, making a disgusted face.

"Oh."

"I mean, are you cool with it? I know it could be weird having your friends date," he asks, turning his attention to me after he's paused his game.

Date. He's using the actual word *date*. Not *hook up*, which I can't even imagine Chris saying, but at the least I'd expected *hang out*, not *date*. It's so official . . .

"I-I don't know. I mean, yeah, it would be kind of weird," I say with a chuckle.

"You're the one who hooked us up," he says, taking a seat on the bed next to me.

"I-I didn't think you'd actually be into her. I just didn't want Aidan to do to her what he does to every other girl he *dates*."

"You know I'm not like that, Lisa." His expression is soft, his warm green eyes staring into mine.

For a moment, I wonder how I could be "just friends" with someone like him: gorgeous, sweet, funny, and extra hot when he picks up a guitar. But even in my moment of jealousy, I feel more territorial about him as my friend than anything else.

"I know, but you told her she could come and see you audition, and you don't even want me and Aidan there," I say, hearing a slight whine in my voice.

He puts his arm around me and pulls me closer to him. "Don't be jealous, Leese."

I fake-punch him. "I'm not jealous," I say, so obviously jealous.

"If I get in, you and Aidan can be my own personal cheerleaders, but if you're there for the audition, it'll just make me more nervous."

I sigh and pout. "Okay, I guess. Speaking of new love connections, I have a date."

He rolls his eyes at me before heading to his closet and pulling out his guitar case. "Who's your next victim?"

I frown. "His name is Brett, and he's premed at Michigan U."

"Well, hopefully he has better luck with you than poor Malcolm," he says, and I throw a pillow at him.

I grab my bag off the floor next to his bed and swing it over my shoulder. "Do you know what you're going to play?"

"Not yet. I'm thinking of that song I wrote last month," he says, pulling out his guitar.

"Cool." Before I open the door, I think back to what Amanda said about him talking to her about his dad. I want to tell him he can talk to me about anything, no matter what it is, but as I look at my best friend, I know he *has* to already know that. "I guess I'll be headed downstairs."

"Have fun."

I shut the door and smile as I hear him strum a few chords. I head down into the study and see Mr. Scott on his laptop. He looks up and smiles at me as I walk in. He's warm and inviting, and I wonder if he's always been like this or if I'm just noticing it now.

"Hey, you ready to get started?" he asks with a wide smile that radiates enthusiasm. He seems excited, and that makes me excited.

"Yeah."

He already has a chair for me on the other side of the desk. Pencils and a calculator are set out along with scratch paper. I can't help but smile. I sit and pull out my homework.

"So I took a look at some of the stuff Chris has been working on," he says, pulling out what looks like copies of Chris's work.

He passes them to me, and I look at them. Chris is in a different class, but it looks as though we're working on the same things. Of course Chris's quiz has a much better grade than any of mine.

"Yup, that's what we've been working on," I say with a sigh.

"So before we get started, I want you to close your eyes," he says.

I look at him to determine if he's serious, and he nods. It seems a little silly, but I let out a small breath and do as he says.

"Repeat after me," he says.

With my eyes closed, I notice the depth of his voice. If it were a color, it'd be a warm hue.

"Math does not scare me or intimidate me," he says, and I repeat after him, holding in a small laugh. "It isn't difficult. I am bigger than it. I will conquer."

I say the same words after him.

"You can open your eyes now," he says.

I almost don't want to, but when I do and see him smiling at me, I forget the thought.

"Okay, let's see what you've got." His voice is still warm, but the magnetism it had earlier is gone.

We go through my homework and worksheets, and he's excited about them, enthusiastic even. He starts from the beginning, breaking down the problems and working his way to the solutions. He walks me through the steps, and as he works, he makes it seem easy. What's crazier is that I find each problem seems a little easier. After about forty minutes, he lets me work alone using the strategy he showed me. I feel nervous but anxious to see if this is legit. For the first time in my life, doing math doesn't feel like pulling teeth, and the person showing me doesn't sound as if they're speaking a foreign language. When I'm done, I let out a small breath and slide the paper across to him.

"You've got it. I know you do," he assures me before looking at the paper.

After he says that, I hope even more that it's right. I play with my fingertips as his eyes scan the paper. I'm on pins and needles waiting for him to look up. When he does, his expression is blank, then he smiles at me, a devastatingly handsome smile that gives me butterflies. I attribute them to the excitement of getting the question right and nothing else, but still I hold my breath until he speaks.

"Perfect." His voice is as warm and melodic as it was earlier, and I'm ecstatic.

"Really? I got it right?" I take the paper from him, and he walks over beside me and shows me how I followed all of the right steps.

I can't help noticing how good he smells. He's wearing a cologne of some kind, and it's intoxicating. Boys my age don't wear cologne—at least not the ones I'm around. It's nice, and I have to remind myself to focus on what he's saying and not what he smells like. We work for another twenty minutes, and by the end, I've gotten four out of five problems right.

"I can't believe this," I say. I'm not getting a headache or ready to quit in frustration. Maybe those mantras really work. Maybe I was psyching myself out, and of course Mr. Scott is amazing. I can be a testament to that. Or I guess I should wait until my next quiz before I speak too soon.

"You've done excellent work today," he says as I put away my homework.

"No, you were great. Nothing in this class has ever been as easy as you've made it. I'm shocked, really shocked."

His wide grin softens, and his cheeks warm up a little.

"I really appreciate you taking the time to do this. I'm so grateful," I say.

"It's not a problem at all. Things are going to be pretty slow around here, so helping you gives me something to look forward to," he says, putting the things away on his desk.

I nod, watching him. "What made you stop teaching?"

He glances at me. He seems caught off guard from the way he drops his items in the desk. Maybe I was being too intrusive. I can be intrusive sometimes. That's what my mom says.

"You don't have to answer if you don't want to," I say immediately.

"My mom says I always ask the wrong questions."

He smiles. It's small one, but it's there. "There's never really a wrong question. It's sometimes just an uncomfortable answer."

I wonder what that means.

"I was young and wasn't sure what I wanted in life," he says, sitting on his desk. He crosses his arms across his chest. It's broad, and through his sweater, I can see that his arms are built in a lean boxer sort of way. "I didn't choose to teach for myself. It was more to piss off my parents." He shrugs.

"Becoming a teacher would have pissed off your parents?"

He nods with a smile. "I didn't have the typical parents."

"So you became a farmer to really piss them off?" I guess.

"No, well, maybe subconsciously," he admits. "I wanted something different, and being a farmer was always sort of a dream. Maybe I watched too many cowboy movies when I was little." He laughs, and I join in. "I did intend to go back to teaching, but when you're young and low on money and you take everything you have to buy a farm, it's a lot harder than you think to make it work. It's not a part-time gig when you first get going."

"You miss it?" I ask, and he seems to think for a moment.

"I'm not sure yet," he says with a shrug.

"I think you'd still be a great teacher," I say, folding my arms around myself.

"Thank you, Lisa," he says, seemingly surprised. My eyes lock on his, and I get lost in them. The same eyes I'd thought were similar to Brett's, but now looking into them, that thought is an insult to the beauty that they are. His eyes are a deep, soulful blue, one that makes you smile but connects to every emotion you've ever had. He has eyes that look like an ocean, one that you don't just want to swim in but skinny dip.

"You guys finished?"

I turn and see Chris in the doorway.

I smile tightly at him.

"Yup, you're right on time," his dad says, standing from his desk.

"What time does Mom get home?" Chris asks, jingling his keys.

"She should be on her way now," he replies, heading toward the front door. "So I'll see you Tuesday at eight?"

"Sure thing," I say happily.

"I'll see you when you get back, Chris. Good night, Lisa." Mr. Scott retreats up the stairs.

"How did it go?" Chris asks as we head to their truck.

"It was great. I actually got some problems right on my own," I say excitedly.

"Good," he says, sharing my enthusiasm.

"Your dad is great. He would have made a really good teacher." I get in the truck after he opens the door for me.

"My dad could have done a lot of things," Chris says when he gets in. He turns on the car. "He taught me how to play the guitar."

My eyebrows rise. "Really? That's so cool."

Chris looks at me a little strangely. "My dad's not cool. He's my dad."

I swat him. "Your dad can be cool, and it doesn't make you any less cool. Does he sing?" I remember how melodic his voice was from earlier.

"Not a lot, but he can," he says, turning on the radio.

He's quiet on the ride to my house, but when Chris gets into his music, he tends to be quiet. I imagine melodies, rhythm, and harmonies running through his head. I used to be the same way when I wrote poetry. That was before I realized there wasn't any money in poetry and if I wanted to do anything besides get stuck here, I had to change my dream. I just haven't come up with another one yet. In college, I plan on majoring in business, a solid choice from what my guidance counselor has told me. Creative writing would practically guarantee I'd remain unemployed or have a useless degree I couldn't pay for after getting it.

When I make it into my house, I call Amanda, but it goes to voicemail. I just leave a quick message. "He likes you. Don't screw it up."

I throw myself in bed, and that night, when I'm having trouble sleeping, from the deepest corner of my thoughts, I hear Mr. Scott's voice singing me to sleep, and I let it.

Gwen

I did it. I got the stupid cap and gown and the piece of paper that shows four years of my life haven't been completely worthless, though time will tell if that's really true. At the very least I've earned my ticket out, or out of my mom's house in Michigan, and the key to Gia's apartment. I did everything I promised. I stopped smoking pot with Zach and only have a wine cooler every now and then. I put a little effort into my classes, and by doing that, I was shocked at how much my mother's attitude changed. I earned a reasonable curfew of nine on weekdays, as long as my school work was done, and eleven thirty on weekends.

But the days of curfews are going to be over soon. Next week, I'll be in Chicago, a certified adult. Well, not really I guess. Twenty-one seems more adult-like since I'll be able to go to bars and stuff, but at least now I'm eighteen and four weeks. Gia mailed me the key, and it arrived with perfect timing. The best birthday present I've ever had.

Today I'm spending my last Saturday with Zach, a boy I was drawn to because he was everything I wanted to be when I wasn't. The boy who didn't care what others thought, who did what he wanted but still could charm his way out of trouble. I'd thought he was my kindred spirit after Gia left for school. He was my first kiss, the person I smoked my first joint with, and came close on a few occasions to being the first man I ever gave myself to. I'm glad we never crossed that line though. It would have been weird, and I know Zach isn't the guy to be anyone's first. He's said that on more than a few occasions.

"I'm going to miss you, brat," he says as we lay in the empty football field.

Okay, we did sneak in and would probably get in trouble if someone caught us, but our last weekend together wouldn't be the proper send-off if there wasn't a hint of danger or punishment.

"I'm going to miss you too." I lay my head on his chest as I look at the stars. "You should come with," I say for the fifth time since I told him I got the okay to move to Chicago.

"And do what? Panhandle on the streets, live out of my van?" He laughs.

"I could always sneak you in the house when Gia's at work," I say semi-seriously as he rubs my back.

"Believe it or not, I don't hate it here. I'm happy where I am *right* now. Everything has its season. I move with the wind."

Zach loves talking in what I call poetic codes. Though annoying, it's part of his charm. He finishes his joint, and I inhale the scent. He won't let me take a puff though. He hasn't since I told him about the deal I made with Gia.

"You're going to be good out there," he says, playing with loose strands of my hair.

"I hope so." I sigh.

"You just be yourself. The real you. Not the you who just wants to piss everyone off." He laughs.

The past year or two, I haven't felt like myself. I didn't really know who I was, so I put on a mask. I played a part that was so different from the person I used to be so I'd feel as though I was escaping—escaping the memories that hurt. The pain never seemed to leave after my dad passed away. It only escalated when my mom married Martin, and it carved itself into my skin when Gia went away. I'd thought I'd gravitated toward Zach because the "me" I created fit perfectly with him, but what it was really is that everyone believed the mask was real. Zach saw behind it and knew it was just a façade.

I kiss him softly and rest my head against his. "Thank you, Zach, for letting me play a part but not become it."

He smiles, showing his pearly white teeth, then gently pushes me off him. "I'm glad you took that crap off your hair." He lays on his side and turns toward me.

I run my hands through my hair. Gone is the charcoal color I'd changed it to. Trying to get it back to my natural red was difficult—at first it was like a light milk chocolate color with auburn highlights—but my mom's graduation gift to me was taking me to a salon and having a colorist correct it. Now it's not far off from the natural red tone of my roots, about three inches of which are showing. I'd forgotten how much I missed looking in the mirror and seeing myself.

"You promise to come visit me?" I prop my head in my hand so that I can look down at him.

"Hell yeah," he says, giving me a dazzling smile. Zach is literally sex on a stick sometimes. He has the smile of a Boy Scout, the swagger of a rock star, and the sex appeal of a soap opera heartthrob. If he could play an instrument or sing, he'd make millions. "So your plan is to not piss off your sister, find a job, meet a nice man, and have a litter of kids, right?"

I frown at him, feigning annoyance. "Litters refer to animals, not babies."

"But that's the gist, right?"

"I just want to have a family. It doesn't have to be a perfect one, but a really good one. And I don't want a guy who's career-obsessed though. You know, I want someone who works hard but can balance his family and professional life. Like my dad. He worked but always made sure he was home for dinner and weekends."

"You're weird." He laughs, and I frown. "You're eighteen, and instead of thinking about all the bars and clubs you'll get to hit up when you find someone to make you a fake ID, you want to be Mrs. Cleaver."

"It's not like I expect all this to happen instantly. It's just that's what I really want. It's what would make me happy," I say with a shrug. "What about you?"

"That's easy—Lisa Bonet on a private island with all the pot I can handle," he says, and I shake my head at him. "Don't knock my dream, brat."

"That's not a dream. That's a fantasy," I correct him.

"Dream, fantasy. It's all the same until you make it a reality." He stands and stretches then reaches his hand out and pulls me up next to him. "Look up at the sky."

I do. It's pitch black with stars littering it.

"What do you see?" he asks.

"I see stars," I say, glancing at him.

He grins then looks at me. "No. That's infinite possibilities."

We stare at them for the rest of the night.

I WALK BACK into the house ten minutes before my official curfew. In one day, I'll be free from it, living in the big city with my sister, an adult with freedom and no rules. I saw no need to rock the boat tonight to make a statement.

Before my foot could hit the first step to go upstairs, I hear my mother call to me from the dining room. I glance at the clock to make sure I didn't break curfew, and I haven't. I hesitantly make my way into the dining room and see my mom sitting at the head of the table with a glass of wine and a piece of chocolate cake left over from my small graduation celebration, which consisted of a few friends from school, two distant relatives, and Martin's staff from the car dealership. It wasn't my idea of a party, but I made off with a hundred fifty bucks. I survey mom's face to gauge her mood. When I see her small smile, her bright eyes, and her hair falling to her shoulders, I let out a small breath.

"Have a seat, honey," she says gesturing to the chair next to her.

I take a seat as she slides the plate of cake over to me. I cut a piece with my fork and pop it in my mouth.

"It's good, isn't it?" she asks, and I nod. "Not as good as your dad's though, huh?"

I swallow the cake and the lump in my throat. Not only because she said the exact thing she was thinking but because it's the first time she's mentioned my father in months. She smiles and sighs.

"I do miss him so, Gwen," she says, her voice lighter than I've heard it in a long time.

"Why don't you ever talk about him?" I ask.

She shakes her head so slightly I could almost mistake it for a tilt. She lets out a long, deep breath. "We all handle grieving differently. Loss can be devastating." She takes another sip of her wine then folds her hands. "Not just loss of a person but loss of love, a friendship, youth. I-I know how close you were with your father."

My eyes leave her face. I feel tears welling up in my eyes and my throat closing in on itself. Why is she bringing this up now? I want to move my hands to wipe the tears coming from my eyes, but I'm afraid to move.

"I am sorry that I didn't know how to be there for you," she says with tears falling from her own eyes. "I want you to have a good life. And I know that when you lost him, you lost a big part of yourself. I want to make sure that—" She grabs a napkin and wipes her eyes. "I want to make sure that your changes are organic and not forged for a reason your father would . . . that I would hate . . ." She adds a smile to her devastated expression. "I'm glad that you're moving in with Gia. I think you'll be great for each other."

I smile and nod. She didn't say Gia would be great for me but that we would be great for each other.

"I'm going to give Gia some money for you so that you can settle in before you start working. I just want you to have the best start there. You're such a special girl. You have a big heart like your father did. You bring light when you let yourself," she says, squeezing my hand.

I squeeze her hand back before getting up and pulling her into a big hug. "Thank you, Mom." I can't control my crying.

We hold each other for as long as we need to, and we forgive each other with words that don't need to be said for the hurt and pain we caused because we were consumed with our own.

THE DAY I'M set to arrive at Gia's house, butterflies have a parade in my stomach from the time I go to bed to the time I wake up. Today is the day. This is it, my first day of real adulthood. "Leaving the nest" is what Martin keeps saying. When I stand at the train station, my bags all packed—three large suitcases to be exact—it's bittersweet.

I sit in the terminal with my mom and Martin.

"Chicago's a great city. You're going to do great things there, Gwen," he says enthusiastically.

I give him genuine smile. "Thank you, Martin."

Since I came back from Gia's a couple of months ago, we've been cordial, sometimes on the edge of friendly. It would still seem false to call him Dad or something sentimental like that, not that he'd expect me to. I think he's grateful enough that I haven't caused any more problems since he's predicted to win the election in the winter. My train is called out. I give Martin a semi-awkward hug and my mom a longish one before I head to the opening in the train where they load my luggage.

"Make sure you call me as soon as you make it to Gia's," my mom calls.

"I promise," I tell her with a little wave.

I see the tears rolling down her face, and I feel wetness in my own eyes. I'd never imagined the day I said good-bye being sad, but I guess things sometimes don't turn out how you imagine them.

I SIT ON a bench at the Chicago train station, listening to the music playing from the speakers. Next to me is a woman reading a book. I flip through the magazine I read cover to cover on the train and glance at my watch. Gia should have been here almost thirty minutes ago. It's not like her to be late. I try to hang on to the anxious energy in my stomach instead of becoming annoyed. It's hard to focus on the pages with all the commotion around me. This city is so different from my town back home. It's as if everything here is constantly moving, and it's exciting but intimidating.

"Gwen?"

My heart tightens when I hear the voice that calls me. I shake it off. That's the voice I run from in my sleep but can't help but yearn to be closer to. It was my only reservation about coming back. When I look up, that only reservation is standing in front of me. Six feet tall, sandy blonde hair, and unnaturally hypnotizing eyes—Will Scott, my sister's boyfriend.

"How are you?" he says with a smile that makes me want to melt.

Shit. This was supposed to be over. This stupid crush was supposed to be gone. Crushes are supposed to go away, especially when you haven't seen the person in months . . . well, except in your dreams.

"Hi," I say, unable to contain my own smile.

He takes my hand and pulls me into a hug. He lifts me so easily. How I fit into his arms feels natural.

"How have you been?" he asks, not knowing the effect his unannounced presence is having on me.

I'd known I would see him of course, but not now. I was supposed to have time to prepare myself, to get ready for him. He wasn't supposed to just spring up here.

"I'm great," I say, his enthusiasm contagious.

"You look great."

I swallow hard at the compliment.

"Your hair . . . you look so different I almost didn't recognize you," he says.

I subconsciously run my hands through it. "You like it?" I need to hear him say it once more.

"I love it. It fits you . . . and now I can call you carrot top." He chuckles, and I roll my eyes. "Let me get your bags."

He grabs the two biggest ones. I take the last and follow him to his truck.

"I can't believe you're here. In the flesh," he says once we're both in the truck.

"You act like I'm a celebrity or something." I feel myself blush. The butterflies return to my stomach just like last time. I'd have thought they'd gone away, but nope, they're still here, making their presence known.

"Shut up," he says playfully.

I try to think of something to say. Talking to him was so much easier on the phone. Talking to him has always been easy, so it only seemed natural that after he took me home, we would continue to talk, to be friends. What isn't natural is that I started to look forward to talking to him more than anyone else. When the phone rang and it wasn't him, I became disappointed. That wasn't natural at all.

"What's the matter? Cat got your tongue?" he jokes.

"I thought Gia was supposed to pick me up."

He frowns, but a smile follows it. "Gia had to work later than she thought, so she called me to pick you up." A moment passes. "You're disappointed?"

My heart beats a little faster. "No."

My eyes stay on my lap. I can't look at him because if I do, I feel like he'll be able to read my mind, to know my secrets and how seeing him has reminded me of everything I'd hoped would change. Somewhere inside me, I'd thought, I'd hoped, that talking to him so much would help. That becoming his friend would change the way I felt.

When I first started talking to him, I thought I'd realize how right he was for Gia, how much he loved Gia, and my stupid little crush would go away. Instead I liked Will Scott even more. Our first phone conversation happened strictly by accident. It wasn't as if I'd meant to talk to him . . . not that there's anything wrong with us talking. Gia knows we talk, though I don't know if she knows how much. I know she doesn't know that I prefer talking to him when she's not around. Not that our conversations are illicit, but they're definitely *not* intimate.

The first time it happened, he was calling Martin back. Martin had wanted to speak with him about something with his dad, but Martin wasn't there. I answered the phone since after I'd arrived home from my impromptu trip to Chicago, I might as well have been under house arrest. Will asked me how things were going, and I complained, of course, that I was stir crazy. Other than school and my mandatory Sundays at church, I had little contact with the outside world. He told me to suck it up, that people had worse problems than being stuck in four-bedroom colonial with a maid named Marta. His playful, sarcastic attitude still intrigued me. He was different. He called me on my bullshit in a way that didn't tick me off or seem as if he was talking down to me. Maybe it was because his voice sounded so good, warm, relaxing, and downright . . . sexy. I could listen to it for hours.

When I was having a bad day, our phone call was what I looked forward to snap me out of my funk, and on the days he didn't call, I felt grumpier, like it couldn't have been a perfect day no matter how well it went because a piece of it, one of the best parts, was missing. Now the best part of my day is sitting next to me, asking if I'm disappointed with him picking me up. How could I be?

Even though technically I should be. I haven't seen my sister in months. I miss her, I really do, but I know when I see her, the twinge of guilt I feel for talking to her boyfriend—not talking to her boyfriend but *enjoying* her boyfriend a little too much—is going to crush me. I'd really, really hoped she would pick me up and I could tell her about it. I could figure out how to casually mention that I've developed a crush on her boyfriend and that it doesn't really mean anything. It's just kind of weird, and I need her help figuring it out. That's what big sisters are for, right?

Except now I'm sitting next to him, and he's asking a question that doesn't seem like what I feel is all that innocent or little. I feel like talking to him so much didn't do anything but make the situation worse. Our friendship is platonic—we've never flirted or talked about anything inappropriate—but looking back on everything and realizing that my feelings are stronger than the last time I was in his presence, maybe this is all inappropriate.

"Hey, what's wrong?"

Will's voice wakes me from my trance. He looks concerned, and I feel bad. I feel worse because he looks completely fine, not uncomfortable, anxious, or tense. That means he thinks we're just friends, that I'm the cool little sister. He has no idea the internal battle I'm having right now, and of course I can't let him find out. Why would he think there was anything wrong? Nothing is wrong. It'll only be wrong if I let there be something wrong. I only have to feel guilty if there's something to feel guilty about, and obviously there's nothing.

"Nothing, I'm just starved," I say dramatically.

His worried look instantly disappears, and the carefree aloofness I've grown way too fond off returns. "Good, we're going to get something to eat."

I feel my stomach flip. "We're meeting Gia somewhere for dinner?" A part of me wants him to say yes, but a bigger part of me wants him to say *no*. The smart part of me thinks I'm being stupid and torturing myself.

"No, she won't be off for another hour or two. We'll grab her something to-go and take it to her job," he says.

I simultaneously feel relieved and tense. "Italian?"

"Of course," he says as if it's obvious.

It is obvious. Italian is *our* favorite food.

WE DINE IN a cute little Italian restaurant on the north side of Chicago according to Will. The lighting is dim but not so dim that you'd think it's romantic even though the restaurant only seats about forty people max. It doesn't have the best décor—it's obvious this place is old—but the smell that greets you when you walk in makes it all too easy to overlook the deterioration. Garlic and butter, the smells of fresh bread and tomato sauce. He orders stuffed shells, and I order fettuccini Alfredo. Will has a beer, and I have a Coke with extra ice.

"So this is the place you're always saying would give my lasagna a run for my money?" I say playfully.

"You'll see," he says jokingly.

"So Gia's still been working late?" I already know the answer.

Gia's interning at the office of a prominent lawyer near her house. It was the opportunity of a lifetime, she'd explained to me over the phone, giddy with excitement. When Will talked to me during her second week there, he'd seemed less than thrilled.

"I know it goes without saying that law school and being a lawyer are going to be hard and take a lot of time, but it's still gonna suck majorly," he says, his disdain apparent. He sighs. "It's sort of my fault. My stepdad pulled strings to get her the freakin' job." He shakes his head. "I'm happy for her. I am. it's just I thought this would give her an edge up on getting into law school, then I bumped into an old friend of my dad's who's a lawyer. He said interning at a law firm doesn't really help you get into law school. It's about the experience."

I don't tell him that I know he approached Gia about quitting, and I know they got into an argument and Gia thought he was being a selfish. I want to tell him Gia doesn't quit anything and if anyone can turn a useless internship into something, it's her, but I can't tell him that because I don't know if he's supposed to know that we talked about their fight at all.

"Well, telling her to quit would make you a big jerk, so definitely don't do that." I take a bite of the garlic bread in front of me. It's fantastic. I look up and see Will's face flush.

"You know I'm a big jerk." He chuckles, and I give him a reassuring smile.

"I'm sure Gia knows that by now." I clear my throat with a sip of Coke.

He grins at me. "Enough about my problems. What's going on with you and Zach?" He leans forward, giving me his full attention.

"You mean the guy you think is secretly in love with me?" I snicker.

"I don't know why you think it's so funny. He's totally in love with you," he says adamantly.

I roll my eyes at him. "Zach and I are just friends. We make out every so often, but he's almost like a brother."

"Except for the making out part," he says sarcastically.

"Except for that," I retort, and he grimaces. "Besides, aren't people my age too young to fall in love? We don't know what real love is, right?"

My eyes meet his, and I instantly regret it because they hold me and don't let go, magical orbs that put a spell on me each time they lock on mine. His mouth slowly turns upward. His eyes smile at me before his lips do, and I fight to look away from him.

"Here you go, sweetheart. Stuffed shells." The waitress has saved me. She gives Will a warm smile. She has coal-black hair with streaks of gray in a tight bun and a strong Italian accent. "And for the beautiful lady, chicken Alfredo. My favorite."

I smile and thank her. As we eat, he tells me about how he feels sad when the school year ends and his students leave. I tell him about how graduation wasn't as big a deal as I'd expected it to be. He counters, saying that he bet it felt good holding that diploma. I admit that it did.

The waitress with the black hair and warm smile returns and asks if we'd like to share a dessert.

"I'm up for it if you are," he says.

Even though I feel stuffed, I can't pass up the chance. We share a big bowl of gelato, and I feel a little more guilty when I compare this dinner to all the crappy dates I've been on. Because *this* isn't a date, it shouldn't feel like a date and shouldn't be compared to one, but part of me does, and the stupid part of me is giddy. I'm reminded of how stupid that part is when Will orders Gia a spaghetti and meatballs with extra sauce, just how Gia likes it. I realize that in my fantasy, or if I were to have a fantasy, my date wouldn't order his girlfriend a to-go plate. In the ideal fantasy, his girlfriend wouldn't be my sister.

"HEY, LITTLE SIS." Gia nudges me awake.

I open my eyes and see her sitting beside me, beaming.

"Hi," I say, sitting up and giving her a hug.

"I'm so glad you're here." She squeezes me tightly.

"You can't be more glad than I am."

"I have something for you. It was for your graduation, and I was going to mail it, but I thought I'd just keep it to give it to you personally." She hands me a small box wrapped in pink paper.

I restrain myself from ripping it open. I carefully untie the ribbon and delicately unwrap the gift, making sure to appreciate the beautiful paper. When I open the box, my eyes well up. "Gia . . ."

She doesn't say anything but just keeps a small smile on her face. I notice the wetness in her eyes. I lift the silver heart necklace Dad gave her when she graduated.

"I can't take this," I say, and my voice breaks.

She only shakes her head, unclasps it, and lifts my hair so she can put it on me. "You will. I have so many gifts from Dad, and I know how hard it had to have been for you to not have him there. I know how much that would have meant to you." She finishes hooking the clasp around my neck. "Funny story—when I graduated, I wanted a car. I just knew that Mom and Dad were looking at this little red dust beater, but to me, it wouldn't have been a dust beater. It would have meant the world." She clears her throat. "On graduation day, Dad handed me that box. I thought—I willed it even—to be a key. A key to the car I had been dropping hints about, that I'd convinced myself they were going to get me."

I nod, vaguely remembering that day. I remember her acting happy, showing off the necklace to me that night at dinner.

"When he gave it to me, I was sooo disappointed. You wouldn't believe how much. I even let it slip." Her voice breaks, and tears flow down her cheeks. "I'll never forget the look on his face. Mom . . . you know how she is . . . she looked angry, like how dare I not appreciate what I was given. But Dad, Dad looked hurt." She sniffs. "I realized then that I was being a brat and if they could have gotten me the car, they would have."

I hold her hand, and she takes a deep breath.

"I would give anything to go back and change what I said. If I had known that was the last gift he would ever give me, give either of us . . ."

I hug her. "You didn't know, Gia. Dad got it. You know how he was. He knew you didn't mean it."

"I know, I know, but I just . . . I want you to have it. I know how much it would mean to you," she says, pulling herself together.

I touch the locket and hold onto it. "I'll wear it, not forever though. It's yours."

She waves me off. "I'll let you know when I want it back."

I get up, and she shows me the small sun porch she's decorated to look more like a bedroom. It's half the size of my old room—not my room at Martin's house but my room in our house with Dad, which was half the size of the house Mom has now—but it's perfect with a twin bed, purple linens, and Madonna posters everywhere. She helps me put away my clothes, and we talk and eat candy for the rest of the night.

Before I drift off to sleep, I tell myself tonight I won't dream about Will's voice. I won't look forward to seeing him. Whatever I feel, whether its curiosity, infatuation, or lust, isn't worth what it could cause between my sister and me. It's nothing. I will make it be nothing.

It will be nothing.

MY PLAN IS to keep busy. If I keep busy, I won't have time to think or analyze my feelings for Whatshisface. I've convinced myself if I refer toWill as Whatshisface, my feelings will cease to exist. I mean, who would have feelings for someone they refer to as Whatshisface?

While Gia is out, I clean the house. I read books, and I watch TV, though Gia doesn't have cable. I talk to Zach as much as I can, but since he's working more hours at the gas station and his uncle isn't keen on him being on the phone, I can't use him to pass the time as much as I like. By day three, I feel restless. With Gia at work and school, she's not home as much as I'd imagined her being. This is actually nothing at all like I pictured life here being. I guess I only imagined freedom—lots and lots of freedom to do what I want—but when I don't have to go to school or work, freedom doesn't really matter. Boredom isn't as glamorous as I thought it'd be. I have absolutely nothing to do.

By day four, after I've watched as much crappy TV as I can stand

and cooked everything in the house, I decide to try my hand at the public transportation system. There's a bus stop on the corner of Gia's block. From talking to a woman in the gas station, I think the bus will take me right to the train station, which would take me into the heart of Chicago. If you can't find something to do there, you're a lost cause, at least that's what the clerk at the gas station tells me.

So I buy a transfer to get on the bus, and with the train fare in my pocket, I start my journey. It seems like a great idea until four hours later, when I somehow end up in a suburb on the opposite side of town from where I live and it's starting to get dark and I'm too embarrassed to ask someone how to get home. Why would *I,* someone who's foreign to the public transportation system in my own hometown, attempt to conquer it in one of the biggest cities in the world?

I finally swallow my pride and head to the payphone, where realize I don't know Gia's work number. I can barely remember the name of the firm she's interning at. Is it Waters and Mitchell or Waters and Michaels? The operator gets frustrated with me, saying she has over a hundred listings of law firms in Chicago with the name Waters in them. I hang up, frustrated, and laugh at myself. The reason I wanted to get out of the house was so I wouldn't be bored and think about the only person in this city whose number I remember, and that's who I'll have to see.

He picks up on the third ring. "Hello?"

I bite my lip. He doesn't sound like a Whatshisface. He sounds anything but.

"Hey," I say quickly.

"Gwen?" he asks, but it's more of a statement.

"Yeah," I say, embarrassed.

"Long time, no hear, stranger."

My heart skips a beat. He's noticed that we haven't talked. I wonder if three days seemed as long for him as it did to me. Of course not. He has a willing girlfriend to talk to. Not a girlfriend—my sister.

"Are you busy?" I say hopefully.

"Not so much . . . what's up?"

I explain how I'm an idiot and lost and ask if he could pick me up. Before he says anything, he laughs at me, which is expected. But he asks me where I am, and once I tell him, he says he'll be here to get me in thirty minutes.

Thirty minutes can't go fast enough, especially when some creepy guy who smells like old cabbage keeps asking for my phone number and saying he's a lot younger than he looks. I couldn't care less how old he is, but he smells as if he's over a hundred. I'm so glad when Will pulls up I could kiss him.

"See, there's my boyfriend over there," I say, jumping up from my seat in the train terminal and practically skipping to Will's truck. When I get in, he can't stop laughing. "Oh, my being harassed by a possible rapist who smelled like an old produce section is so amusing to you."

But his laughter is a sound I always welcome. It has a way of making me feel better.

"You want me to go kick his ass?" he says in a coddling voice.

"Yes, that would be nice," I say sarcastically.

He rolls down our windows and looks at Mr. Cabbage. "Hey, you," Will says in an angry voice, which surprises me.

Mr. Cabbage flips him off. When Will opens the car door and starts to get out, my heart races, and I grab his arm.

"I was kidding!" I say, and when he flashes me a breath-stealing smile, I realize he was only kidding too.

"I wasn't going to hurt him. Look, he's gone."

I look over and see that Mr. Cabbage has run clear across the street and hasn't stopped. I swat Will with pretend anger. He winks at me, and my heart nearly stops. I grasp the chain Gia gave me and remind myself of the reason I've been avoiding him in the first place. When he pulls off and turns the radio down, I know he wants to talk. Talking is what we do after all, but talking has caused so many problems.

"What made you decide to go downtown?" he asks.

I shrug. A valid response with no words spoken. He glances at me expectantly, waiting for me to follow up with a verbal answer, but I don't.

"You don't know . . . ?" he prods, and I shake my head. He looks a little confused. "Are you okay?"

I only nod. He doesn't say anything for a while.

Suddenly he asks, "Have you decided take a vow of silence?"

I can't help but crack a smile.

"You're being kind of weird," he says, turning the radio completely off.

I turn it back on, and he turns it back off. When I reach for it again, his fingers land on mine. I snatch mine back, trying to ignore the jolt of electricity that shoots through me.

"What, do I have rabies or something? Is this about that guy back there?" he asks.

I realize how ridiculous I must look. I can't become completely mute around him. That's not going to look normal at all.

"What's up?" he asks, genuinely confused.

Of course he's confused. He has no clue what's going on in my head, and I'm pretty sure that aside from that brief lapse in his judgment at the carnival, my feelings are completely one-sided.

"I just don't feel like talking," I say, forcing the words out.

When we get to a stoplight, I feel him staring at me, probably trying to figure out what the hell my problem is. Little does he know *he's* my problem.

"Gwen. Can you talk to me?" His usually playful voice is serious, and for some reason, the tone makes something move in me.

I suddenly feel my throat burn, and I feel as though if I do or say anything, even one word, I'll start to cry.

"Please," he says in a soft tone that makes my stomach flip. "Did I do something wrong?"

I want to tell him that I'm wrong, that the feeling I have for him is wrong and I hate it . . . so much that he's driving me crazy.

Instead I lie. I take a deep breath, and my voice breaks as I tell him, "I just miss my dad." My voice is so weak it sounds like a six-year-old's. It's a lie but partly true. I could never talk to my mom about this. She'd look at me as if I had two horns growing out of my head, but my dad, he would listen. He would give me the right advice. He wouldn't judge.

What happens next surprises me. Will pulls over to the side of the road. He takes my hand and pulls me into a hug. He holds me close and tight, which makes me cry harder because this closeness, his touch, is so comforting. As he strokes my back, I yearn for him to touch my skin, but at the same time, my skin crawls, and I cry more. I think about when my English teacher asked us for an example of an oxymoron, and I realize I'm smack dab in the middle of one. My problem is right next to me, and my solution is being wrapped in his arms with the little silver necklace between us.

chapter seven

lisa

CHRIS AND AMANDA are officially dating, or so it would appear. Something I never in a million years thought I would say. It's been five and a half weeks since I had the bright idea to put them together, not thinking it would turn out like this, and now they're officially an item.

"You should have seen him. He was amazing. Those other guys didn't stand a chance," she says in excitement before kissing Chris's cheek as she sits on his lap at lunch, recapping the audition Aidan and I weren't allowed to attend.

I really think his reason is a crock of shit right about now. I glance at Aidan, who has the same sneer I'm hiding behind a weak smile.

"It was stiff competition. I'm just lucky," Chris says modestly.

"They play their first set this weekend at the Deegan's in Sheridan.

You have to come see how good he is," she says in a sickly sweet voice, almost like the mother of a five-year-old.

"Sweeet! Chris!" Devin slaps Chris's back, giving his approval.

"We'll be there," Mike and a few others at our lunch table chime in.

"What about you, Lisa? Maybe you can ride with me. That is if we can remember to not embarrass our town rock star," Aidan says with a sarcastic snarl.

Amanda frowns, and Chris grimaces.

"You know it wasn't like that," Chris says, his tone apologetic.

"I don't know what it was like. I just think it's weird that you wouldn't want your two best friends to come support you but you let cheerleading Barbie be front and center." Aidan's tone is joking, but the undercurrent is bitter, and I can't say I don't feel the same way.

"Hey chill out, Aidan," Amanda says, glaring at him.

Aidan rolls his eyes at her and laughs before getting up from the table. The phrase "three's a crowd" has never seemed to apply to Chris, Aidan, and me, but with Amanda added to the mix, a better saying would be "four's a disaster." She just hasn't gelled in, and it sucks because she's my best friend. She and my other best friend being together has really thrown my life out of balance.

"I'll go talk to him," I tell them, unable to muster up anything other than the artificial grin I've had plastered on since this whole thing started with them.

I think about how a few weeks can change things. Since when am I the one to go coddle Aidan? He's at the table across from us, flirting with one of the junior cheerleaders.

"Can we talk a minute?"

He looks at me in annoyance. "I'll be right back, Jada." He follows me out.

"Kayla," she calls after him.

"What's up?" he asks.

"Look, I'm not thrilled about Chris and Amanda any more than you are," I say, and he grimaces.

"You're the one who had the bright idea to set them up."

"Yeah, but I didn't think they'd actually do this . . . I was just trying to stop my best friend from becoming one of your wham-bam-thank-you-ma'ams," I say defensively.

"Amanda's not an angel. You act as if she's a virgin or something, like she's not aware of my reputation. If you would have just let nature take its course, we wouldn't be having this issue. She's got Chris wrapped around her bipolar little finger! And what the hell is with him not inviting us to see him play? *She* invites us like we're the pity friends!" he says angrily.

"I'm not happy about it either, and yeah, my feelings were hurt a little bit, but I know Chris isn't embarrassed of us. I think he just would have been embarrassed by us being there."

He looks at me as if I'm crazy.

"I think he wanted to do something on his own," I say, and Aidan crosses his arms as if nothing I'm saying is getting through to him. I sigh in frustration. "Okay, you're right. He was an ass to not invite us, but are you going to act like a mad little girl for the rest of our senior year? This could be our last year together for a long time. Don't let your ego ruin it." I walk off and leave him where he's standing.

EVEN WITH EVERYTHING that happened earlier today with Chris and his new girlfriend—gosh, that sounds weird—today is still going down as an awesome day. I woke up for the first time in a long time without a strange guy, or one I didn't like, in the house with Evie and me, which was unusual, but I didn't question it. And for the first time since I was a freshman, I received a B-plus on a math quiz, even getting a "Keep up the good work" from Ms. Gregory.

I can't help glancing at my quiz every so often to make sure it was real. It isn't an A, but for math, a B-plus is a big accomplishment. I didn't manage a grade that good even the one time I tried to cheat or when I worked with a partner. The first person I want to share the news with is Mr. Scott . . . Will. When he told me I could call him that, I felt like I was on cloud nine. Our three-time-a-week tutoring sessions have paid off. Not only that, but they're something I've begun to look forward to. Something about him makes me feel warm inside. He makes me feel as though I can do anything, be anything I want. Even though he's tutoring me on a subject I hate—well, used to hate—I can't help looking forward to them more than most things.

"Hi, Lisa," Will says when I arrive. Today he's wearing a grey sweater that brings out his eyes, not that they need any help being the center of attention. The sleeves are pulled up to his elbows, showing a gold watch.

"Hi. I like your watch," I tell him as I sit in my regular place.

"Thanks. I bought it last week. It was on sale." I notice that his cheeks turn a bit pink.

"I have something to show you," I say, trying to contain my excitement.

His eyebrows rise slightly, and his lips turn upward. I pull out the quiz I haven't been able to stop looking at today. I put it on the desk and slide it over to him. When he looks at it, he lets out a big laugh with a wide, glorious smile, and I feel my heart skip a beat. It's been doing that lot when I'm around him lately.

"Lisa, that's great!" he says, his excitement matching my own.

I laugh at how excited we both are. "I couldn't have done it without you."

He smiles warmly at me. "It has been an absolute pleasure."

I fight the urge to close my eyes and replay his words and wrap myself up in his tone. Then I think of what he's just said. It sounds so final. This can't be it, right?

"We're still going to see each other, right?" I say, then I realize how that sounds. "I mean, you're still going to tutor me?" I feel my own cheeks heat up.

"Of course, I think there's a lot more math for you to still get before the end of the year," he says with a chuckle.

I can't help the smile that spreads across my face. "I got you something to kind of say thanks."

He smiles, seeming surprised. "You didn't have to do that."

I ignore him and pull out a book of positive affirmations. I bet he knows most of them.

His eyes widen. "Thank you."

I wonder if he gets it or if he thinks it's stupid.

"Do you like it?" I ask, feeling self-conscious about it now that it's in his hand.

He chuckles, low and rich. "It's perfect." He smiles at it then glances at me. "Thank you."

He opens it and reads the first page. I think of the inscription, which I'm a little embarrassed about it. I didn't expect him to read it while I was here.

"'To the man whose words can awaken part of you that has long been forgotten where you remember that you can be great.'" The words roll off his tongue quietly.

They sound so much better after he's said them. He says each word as if he's savoring it, and when he looks at me, I can't meet his eyes. I don't dare.

"Do you like to write?" he asks, and it catches me off guard.

"I used to." I watch him as he carefully puts the book in his desk.

"Why don't you like it anymore?" he asks.

I shrug. "There isn't a high demand for poets."

He nods in understanding. "That shouldn't stop you from doing what you love though."

He leans on his elbows, his gaze directly on me. His stare is intense, and I know he doesn't mean it to be, but I can't help but feel intimidated when someone with eyes like his stares directly into mine.

"My mom says it's a ridiculous hobby," I say, taking out my paper from math—anything to release my gaze from his. I think if I look for too long, there'll be no coming back.

"Don't tell Chris, but there are times when parents can be very wrong," he says playfully.

I laugh. If anyone's mother was wrong, it'd be mine. I don't tell him that her words are just an excuse. With how horrible it would be to fail at something that my heart and soul was wrapped around, I'd chosen to just keep it a secret. A secret never gets lost. There's no measure of success for it. You just have to keep it. That's the only thing you have to do right, and besides Chris and my mom, it's a secret I've never shared. But things you love should never be a secret. You should be able to share them with the world regardless of what people think. But what's worse than failing is being stuck with Evie and having no chance of escape because I chose to be a starving artist.

I don't tell him that. Instead I smile and pull out my homework. Then my mind drifts back to something he said when we first started working with one another. "You, you knew my dad, right?"

I see him swallow, from his nerves or the awkwardness of my question, I'm not sure. But if he does know, I know he'll make whatever the truth about my dad is easy, just as he did the big bad math problems.

"I did," he says.

I focus on the notes on my scratch paper. "What was he like?"

The question sounds forbidden. He's a man I haven't brought up or spoken about since my mom said, "He's an asshole who you never give the satisfaction of thinking about." That was when I was six.

Will leans back in his chair and crosses his arms. I expect him to let out a deep frustrated sigh, but he doesn't. "The man I knew, when I did, was a good man."

I feel myself frown. I try to imagine a good man leaving his wife and two-year-old daughter, for him to never come back, to never wonder about me as if I were a forgotten sock in the washing machine at a Laundromat.

"Time has a way of changing people," he says quietly. The comfort in his tone tries to soften the blow, but it doesn't. "He loved you both, but sometimes life can suck out the person you are and leave a shell behind."

I nod. I guess it'd be easier to be mad at the shell rather than the man. I look at Will, his eyes warm and full of understanding. His presence is comforting, easing me from my thoughts.

I wish I could hate my dad, but I don't. I hate myself more for not hating him, for wanting to know him. How could he leave me if he loved me, if he thought about me ever? I smile, letting him know I'm fine. Shaking my absentee father from my thoughts has become a lot easier. He only infiltrates them every once in a while. I won't let him defile this place though. Here, I am happy.

My homework tonight is only one sheet. It's a sort of new concept, but like everything else, he makes it easy. The concept goes down smoothly, and his words stick in my memory like candy. I hang on to each one.

Everything he says is interesting. I'd wondered if that would wear off, but it doesn't, and I've become nervous that I'm paying too much attention, that I'm too interested in him. I've never listened to a teacher the way I do with him, I've never felt the wonderful anxiousness that I do around him, and I realize that this is bad. Do I have a crush on Mr. Scott? I shake the thought from my head. I can't. It would be wrong, not to mention weird. Not only is he my best friend's dad, but he's married. I don't crush on married men, especially married men who are twice my age . . .

If only he looked it, but he doesn't. If only he had gray hair or was balding or smelled like Bengay. Isn't that what dads are supposed to look like? No one's father should be as hot as Will is. They shouldn't have the magnetism he does, and everything that distinguishes him from boys my age is exactly that—distinguished.

His full unkempt beard is just long enough to be sexy but not look like a caveman's. His body's fully grown and matured, not still in transition, and his voice . . . I think aside from his eyes, his voice is what does it the most. It's the icing on the cake. It doesn't matter how he looks with the tone that comes out of his mouth. He should be one of the guys who narrates movies, the sensual kind.

Oh my GOD, what is wrong with me?! This is something else, something weird but great at the same time. I drop my pencil, and he hands it to me, and I get butterflies when our fingers touch. I realize absolutely, without a doubt, I have a crush on my best friend's dad. I'm suddenly distracted, unable to concentrate. The comfortableness I'd felt earlier has vanished from the room, and I feel tense and awkward.

"Lisa, are you okay?" he asks, concern filling the eyes I so badly want to swim in.

Oh no. No no no no no.

"I-I'm not feeling well."

"Do you want me to get you some water or something?"

"Yeah, but I think I need to go home. If that's okay," I say, rubbing my head. I stuff my papers in my book bag, avoiding looking at him.

"Let me help you," he says, noticing my frenzied movements.

When he nears me, I feel my skin warm. Our arms brush, and I let out a small sigh.

"I've got it, Lisa," he says, putting my textbooks, pencils, and papers in my bag. He hands it to me, and I keep my eyes on his chest. I don't look up at him.

"Thank you." I quickly make my way out of the room. Before I do, I look back at him.

He looks puzzled.

"Thanks again, Mr. Scott," I say quickly before getting through the door in what has to be record time. I don't think I should keep calling him Will. I need everything I can to remind me that he is off-limits, and calling him Mr. Scott helps just a bit to remind me he is my best friend's married father.

I've never been so thankful Evie called off tonight and I have her car. I head to Amanda's house, hoping she's free. Because if there is any time I need my girl best friend, it's now.

AMANDA'S SURPRISED TO see me. It's nine o'clock on a school night, and I usually never show up at her house without calling her first because, one, I'm pretty sure her parents don't like me; two, I'm positive her sisters hate me and are grand bitches; and three, she usually always picks me up. She's happy to see me though. She loves surprises. She pulls me into her room, away from her mom's questioning look.

Amanda covers for me. She has a way of being able to come up with a lie on the spot. "Lisa's staying over to work on a project due tomorrow. We have to put the finishing touches on it. I'm sorry I forgot to tell you, Mom."

She pulls me into her bedroom, her eyes wide with anticipation. She knows something's up for me to show up like this. "What's up? Did you and Evie get into a fight? Is Chris ready to take the next step? Did you do it with Brett?" Her excitement grows with each assumption.

I roll my eyes and calmly sit in the pretty pink rolling chair near her desk. "How are you and Chris?"

She instantly starts to fawn over how great Chris is, how talented he is, how they make such a cute couple, how jealous all the girls are of her and Chris. While she talks, I try to think of the best way to talk to my best friend about something I can't talk to her about because she's now dating my other best friend. Because Amanda, love her to death, would spill her guts to a boy she likes. They become a part of her newest persona, and right now, her persona is Chris's doting, loving, loyal girlfriend.

"I have feelings for someone," I say, finally cutting into the Chris lovefest.

"Brett," she says as if it should be obvious.

I think of beautiful, blue-eyed Brett. Our date was *nice*. If it was Brett, things would be perfect. He's sweet, nice, smart, and charming. He's a good guy, and I enjoy spending time with him . . . more as a friend than anything. I shake my head.

"Who?" She flutters around her room to the very edge of her bed, ready for me to spill.

I let out a small breath. While Amanda is an excellent liar, I have a hard time keeping a straight face when I'm just stretching the truth.

"Come on, Lisa, you have to spill. Since when do you like boys? When do you have feelings? When did you become such a girl?" She giggles, not realizing how completely mortified I feel. I must be doing a good job hiding it.

I run through every boy in school in my mind, trying to think of someone she wouldn't feel the need to tell Chris or anyone else about, but I come up blank.

Then her eyes grow big. She's obviously figured out a candidate for herself. "It's Aidan, isn't it?"

I have to keep from laughing out loud. "Ugh, no, it's not Aidan."

She frowns, disappointed. "Then who? And why do you look like you're about to throw yourself off a bridge instead of giddy in love like every other girl would be?"

I guess she is reading me right. "Because . . ." There are a thousand reasons why, but how can I tell her and make her understand without saying too much?

"Is it a girl? Because if you like girls, I'm totally okay with that.

Unless you're in love with me, because I'm strictly into boys," she says, touching my shoulder.

"No, Amanda, I'm not a lesbian," I say, exasperated.

"Oh, thank God. You being in love with me would be way too awkward." She giggles, and for a moment, I love her for being so vain.

"He's-he's not available. In the worst way," I say.

Her blue eyes are focused on me as if she's trying to solve a mystery. "He has a girlfriend?"

"Yeah." *Try wife.*

I know it's wrong. I imagine myself as the trashy homewrecker on some daytime TV show, but the truth is, I haven't really thought about Mrs. Scott in all of this at all. In reality, she's the reason I've been having these feelings. She set me up . . . okay, I'm being unreasonable. I know this isn't what she wanted. It's not what I wanted, but I can't help the way that I feel.

"And he doesn't even know I like him," I add, and she shakes her head sympathetically. "The most messed up part is he's not someone I should like. He-he hasn't flirted with me or tried to impress me. He's just naturally amazing." I stand from the chair and turn away from her. "I've dated so many guys, and none are as interesting or smart as he is. I got butterflies!"

"You don't get butterflies!" she says in shock and disbelief.

I nod profusely. "It's fate's cruel trick. The one man I feel something for is completely off-limits." I feel tears in my eyes.

She pulls me down next to her on the bed. I know she's not used to seeing me like this. I'm not used to feeling like this.

"Oh, honey. A girlfriend . . . I mean, it sort of sucks, but maybe you should tell him how you feel. It's possible he could feel the same way."

I chuckle at that. "There's no way he feels the way I feel. There's no possibility for us. He'd probably laugh in my face. Or be horrified."

"Honey, are you crazy? You are hot. You're smart, and you have a kick ass personality. The kind guys like to be around and not just to get laid," she says, rubbing my back. "You have to tell him. What's the worst that could happen?"

She has no idea.

"It's just a stupid crush. I'm imagining feelings that aren't there," I say, trying to convince myself and her. But by the look on her face, she's not buying it.

"Okay. This is what you're going to do. You're going to have sex with Brett," she says.

"What?" I ask her as if she's crazy.

"I think you have a wall up with guys. Maybe because of your dad, I'm not sure, but if there's any guy you should give a chance, it's Brett. He really likes you. He told Claire's boyfriend that. I heard Claire bitching him out when she was home this weekend. I bet if the sex is amazing, then you'll forget all about he-who-shall-remain-nameless."

"How can the sex be amazing when I don't feel anything even when he kisses me?" I ask, irritated.

"Sex and kissing aren't the same thing," she says as if it's obvious. "Oh, come on, can you just tell me who it is?"

"Maybe I can try a little harder with Brett. Maybe you're right. I'm just not giving him a chance," I say, trying to convince myself. Deep down, I know it won't help.

"Don't sound so down about it. You act like you're going out with the hunchback of Notre Dame." Amanda's going through one of my favorite stages yet—she's a literature buff with a pair of cute black frames. "Who is this guy? Where did he come from? Who got the unattainable Lisa to fall this hard out of the blue?"

He's always been there. I guess I just never noticed.

I FOUND OUT why there was no guy at our house last night and why our fridge is fuller than it's been in . . . since I can't remember. My aunt Dani is visiting. If I had one wish, it would be that Aunt Dani would live with us. She's the one person who makes my mom get her shit together. The one person my mom seems to respect—maybe the person ,my mom wishes she were. At first glance, you'd think they were twins with their light-almost-white-blond hair and perfect lips and asymmetrical noses, but my mom's eyes are blue like ice, and Dani's are emerald-green. Ten months apart—Irish twins—they couldn't be more different.

"Aunt Dani!" When I see her in the kitchen while my mom makes breakfast, I'm almost giddy. I run to her like a six-year-old, and she pulls me into a bear hug.

"You get more beautiful every time I see you," she says, taking my hands and giving me a once-over.

"Lisa bear, sit down. We're about to have breakfast," my mom says, her tone sweet but teetering on the edge of bitter.

Aunt Dani gives her a sideways glance. When I was younger, I didn't recognize the way my mom looked at my aunt, but as I grew older, I did—love mixed with contempt, contempt that Evie should have for no one but herself. Aunt Dani and Evie grew up in the same household, with the same parents and the same opportunities. But as my grandma used to say, some people could pick a bad decision out of a barrel of crabs with their eyes closed and one hand tied behind their back. She'd always eye my mom whenever she said it too, and I could sense my mom glaring daggers at her. Evie's worst decision in her parents' eyes was marrying my dad. When he left us high and dry, it didn't help her case.

My grandparents never let her live it down. My tenth birthday party was the last straw for Evie. My grandma said that I was the best mistake out of the worst decision she ever made in front of everyone, and Evie was livid. She unleashed so many curse words I didn't know what they all meant. She told Grandma she never wanted to see her again and to stay away. Now I only see Grandma when Dani sneaks me for a visit.

Evie likes to pretend things are great when Aunt Dani is around, knowing she'll report back to their mom. While my mom worked two jobs, one as a waitress and the other as a bartender, and continued to make bad decision after bad decision, my aunt Dani went to college and earned her degree in nursing. She married her husband, Dr. Grant, and moved to a well-to-do part of Chicago. She has bested my mother in every way except one.

Me.

My aunt has been trying to have a child since before I was born, and she's never had any luck. I don't know the medical terms, but in Evie's language, "her well's dried up." I can't imagine how my aunt would feel if she ever heard my mother say that. I wonder what my mom would think if she knew how many times I'd wished Aunt Dani was my mom.

"Why didn't you tell me she was coming?" I say, sitting beside Aunt Dani and stuffing a piece of toast in my mouth.

"I wanted it to be a surprise," Evie says, setting a plate of eggs on the table. It's my favorite—scrambled hard with cheese.

"So tell me, how is everything? Do you have your eye on any schools, any special boys? I want to hear all about it," Aunt Dani says.

I tell her about Brett—not the man who gives me butterflies—then I tell her how I'm pretty much getting As in everything except math, that I'm working on bringing up that grade. I don't tell her that the man who gives me butterflies is the one helping me do that, and I definitely don't tell her that I'm trying to figure out how to keep a handle on my grade without ever seeing him again. That'll be hard since he's my best friend's dad, but it'll be better for everyone.

"This Brett sounds like a keeper," my aunt says enthusiastically.

"No college boy is a keeper for a high school girl. You know they only want one thing, and I told Lisa if she gives that up, she better be using protection," Evie says, leaning on the counter and eating from her plate.

Aunt Dani rolls her eyes at my mother. "You're so crass sometimes, Evie."

"Brett and I are going to a poetry reading tonight. I wish you would have said something, Mom." I'm disappointed. Aunt Dani and Mom can't stand being around each other for longer than two days max, so I try to soak up as much time with her as I can.

"Oh, don't worry. We'll go downtown and pick you out something really cute to wear tonight and just have a regular girls' day this afternoon," Dani says excitedly.

I feel like a kid again.

"So go ahead and get showered. We're going to leave around ten," she says.

"You spoil her, Dani," my mom mutters as I head to the bathroom.

"Someone should. I can't believe you haven't done more to this place since the last time I was here," Aunt Dani replies.

A part of me feels sorry for my mom. She definitely makes mistakes, but if it weren't for that, I probably wouldn't be here.

IT'S COOL OUT today. The sun is bright though, tricking you into thinking it'll provide some warmth against the chill. I don't mind cold days. Something about them makes me feel grateful about life, more so than when it's hot. My aunt Dani and I are walking though Madison's quaint little downtown. It's nothing like where Dani lives in Chicago, with thousands of stores and people bustling. When she took me there, it was like being on another planet. Even now, at the prime time for shopping, the amount of people isn't anywhere near what I saw there.

"So tell me all of the things that are on your mind that you haven't said," she says as we sit on a park bench and sip the caramel lattes she bought us. Working at a coffee shop hasn't stopped me from loving them.

"Nothing, things are great here." I swallow the hot liquid.

She eyes me knowingly. "Your mom told me she think she's in love again." Her tone's a mix of amusement and contempt.

I laugh. "With who, that Jack guy?"

She nods and lets out an exasperated sigh. "I didn't say anything because I wanted to come and see you guys, but I wanted to tell her that he sounds just as worthless as every other man she's let pass through. She says he owns his own truck company."

That's a complete stretch. I think he just started driving a truck last week. I doubt he owns anything, but maybe he does since he skims off our food, electricity, and everything else when he's around. If you never have to spend your own money, you'd have enough to own a lot of things.

"I wish she'd just wake up, realize that it's not too late for her. She's still beautiful. She was smart at one time. You'll be going away to school soon, and she can start living a real life again, not this trailer park fantasy she has going on," she says.

I fiddle with my cup. Evie isn't one of my favorite people, but she's still my mom, and listening to the only woman I love as much as her badmouth her is uncomfortable. I know Dani means well, and I feel the same way, but listening to her and not saying a single thing in Evie's defense feels like a betrayal. I wish I had something to say.

"Enough about your mother. So Brett. I get to meet him tonight?" she asks.

I nod with a smirk. "Yeah. I think you'll like him." Why wouldn't she like him? He's handsome, smart, polite, and charming. Of course, only I wouldn't be attracted to a guy who has it all going for him and is available. That would be too easy.

"What's wrong?" Aunt Dani asks.

"Nothing," I say quietly.

She turns me to face her. "Something's wrong." Her eyes meet mine like she's trying to read them.

I let out a sigh. "When you met Uncle Ryan, when you first met him, did you know right then that you liked him?"

Her face softens, and I can tell she's reminiscing, a memory wrapping around her. "Your uncle was very handsome but a little bit of a jerk. At work, that is. I guess as a new doctor, he had to be tough, curt. Most of the nurses hated working with him. He demanded perfection, zero mistakes. He never laughed or joked around like most of the doctors did with the staff. He was oh so serious all the time. He never let anything get to him." Then she sighs.

"Then one day, he had a patient in the ER, a young woman. She was beat up so badly the pale thing was black and blue. Her face was . . . I walked into the supply room, and he was sitting on the floor, his head between his legs, silently weeping. I knew then he wasn't made of stone. He wasn't just a heartless prick. He was more human than most people in that entire hospital.

"When he looked up at me, his big brown eyes wet with tears, my heart stopped and melted at the same time. I sat next to him and laid my head on his shoulder. I knew I wanted a man with a heart like his."

I smile.

"Why'd you ask?" she says. "Do you think you're in love with Brett?"

I laugh. "No. He's really nice and sweet. I just . . . I don't feel how I think I should feel with him." I feel as if I sound ridiculous.

"And how do you think you should feel?"

I shrug, almost embarrassed by what I'm about to say. "Butterflies." I laugh.

She cracks a smile and shakes her head. "You are Evie's daughter." She chuckles and sighs. "When your mom met your dad, she was so excited after their first date. She ran into my room and said, 'Dani, I've found the one, the man I'm going to marry.'" She mimics my mom's voice. "She said, 'He makes my knees weak. When we kissed, it was one of the most amazing things I've ever experienced. He set my body on fire.'"

I hang onto her every word. My mom doesn't say much about my dad. She certainly would never tell me about how they met.

My aunt shakes her head. "Your parents had heat. They had chemistry and, according to your mother, mind-blowing sex. But that was all that they had. They didn't share common interests. They didn't have a friendship. I doubt your dad even knew your mother's middle name. I'm not saying that chemistry isn't important, it is, but I think so many people get lust confused with love. It's hard enough to build a relationship with love. You're fighting a losing battle if you only have lust. Lust is spread around easily and indiscriminately."

I bite my lip. "What if it's not lust though? Don't you believe in a connection, like mentally, that transcends everything else? Race, gender, age . . ." I feel as though I may have given away too much.

She eyes me and laughs. "You're young, Lisa. If you want to experiment, that's fine, act on your physical urges—with protection of course. I don't need to show you the video on STDs, do I?"

I shake my head.

"But when it's time, you don't act off just this," she says, gesturing to my body. "You use this to guide you." She touches my head.

I give her a smirk.

"Come on, let's go find you something pretty to wear," she says, pulling me out of my seat.

We stop in several shops, browsing and trying on a few things. She ends up with a couple of blouses, and she picks me out a cute navy bandage dress and a white blouse to go over it. Wearing it without the blouse would be more my style, but I don't tell her that.

As we leave the store, she's showing me the cell phone she just bought. It nearly drops out of my hand when she yells, "Will Scott!"

"Danielle, is that you?"

"Yeah, it is."

She walks, I assume, to meet him, but my legs are frozen in place. I command myself to follow her and do my best not to look at him.

"How long has it been?" she says.

Out of the corner of my eye, I see them hug. I hate that I wish I could hug him like that.

"At least six years," he answers.

"You know my niece, Lisa?" she says, gesturing to me.

"Yeah, she and Chris are best friends. I'm actually tutoring her now. How are you feeling?" he says.

I swallow hard, my eyes still on the ground. "Good."

"What are you staring at your feet for?" My aunt nudges me.

I look up at him. He's even more beautiful in the daytime, the sun highlighting his every perfect feature, especially his eyes.

"It's funny how time passes, isn't it? You have a practically grown son, and my little niece is about to go to college. Lisa didn't mention you were tutoring her."

"I didn't think you knew him," I say. It's partially true. I know they all went to school together, but if I mentioned him, I thought she'd see all my illicit thoughts in my face.

"We go waaay back." She giggles, and I can't help but look at her strangely. She's twirling her hair and smiling way too wide. Is she flirting with him? "Lisa and I were about to have lunch. Why don't you join us?"

My heart is about to beat out of my chest. I don't know what I want. My brain wants him to say no, but every other part of me wants him to say yes. I want to see what he's like outside of our little bubble. Is his laugh just for me, or does he share it with everyone?

"Are you sure? I don't want to intrude on you ladies," he asks, giving a lazy sexy grin.

"Don't be silly. We'd love to have you. Wouldn't we, Lisa?" she asks.

My eyes meet his, and I feel my heart clench. If only he knew the effect those small glances have on me. "No, I wouldn't mind at all."

We sit down at a little pizza parlor I used to hang out at with Chris and Aidan when we were freshman. We order a large pizza with sausage, peperoni, and cheese.

"So how's the big city treating you?" he asks.

Aunt Dani beams. "Like it's treating everyone. Ryan's practice is doing well."

"Is that your husband?"

"Yeah, five years now," she says proudly. "What about you and Gwen? We're amateurs compared to you guys."

He laughs and lets out a little sigh. "Yeah. We're great."

But I notice something else behind his words, a second where he stopped to think about what his answer *should* be.

"How many years has it been?" she asks, not knowing each question she asks reminds me of how terrible I am for feeling this way about a married man.

"Twenty-two." He runs his hand through his hair, as if for the first time realizing how long it's been.

"That's so great. You don't hear about marriages lasting that long anymore," she says.

I take a big sip of my Sprite.

"When William and I were in high school, well, before he upgraded and started going to that ritzy prep school his dad put him in," my aunt says, and Will playfully rolls his eyes. "He was the catch of the high school. Quarterback, homecoming king. I think your mom even had a crush on him." She nudges me, and I feel my stomach flip.

"She did not," he says, his eyes falling on me, and I let out a small breath.

"Okay, maybe that was me," she says, and I glare at her. She is flirting! "Oh come on, Lisa, I'm not embarrassing you in front of your tutor, am I?"

My face turns red. I hate that she referred to him as just *my tutor*, but what else could he be?

"Lisa's been great to work with. She's really intelligent and a quick learner," he says.

I should feel good about his compliment, but I'd rather him say

I'm beautiful and mature for my age and he loves spending time with me, but I realize how inappropriate that'd sound. We would always be inappropriate.

"She is. I'm so proud of her," Dani says, pinching my cheek as if I'm five years old.

I'm about to die of mortification when her phone rings.

"Would you guys excuse me? It's your uncle," she says, glancing at me before walking away from the table.

Now it's just Mr. Scott and me. I play with the straw in my drink to distract myself from all the energy buzzing through me.

"How are you doing?" he says.

I look at him and only stare for a second. Why him out of all the people? He's trimmed his beard much lower than usual, but his hair is still long, reaching past his chin. It's thick and full, and I think of all the times I've wanted to run my hands through it. "I'm good."

He looks perplexed. "Are you sure?" He leans in on the table. He does that a lot when we're studying.

I think it's a habit, but I wish he wouldn't. It makes me want to lean forward too, and his lips being the magnets they are, it wouldn't be good for either of us.

"Yeah," I say nonchalantly.

His eyes peer into mine. "I was worried about you."

He's never used that tone before, one that soothes my nerves, one I wish was only for me. Can he see what no one else does? The conflict, the turmoil boiling within me when he's around. There's no way out.

"Why would you be worried about me?" I ask, making my eyes meet his.

He actually leans back as if my look pushed him away. "You seemed upset the last time we were together." He seems genuinely concerned, and I feel bad for making him feel that way.

"I didn't mean to make you feel that way," I say quietly.

"Did I do something wrong?" he asks hesitantly.

I feel my eyebrows rise.

"How could you do something wrong? You're perfect." I hadn't meant to say that out loud.

He looks bewildered. He adjusts his position in his chair, and the flush of his face tells me the words actually came out of my mouth.

I try to think of how to recover. "I-I mean . . . what I meant . . ."

But the waitress appears with a steaming pizza and sets it in front of us. "Large pizza with sausage, cheese, and extra pepperoni."

"Thank you," he says to her with an uncomfortable smile.

I can't believe I just said that!

"Anything else?" she asks, and I glance from her to him.

"No, that's all, thank you," he says, and she smiles before leaving.

I can't sit here with him, especially not with him and my aunt after I've completely embarrassed myself. I shoot up from my seat. "I've got to go."

"Lisa, wait!" he calls.

I keep walking and barge out of the restaurant, letting out a deep breath.

"Lisa, what's wrong?"

I forgot Aunt Dani was out here. I try to think of a reasonable excuse as quickly as I can. "Nothing. I started my period, and I don't have any tampons. I've gotta go." I give her a tight smile and quickly walk away from her.

"Hey, wait, I can go grab you something," she says, looking confused.

"No, I'm fine. Have fun. I'll see you back at home." I walk frantically away.

"HEY, BABE, YOU there?"

Brett's voice wakes me from my daydream of the nightmare of events that happened earlier. I can't believe I said that to *Mr. Scott*, and not just what I said. My voice sounded like a nymph's in heat. I cringe just thinking about it.

"Nothing, I'm fine," I say, giving him an artificial smile.

He looks at me as if he doesn't believe me. "It's like you're somewhere else."

The crowd applauds as the performer finishes his piece. He was good. I would have enjoyed it more if I didn't have so much on my mind.

"I'm fine." I kiss his cheek and take his hand and squeeze it.

His smile is bright and real, unlike the ones I've been wearing all night. He lets go of my hand and put his arm around me. I close my eyes and try to feel *something*. I pray to feel anything but I don't. Still, I rest in his arms. I zone in on his touch, how his fingers are caressing my arm. I should feel something! Brett is handsome and available. Our waitress comes over way too frequently, throwing him cutesy glances and carefully refilling his cup. He's desired. He's desirable, just not to me.

The next performer on stage is a redheaded girl. She's really pretty with long hair that's so red it has to be a dye job—a really good one, but no one's hair can be that color without some type of aid.

"I think you're going to like her. She's really good," Brett whispers in my ear.

She grabs the mic and clears her throat. "My name is Shelly, and I'll be reading a poem I wrote titled 'The Recipe of She.'"

The petite redhead takes a deep breath, and the small room of about thirty is quiet. I hope she does well. Most of the people who've performed here tonight have been singers and comedians. She's the first one to read poetry, and I immediately connect to her. Poetry is different. It's like baring a little part of your soul. I wish I could get up there and do what she's doing. I can tell she's changing, becoming what she's about to speak.

"She's just a girl, maybe not eighteen, nineteen, or twenty *they* think. She sits there, no longer a girl but a woman, the only woman noticed in the room.

Still the girl with a past. Who is she, they wonder, what has she done, how many hearts has she broken?

More than you'd think.

More than you could ever know.

That girl has a secret a secret that can only be told if you kiss her lips, slide your hands across the swivel of her hips.

Rocking- rocking faster and faster, the pleasure only leads to disaster. So many had to know, had to taste, had to see the recipe of she.

Who she is, what she knows, what she can give, but they give nothing in return, each time taking a peace of her soul, her energy goes and goes.

Until there's nothing left, that recipe that they so wanted, her secret that they promised would never be told, and then they are done, that juicy news now old.

She's just a girl, maybe a woman, she was noticed

Now no more."

The quiet room bursts into applause. I stand, clapping excitedly. She smiles shyly, returning to who she was. The bold, vibrant presence she displayed as she read has evaporated back into her.

"Thank you," she says before leaving the stage.

"That was amazing," I tell Brett.

He smiles at me, and I hug him.

"I thought you'd like it. You can do that. You should do that," he says, and I feel myself blush.

He remembered me mentioning I liked writing poetry. It was an offhand comment—I only mentioned it once—and maybe he notices all the writing I do in my journal before I rip up the pages and throw them away. He kisses me. It feels like a quick kiss but one that starts to linger, and though I don't get butterflies, it's nice. This time I don't pull away.

IT'S BEEN TWO weeks since the disaster at the pizza shop and the poetry reading. Brett has grown on me. I still don't have butterflies and just being around him doesn't make me feel all warm inside, but he's sweet and I enjoy being around him. He's a good kisser, even if there's nothing behind the kiss. I keep going back to the conversation I had with Aunt Dani, how she said that you don't build a future based on lust, but that means that lust exists. If it does, why have I not felt it with anyone except Mr. Scott?

Brett asked me to go out with him . . . officially. It's the first time I've ever been asked to be someone's girlfriend. I've gone on a handful of dates, the normal amount for a teenager and maybe a little above average with my best friends being so popular. I've made out with some, refused to kiss others, but never, not once with any of those guys, did I feel what I feel when I'm around *Mr. Scott*. That means something, right? Or it means nothing. I like the idea of being Brett's girlfriend, so I say yes, and afterwards I feel depressed and downright terrible.

His eyes see into my soul, or I fall into his. His voice wraps around me like a blanket when all else is cold. I don't get his touch. It is too far and away . . .

I rip up the third piece of paper in my notebook. I have writer's block . . . or Will block. Everything I write segues into being about him. Which is now starting to affect my grade in my creative writing class, and my math work hasn't been stellar since I stopped seeing him for tutoring. I haven't even been hanging out at Chris's since I don't want to see his dad.

"Hey, bestie!" Amanda whispers loudly, nearly scaring the crap out of me as she plops beside me in the library.

"Hey," I say, trying to sound chipper and not like the killjoy I've become.

"You writing something?"

I sigh. "It sucks."

When she reaches for the crumpled paper, I try to beat her to it. She sticks her tongue out at me when she grabs it first. She straightens it and her eyes skim it and her face frowns.

"Are you still pining about this mystery dude? Is that what's been wrong with you?" she asks impatiently.

I don't answer. I just snatch up the crinkled paper and stuff it in my bag.

"Leese, you got to quit acting like this mopey zombie." She pouts and sighs. "We're worried about you."

I roll my eyes. "Who is we?" But I already know the answer to that.

"Chris and I—and even Aidan."

I have to chuckle at the fact that Aidan's worried.

"Come on, spill it. I'm your best friend. I'm starting to be offended that you won't tell me who this dude is," she says with a slight frown

"I can't."

She rolls her eyes and sighs dramatically. "You're selfish. And I'm not going to feel sorry for you," she says in a forceful tone resembling someone's mother.

My eyebrows rise as I give her an amused smirk.

"I'm serious. Here you are living in the greatest country in the world, you're smart, and you have great hair and a perfect set of real boobs that I have to wear a push-up bra to get. You have this super cute college guy who wants you to be his girlfriend—and why wouldn't he? You're amazing—yet you've been moping and being a complete killjoy over some guy because he gives you butterflies but you can't be with him because of some reason you won't tell me, and you haven't even done anything with this guy. It's annoying!"

I laugh. I laugh hard, and it feels good. She grins at me. The librarian shoots us a warning glare, and we quiet down.

"You know what I think you should do?" she whispers.

It's not often that I take Amanda's advice, but she's just made me feel better. What's the worst she can say? She waits for me to ask her, and I oblige.

"What do you think I should do?"

"I think whoever this guy is, you need to push him out of your life," she says.

"If it was that easy, I would have done it already," I say.

"No, I think you have built up this boy and whatever you feel to be so much that your expectations won't possibly live up to what it really is. Once you see that, you'll be able to get over him," she says.

I look at her, confused.

"You said this guy makes you feel all these crazy and surreal ways by not even touching you, right?" she asks, and I nod.

"Well, *touch* him."

My eyes widen.

"I can't," she says with me in a teasing voice.

"You don't understand. It's a lot more complicated than you think," I say adamantly.

"What I know is it doesn't seem like you're getting over this any-time soon. Your life has been at a standstill. You lied about being sick for homecoming—I know you weren't—and I'm sick of it. I don't care how complicated it is. Put your lips on his so you can see that whatever you think you feel for this guy isn't real and you can move on!" Her big bright eyes narrow on mine.

It sounds crazy, but then I think I've always done things that are a little crazy. I bet Amanda is right. Maybe I have worked myself into such a frenzy that I've imagined what I've been feeling. It wouldn't take much for me to figure out if what I'm feeling is real or imagined. A quick peck on his lips is all it would take. Of course he'll probably freak out a little, but Will seems pretty laid-back. Afterward I could apologize and say I had no idea what I was doing and make up something about how I was upset with my boyfriend and it'll never happen again.

Then I can stop imagining what it would be like to kiss him and stop wanting him, stop writing a story in my head of what it would be like. I just have to make sure no one's around and that I have enough time to convince him afterward that it was silly, not premediated, a mistake, and get him to never say anything to Chris or Mrs. Scott.

It sucks. I've been trying not to think about her in all of this. . . .

Yeah. That's what I'm going to do.

I'm going to kiss Will Scott.

during . . .

chapter eight

will

"DO YOU KNOW how much I love you for bringing me my absolute favorite dish while I'm in the midst of starvation?" Gia says as she savors the pasta.

She means it as a rhetorical question, but the funny thing is, I don't know how much she loves me. I know she loves me, but is she in love with me? Does a girl in love act like her? A woman in love says yes when you propose.

"Babe, what's wrong?" she asks, her voice cutting into my thoughts.

I look at her, her long, dark hair tied in a bun at the top of her head, dark green eyes. When I saw her, she was one of the most beautiful women I'd ever seen. She had a presence that made me take notice. She was smart, feminine, and looked as if she could be from a different time. If I had to describe her in one word, it'd be elegant or regal—something like that.

When I introduced her to my mom and stepdad, I knew whatever it was was real because they saw it too. Dexter Crestfield, who doesn't think anyone is good enough, was impressed, impressed by *my* girlfriend. I was just the son he put up with because he'd fallen in love with my mother. Then he grew to love me and make me miserable my whole entire life. I remember what he said: "You've found something special, son. Don't let her get away if you can." His backhanded compliments were normal, but with her, there was no twisted insult in his words.

Gia's an amazing woman, fit to grace anyone's arm, yet she's chosen mine though not officially. She wears my ring but not on her engagement finger. She had a way of turning down a proposal without making me feel like a loser—until I realized that maybe she hasn't accepted because she's looking for something better. But then she looks at me with those big green eyes and convincing smile, and I think, *No way. She's all in. She's just waiting for the right time, then she'll say yes.* Then I realize it's been nine months and counting, and she still hasn't said yes.

"Babe, what's wrong?" she says again. Her voice interrupts my thoughts.

"Nothing, just thinking." I hear the dryness in my own tone.

Her eyebrow arches. She puts down her food, takes a drink of water, and sits on my lap. "About . . . ?" she says with a giggle, rubbing her hand up my arm.

"Gwen," I say.

She looks perplexed. "What about her?"

I lean back into the couch. "She started crying today in the car about your dad."

My eyes leave hers because I feel guilty about bringing up her sister while she's sitting on my lap, because I've been thinking about her sister a whole lot more than I should be. We met while she was in the shower, go figure. Our meeting was a surprise, a mistake, unexpected, wild, and frenzied, which is fitting. That's exactly how Gwen is—unexpected and wild. I thought she was Gia at first since she had long dark hair and she's small framed just like her sister, but those eyes . . . something behind them was different even in the brief moment our eyes met. It shook something in me.

When Gia spoke about Gwen, it was always as if she was a little girl. I'm sure she mentioned her age at some point, but she always referred to her as little sis, little Gwen, cutesy nicknames that just sort of conjured up the image of a six-year-old in a pink fairy dress—the way Gwen was in the picture Gia kept on her wall.

When I saw Gwen, she was everything my imagination hadn't thought of, and it caught me completely off guard. When we met under better circumstances, she'd opened the door to me, her bravado off the charts. She stood there, hands on her hips and unshaken confidence, but in those eyes, I saw something different again. She wasn't all bravado and attitude. I know because I see the same thing in mine.

"I think it's because of the move, then I gave her Dad's necklace. She's sleeping well, so I'm sure she'll be fine," Gia says. She shifts on my lap. "I'm glad you guys get on so well."

I smirk. I search her face to see if there is any sarcasm in her comment, but there isn't. No double meaning or jealousy there. She's genuine, and that's what I like so much about Gia. She's forthcoming, no games or drama like I had with girls before I met her.

I do get on well with her sister—it's the exact reason why I feel guilty. Not that we've ever crossed the line. Though we almost did that time at the carnival. We were sitting there, just talking, and the ride shook, and she landed right on me. We were close but far away, and if that ride had been still just a second longer, I would have kissed her. Her lips were like magnets drawing me in. I thought it was just because of us having a near-death experience, that biologically our instinct was to long for human closeness before our demise, which is being dramatic, but I latched on to that. I couldn't regard the experience as anything else *then*.

But after getting to know her, I know it wasn't just that. Around her, I don't have to pretend. I don't feel the need to be better, to be different. I can just be me, and she prefers me like that. Not that Gia doesn't like me for who I am. I know she does . . . sometimes.

Gia keeps me on my toes. She pushes me to be a better man, or a different man, and that's good. I think. I know I have bad habits and there's definitely room for improvement, but it can be exhausting. With

Gwen, I feel like I can breathe. I can be myself, the person I am when I go home and take off the tie and kick off the shoes. I can talk to her without worrying about if I sound smart enough or considerate enough, or if I'm interesting enough, which is why I like talking to her, hearing her voice, being around her.

And Gia's cool. She's not possessive or jealous. She's fine knowing that we talk. What she probably wouldn't be fine with is how much we talk, how much I look forward to talking to Gwen, how she's started to cross my mind when we don't talk, how I think about her a hell of a lot more than I should. How I found myself feeling slightly jealous when she talked about that Zach guy, her weird best friend/make-out buddy. I told her she deserved better than that, and I drowned out the small voice in my head that said I could give her better than that.

"I'm glad we get along too." I fake a yawn.

"Tired?" she asks.

"Yeah. I'm going to head home in a little while." I see a flash of disappointment on her face, but it doesn't stay long. Nothing affects Gia for long.

"I have a lot of work to do, anyway," she says with a smile and gets off my lap. She starts to put away her dinner. "I wanted to ask you something. Gwen is going to go stir crazy in our house. I know there has to be some department position she can be squeezed into if you asked someone, right?"

I feel my heart speed up. "Yeah, they're doing this big project in the library they need help with before school starts back up. It wouldn't be a problem." I try to hide my excitement, then guilt sets in. "You'd be okay with it?"

I realize my question sounds suspicious. Why wouldn't she be okay with it? Really, there's no reason she shouldn't be. Or maybe I should be worried. I haven't done anything too wrong, outright at least. Gwen and I have never crossed the line, and we never will. She loves her sister too much.

"Of course, why wouldn't I be?" she asks and looks at me questioningly.

I don't answer her, but I rest my hands on her hips and give her a quick kiss.

"She likes you, and I know she doesn't like a lot of people. Hopefully she'll make some friends, and it'll be good for her," she says, pinching the bottom of my chin.

"As long as she's okay with it." I try to sound casual.

As I walk out of the house, I notice how my mood has changed, how I can't stop smiling. I know it won't take much to get her hired—the department head loves me—but is it a good idea? Something tells me it isn't, but I ignore that.

gwen

"HOW'S MY WORKING girl?" Zach asks.

I sit in the empty classroom, using the phone on my break. "Fabulous, da'ling." I twist the cord around my finger.

"That boring, huh?" He chuckles.

"Yeah," I say with a laugh.

"Well if you're bored, that means there isn't much to do. So enjoy it."

I miss Zach. I sort of miss home and lying in my bed when I thought my biggest care in the world was what I was going to make for dinner. Not much has changed—I'm not responsible for bills or anything like that—but things are so different than they were. I love living with Gia, having my big sister around and sort of being on my own. I like getting my own paycheck and not having to rely on anyone else for the things I want. Still, the job is boring. No one comes to the library in the summer, and it's usually just Ms. Carmine and me cataloging books all day.

"I miss you, Zach. I wish you'd come down here," I say for the hundredth time.

"Maybe I will."

My eyebrows shoot up. "Really?" I sound way too excited, but I am. If Zach comes, it will be beyond great.

I haven't really made any friends here, and hanging out with Gia is practically out of the question with the way her schedule is. The other person I get to hang out with is fantastic, but at the same time, it's gut-wrenching. I can't tell Zach that though. It's the one thing I feel uncomfortable bringing up. Not that Zach would judge me—he's not the judgmental type—but he'd definitely tell me to do something. He gets irritated by inaction. And if there's anything I can't take action about, it's this. It wouldn't be so bad if I had a distraction, but there are none. The job I hoped would keep me busy gives me way too much time to think and wallow.

"I'm thinking about it." He chuckles, and I pout.

"Come on, seriously. Don't get my hopes up if you're not going to come," I whine.

He laughs. "Maybe in the next two weeks, possibly."

I squeal.

"You must really be bored," he says, sounding flattered.

"I am."

LUNCH IS UNFORTUNATELY something I look forward to. A little too much maybe. I pull out a bowl of the potato and bacon soup I whipped up yesterday. One of the best things about a job is having money to buy CDs and whatever food I like and try whatever recipes I want. I put the soup in the microwave, then I feel two hands grab my sides. My nerves shoot through my body, and I almost jump out of my skin. When I turn around and see Will laughing, I'm not surprised. I punch him playfully anyway.

"Why do you always do that?" I say, feigning anger, but unfortunately, I enjoy any reason we have to touch.

"I can't believe I still get you with that." He chuckles, leaning on the counter and looking at me with a lazy, sexy smile.

I quickly look away and concentrate on the microwave heating up our food. "Potato and bacon soup. I think it turned out okay." Not to pat myself on the back, but it was delicious last night and smells even better today.

"I'm sure it's okay," he says with half smile.

"Okay?" I ask.

He sighs. "Okay, everything you make is finger-licking good."

He winks, and I turn back toward the microwave, hoping my cheeks haven't changed colors.

"You seem happy today. Is the job getting better?" he asks, and I shake my head.

"No," I say with a smile.

He looks at me curiously. "Then what?"

I grab the container of soup and two bowls, and we sit at the little table in the employee lounge. It's funny how I went from high school student to an employee at a school in a matter of weeks.

"Nothing," I say secretively.

I see from his expression he's getting more curious as I pour the soup into our bowls. He's brooding, eyeing me, and it gives me tingles.

"Come on, what's up?" he asks, giving me a mischievous grin.

I look up as if I'm contemplating whether or not to tell him, but he knows it's a ruse. I tell him practically everything—except for what's most important.

"Zach might be coming to visit," I say, unable to contain my wide smile.

As soon as I say it, his smile disappears, and he sort of frowns.

I look at him questioningly. "What's that look for?"

"I don't see why you still even talk to that guy," he says, not even trying to mask his disdain.

"He's my friend," I say as if it's obvious.

"A friend who likes to feel you up whenever he feels like it." He pops a spoonful of soup in his mouth.

"It's not whenever he feels like it. It's whenever I feel like it," I say defensively.

Of course Will and I have talked about this before, and he's always expressed his disapproval of my relationship with Zach, but he doesn't understand it. And really, it shouldn't matter if he understands it or not. The difference today though is that instead of just stating what he thinks, he has an attitude. Like he's sort of pissed. I know when he's pissed because he gets that way a lot when he has to do administrative paperwork or when he talks about Gia still not accepting their engagement.

"What's your problem?" I ask, a little annoyed.

"I don't have a problem," he counters, so obviously annoyed.

"It doesn't seem like it," I say, taking a spoonful of my own soup.

Then his face softens as if he knows he's being ridiculous. His blue eyes focus on mine, and my annoyance instantly dissapears. "I just think you deserve better than that. A guy who wants you to be his . . . and not in some twisted friendship."

His tone is almost intimate, and I grip my spoon tightly. Why does he have to be like that, so . . . so heart-wrenchingly sweet?

"Maybe one day I'll find a guy like you, Will. Cross your fingers for me," I say quietly.

The rest of our lunch is quiet and awkward. I don't understand why he cares so much about what I do with Zach. I don't insert myself into his and Gia's business. I don't tell him that I think he's stupid for waiting around for her to decide when he's good enough for her to marry, that so many girls would say yes to him in a heartbeat if he gave them the chance. I want to tell him that one of those girls is right in front of him.

No, that's *crazy*. I don't want to marry Will. That's going too far. I have feelings for him, I care about him, and I love being around him, but marry . . . what type of a person wants to marry her sister's almost-fiancé? I guess that's as bad as wanting to kiss your sister's almost-fiancé. I swear, there are times, though brief, when I think just for a moment that he has feelings for me too, but thinking like that doesn't help things.

The awkwardness passes, and we're back to us—whatever *us* is. I'd rather have us than nothing even if it's not exactly everything that I want.

TONIGHT I'M MAKING pork chops with garlic scalloped potatoes and asparagus. Evening is one of my favorite times here. It's the one time I don't mind that I'm alone in the house most of the time. In the evening, when I get to cook and turn on the radio and the sun sets, it's like the house is mine. I'm surprised when I hear the door open and Gia walks in. It's a Tuesday, and so far Tuesdays are usually her late nights.

"Something smells good," she sings.

I smile. "It's going to be. What are you doing home so early?" I check on my roast.

"Class let out early today, believe it or not," she says as she peeks into the pot I have going.

I shoo her away. She knows I hate when people look in on my dishes.

"And you didn't stay at the library to study?" I ask, surprised.

"No, I'm going to be there all weekend, studying for this exam next week." She takes a seat at the table, and I sit across from her. "How's work going?"

I like how she says work as if my job at the library is a career.

"Another day, another dollar." I laugh.

"How's Will?" she asks.

I look at her a little awkwardly. I'm surprised by her question, but I try to play it cool. "Good, I guess. Why would you ask me?"

"He's just been acting kind of . . ." She grabs a pop out of the fridge.

"Kind of what?" Now my curiosity is piqued.

"I don't know . . . distant," she says with a sigh before she sits back down.

"Do you think it's because you still haven't said yes to marrying him?" I ask as if it's obvious.

She shakes her head. "No, I mean, I don't think so. Will understands my feelings about that."

Really.

"I think it's because we haven't been able to spend that much time together. My schedule is just so crazy right now. It sucks. I wish I had more time for him, but things are just super hectic." She twists the cap back on her bottle of soda. "The thing is though, I'd think since we haven't been spending much time together, he'd kind of soak up the opportunity too, right?"

Right then I see a flicker of what might be worry behind her confident façade.

"I think that you should make time for someone you care about before they stop caring," I say. I defeat the urge to tell her that nothing's wrong and she's exaggerating, I won't be that person. I'm already the person whose feelings I loathe.

"You wouldn't understand, Gwen. When you're an adult and you have plans you've made, it's important to stay on track with them. Will should understand that. At least he would if he was a little more driven, a little more of an adult. Sometimes he acts like a kid."

At that moment, I realize Gia wants Will to be William and she won't be happy unless he's exactly that.

"Has he said anything to you?" she says flippantly.

"No."

"Have you noticed him not being himself lately? Right now you see him more than I do," she says with a sigh, and I shake my head. She lets out a deep sigh then giggles to herself. "You know, you're absolutely right Gwen. I have to make more time for him. Do you mind if I pack up some of this and take it over to him? I think I'll spend the night there."

I try to force a smile, but I feel as though I'm going to vomit. *What is wrong with me?!*

"Sure," I say quietly, and she beams at me.

She kisses my cheek and heads to her bedroom. "I'm going to go shower first. How long will it take for it to be done?"

I swallow hard. "About an hour." But I feel as though my voice is about to crumble.

I feel as if my puppy just died. I want Gia to be happy, but why does it feel like her happiness is crushing my own? I try to clear the swelling in my throat, and the doorbell rings. I gather myself and go open the door, and my heart nearly jumps out of my chest.

"Hey, brat," Zach says, standing there looking as sexy and annoying as ever.

I jump into his arms, and he spins me around. "You knew you were coming when you talked to me today!"

"Yeah, I already had my stuff packed. I was waiting for you to call so I could leave," he says after he puts me down.

"Gwen, who is that?"

"This is my best friend, Zach," I tell her excitedly as she approaches us.

She gives him a once-over and smirks. "Oh, wow!"

Zach's look can do that to a girl. He gives her one of his sexy, breath-stopping smiles.

"I remember you. You're still beautiful as ever," he says as I pull him into the house and shut the door.

Gia's face reddens. He's wearing a black knitted cap over his long black curls and a grey sweater with skulls all over it. I wouldn't say he's even remotely close to Gia's type, but Zach's looks and disarming attitude would definitely qualify him for a roll in the hay. Not that I could see Gia ever doing that type of thing.

"Thank you, come have a seat." She gestures toward the living room.

He follows us and sits on her couch, setting his backpack between his legs. I sit next to him, and when he pulls my leg over his and massages it, Gia's eyes widen. Zach doesn't notice.

"How long are you staying?" I ask, squeezing his hand.

"I only got two nights off, so I'll be headed back after that," he says in his slow, dragging tone.

"Where are you staying?" I ask. I know he doesn't know anyone here but me.

"Maybe a motel or something." He shrugs.

"No, that wouldn't make sense. You can stay here!"

Gia clears her throat, and Zach's and my eyes fall on her.

"Umm, can you excuse us one minute, Zach?" She gestures for me to follow her to her bedroom.

I kiss his cheek before following her. She's all smiles until we're in her bedroom with the door closed.

"He can't stay here, Gwen," she says indignantly, and I frown at her.

"Why not?"

"Because he's a guy, I don't know him, and you two can't keep your hands off each other," she says as if it's obvious.

"That's so unfair! He's my friend. Our relationship is a little unique, but if you're worried about us getting it on, that's not happening. But even if it was, I'm an adult. I'm not a little girl, and isn't this my house too?" I ask indignantly.

She sighs and runs her hand over her face. "Mom wouldn't like it."

"Who the hell cares what Mom thinks? Gia, I live with you. I'm not a houseguest. I moved here so that I could have freedom, not be treated like a little kid."

She lets out a gruff sigh and shakes her head. "He can stay at Will's. That's the best I can do," she says with a huff.

I feel myself turning red. "He can't stay at Will's. Will hates him."

She looks perplexed. "Why would Will hate him? Has he ever even met Zach?"

"No, it's just . . . maybe some of the things Will knows about him," I say guiltily.

She squints at me, and for a moment, I swear she sees through me, right into my guilty little soul, that she sees every thought I've had about her boyfriend, and she's going to haul back and slap me into tomorrow. Actually no, Gia's not like that, but she'd have every right. But she just shrugs, and I relax.

"I'll call Will and set everything up. We can all have dinner over there tonight," she says, and before I can answer, she storms out the room.

Ugh! I go back out, and Zach's sitting with his feet up on her coffee table. Gia would *love* that. I knock them off.

"What's your problem?" He chuckles.

"Apparently I'm still sixteen and need permission for boys to come into my room," I say sarcastically.

He laughs, a deep chuckle that I've missed, then he rubs the top of my head, making my hair look crazy.

"Stop being a brat," he says as I push him away.

"How am I being a brat? I live here. I'd like my friend, you, to stay, and she won't let you. I might as well be living back at home, asking permission for things."

Zach is calm as ever. "Well, I kinda am some strange guy she doesn't know, and she probably knows that if I stay, we're going to make out, and I'm pretty sure your check is as pathetic as mine and can't pay even one utility bill, meaning big sis is still in charge."

I pout. I hate when he makes sense. "It's still not fair."

"I got a couple of bucks to stay at a motel—a really bad one." He chuckles.

"Oh no, she's going to get Will to let you stay at his place," I say bitterly.

"Cool, more money for us to party tonight," he says with a nudge and mischievous smile.

My eyes widen in excitement. Lord knows I need to let loose a little. Before I can ask him about it, Gia's back in the room.

"Okay, Zach, if you don't mind, my boyfriend would love for you to stay at his place. I was thinking we can all have dinner there, then you and Gwen can have the whole day together after she gets off work," Gia says brightly.

I roll my eyes.

Zach only says, "Cool."

I'VE ONLY BEEN to Will's house once, and it was brief. Gia had left a book she needed, and we stopped to pick it up on our way home from work, and I had to go to the bathroom. Will's house is closer to the city than Gia's, and it's in a big apartment building with five floors and a doorman.

"Classy," Zach whispers into my ear as Gia greets the doorman by name.

"Can you try to be nice?" I whisper as we walk a few feet behind Gia.

"I'm always on my best behavior," he says sarcastically.

I eye him, calling him out on his BS. His eyebrow arches.

"What do you care about my behavior? You didn't even care what impression I made on your mom," he says suspiciously.

I avoid his questioning glare.

"Come on, guys," Gia says as she holds open the elevator.

When we make it to Will's floor, we see his door is already open. We walk in, and Gia calls his name while shutting the door.

"This is kick ass," Zach says as he looks around the apartment.

Being at Will's apartment is the only time I'm reminded that Will does indeed come from money. He has a big screen TV and a pool table. His kitchen is bigger than Gia's, and he even has a dining room.

He appears from his bedroom, his hair wet. He must have just gotten out of the shower. He has on a short-sleeved T-shirt that clings to him, revealing his sculpted arms and giving me a better view of the tattoo on his arm—it's a moon with clouds around it. I've seen pieces of it, but this is the most revealing look yet. My eyes run over his stomach. I think he may have six-pack underneath that shirt, and I feel my body temperature rise.

"Hey, guys." Will's eyes drift over to Zach, and he gives him a once-over.

Gia gives him a quick kiss on the cheek. "This is Gwen's friend Zach."

I hate that she didn't let me introduce him. She heads to the kitchen to put the food on the table as Will approaches Zach and me. He gives us a tight smile and sticks out his hand. Zach gives him a tense handshake.

"What's up?" Zach says nonchalantly.

For some reason, it seems as if there's tension between them. Zach wears his smug grin, and Will gives him an "I call bullshit" glare. These two will be awesome roommates.

AS WE SIT at the table and eat, the room is quiet and seems a little chilly. Zach and Will's attitudes toward each other haven't changed, and I'm still sort of pissed at Gia, who seems oblivious or just doesn't care. Will and I have exchanged a few glances, and I feel annoyance and disapproval radiating from him.

"So, Zach, are you in school?" Gia asks, trying to strike up a conversation.

"Nah, school's not for me. I only finished high school because my parents would have kicked me out if I didn't," he says before putting a spoonful of mashed potatoes in his mouth.

"So what're your plans going forward?" she asks.

Zach shrugs. "I like to take things as they come."

If Zach was my boyfriend and I cared about things like impressing people, I'd be absolutely mortified, but since he's my friend and I couldn't care less what Gia thinks, I'm not as uncomfortable as I could be.

"Oh." Gia sounds a little puzzled. Anyone who doesn't have their entire future mapped out is puzzling to her.

"So you guys getting married?" Zach asks, looking at her engagement or promise ring. Leave it to Zach to ask the most awkward question in the room.

"The date isn't exactly set as of yet," I answer for Gia since she's been answering for me all night.

"So you and Gwen are just friends?" Will asks, sarcasm evident in his voice.

I feel my stomach flip. What the hell is he doing?

"Really *good* friends," Zach says, his eyes narrowing on Will with a teasing smirk.

Will's jaw clenches. Zach has a way of reading people and homing in on the one thing that grates on their nerve. I have no idea why he's choosing to grate on the nerves of the guy he's staying with, but I shoot Will a glare to drop it.

"These pork chops are amazing, Gwen," Gia interrupts.

"Yeah, brat, you can really cook. I thought you just made good brownies," Zach says.

I can't help but laugh. Will's face is hard like stone . . . *geesh*.

"I love her brownies. They are so good," Gia says, clueless.

"Yeah, Gwen's brownies are special," Zach says again, smirking at me.

"Cool it. Nobody's stupid here," Will says, his tone cold. He's staring at Zach, who raises his hands in a truce with a laugh.

"What? I don't get it," Gia asks.

"He's talking about brownies with pot, Gia," Will says, exasperated.

Gia's eyes widen before she frowns at me disapprovingly.

"Hey, she hasn't touched anything in a long time. Besides it's all natural . . ." Zach goes into the history of pot and the real reasons why it was banned and all the politics involved.

I can recite his argument by heart I've heard it so many times. It's one thing he's passionate about, and Gia listens intently and seems impressed. He's pretty articulate when he wants to be.

"Well, at least you're well-informed." Gia smiles, and I can see her view of him change.

Will rolls his eyes. "Excuse me." He gets up and heads into the kitchen.

I excuse myself as well. Will's in the kitchen, drinking a pop near the fridge.

"Hey, what's your problem?" I ask.

He glares at me, a look I've never seen before. He looks angry. His cheeks are flushed and his eyes narrowed. "That's your best friend—a smug little druggie?"

I squint at him. "Wow, I can't believe what an ass you're being. You don't even know him."

"I know enough. He's not good enough for you," he says a little too loudly.

I look at him in disbelief. "Are you serious right now? He's not coming here with a marriage proposal. He's my friend, someone I care about, and don't ever say anything that rude about him again or we won't be friends," I say sharply before turning around to leave.

He grabs my hand, and my stomach flips. He turns me toward him. I look up at him, nerves in the pit of my stomach, and his expression softens.

"I'm sorry," he says with puppy dog eyes.

I look at his hand holding mine, and our eyes lock. He steps closer to me, and my heart skips a beat. My entire body tingles, and my breathing slows down. Does he feel this? Is it not just me? When his eyes drift from my eyes down to my lips and he licks his, I feel as if I'm going to pass out. But then he lets my hand go, and the look I thought I saw in the eye is gone.

"I'll be better," he says quietly before leaving me in the kitchen with my heart dropped to the floor.

Back at the table, Will does do better, his ice-cold demeanor melted. He's more involved in the dinner conversation, but I'm silent. My heart has gone from the floor to my throat, my thoughts still on what transpired in the kitchen. Will and Zach have found a common interest in the class system in the country . . . and on farming of all things. It turns out that Will's uncle, his mother's brother, had a farm, and the summer he stayed with him was one of the best summers of his life.

Zach's biological dad has a farm, and he talks about how peaceful it is and how fulfilling the work is.

Gia looks on as if they have ten heads growing out of their shoulders. "I can't see why anyone would ever want to do that. You guys are on your own." She laughs.

Zach shrugs with a grin. "It's not for everyone, but don't knock it until you try it."

She shakes her head. "Nah, not for me. The animals, the crappy pay, living in the middle of nowhere?"

I wonder if she sees the disappointment in her future—well, possible future—fiancé's face. My thoughts drift back to that night Will dropped me off at my parents' and how he asked me about Gia living on a farm.

"So, Zach, what's the plan tonight?" I ask, wanting to change the subject.

"I've got us tickets to this after-party a band's having," Zach says, and my eyes widen.

"Really! That's so cool," I say, excited.

"What time is the party? It's already kind of late," Gia asks.

I shoot her a "don't embarrass me" glare.

"Well, it starts at ten. That gives us, like, an hour to get there. It's in Wicker Park," he says.

"That's not too far from here. I can drop them off," Will says, and I shoot him a half smile.

"I guess . . . what time would you guys be back?" Gia asks as I start clearing the table.

"I won't keep her out long. Like around one," he says, and Gia frowns a little. "Or twelve." Zach chuckles.

I stop midway to the kitchen. "One is fine. Gia knows I'm eighteen now—nineteen in a couple of months—and she wouldn't do anything as embarrassing as trying to give me a curfew knowing what a disastrous and unnecessary argument we would have if she did," I say in a cheerfully sarcastic tone.

She sighs. "Only if Gwen agrees not to do anything that would jeopardize her life or freedom because Chicago is nothing like the little city she grew up in, and if she gets arrested or kidnapped, I won't be offering any money for her return," she says in the same tone I used.

"Great, it's settled," Zach says happily.

IT TOOK TEN full minutes of arguing with Gia for her to agree to let us take a cab. I felt like a sixteen-year-old fighting with Mom again. When I glanced at Will for help, he finally stepped in and told her we'd be fine.

As soon as we made it to the party, Zach showed me his surprise for the night—Zach had gotten us fake IDs. My name was Lita Maldanado, a twenty-three-year-old redhead, and Zach was James Garvin, twenty-one with bangs. They didn't look much like us, but Zach swears the bouncers won't glance at them for more than a second before letting us in.

"Your sister is hot," he says as I apply eyeliner, lipstick, and mascara while he holds up my pocket mirror for me.

"I think her boyfriend wanted to break your face." I chuckle.

"Yeah, he did, but it was weird. He was acting like he was your big brother or something," Zach said, irritated. "He's kind of a jerk."

I don't comment. I've never talked about my feelings for Will with Zach. I've never even told him how much time Will and I spend together, but as I sit next to Zach holding my mirror so I can do my makeup, I can't help feeling a little guilty.

"Do you like him?" he asks, and I look at him nervously.

"No," I say, sounding more dramatic than I intended.

"Why did you get so defensive?" he asks, giving me a suspicious glare before we walk up to the bouncer.

Just as he said, they glance at our IDs for a second before we get in. The club Zach chose is pretty nice. The music is good, and there're a lot of people, but it's not too crowded. The music makes me feel invigorated. I move my hips to the beat as we push through the crowd. Zach takes my hand, and I see we're headed to the bar.

"I'll have two shots of Jose Cuervo. Training wheels for the lady," he says to the cute blond bartender. She gives Zach a flirtatious smile.

"She likes you," I say in his ear, and he winks at me.

"Here you go, cutie," she says, sliding over two little glasses with clear liquid.

"It's tequila. Lick it, shoot it, suck it," he says. "Put the salt on the back of your hand and lick, do the shot, then suck the lime."

I salt my hand as he says, and we take our glasses and clink them together.

"To you being a big city girl," he says with a sarcastic smile.

I do the shot just how he said, and when it's all over, I feel my face contort. I've never drank alcohol except for a beer here and there and the occasional glass of wine my mom let me have with dinner when she was in a good mood.

"That's disgusting," I say, making a face.

"The second one's always better."

"I don't ever want to drink that again. What is wrong with people? It tastes terrible," I say, sliding the glass away from me.

Zach only shakes his head and laughs. He motions for the bartender.

"Yeah, sweetie?" she says in a disgustingly cute tone.

"Something sweet for lady, and a shot of the house tequila for me," he asks.

Her eyes glide to me. "Girlfriend?"

I laugh and bump his hip with mine. "Sister."

"This drink's on the house then," she says, smiling widely.

When she turns around to make our drinks, Zach looks at me with a seductive grin.

"What?" I ask playfully.

"You're different here," he says into my ear.

"Why do you say that?" I ask.

He shakes his head. "You've always been cool but not cool enough to do what you just did and score a free drink."

I wink at him. The bartender is back in front of us with a cute pink drink.

"What's it called?" I ask, lifting it to my mouth. It's fruity, sweet, and tastes like a smoothie.

"It's an Amarillo Sunset. You like?" she asks, and I nod, slurping it up.

"Really good," I say in surprise.

"If you're a novice, don't drink it too fast," she adds before giving Zach a grin, sliding him his shot, then making her way to the next customer.

"Why do you think she thinks I'm a novice?" I ask, and Zach chuckles.

"The way you looked downing that shot isn't exactly what an alcoholic would look like," he says.

Can't argue with that. After I finish my drink, my legs feel warm, and I can't stop moving to the music.

"Let's dance!" I say, pulling Zach to the dance floor.

We dance to fast songs—Zach's just as into it as I am. We dance to slow songs, and he grabs my ass, though I move his hands up to my back. He eyes me, a little surprised. I just want to move and have fun, and for some reason I can't help but think of Will's disapproval about letting him touch me that way. Then I have one more of those fruity drinks, and the music sounds even better and Zach looks even cuter. The more we dance, I stop moving his hands from my butt, and I hug him a lot more. I kiss him on the cheeks then the lips, and I realize I'm about to make out with Zach on the dance floor of a club. What's worse is I feel guilty because I'm imagining he's Will.

"What's wrong?" Zach asks.

"I-I can't do this. It's wrong," I say, hearing my words slurring a bit.

He giggles and moves to my ear. "You're a little drunk, I think."

I frown. I'm not drunk. Before I can tell him that, he's pulling me back over to the bar. The same flirtatious blonde who served us is back.

"Water, please," he tells her, and she smiles.

Zach looks at me, and I lean on the bar to steady myself. He has such a sexy smile. He shouldn't be wasting it on me when someone else would appreciate it.

"Do you think she's cute?" I ask, and he grins with a nod. "You should ask her to dance."

He looks at me skeptically. "Really?"

I nod adamantly.

"Nah, I can't do that. You're my date tonight," he says with a grin.

I shake my head. "I wouldn't make a really good date. You should enjoy your night in Chicago. I wish I could."

"What's wrong, brat?" he asks, searching my eyes.

I look away. When the bartender comes back, I smile widely at her. "Do you think my brother's cute?"

She laughs, her eyes cutting over to Zach. "I do actually."

I look at him, and he smiles, looking almost a little embarrassed. He not usually embarrassed.

"I think you should let him dance with you. It's his birthday," I say, laying it on thick. I know I don't have to do much of that though. She's obviously into him.

"Well, I'm off in five minutes, if you can wait," she says to Zach.

"Uh, sure." He sounds surprised.

"Okay, I'll come find you," she says before going to help another customer.

He grabs the glass and hands it to me. "Drink."

He lifts it to my mouth. I do as he says, then he sets it back on the bar.

"You going to tell me what's wrong? Something is definitely wrong with you," he says not as playfully.

I laugh. God there is so much wrong with me—what isn't wrong? "I'm here without any friends, I have no clue what I want to do with my life, my sister is perfect—smart, beautiful, sweet—and she's fun but acts like my mother, and I'm in love with her boyfriend." I hiccup.

As I spoke, the words sounded so normal coming out of my mouth. I'm in love with my sister's boyfriend. That's what's wrong with me. I laugh at the revelation, and everything seems easier, better—until I look at Zach's face. He looks horrified, then the realization dawns on me what I just said. Aloud.

Oh shit!

"You're what? With the guy, with the Will dude?" he asks frantically.

"I-I—" I try to think of how to make what I just said sound like a mistake or a flub, but I can't think of anything. "He doesn't know, and he's not in love with me, so it's not as bad as you think." I try to sound as if I'm joking, but his face is hard. "Why are you looking at me like that?"

He shakes his head and signals the bartender over again. This time it's a dark-haired slender man with a noise piercing.

"Double shot of 1800 please," Zach says.

ZACH TRIES TO hit me with a thousand questions about the bomb I've dropped on him—like when did this happen, how did this happen, why am I in love with Will? He asks them so rapidly that they sound like one question. Before I can explain, the bartender from earlier approaches us. She's even prettier up close, with ice blue eyes and perfect skin. Zach looks a little taken aback. I'm so glad his attention isn't on me anymore so I can have time to think.

"Are you ready for a dance?" she asks, a little shyer than she appeared earlier.

Zach glances at me. I see he's about to back out of it.

"Yes, yes, he is," I say, nudging him toward her. "I'll be sitting over there." I point at an empty table nearby.

She takes his hands and puts them around her waist before he can protest, and I'm grateful. I sit and think about what I just said. That I just said out loud to another person. That I admitted it to myself.

WHEN WE GET in the cab, there are three of us. I vaguely remember us all being back at the bar. Ashlyn got us free drinks, and Zach had a whole lot. He's super touchy-feely now, and he and Ashlyn are on the verge of making out right in the cab. Luckily Will's house is only a few minutes away from the bar.

When the cab pulls up in front of Will's building, I open the door and welcome the air. I feel a little warm and a tad dizzy. I step out and wait for Zach to join me. Ashlyn whispers something in his ear, and he turns and looks at me with a super goofy smile.

"I think I'm staying at Ashlyn's tonight," he says with a slurred voice.

"Ooh okay," I say, getting out of the cab. I hear him get out behind me.

He leans back into the cab. "I'll be right back. Just going to make sure she makes it in safely."

"You're such a gentleman," she says, slurring even more than him.

"I think I have a better chance of making it up without you," I say.

We walk into the building, Zach singing a jingle from the Frosted Flakes commercial too loudly. When we get to Will's floor, I shush him.

"You're drunk, Zach. Maybe you should come inside and just crash," I tell him, and he nods.

"Nope, I'm not going to sleep on that jerk's couch," he says with a pout.

"He's not a jerk," I say defensively.

"Yes, he is!"

He's so loud I shush him, sounding loud myself.

"Damn it, do you remember what apartment he lives in?" I say, scratching my head.

"That one," he says, pointing at a door.

I walk over to it and knock and wait. When the door opens across from the one we knocked on, we see it's Will.

His face is red, and he's glaring at us. "Are you drunk?" Will's hair is disheveled, and he has on a wife beater that displays the tattoo on his arm in all its glory.

I feel as if my eyes are glued to it. "No, no, I'm not drunk." I expect Gia to storm out in full mom mode.

"Okay, brat, I'm out. I'll be back tomorrow," Zach says with a slur, heading to the elevator.

"Where the hell is he going?" Will asks.

"He has a date," I say, walking into the apartment.

Will looks at me with a perplexed expression. "Ugh."

He's so cute, and I giggle.

"Okay, you stay here. Let me see where this guy is going," he says, walking out and shutting the door.

will

I CAN'T BELIEVE this Zach guy. He's drunk as hell and taken off in a cab with a girl he doesn't even know in a city he's never even been to. God, was I that stupid at his age? I stalk back to my apartment. I'm so pissed, mainly at myself. I let that little shit take Gwen out by herself, and he didn't even stay sober enough to know what the hell was going on with him or Gwen.

I breathe a sigh of relief when I make it back to my apartment. So many things could have gone wrong. I'm pissed at him for not being coherent and ditching Gwen, but a part of me is glad I don't have to stay up all night to make sure he didn't crawl into Gwen's bed. Not that I should be worried about that. It shouldn't bother me. She's not my little sister, and I really shouldn't care, but I do, and if I caught him in her bed, I probably would have probably broken his pretty-boy face.

"Your friend is a dumb asshole," I say angrily.

I walk over and see her slumped into the couch. I can tell she's been drinking too—not as much as her asshole friend, but she's definitely tipsy. Thank God I convinced Gia to go home. Hopefully Gwen can sober up before I get her back to her house.

"Come on, I'm taking you home," I say, trying to keep the edge in my voice, but it's hard looking at her.

"Where'd Gia go?" she asks, her voice lighter than normal.

Her usually pink lips are stained red. She has on heavy makeup like she did the first day I met her. She looks good as always, but she looks different.

"She went home. I told her you could stay in my extra room and Zach could sleep on the couch since I'm closer to the city. I figured you'd want to hang out downtown or something," I say, unable to stay mad at her.

"That was thoughtful."

Her big green eyes are on mine, and I feel my chest warm. I clear my throat from the way she's looking up at me like she's willing me to see into her eyes, to get closer and kiss her lips. I shake off the haze. It's late, and I'm obviously tired.

"I'm gonna go put on my clothes, then I'll take you to Gia's," I say, starting to head toward my room.

"Wait." She sounds desperate as she sits up. "Why do I have to go home?"

Now her voice sounds almost innocent, but the way she looks in those tight jeans, and she's put on some type of push-up bra because her breasts look fucking fantastic, and she's tied her shirt in a knot, showing her belly button . . . she looks like temptation personified.

"Your friend's not here." My voice has a little bit of a tremble in it, and I glue my eyes to the floor. I want to look anywhere but at her. If I look too long, she'll be able to see the lust in my eyes.

"So you're going to kick me out?" She giggles, folding her arms across her chest.

I don't say anything. She stands and walks toward me. If I didn't know any better, I'd think she was swinging her hips more than normal. She walks over to the table and grabs the glass of water I was drinking. When she's done drinking it, she licks her lips, and her angelic eyes find mine.

"I'd like to stay," she purrs.

God, is she serious? Please don't let her be. I groan and run my hands over my face. Is she trying to be sexy as hell, or am I imagining this?

"Okay, you can sleep in my room. I'll sleep in the guest room since your buddy's gone MIA," I say with a shrug.

I sit on the couch and try to fix my attention on the TV. I hear her behind me, then the lights go off. I look behind me and see that she's flipped the switch. When we're at Gia's house, Gwen's always turning out lights that we leave on. I expect her to head to the bedroom, but instead she sits on the couch. I swallow hard. The energy that was between us at the carnival seems to have multiplied a hundred times. She's quiet, but I feel her eyes on me. I feel her move, and my whole body stiffens when she reaches across me and turns on the lamp beside me.

"I could have done that," I joke to lessen the tension.

She looks at me, her eyes hooded. She only smiles. "What does your tattoo mean, Will?" She sounds more like herself than the little nymph sent here to test my restraint earlier.

"It's a reminder that even in the dark, there's light."

Her lips stay parted, but she smiles with her eyes. I get up and head to the kitchen for another glass of water. It's getting pretty damn hot in here. If she's not going to go to bed, I will, because the energy around us, the looks she's giving me . . . I know I'm reading things wrong. The way she's looking at me—it's as though she wants me, as though she's willing me to touch her, to do things I need to block out of my mind.

"I'm gonna jump in the sack," I say.

"Will?"

My heart races.

"Do you ever think about that night at the carnival?"

Then my heartbeat goes into overdrive. Of course I do. I think about it all the time.

"Gwen, you're drunk. We should talk about this in the morning." My voice sounds shaky and unfamiliar to me.

She shakes her head. "No, I'm not." She gets off the couch and walks toward me.

I fold my arms across my chest, and she stops only inches away from me.

"Are you going to answer my question?"

I can see the necklace on her chest moving up and down at rapid speed. Her heart's beating just as fast as mine.

"I do," she says, looking up at me with big sad eyes. "I think about it all the time, and I wish I didn't. Even worse, I wish that ride would have never started back up. If it hadn't started, I would have kissed you, Will."

I look down at her, not knowing what to say.

"I think you were going to kiss me too," she says nervously. She inches toward me. "I have to get that night out of my mind. What if you had kissed me? I want to stop imagining what it would have felt like. I'm sorry, but I have to know."

She brings her lips to mine. The moment they touch, I feel something, *everything*. I know I should pull away, she's been drinking, but I can't. Because as much as she wants this, I've wanted it too. Her arms wrap around my neck, and she presses herself into me more firmly. I pull away slightly, and she sighs.

"Kiss me back, please, Will. Do this, and I'll never ask you again," she pleads.

It's like time's stopped. I know what I do next will change everything. Even now with what she's done, I can tell her she's drunk and to go to bed, and in the morning, things can be the same as they have been. But do I want them to be the same? I've never felt this way about anyone, even her sister.

"I understand," she says.

I hear her voice break as she lets go of my face, and I see tears in her eyes. I won't let another one fall. I pull her toward me and make her lips mine. We move together, consuming each other as the room spins. My body's on fire when she sucks on my tongue. The wall between us was crumbling, but now it's collapsing. I pull her as close as I can get her.

She moans in response, and I lift her. She wraps her legs around my waist in response, and I carry her to the couch. I pull her onto my lap, and her hands run up and over my chest as we continue to kiss, each one deeper than the last. She pulls away, gasping for air, and I do the same, our foreheads resting against each other's. She holds my hand on her cheek and kisses me softly. This one is slow, tender, and innocent, and I can feel her emotions. I wrap my arms around her back, pulling her as close as we can be.

"What happens now?" she asks. It's dark, but I know her eyes are on mine, searching for answers.

"I-I don't know. What do you want to happen?"

Her hands leave my chin and slide down my chest and stomach. She begins to unbutton my pants, and I lose my breath.

"We can stop now. It's not too late to stop," I say. I try to be strong, even though my body is weak and already giving in. I know she can feel how much I want her.

"I want this," she says. She leans back and pulls her shirt over her head, revealing a pink lacy bra holding her breasts up perfectly. "Do you want this?"

I bring her lips back to mine. For the rest of the night, I show her that I want her more than anything.

chapter nine

lisa

EXECUTING THIS PLAN was a lot easier in my mind than it has been in reality over the last three weeks. Amanda unwittingly planted a seed that I doubt she would have had she known who my mystery man was. There is no way she would have encouraged me to kiss a married man. I know she wouldn't have, but it was good advice all the same, advice I needed to hear. Now I have a plan, something to get me out of the blue period I've been stuck in for the past month.

I've planned on doing this before but chickened out. The timing never seemed right, not that there will ever be a right time to do this, but tonight it seems as though everything is falling into place. Tonight, Chris and his mom are going to see his aunt. That means that Will will be home alone, and I can make my move. I'll get my freedom, and I can go back to being my best friend's actual friend. Maybe I'll make things work with Brett. He'll make a great prom date at least, and I can stop carrying around this backpack full of guilt that feels glued to me.

Evie is working a double shift. She's been doing that a lot since she met Jack boy. I'm starting to think she's working to pay our bills and his, but that does allow me to have the house to myself. Not having to carry a blade or pepper spray around the house feels so great.

I was nervous all through my shift, and the extra two cups of coffee haven't helped. I'm still jittery even though I've been off work for an hour. I look at myself in the mirror to make sure I look nice but not like I'm trying really hard. I've straightened my hair and applied some eyeliner and pink lipstick. I take a bottle of Evie's perfume, the really expensive kind that Aunt Dani bought her, and spray it on my neck, behind my ear, and between my breasts like I see Evie do.

"I am wanted. I am desirable. I will get what I want today," I say into the mirror. I ignore how much I look like my mom all done up like this . . .

When Will taught me about positive affirmation, I wonder if he knew exactly what I'd be using it for one day . . . even now I'm not sure what I want. I don't know what to call what I'm doing. I don't want to seduce him. I'm wearing a pink sundress that isn't tight or anything, but it displays my cleavage. I made sure my bra matches my underwear, and to be honest, this is the most primping I've ever done, even when going on dates.

I throw myself on my bed and rest my head in my hands. I'm really doing this? I'm wasting time moping. Whatever happens after this will be better for me. I can't keep feeling like this. It's like being in prison or, worse, when you're released from prison but feel like you're still there. I don't even know how I want to feel, if I want to be let down . . . that would make things a lot easier. But what if I'm not let down? What if it's the best kiss of my life and he pushes me away . . . or what if he doesn't? That's the place my brain won't let me go. It doesn't seem as if I'll win in any situation, but at least I'll know. I take solace in that the next time I enter this room, I'll have answers and not more endless questions . . .

MY STOMACH FEELS as if it's on a roller coaster as I stand on the front porch after I've rung the bell twice. I hear his footsteps approaching. When he opens the door, I swallow my nerves. His eyes widen, and a bright smile spreads across his face.

"Lisa, it's good to see you," he says.

I feel relieved that he's excited to see me after I practically ran away from him like a crazy person the last time I saw him. He had to have been as embarrassed as I was because Chris didn't bring it up. Will's beard is now closely shaven. His hair seems longer, a little wilder, and I want to tame it for him. He's wearing a wife beater, and I see a tattoo on his left arm. It's the moon with clouds around it.

"I'm glad you said that. I just wanted to apologize for how I acted at the restaurant," I say, folding my hands together.

He gives me a sexy smirk—I wonder if he knows it's sexy.

"No, you were fine. I just—I was a little confused." He chuckles while leaning in the doorway.

"I can see how you would be," I say with a giggle, sweeping my hair over my shoulder. I rub my arms to signal I'm cold. "Can I come in?"

His eyes meet mine, and I see him swallow hard. Does he know? Do his years of life experience—he's so much older than me—give him superpowers to read my mind?

"Sure," he says after a moment of hesitation.

I smile gratefully. He steps back and allows me to pass. It's been a long time since I've come into the house through the front door. I don't know what made me use it. The TV is blasting one of those sports stations Chris and Aidan watch. He has a pizza box open on the table and a bottle of Jack Daniels sitting next to it.

He walks past me and turns down the television. He looks a little embarrassed, and it's cute. He runs his hands through his hair. We stand around awkwardly for a minute. In my wildest dreams, I'd just walk up and kiss him, but I didn't factor in that he's so much taller than me. He'd have to let me pull his head down or lift me up to kiss him, and I'm not strong enough to force him without this going extremely wrong. Shoot, I should have worn heels, but that would have been stupidly obvious.

"Can I sit?" I ask, feeing all the butterflies that lie dormant when I'm around any other boy wake up and parade around my stomach.

"Sure," he says, gesturing to the couch.

I sit and try to inconspicuously let out a deep breath. He sits in the chair across from me and leans forward, his elbows resting on his knees. He's so relaxed, more than I've ever seen him before.

"So that day at the restaurant when you ran out," he asks, but not in a way that makes me feel awkward. He's not stiff and distanced as he was that day. He seems . . . *curious* maybe.

I smile. "I shouldn't have run out like a little girl."

He smiles one of his glorious smiles that makes my heart flutter.

"I was kind of embarrassed," I say, feeling my nerves getting the best of me.

He nods with a glimmer of a grin. He clasps his big hands, and my eyes drift to the tattoo on his arm. I want to touch it. I want to rest on it. I want to live there on his moon hidden away behind the clouds.

"I figured that," he says, his voice like a lullaby. "I never meant to make you feel that way." He sighs, and I can see clouds form behind his bright eyes. "I don't know if I did something to make you feel too . . ." His eyes are glued to his hands. He's moving around in his seat . . .

No, no, no. This conversation is about to go in a direction I definitely don't want it to go.

"You didn't do anything," I say. I'm afraid he'll say something that will destroy the courage I've mustered to come here, killing any spunk I have now. "It's not what you do."

His eyes reluctantly meet mine. Color rises in his cheeks.

"It's just who you are. It's how you make me feel—your voice, your energy. Everything about you made me say what I said that day," I say, begging his eyes to meet mine.

They do but only briefly. He sits back in the chair and lets out a deep sigh, picks up a cup near the Jack Daniels bottle, and takes a swig from it. He shakes his head. "You don't know what you're saying. You have a crush. Maybe I remind you of your dad."

"That's not it!" I shake my head.

"Lisa, I-I'm flattered, believe me," he says, his blue eyes on mine, and I feel my heart sink. "But I can't—you can't, you can't say things like that to me." His voice is soft, caring, and it warms up every part of me regardless of his words.

"I meant every word! No one makes me feel how I do when I'm around you." At this point, I'm desperate. I have one shot, and since I'm going to walk away from this embarrassed no matter what, I want to leave with no regrets.

He looks at his feet.

"I'm not saying that I'm in love with you. I really don't know what I feel because I've never felt it before—for anyone. And I know you're married and you're my best friend's dad, but I can't go another day without knowing if this is all in my head," I say pleadingly.

His head snaps up. "It is. I promise you, Lisa. You need to leave before you do something you'll really regret," he says as if it pains him.

I stand and take a deep breath. My heart feels as if I'm running a marathon. I walk to him and stand between his legs. He looks up at me confused, almost afraid, but there's something else I can't read. Whatever that is, even if it's just curiosity, it drives me onward.

"Do you not feel anything?" I ask, my voice barely above a whisper.

I'm standing over him, and he leans back, looking at me. I've never been this close to him. My legs are against his knees, and even though he's not touching me per se, my entire body is on edge and warm. I can't leave this house without kissing those perfect lips that seem to be quivering right now.

"Lisa, please." His voice has dropped an octave, and I feel as if it's vibrating through me. His eyes drift over my body, taking in every inch of me, and my stomach clenches. Just the way he's looking at me has made me hotter than anything any boy has ever done to me. He swallows hard. I see the conflict in his expression. He's fighting a silent battle with himself, and I want him to lose.

"You're a very beautiful girl, but what you're saying—doing—is crazy—"

That's the last word he says before I silence him with my lips. The second I do, it's as if my body wakes up. I feel every nerve in it. His lips are so soft, and they're still but parted just enough for me to take his upper lip in my mouth. I gently bring my hands to the back of his head and run my hands through his hair. Our lips fit perfectly together, and even though he's perfectly still, it beats every other kiss I've ever experienced.

I feel the anticipation building. He hasn't pushed me away, and that's all the invitation I need for more. I climb on his lap, wrap my arms around his neck, and feel fire move through my body as I kiss him a little more tenderly. When his hands move to my waist and he pulls me closer, I feel faint. His mouth opens, and his tongue enters my mouth, filling it. His kiss is artful and more experienced than any other I've had. I feel heavy but light-headed as our kiss gets deeper, so deep I feel as if I'll be one with him soon.

The longer I kiss him, our tongues devouring one another's, the more heat comes between my legs. It's frustrating but the best feeling I've ever had. I feel his length press against me, and when I would usually move away from it, I lean in and feel it pressed between my thighs. I let out a soft moan while our tongues wrap around each other's. I press against it again and faster and faster. I can't control the whimpers coming out of my mouth.

He starts to guide my hips against him, aiding me in the absolute pleasure building and building. His own breathing becomes deeper. It's coming faster and faster. I'm no longer kissing him. My head is thrown back as I concentrate on feeling him through the hard, rough jeans that feel like heaven through my cotton underwear, which is soaked. He squeezes my butt and presses me hard against him, and his mouth starts to devour my neck, sucking in my skin like it's air he needs to breath. We move in sync, rhythmically, more rapidly, *desperately*. I dig my fingers into the couch, clawing it as I move against him. Then, I feel an explosion that no boy has ever been able to make me feel, and as I tumble over the edge, I moan his name loudly, and I can't stop panting. My legs are quivering, and the hardness I felt underneath me is gone.

We sit there, both catching our breath, my body still reeling. I rest my head in the crook of his neck and feel our hearts beating in sync. I lean back to look at his face. His gaze is on the ceiling. Tiny sweat beads are on his forehead, and I wipe them. His eyes are closed, and his breathing normalizes. When it does, his eyes almost snap open, and he looks at me. For the first time, his eyes don't smile at me. They're like glass. I think there are tears in them, and that scares me.

I climb off him. He stands and glares at me, not with anger just confusion. He walks quickly out of the room, and I hear him cursing. I can't exactly understand what he's said, but I know he's upset. I sit there, unsure of what to do. Should I say something to him? I can't think of anything that will comfort him. Will he be mad if I'm still here when he comes back? What the hell did I just do? I feel more confused than before because the answer I wanted is clear. What I feel is real, and what we just did, what I just experienced with him, I won't be able to just forget. I don't want to forget it. I want to relive it over and over.

"Lisa?" he calls.

I think he's in their bathroom. I take a deep breath. "Yeah?"

"Can you please go home?"

My heart drops, and I feel tears in my eyes. "Uh, sure." My voice sounds weak and broken.

I slowly get off the couch and look back to where he is in the house. I can't see him, but I know he's there. A part of me wants to go to him and make him look at me, another part of me says I don't deserve to make demands, and the other part of me just wants to slink away. Once my legs regain their balance, I practically run out of the house.

The whole drive back, I feel as if I'm holding my breath, and I don't let it out until I'm in my room and on my bed. I cry because I feel like I hurt him, what I'd intended went too far, and I'll never be able to look at him the same way again. When I left this room, I'd promised myself I'd have answers. What I didn't think was that those answers would only bring more questions. I cry myself to sleep because I know I've made things a whole lot worse.

will

I CAN'T PINPOINT the moment my life became not enough, when it didn't seem good enough, when I felt trapped. When I began hating myself for it, questioning every vital decision I've ever made. The worst part about feeling like this is knowing that something is wrong with me, that I can't blame anyone else for the way I feel.

I'm forty-one years old. I have a great family: a beautiful wife who loves me, whom I love, who is the love of my life; a son who doesn't cause trouble, does well in school, and is just a good kid. I have a thriving business that, even if it's not bringing in buckets of money, keeps our monthly bills paid. We have a nice amount in the bank, and we can buy a few things that we want every now and then without living beyond our means. Life is nice, quiet. It's everything I imagined it to be when I was younger and overwhelmed by my stepdad pushing me to join his business. Stepping onto the property my dad's brother left me when he passed felt like home. I felt as though I had a purpose, and I could see spending the rest of my life here with Gwen, the love of my life. Everything has gone according to plan . . . almost.

My son, Christopher, is a blessing to us. He came into our lives when he was just five years old and Gwen and I were lost, devastated. My wife had always dreamed of having a house full of children. It was a simple dream—or so we thought. We never wondered why, before we were ready for kids, we never had any surprises even though we didn't take any precautions to prevent pregnancy. After three years of being married, Gwen was ready to fill the farmhouse we'd made our home with children. When it didn't happen, we became worried. We were both young, healthy, and happy. Those should have been the only requirements.

We learned that wasn't the case on that trip to the doctor. His news broke my wife. She was a ghost of herself after learning the one thing she'd always wanted would most likely never be hers. She cried for weeks, and her tears made me go to the one person I'd really started to loathe who'd basically exiled me when he found out I wouldn't marry the girl he wanted me to after not choosing the career he thought I should have. I knew with the right amount of money, anything was possible. He laughed in my face and told me I bet I wished I had "Crestfield" money now.

But a year later, when Gwen was sort of getting out of her funk, my stepfather showed up with a five-year-old boy and the papers already completed, the adoption done.

Only stepfather Dexter Crestfield could make something like that happen.

Just like that, we were parents. My wife became alive again, and we were happy.

We stayed that way until last year, a few weeks after my fortieth birthday, when I woke up with a feeling I couldn't shake. I wasn't happy. I wasn't sad or angry, but I felt as though something was missing. Doubts and fears I'd never had started to play in my head. Things that had never bothered me started to, stupid things like the one strand of gray hair that has been there since I turned thirty-five. Or the fact that I used to be able to work ten hours straight and still be up for a round or two with Gwen before bed without blinking an eye, and that was becoming a whole lot harder.

What really started to bother me was that as much as I loved my son with everything in me, when he had children, they wouldn't share my blood. I was an only child, my father's only son, and after me, there would be no more. It ate at me more and more, especially as Chris started to apply to colleges. It gnawed at me, and I couldn't tell Gwen, my wife, my best friend. If anyone could have gotten me through it, it was her, but at the same time, these feelings would have destroyed her, devastated her. She'd have felt it was her fault, that I blamed her, and I didn't—not for a second.

I never ever regretted making her my wife. She's my other half, and being with her is enough. That's what I told myself over and over and over, but she felt me growing distant, withdrawn. I distracted myself by reaching out to my stepdad and getting contracts for the farm in his commercial division. It helped distract me from all the inadequacies smothering me. She loves me so much. Even after all these years, I see the love in her eyes, feel it in her touch. When other guys who've been married as long as we have told me that their wives denied them, seemed to resent them, only tolerated their presence, I looked at them as though they were crazy.

Gwen and I were still in love, our feelings still fresh as the day we met—until these stupid feelings and thoughts and crap interfered. Gwen tried so hard to make me feel better. I never acted as if anything was wrong, but she could tell—your soul mate isn't stupid. She complimented me more, told me how much she loved me more often; she even offered counseling. Like an idiot, I was too proud to talk to someone, to admit I had a problem. Talking may have helped. It may have helped me come up with a solution. Instead, I held everything in. I could handle it, I thought. But nothing helped.

Chris saw the changes too. He saw the changes affecting his mother, and he grew distant. I saw it all happening, and still I was broken. No matter what I did to try to fix myself, nothing worked. I was losing their sympathy, Chris and Gwen's. I didn't blame them. They wanted to know what was wrong, and I couldn't tell them. Gwen channeled her frustration constructively—she decided to go back to school, taking night classes to get her associate's degree. Chris threw himself into his music, and I floated around from project to project, feeling useless.

I remember clearly the day things changed. We were all eating dinner.

"Lisa needs help with her math. With Chris starting his music again and his clubs and me going back to school, tutoring her could give you something to do," Gwen said.

"Who's Lisa?" I asked dryly, somewhat annoyed. The fog of my problems clouded my memories, faces I should know, faces I didn't care to recall. I saw the disappointment in Gwen's face, disappointment that I was being an asshole.

"Lisa, your son's best friend since they were knee-high. She really needs the help, and you certainly need something to inspire you, or at least motivate you to yank the stick out of your butt," she said sharply before leaving the table.

I realized I was turning into an jerk. That night I apologized. I told her I'd give tutoring a try, and she smiled, easily forgiving me and wanting to really have hope for me. I wanted to give her hope. I had hope too. When I was a teacher, I enjoyed it. I felt as though I was making a difference in the world until I realized how screwed up the schools were. One of my best and favorite students at the inner city school I worked at was shot in the chest after leaving an honor society dinner. After that, I realized the difference I made was shit.

I couldn't stomach being in that building or that neighborhood anymore, and Gwen and I packed up, moved to the farm, and slowly but surely, I became a farmer. My teaching days were far behind me. The closest I came to it was coaching some of Chris's sports leagues when he was younger and helping him with his homework. I thought maybe tutoring could do me some good, and for the first time in a while, I imagined what could happen, allowed myself to dream. If it worked out, maybe I could tutor more kids. If I couldn't leave my mark on the world biologically, I could leave my mark in memories. I was hopeful.

I tried to conjure up an image of Lisa, Chris's best friend, but for some reason, I couldn't get the vision of a ten-year-old tomboy who wrestled with Chris and Aidan and had scars on her elbows and knees out of my head. A couple of days before I was to start tutoring her, Chris called me, sounding a little slurred, and I was fuming. I had to calm myself down—I had a good kid and he didn't sound dead drunk and he'd called me instead of letting some other drunk kid bring him home.

I remember fiddling with the radio when the car door opened and I looked up, and to my surprise, it wasn't Chris. It was a beautiful girl with long almost-white blond hair, big green eyes, and a smile that reminded me of when I was younger and got smiles like the one she wore easily. She greeted me as if she knew me, and I had no clue who she was. Then it hit me—Lisa, and a ten-year-old tomboy she was not. I had to have seen her around the house, though I'd never paid her any attention, but sitting next to her in the car, she imprinted herself on my brain—her eyes, her lips, her voice, her laugh.

I'd never forget the way she looked at me before she got out of the car. She didn't look at me as though I was her friend's old dad. She looked at me in a way that made my heart speed up, that made blood rush to a place it shouldn't have gone, in a way that let me know she was anything but a little girl. I should have known just from that look and the little voice in my head then that tutoring her was a bad idea. I should have made up an excuse to put it off or have Chris join us or only meet on days when Gwen was around, but I didn't. I didn't because for the first time in almost a year, I didn't feel like a zombie slogging through life.

I felt alive.

chapter ten

lisa

IT'S BEEN TWO weeks since the night I decided to take destiny in my own hands and force myself on Will.

Two weeks since it exploded all over me, right in my face.

In a way, I was right. I knew what I felt wasn't imagined—it was more than I could have ever have dreamed. Kissing him was surreal. He was magnetic and made my body feel things that only I've been able to make myself feel, but he made them happen faster and at a whole different level.

I foolishly tested this theory with Brett. It was one of the dumbest decisions I've ever made. I drove to his dorm the night after I was with Will, and when he opened the door, I threw myself at him, clumsily, frantically. I wanted to feel something, anything like I had with Will. I went further than I ever had. I handed over my virginity while searching for the same feeling. Needless to say, it was nothing like that, not even close. Brett couldn't make me feel anywhere near the way I did with Mr. Scott, and we'd had our clothes on.

It could have been worse, I guess. Brett tried to be tender and slow and considerate when I told him I was a virgin. He kissed me with passion. I know because I saw the passion coming from him, but I just didn't feel it. It hurt like hell, even with him going slow, and all those books I'd read where the virgin has seven thousand orgasms her first time turned out to be a crock of shit. It was nice though, and it wasn't in the back of some car with a dude who wouldn't call me again. In fact, Brett assumed that our consummation made us official. I'm now his girlfriend, and what would have made any other girl giddy threw me into a sea of depression.

"Hey, what the hell is wrong with you?" Aidan asks, sounding completely annoyed.

We're in physics with a sub, so we can pretty much do what we want. I only sigh at Aidan's puzzled expression.

"I used to joke about you being a buzzkill, but you really are now, and I'm sick of it," he says sharply, coming off as oddly charming in a way only Aidan can.

"Nothing is wrong with me," I say dryly.

He throws up his hands. "That's the best you can come up with? You're the comeback queen—this is what we do, our funny banter. I call you something insulting, then you do it back."

I do let out a little chuckle, and he grins.

"Is this about Chris and Amanda? They're annoying the hell out of me too," he says, drumming his fingers on my desk to some solo in his head. "He hardly gets to hang out with us anymore."

I can see that his feelings are really hurt. Between Chris's new girlfriend and being in the band and homework, he doesn't have much time for his besties. Which sucks for Aidan but is great for me since whenever I see Chris, I get overwhelmed with guilt and I can't avoid being questioned about why I won't even walk near his house.

"You know what? Screw Chris. You should get one of your minions, and we can do a double date with Brett," I say, trying to make him feel better.

Aidan is one of the most popular guys in school with no shortage of date possibilities, but Aidan is an asshole. He doesn't like most people, and even though we fight, I think we've grown to genuinely like each other in our own twisted way.

"I'll let you know," he says with a shrug and a smile as the bell rings.

THE COFFEE HOUSE has gotten busier since the temperature is starting to drop. I like it since the busier I am, the less I think about Mr. Scott and how I may have made a mistake. What did I expect really—for him to tell me he wanted to run away with me and leave his family, which happens to include my best friend?

I'm surprised when I see Amanda walk in. She sees she's caught my eye, and I conjure up a weak smile. I know it's not her fault I followed her advice, but I do blame her at least a little. I think it's human nature to not want to blame myself. I let my manager know I'm going on break, and I grab her favorite drink—a caramel latte with nonfat milk and extra caramel, which totally negates the non-fat milk. I sit down, and she greets me with a wide "I'm in love" smile. She's had it since she started dating Chris.

"What's up, hon?" she says, taking the latte.

I sigh, and she pouts, obviously as sick of my moping as Aidan is.

"I'm sorry." I flash her a wide fake grin.

"That's better," she sings. "Student council got canceled, and Chris is in writing mode," she says, explaining her presence. "I don't see how you're so unhappy. You're officially in a relationship with one of the most wanted guys at his college. I repeat college again, and you look like you're the girl who hasn't gotten asked to any dances."

"I slept with Brett, and I didn't feel anything."

Her eyes widen. "You what? How could you lose your V-card and not tell me? When did this happen? How was it? Lisa, I can't believe you didn't spill the second you finished!"

I give her the details she wants and tell her it would have been kind of awkward to call her the *second* after.

"Leese, the first time isn't going to be fireworks and rainbows or whatever you read about in those books you carry around. It will get better, trust me. One time is just like breaking the seal. The rest can feel pretty good with the right person."

I can't help letting my curiosity get the best of me. "Did you . . . have you and Chris?"

She shakes her head with a small grin. "Not yet. We've come close but haven't actually done the deed, if you know what I mean."

I realize I definitely didn't want to know that.

"So I know what you're thinking," she says, and I look a little suspiciously at her. She can't know what I'm thinking. "I bet you're thinking that if you did it with Mr. Mystery Man, it would have been better."

I frown. That's actually the thought I've been trying to block out of my mind, seeing as Mr. Mystery Man basically told me to get out of his house. I plan on avoiding him at all costs. I'm only some months away from summer break, then I'm off to Michigan State. Well, if I can figure out how to pay for it, I will.

"It wouldn't have been. I can tell you it would have sucked regardless. Usually the first time with any boy is going to suck. You get better with practice," she says.

I sort of roll my eyes. Amanda acts as if she's a sex guru, and as far as I know, she's only done it with three boys at the most. I fight the urge to tell her that my mystery boy isn't a boy but a very experienced man who made my body feel things without even taking off my clothes that her boys couldn't even dream about doing.

"Give Brett another shot. It'll get better," she says.

I change the subject, and we talk until the end of my break. Afterward, she swishes out, carrying her cute little Kate Spade bag, and heads back into her happy bubble.

IT'S ALMOST CLOSING time, and I'm the only one working. I'm studying for my AP history class when the bell above the door rings, then I see him walk in. What are the chances? Does he know I work here? Was this an accident or coincidence? I want to slink behind the counter and hide, but since it's just me, I can't do that.

"Hi," he says, his voice still warming my chest even after he was so cold.

"Hey." My voice is tremulous but light.

He looks around the shop. The store is empty except for one stoner kid with his headphones on, and he's fallen asleep at the front of the shop. As Will approaches me, my heart speeds up. Thoughts of how horrible I felt that night make my chest tighten, colliding with the sensation between my thighs as I recall the memory.

"Can we talk?" he asks hesitantly.

I want to tell him no and ask him to leave, just how he did me that night, but I don't. Instead I nod. "Give me a minute."

I walk over to the stoner kid and nudge him. "Hey, we're about to close, okay?"

He checks the time on his laptop with an irritated glare. "I have fifteen minutes." He puts his head back down.

I sigh. "I'll give you a bag of cookies and a free coffee if you head out now."

He gathers his things as I fix his bag of cookies, and he asks for a hot chocolate instead of a coffee. Then he's gone, leaving me alone with Will and the butterflies in my stomach. I let down the curtains in the front of the shop and flip the open sign to closed. He's sitting at one of the coffee tables, and I sit in the chair across from him.

"I wanted to apologize to you," he says, his blue eyes on mine. They look sad and apologetic.

I forgive him just from that look, but I let him finish.

"I-I—you have to understand that what happened was wrong." His voice sounds stern but compassionate.

I fold my arms and feel myself frown.

"It was, Lisa," he says again.

"It didn't feel wrong until you left me alone and told me to get out," I spit at him.

He looks surprised, and I'm surprised when I see the hint of a grin.

"It's not funny," I say angrily.

"I'm not laughing at the situation obviously. I-it's just—you're sort of a firecracker," he says, looking a bit stunned but amused at the same time.

I roll my eyes. "Did you come here to tell me how sorry you are and how it can never ever happen again?"

He looks down guiltily, and I let out a frustrated sigh. Because of course I could have guessed he would say that. Just being near him makes me think of that night and makes me a different kind of frustrated.

"It can't. We—you know why," he says as if it's obvious.

My head shoots up, and I glare at him. "Just tell me, how did you feel? Setting aside everything your mind is telling you, how did you feel?" I don't want to mention his family.

He lets out a frustrated groan and shakes his head. "It doesn't matter! We can't do what you're asking me to."

I'm quiet and feel tears welling in my eyes. His expression softens, and when it does, I clear my throat. "What do you think I'm asking?"

He runs his hands across his face.

"It's not illegal. I'm eighteen. I'll be nineteen in six months," I say desperately.

"Lisa, I'm married. It doesn't matter if you're legal. If anyone found out, my family would be destroyed. Your reputation would be shredded. This wouldn't be good for either of us," he says frantically.

I know he's right. I'm not stupid or that immature, but I am selfish. That's why I say, "What if no one found out?"

I beg his eyes to meet mine. When they do, I see they're conflicted but not dead, not stubborn, and I know there's a chance.

"Someone always finds out when things like this happen," he says quietly.

"I would never say anything. I don't want to break up your family." I start to add that Chris is my best friend and I'd never want to hurt him, but I think that'd only hurt my case. "No one has ever made me feel the way you did, Will. The way I feel now just sitting across from you." I soften my expression. "Please just tell me. How do you feel being here with me?"

He closes his eyes and sighs. He gets up from the chair and walks toward the door. Each step feels like a stomp on my heart. I feel tears streaming from my eyes, and I whimper.

Then he stops. "Alive."

Even though he's not facing me, my heart starts again.

gwen

I HAVE NEVER felt so conflicted. Waking up in Will's arms feels like heaven. We fit as if we were made for each other. I take in his scent, his touch, his strong arms wrapped around my nude body. Last night was incredible. A night that seemed impossible, or at the very least distant or imagined, came true. I feel as though I'm on a cloud.

When there's a loud banging on the door, I'm in hell—instantly in hell! We both jump up, our eyes wide, and we each know what the other is thinking—is it Gia? I don't even know if Gia has a key. There's another knock. I pick up my clothes, run to the bathroom then the guest room, and throw them on as fast as I can.

"One minute," Will yells at the loud knocker.

I'm sure he's throwing on his clothes. I hear the door open, and I pray to God it's anyone but Gia. I can't see her now, with Will's scent all over me, after what we just did. I'm a terrible liar—I'd blurt it out. Gia's smart. She'd figure it out just from the look of us.

"What took so long?"

My heart slows down when I hear Zach's voice.

"You leave in the middle of the night with some stranger, then you have the nerve to expect immediate service in someone else's house you're staying in for free?" Will asks sarcastically.

"Yeah, that's about the gist," Zach says arrogantly. "Where's the brat? I know she's not still asleep. She's an early bird, and she didn't drink as much as I did."

"She's still sleeping, I think," Will says.

"And no breakfast? God, I thought she'd be whipping up a farm," he says.

I glance at myself in the mirror. My skin's flushed, and I have on last night's clothes. It doesn't look suspicious though since I just got up from a hangover, right? To look any way else would be suspicious. I finally work up the nerve to leave the guest room.

Zach's sitting on the couch, looking as though he didn't have one drink. He's alert, pretty as usual, with a freshly showered look. He grins at me. "You look like you've been fucked three ways from sundown."

Will's cheeks turn red. "Language," Will says authoritatively as though he's in teacher mode.

"You're not that much older than us, dude. Relax," Zach says.

When my eyes meet Will's, I shoot him a "please be nice" look, and he sighs with a small grin.

"Aren't you a teacher? Shouldn't you be in someone's classroom?" Zach asks.

Our eyes shoot to the clock. Oh my gosh, it's eleven thirty.

"Shit!" he says, running to his bedroom.

Zach laughs. "Did he get drunk last night too?"

Zach turns on the TV and puts his feet on the coffee table. I sit next to him, in the same spot where Will and I just shared the best night of our lives, and grin. Zach looks at me suspiciously.

"You seem to be in a pretty good mood for someone who's hungover." He nudges me in the side, and I laugh.

When he tickles me, I can't stop laughing, and he's on top of me.

"I can't breathe," I say between giggles.

"What the hell are you doing?" Will's voice booms, and the tickling and laughing immediately stops.

"What do you think I'm doing?" Zach asks, irritated.

"She was telling you to stop," Will says sharply, approaching us.

Zach stands. I jump up and get between them.

"We were just playing. He was tickling me," I say. "It was nothing."

"I'd hate to kick this guy's ass in his own house," Zach says cockily.

Will laughs at him. They're about the same height. Will has two inches on Zach, but I've seen Zach fight his brothers, and he probably fights more frequently than Will has in his life. But Will's build is bigger. I'm not sure who would take who in a fight, but I sure don't want to find out.

"Aren't you running late?" I say to Will giving him a "you're acting really weird right now" look.

His anger drops several notches, though it lingers in his expression. He tosses me his keys. "Lock up when you guys leave and call your sister. She's probably worried."

After Will leaves, Zach steps in front of me, his arms folded.

"You're doing your sister's boyfriend," he says as if he just figured out a big mystery, and I feel my stomach drop.

I'M A TERRIBLE liar and, I've found out, a terrible denier. Zach pesters me the whole day, continuously asking me if I'm *doing* Will while we sightsee and stroll through downtown Chicago. After four hours of him not letting up, as we're sitting by the lakefront, I admit it.

"It just happened last night. I feel terrible," I say, but I don't.

I don't feel terrible. I feel terrible about Gia finding out—that's actually terrifying—but after what happened between Will and me, I don't feel guilty. I'm too happy to feel anything else. The knot that's been in my stomach has finally untied. I feel as if I'm floating, and I know the other shoe is going to drop. But right now, I want to just enjoy this feeling, though I don't want to sound like a terrible person and say it out loud.

Zach shakes his head and laughs and laughs. I thought he'd be upset or disapproving, but he isn't. "You don't feel terrible. You look happier than I've ever seen you."

I cover my face, embarrassed. "I am. God, I am, and *that* feels terrible." I can't stop myself from smiling.

"So what happens now? Are you two going to sneak around, is he going to break things off with your sis, or are you going to pretend it never happened?"

I feel my happy bubble starting to burst. None of those options sound good at all. I feel my face fall.

"I don't mean to be a buzzkill, but you got to think about these things. Not only is she your sister, but you actually like her. I'd fuck one of my brothers' girlfriends in a heartbeat, but I can't stand them. I couldn't care less if they stopped talking to me. Plus you live with her. Can you imagine going back to your mom's place?"

I shoot him disbelieving glare.

"You're right. I'm sorry. Don't think about it. Enjoy the bubble," he says, patting my back.

But it's too late. Zach's burst it.

WE EAT AT a pizza place near Will's house—well, Zach eats. My stomach's too queasy for me to eat anything. Each hour that passes reminds me that soon I'll have to face Gia, and I don't know what I'll do or say. Will one look at me tell her everything? Zach tells me to just play it cool and keep my mouth shut until I talk to Will about his plans.

It'd be nice if I knew what his plans are. Everything was so hazy last night—wonderful but hazy. Until now, I didn't know he had any feelings for me, I just hoped, and now I really hope he does. With my best friend being the lady-killer he is, I know better than anyone that guys don't look at sex the same ways girls do. Will's sleeping with me doesn't mean he feels anything for me. Maybe I just made him really horny. I'm still not sure if Gia's sleeping with him. The image of him and Gia having sex makes me want to vomit.

Around seven o'clock, we head back to Will's. He should be home by now, the doorman has probably let him in. I ask Zach to please be nice and not let on that I told him what happened. As soon as we walk in, Will glares at us. It's a mixture of annoyance and something I can't put my finger on, but I think he's jealous.

"You guys have fun?" he says in a sarcastic, dry tone.

"Not as much as you guys had last night," Zach mutters, and I shoot him a look.

"What did he say?" Will asks me, and I shoot him a look to drop it.

"I gotta use your phone," Zach says, picking up the cordless and carrying it into the guest room Will assigned him.

Will and I sit in a comfortable but anxiety-filled silence.

"Did you talk to Gia?" I ask, and he nods quickly. "About what?" I'm paranoid. I want to make sure he didn't talk to her about what I think he wouldn't talk to her about.

"Just told her you and Zach had made it home safely and apologized for not calling her last night," he says quickly.

I let out a little sigh of relief. "Was she suspicious?"

"She has no reason to be," he whispers back, still unaware that Zach knows what happened.

"Is she coming over?" I swallow my nerves.

"No, she said to just keep an eye on you here," he says, looking away from me.

Zach reappears and gives us a peace sign. "Well, I'm out."

"Ugh, where are you going?" I ask, surprised.

"Over to Ashlyn's. She's off tonight," he says with a grin, opening the door.

"You're spending the night?" Will asks in a disapproving tone.

"Yeah, that should give you two lovebirds some time to talk," he says with a wink before leaving. "See you later, brat."

Then he's gone. When I look at Will, his eyes are practically popping out of his head.

"You told him?" he yells.

"He knew already. I didn't just volunteer the information!" I yell back.

He sits on the couch and rests his head in his hands.

"What are we going to do?" I ask nervously, though I don't know what he's going to say. I still don't know if last night meant to him what it meant to me.

He sighs and sits back on the couch almost sinking into the sofa. "I've been thinking about that all day." His voice is low and strained. "I don't know what to do."

My heart sinks. I want to be mad at him, to yell at him, but when his eyes find mine, they're sad and full of uncertainty.

"Do-do you regret what happened?" I ask, and I feel my chest tightening, trying to cushion my heart, because if he says yes, it'll break into a thousand pieces. "Do you think it was a mistake?" This time my voice is weak and breaks.

He looks at me for what seems like an eternity before he comes over and rests on his knees, pulling me toward him. He holds my face so that I look him directly in the eye. "You're not a mistake. I don't regret what happened, and if you want me to break it off with her today, I will. I want to be with you, Gwen."

I smile, but it's weak. As happy as I am to hear his words, they change everything. Words that have made my day and could possibly make my life will destroy my sister. The reality of the situation is really kicking in. What used to be just unrequited feelings, what ifs, dreams, fantasies are hitting me in the face as reality. I want him so much, but I know it's a trade-off—if I get Will, I lose Gia. She won't understand that I didn't mean for this to happen, that we couldn't help it. She'll see our love as the ultimate betrayal, and no one will blame her. I can't even blame her. Why, out of all the people in the world, did I have to feel like this about him? But looking into his eyes, I feel alive and I know it can't be anyone else.

"I know this sounds silly and trivial now, but I don't want to hurt her." Tears fill my eyes.

He wipes them away, pulls me close to him, and strokes my back. "I know. I-I love your sister."

I feel a stab of pain in my chest.

"But me and her, we aren't meant to be. We don't fit. She knows that—it's why she hasn't accepted my proposal. Since I met you, since I've fallen for you, I've prayed every day she wouldn't change her mind."

I pull back from him and rest my forehead on his.

"I'm going to tell her I met someone else," he says, and my heart stops.

"You can't say that," I say, my eyes wide in terror.

"I won't tell her who," he says, and I shake my head.

"That will hurt her too badly," I say, trying to think. I grip the necklace resting on my chest. This is a terrible mess. "Okay, you can tell her that you know you two aren't working out, that she deserves better, that things just aren't working. It will hurt her, she's going to ask questions, but she'll find comfort in school and work. Gia's strong. She'll get over it I'll keep working at the school—she shouldn't suspect anything—and I'll tell her I met someone or something. I can come and see you and . . ."

His face falls. "I know you don't want to hurt Gia, but I want to be with you, Gwen. I don't want us to be a secret . . ."

I shake my head. "No, it won't be like that, not forever. We just have to let enough time pass."

Gia's reasonable. Maybe in a year or two she'll understand. She'll feel some type of way about it, but she won't hate Will or me. By then, I'm sure Gia will have charmed another guy into marrying her even. I don't say that to Will though. I've learned that when Will gets involved in something, he's all in. He throws himself completely into it, and making him feel as though we'll have to wait so long to really be together will make him angry or he'll shut down.

"Okay, whatever you want," he says before kissing me softly, tenderly, so differently from last night.

He pulls me to him and guides us to the floor, kissing my soul out of me. While his hands and lips explore me, I don't think about her or what will happen. We're only us, and I've never felt so good about being so selfish before.

GIA'S BEEN SO busy with school and work that Will just hasn't had the chance to talk to her. I'm disappointed and relieved at the same time. The day after Zach leaves is so nerve-racking.

Walking back into our house feels utterly strange, as though I don't belong here. Guilt crawls up my spine and rests there as I walk past Gia's room to the bathroom. I shower for almost an hour, trying to wash away my guilt.

I walk to the grocery store and buy food for her favorite meal—baked chicken with white rice and spinach salad. She'll be home in about an hour or so. My stomach feels as if it's on a seesaw as I wait for her to come in. It seems as if the minutes have slowed down and simultaneously sped up. I want to get seeing her over with, but the delay is also comforting.

"Oh my God, is that baked chicken with rosemary I smell?" she calls.

My stomach drops, and I turn around to face her. "Yup."

She walks up beside me and peeps into the oven. "Have I told you how much I love having you here?" She bumps my hip with hers.

My stomach starts to feel queasy.

"How was your visit with Zach?" she asks as she heads into her room to put away her stuff.

"It was good," I say, wondering if I sound timid.

"So good news," she says with a wide grin.

I smile back at her, and she looks at me a little curiously.

"Dad's necklace fits you," she says warmly. I want to punch myself in the stomach. I fiddle with it and giver her a weak grin instead. She continues to look at me in a probing way. Maybe I'm just paranoid.

"What is it?" I ask, sitting at the table.

She does the same, tilting her head to the side, her eyes glossing over me. "You look different."

"What do you mean?" I ask, trying to control my breathing.

"I don't know. It's not bad, it's good." She grins at me, and guilt washes over me, then her eyes widen with excitement. "Did you sleep with Zach?"

Double load of guilt now. "No." But I feel my cheeks heat up.

"You did, didn't you!" she says, swatting me playfully.

"Maybe," I say, feeling terrible about the lie.

"Wow! What happened? Tell me everything!" she says excitedly, then her face scrunches up. "You didn't do it at Will's, did you? He'd be mortified." She chuckles, and I look away from her. "You did! Oh my gosh!"

She laughs, and I feel as if I'm on a roller coaster.

"How did you pull that off? I can't believe Will didn't stay up and stand guard while you slept. You should have seen how on edge he was when you guys left. He was acting like he was a knight trying to protect your virtue. It was so cute." She giggles, and I give a fake laugh. "Hey, what's wrong?"

"Nothing, I just don't feel real good. I think it's something I ate earlier." It's the truth and a lie.

"Oh. Do you need me to go grab you something from the drug store?" she asks.

"No, I'm fine really." I stand and turn off the oven. "I'm just going to lie down for a few minutes."

"Okay," she says, rubbing my shoulder.

I fall into my bed, and I do feel sick. Sick to my stomach, a feeling I hope goes away soon, it's definitely nothing Pepto Bismol can cure.

will

TODAY IS THE day. It's been four weeks since the night Gwen and I gave in and stopped fighting what we've both been feeling. I've been searching for the right way to tell Gia that it's over. It hasn't been easy, but I know the guilt Gwen feels about us sneaking around at work, coming here and doing what we're doing while Gia and I are officially together, is starting to get to her.

I asked Gia over for dinner today, telling her I needed to talk to her about something important. I've never broken up with anyone before. I've dated girls but never seriously, and they always kind of fizzled out or we grew distant. Gia is my first real relationship. For almost two years, she's been a part of my life, and I guess what makes this different is that even after tonight, she'll still be a part of my life because she's the sister of the woman I love. I don't know what she's going to say when I tell her. I hope I don't blindside her. I mean, of course she wouldn't expect this, but we've been distant; she's been distant. Or not really distant. Just busy—busy with school, busy with work. We haven't had a real date in almost three months.

I hear her come in. She has a key. My stomach feels as if it's dropped eight floors.

"Hey," she calls.

She takes off her coat and folds it neatly before laying it across the couch. She walks over to me siting on the sofa and kisses me softly, and I feel guilt surge through me. I pull away. She looks at me questioningly then giggles without saying anything.

"Chicken chili," she says, walking into the kitchen. It's the only thing I'm good at making.

"You know it." I hear my voice waver.

She dishes us each a bowl. "So I have some good news."

I force a smile as we sit at the table. I try to think if it's crazy to let her eat before telling her what I have to. I know she won't eat after, so is it wrong to let her eat and let us talk without her knowing? I feel each second I don't tell her will make things worse.

"What?" I ask before putting a spoonful of chili in my mouth.

"Gordon has a new assistant," she says happily.

"That's great."I smile but am unsure why her boss getting a new assistant is good news. I try to sound excited though. I want to make sure the time we spend together before I break up with her is good, bearable.

"But you don't know why it's great," she says with a chuckle, and I do the same. Her face is lit up.

I know this news has to be something that makes her happy. I hope that what I tell her next won't wipe that away.

"That means I won't be working as many hours, that we'll be able to spend more time together," she says.

My chest feels as if someone is standing on it now. Her smile is warm, good energy radiating off her, and I feel gutted.

"I know we haven't been spending as much time together, and I hate that. I don't want us to grow apart. You're really important to me, William." Her voice is warm like honey, and I feel like complete shit.

I push my bowl away and think of what to do next. Should I sit here and tell her while we eat chili that I don't want to be with her anymore? Should I stand? Is there etiquette for this sort of thing?

"William, what's wrong?" she asks.

My thoughts must be playing out on my face. What do I say? What are the right words to soften the blow? I rub the back of my neck, hoping to release some of my tension. My throat has gone dry, and I clear it. Her gaze is on me, and I break away from it by staring at the steam coming from my bowl of chili.

"Will?" she says, her tone alarmed.

My eyes drift to her face, but then I focus on the engagement ring I gave her almost year ago. I think about all those feelings I had for her, the dreams and plans I made for us, and how it crushed me when she told me she wasn't ready but would be one day. Even now, *one day* hasn't come, and that gives me a small piece of courage.

"I can't do this anymore, Gia," I say quietly.

She squints at me as if she didn't really hear what I said, as if I mumbled it. For a second, I wonder if she did hear me, then she sits up straighter, dropping her spoon. I hear her suck in a small breath, but her face stays still, perfectly so.

"I'm assuming you mean us?" she says slowly.

Our eyes meet. I tear mine away from her, and I nod. There's a stretch of silence, and I see her eyes move to her ring. She rolls it between her fingers. I feel as though I should say something, that she's waiting on me to say something, but "I'm sorry" seems trivial and nowhere near enough, yet I can't give her the real explanation. If I speak, I'll have to lie, and I don't want to lie to her, not after everything that's happened.

"Did I do something wrong? Is it because we haven't spent a lot of time together?" Her voice is strong, but her expression is weak and vulnerable in a way I've never seen on her before.

"No, Gia. I think that when you really think about us, we don't make sense," I say, and her mouth moves into a tight line. She pulls off her ring and sits it on the table.

"Is that why you proposed to me?" she says sarcastically, but I know she's hurt.

"I think that's the reason you didn't say yes," I say softly.

Tears roll down her face, and my eyes water too.

"Is there someone else?" she asks the question I've been dreading.

I can't lie to her. I start to tell her, but she raises her hand, stopping me. She smiles, but it's a sad one.

"I don't want to know. I'd rather not know," she says quietly. She stands and rubs her hands down her thighs. "I'll get my things."

Her face is red, her eyes are wet, and her voice is shaking. I nod and sit at the table, looking at the ring she's left on the table. My head feels clouded, but the tension in my chest starts to leave. I feel guilty but free. I hate that Gia's hurting, but she's smart, independent, and beautiful. She'll find someone who will be in love with her, someone she'll say yes to the first time they propose.

Gia is reasonable. Gwen's right—after a couple of months, we can ease her into the fact that we've fallen in love. She won't like it. I know it'll be awkward at first, but she'll accept it. She doesn't have to feel betrayed. She doesn't have to hate her sister or me.

"William," she says. Her voice is sharp and high.

I stand from my chair immediately because it seems urgent. Before I can make it to the bedroom, she's standing in the hallway. My eyes move to her hand, where her silver necklace dangles.

"What's wrong?" I ask.

Her face is beet-red, and I can tell she's breathing hard from the way her chest moves up and down.

"What. Is. This. Doing. Here?" She says each word pointedly but almost as if she's breathless.

I frown. "That's yours. You left it here the last time you were here."

She shakes her head and runs her hand over her head. "I haven't worn this in months."

"Then what is it doing here?" I say, a little exasperated and confused as to why she's so upset that she's questioning me about this necklace. She seems more upset about it than about me breaking up with her.

"It was under your bed!" she shouts.

"What are you talking about? Why are you upset?" I say frantically.

She walks closer to me and looks me straight in the eye. There's a fury on her face that I've never seen, then her hand is across my face like ten bee stings at once. I've gotten into a lot of fights, but I've never been slapped.

"I gave that necklace to Gwen," she says in a low growl, and I feel my eyes widen. "What is it doing it here?" Tears fall from her eyes.

"I-it's not what you think." The words fall out of my mouth as if I was programmed to say them, as if they were embedded there—maybe from hearing stories or seeing movies about someone cheating and getting caught.

She gazes at me, waiting for me to say something else, but words don't come.

"I hate you," she says in a vicious growl before storming past me and out the door.

I'm frozen. Gia knows. *She knows.* I snap out of the trance I'm in, pick up the phone, and call the house. I have to tell Gwen, to warn her. I don't know what a warning will do, but it'd be better than her being blindsided. I dial her number, but all I get is a busy signal.

"Get off the phone and pick up!" I yell. I call five times and get the same signal. "Shit!"

I slam the phone down, grab my keys, and head out the door.

gwen

"YOU'RE REALLY THINKING of moving here?" I ask in disbelief, twirling the cord between my fingers.

"I know, but I think I'm in love. Ashlyn's amazing," he says. I can hear his smile.

"That's pretty awesome." I'm happy my friend has found what I have, even if it's just for this moment.

"What about you? You and the big brother still sneaking around?" he says.

I sigh and roll my eyes. I keep telling him not to call us that, but he still does. "Yeah, but she's over there now. He says he's going to break it off with her today." I've had a headache since he told me this morning. It goes and comes, and my chest has been tight, and my stomach is queasy.

"Wow. That's a good thing, right?" he asks.

"I mean, in one way it is. I love him, and the thought of them together makes me crazy, but on the other hand, I know it's going to hurt my sister. Who wants their sister hurt?" I let out a deep sigh.

"You do know that what you two are doing is going to hurt her?" he says, but his tone isn't sarcastic.

"I know, but I really don't think Gia is in love with Will. I think she loves him, but she's not in love with him. She doesn't feel the way I do about him. She won't be devastated by him breaking up with her, and

Gia's a guy magnet. She'll meet a guy that she fits with better, who is more like her, and she'll be happier," I say, trying to convince myself.

"And how long do you think you guys can keep what you're doing a secret? How much time do you think she needs to be okay with you guys as an item?"

That's the question. I'm hoping in about eight months I can tell her that I've grown to have feelings for him. It wouldn't be so farfetched. We work together, and people fall in love in the workplace all the time. At least from what I've seen on TV.

"I guess my question is, Gwen, is he worth it? Is he the one? Is it worth the risk if she finds out?" he asks the question I've asked myself a thousand times.

I give him the answer I've come to each time. "Yes. But hopefully it never comes to that."

"I'll be back in two weeks, when I get paid, to see you and Ashlyn," he says.

I'm grateful he's changed the subject. I've been on pins and needles all day and need to be distracted. I hear Gia's car pull up, and my heart speeds up.

"Hey, she's back. I'll call you later, okay?" I say nervously and hang up.

I feel as if I should look busy. If I was just sitting here, that'd be suspicious in some way. I quickly turn on the TV and sit cross-legged in front of it. I should have told Will not to tell me when he was going to tell her so my reaction would be more natural.

The door opens, and she comes in. I look for signs of sadness, anger, depression, but there's nothing. No running mascara or tears in her eyes. I'd thought their breakup would take longer than it did. She's only been off work for maybe two hours. It had to take her a little while to make it to his place and then for him to tell her and for her to make it back here.

Maybe he didn't tell her. I feel relieved and relax a little bit, even though I feel a tad angry. What if he chickened out? Then my stomach drops. What if he changed his mind?

"Hey, sis," I say cheerily, but I keep my eyes glued to the TV.

"Hi," she says shortly and walks past me into her room. Maybe she did talk to him and she's in shock or something.

"I-is everything okay?"

"Yeah," she calls, sounding more like herself from the bedroom. "I was wondering though—could I borrow your necklace?"

"Which one?" I ask, flipping through the television channels.

"Dad's."

Ugh, I actually haven't been able to find it. I've been destroying my room, and it's nowhere to be found. "I actually haven't been able to find it. I didn't want to tell you because I didn't want you to think I was a careless."

She walks back into the room, sits on the couch next to me, and crosses her legs. "Where do you think you lost it?" She's mad. I can tell.

"I think at work or somewhere in my room. I'm going to find it. I promise."

"And there's nowhere else you can think of you took it off?" she asks calmly.

There is one place, but I can't tell her that.

"No, it has to be here somewhere."

She nods, and I notice her leg is shaking. Actually her entire body is.

"Are you okay?" I ask.

When she looks at me, her face is flushed and tears are starting to fall rapidly down her cheeks.

"Gia, are you okay?" I ask her, and I realize Will did tell her. Maybe it's just hit her now.

She squints at me and moves her hand off her trembling thigh, revealing the necklace. "I found it under Will's bed."

I lose my breath. I can hear my heart beat in my ears. I try to think of what to say to explain it. Has she noticed I've worn it since the night I stayed at Will's with Zach? Of course she's noticed—she's Gia. I try to think of something to say, something to defend myself, but the tears in my eyes are a dead giveaway.

She shakes her head and sniffs, wiping her face, and turns away from me, back to the television. "I need you to leave."

"Gia, please." It's all I can say. I take her hand, and she snatches it away from me as if my skin is scalding.

"Have you slept with him?" she asks as if it chokes her to speak the words.

I want more than anything to say no. Right now, I wish it hadn't happened yet. I try to make the right words come out of my mouth, but none do.

"How could you?" she asks, looking at me. Her lips quiver, and I feel light-headed as tears pour out of my own eyes.

"I'm sorry," I say, but it's weak and barely gets out of my burning throat.

She stands. "I will never forgive you for this. How could you choose him over me? My heart is broken." Her voice is strained as she touches her chest. "And you broke it. Not him." She's crying so hard her body is trembling again, and mine is too. "You have one hour to get your things and get out. I'm sure William will welcome you with open arms."

She quickly goes to her room and slams the door. My head is pounding, and I keep trying to catch my breath and stop crying, but I can't. My whole world is collapsing. I don't know what to do, what to say, and nothing I can say will make this better. I've lost my sister. When my mom finds out, she'll hate me too. She'll take Gia's side, and she'll be right.

will

WHEN I PULL up in front of Gia's, I see Gwen sitting on the curb in front of Gia's neighbor's house, sobbing. She's crying so hard her body is trembling. When I open the door, I hear her whimpering. I hop out of the truck and run to her. I pull her into my arms, and she continues to break down.

"She's never going to forgive me. Never. She kicked me out. She's going to tell my mom. She's probably going to disown me. She hates me," she says between choked gasps.

I hold her tight then grab her bags and guide her to my truck. I put her into the passenger side and walk around to get in. As I do, I look toward the house and see Gia in the window, glaring daggers at me. Even in her anger, she watched to make sure Gwen was okay. Gwen is too upset, her eyes probably too blurry, to see anything though.

On the ride to my house, Gwen continues to cry. I hold her hand and stroke it, and she finally goes to sleep from sheer exhaustion. I can feel her desperation, her spirit shattering. Her joy, her spunk, her hope dissolves with each tear she sheds.

When we reach my house, I pick up her small body and carry her into my apartment, ignoring the questioning glances from some of the other tenants. I shift her in one arm to open the door to my apartment, and she stirs. But she doesn't say anything—just nuzzles her head in my chest and clings to me tighter. I take her to my bedroom and lay her down. I put away her bag and go get her a glass of water. When I return, she's awake, curled into a ball, and still crying tears. I sit at the end of the bed, my own head pounding, my heart breaking for her. I want to help her to do something that will make her feel better, but I know it's a lost cause.

"Do you want some time alone?" I ask, unsure if my presence will smother her or make things worse. It's my fault. I'm the reason she's hurting so badly. I'm terrified that this could be the end for us, that this will all have been for nothing. She'll only associate me with pain, hurt, loss, and we'll never be the same.

"Hold me. Tell me everything is going to be okay," she whimpers. "Even if it's a lie." Her eyes are glossed over and wet, and a shadow of a smile crosses her face.

I make my way to her and pull her close. She rests her head on my chest, and I stroke her head as she cries into me.

"Gwen, I love you," I whisper. I don't know if it's the right time to say it, but I can't sit with her for another second letting her think I don't love her, that this is all for nothing.

"I knew there was something special about you when I first saw you. I love everything about you, and there isn't one thing I'd change." I lift her chin so that I'm looking her directly in eye as her tears fall. "They will forgive you. They have to. It'll take time, but they will. In the meantime, I'll do whatever it takes to make you happy as I can. I'll love you times two if I have to. It can be us, forever, against the world. I promise."

She cries harder, but she kisses my lips even though they're trembling. She lets me know, even though she doesn't say anything, all is not lost. She's still there, not broken beyond repair, and I'll make sure she never is.

lisa

Jealousy. . . .
It's a poisonous feeling.
One that grows and grows,
wraps itself around you
and takes over your soul.
~ Lisa

FALL CAME AND went as quickly as a leaf falling from its branch, and winter took hold, sending a chill through our little town, freezing what was old to make room for the new.

He's inside me, taking over me, consuming me, hypnotizing my thoughts, claiming my body as his. I moan his name, and my fingers dig into his back as he pushes rhythmically inside me. He plays me as if I'm his favorite instrument, and I make every sound before I crescendo. This is when he's mine, when I'm the only thing in his thoughts, where time outside of us doesn't matter.

He grabs my wrists and pins them down—it's a rule I break often.

No marks.

I can't mark *him,* but he marks me.

"Will," I moan.

The tension between my thighs builds, ready to throw itself off the cliff that is us. I rock beneath him. His body is hard and his skin wet. His eyes look into mine. That's become one of my favorite parts, when he not only gives me his body but shares his soul. His clear blue eyes clouded with lust, with need. He needs me. I free him. This is when he's alive. I can feel him coming close.

"Don't stop. I'm almost there," I plead, begging him to keep going, to not stop or pull away.

He moves faster and faster, granting my request, and his lips kiss mine, taking them in a slow, passionate kiss I usually don't get from him but I give him all the time. It's so natural, so wonderful, but he usually keeps it from me. *This* kiss, even if his words never say it, lets me know how he feels, what he can't say , and it's what pushes me over the edge, relieving all my tension. My toes curl, and my eyes roll to the back of my head. I pant to catch my breath, and my body quivers before he follows.

His body rests on mine, our breathing frantic, our hearts beating rapidly but as one. My fingers trail up his back, and I kiss his shoulder. He rolls off me, catches his breath, and pulls me against his naked body. I revel in the small amount of time we have, the moments when he's guilt-free, when I pretend that it's just us with no *complications*. I pretend my heart isn't going to break the moment he leaves, that reality doesn't end the best part of my world.

Those moments, that small window when he's like this, are short, and when he removes his arm from across my stomach, I know it's over. The bed shifts, and he gets out of bed and grabs his clothes. His body is beautiful, sculpted and hard, and I feel lucky that he shares it with me. His eyes find mine. I try to smile even though I want to cry. I hate this part. He knows I do, and I don't want to ruin what just happened, but I know the words I'm going to speak will. I can't hold them in anymore, so I try to prolong the time by trying not to say them. I try to think of everything else to say.

"Evie's going out of town next week. She and Jack are going to Vegas."

His eyes widen, his jaw clenching, his guard coming up around him.

"Could we spend the night together?" I'm hopeful even though his expression gives away his answer before he opens his mouth. I know the rules, I know what this is, but we've spent the night together before. Only once when he told them he was going out of town for business and got a room for us outside of town. It was one of the best nights of my life.

"Lisa, you know I . . ." His voice is stern but soft.

His eyes, which had been free and clear and full of me, now avoid me. I see distance in them, guilt weighing on him, and my eyes start to water. My tears don't usually make an appearance while he's with me.

"I'll see what I can do," he says quietly. It's as noncommittal as we are, but I'll take it. He doesn't say things he doesn't mean, so I know he'll try, and that means so much. "Are you okay?"

It's always the same question every single time. He looks at me with his eyes full of sadness, his expression full of embarrassment, and I hate it! That question always makes me feel terrible, as if we just did something wrong . . . which we have, but I hate that he's conscious of it, that he reminds me of it. As if I said 'no this is wrong, terribly wrong, I'm in love with you, and I want to be with you,' it's something he wants to hear.

"Yeah," I say, my throat burning. He looks at me, and I turn my face away, feeling a tear escape.

"Lisa." His voice is full of sorrow, fear, and every other depressing feeling that makes me want to vomit.

Anger starts to consume me, and it replaces the hesitancy I usually have to say the words I've wanted to say for so long. "I love you, Will."

There's silence, and each second cuts through me. When my eyes meet his, I see a storm in them, and I don't care. I want him to say something. Anything.

"You know I . . ." His voice is weak, his expression full of confusion as if to say *Why on earth? How dare you?*

"I love you, Will!" I say louder.

He doesn't say anything but sits on the edge of the bed, as if my words have knocked him out. I cry, and I know it's making things worse, but I can't help it now. My resolve is in tatters.

I get off the bed and stand in front of him, naked and vulnerable. "I know it's wrong. I know you said that this would happen. I know all of this, but can you at least say something? Can you at least try to make me feel just a little bit better about it?"

I only see deadness behind his eyes, as if he's left himself and only his body is here with me.

"I want to be loved how you love her! Is that too much to ask? Does just wanting to be loved make me terrible person?" I ask desperately, and his eyes water.

"No, it doesn't," he says softly. "But it makes *me* a terrible person." He stands up from my bed, grabs the sheet, and wraps it around me. He kisses my forehead and looks into my eyes. "I can't love you how you want me to, Lisa, how you should be loved."

I feel my heart race. Why did I say that? I feel anxious and angry with myself. "I'm sorry."

I hug him, but he doesn't hug me back. Anxiety courses through me. It was too much, I knew it was, but I couldn't keep the words from leaving.

"I won't ever bring this up again. Just please don't be mad. Just forget I said it."

"I think we . . . this is destroying you. I can't do this to you anymore," he says, going to the door.

I jump in front of it. He looks at me sympathetically but gently moves me out of the way. I follow him through my quiet, dark house to the back door. When he opens it, the cold air hits me. The sky's still dark aside from the tiny light on my back porch. He goes down the porch and looks back at me.

"Good night, Lisa," he says quietly before disappearing down the street into the darkness. His truck is parked almost four blocks up in its usual spot.

I get a sick feeling that it won't be there again, that my words have pushed him too far and his good night was really a good-bye. I cry and cry into my pillow, in the bed that smells like him, and wish for things to be different. The worst part is that I'm angry. I think stupid thoughts about if it wasn't for her, things wouldn't be like this, and that's silly and ridiculous and makes me feel a thousand times worse.

I HAVEN'T HEARD from him in two weeks, the longest we've gone without seeing one another since that night in the coffee shop when it all started, where we first made love and it felt the way I knew it should have felt, the way I'd read about in books. I've lost a part of myself. I'm empty. Something is missing. I frequently check the cell phone he bought me, hoping for a call, a text, something, anything, but nothing comes. The worst part is that Evie and Jack got married in Vegas. I now have a lazy slob of a stepdad, but my mother's been blissfully happy, and I hate her for it. I hate her for being happy while I'm miserable. I hate myself for being such a miserable envious bitch.

Everyone notices. Chris and Amanda, they can both see that something's bothering me again. Even the acceptance letter to my second-choice school doesn't make me feel better. They both think that Brett and I are fighting, and I feel badly about the deception. Brett's still great and technically my boyfriend even though we've only had sex twice in six months. I lied and told him I didn't think I was ready for what we did, and he was sweet and understanding and didn't force the issue.

I trudge through my classes, glancing at my phone, the one I lied about and said Brett bought me that Will really did, between each period. A ritual that's completely torturous. I head to the library at lunch. I've started avoiding the cafeteria because lunch is overwhelming. It's become so hard to look at my friends, the people I usually share my secrets and deepest flaws with. I can't look at them, especially Chris, because of my guilt and because he reminds me of Will.

"Hey."

I look behind me and see Chris. He's wearing a concerned smile, and he sits at the table with me.

"Hey," I say back as he takes out a notepad and textbook.

Chris is very subtle. He'll sit in my presence until I spill. I know he wants to know what's going with me because it's lunchtime and he's here instead of stuffing his face. One of his favorite pastimes is eating, and I have no idea where it goes. I can't spill though. He can't know what's wrong with me. Not this time.

"What's up?" I ask, and he shrugs.

"Nothing, things are good. Except my best friend's gone MIA on me." He gives me a small grin.

"That Aidan is such a bastard, huh?" I joke, feeling a teensy bit better when he laughs. I sigh.

Aidan's been gone for the past three months, since his mom had one of her itches to move again. It happened all the time when we were younger, but she really picked the worst possible time to jump up and move again.

"He isn't the only one," Chris says, and his voice is sullen.

"I'm sorry. I just have a lot going on."

"We're best friends. If we can't be there for each other when it counts, what's the point?" he says, looking at me with those beautiful green eyes of his. I hold his hand, and he squeezes mine.

"Sometimes just being there helps," I say.

He goes into his bag, looks around for our nosey librarian, and hands me a bite-sized Snickers. I laugh and pop it into my mouth, and he does the same with his. We sit and eat in silence, and I get the feeling I'm not the only one with a problem.

"What about you? Want to talk or eat another piece of candy?" I ask.

He gives me a sad grin. "It's my dad."

My heart starts to pound. "What wrong?" I ask, trying to contain the desperation in my voice.

"He-he's been walking around like zombie again," he says.

I feel my insides tighten.

He shakes his head. "He was doing good. He was being himself again, the dad I missed. I heard my mom talking to my aunt. She's worried about him."

I can see the worry in his eyes. "Everything's going to be okay. Your dad loves you guys more than anything." I know my words are truer than he knows.

He nods. "Yeah, but . . ."

Instead of finishing, he takes out two more bite-sized Snickers, and we eat them together, and a little piece of my soul crumbles from knowing that my best friend is hurting because of me. At the same time, a little piece of my heart becomes alive again because I know Will is hurting just as I am. But when he's hurting, everyone else is hurting. I don't want to hurt anymore. I want to be fixed, and we can fix each other.

I can fix Will.

will

THE HOUSE IS empty. Gwen is gone, escaped to my stepsister Clara's house. She's hired Gwen to help with some decorating, so Gwen's staying in Chicago to finish up the job. Chris is over at his friend's house, setting up for someone's birthday party, I think. I hear a lot these days, but it's all jumbled together. It's better that way. I try not to think because thinking reminds me of what I've done, what I've let happen to me.

I've become that guy, that terrible stereotypical man who's cheated on his wife, who's betrayed his family with a younger woman, and I hate myself for it. I hate myself because I was weak and let it happen. I hate myself because there is no tangible reason as to why I've been unhappy. I hate myself because being with her made me happy, made me feel alive again. She brought me back to my old self, but my old self would have never done anything like this.

My old self loved Gwen with every part of him every second of the day. My old self would have died before hurting Gwen. My old self promised he'd protect her from the pain he caused her so many years ago, that she'd never have to experience it again.

The smartest thing I've done in the past year was walk away from

Lisa that night, and I didn't do it until after she'd given me her body willingly, unselfishly, and made it mine. I took her each time knowing that I took a piece of her with me when I left. I saw it in her eyes even when she tried to hide it. I hid from myself that each time I left, I left a part of myself with her.

She looked at me with her big, wide eyes full of tears and told me she loved me, and I couldn't say it back. I felt terrible—I wanted to be able to say it back more than anything. She wouldn't have understood that would have made things worse. If I'd said those words, it would have made everything worse, intensified things that much more. I care about her, I crave her, I want her, but love . . . I can't love her the way she needs me to. You can't love two people at the same time, and even in the state I'm in, my heart belongs to Gwen. It's ridiculous, I know, because I shouldn't be able to cheat if I love Gwen.

I've grown selfish. This year has made what I want come first—my priorities have shifted. It's been two weeks since I've had Lisa, and I miss her. Like an addict, my withdrawal turns me into an asshole. I just have to detox, forget about her, learn to handle things the way I should have in the first place, not like a fifteen-year-old boy with a boner. I have to get back to who I was, fall in love with my family again. Maybe we should go on a trip. We all need a vacation, especially before Chris starts school. I have to let Lisa go. She deserves more. I don't want to ruin her. She got a shit deal with her dad, and I'm already adding to her view that men aren't worth shit.

I've been staring at the inventory book, but my mind keeps jumbling everything together. I shut it—I'm not getting anything done tonight. I head to the kitchen and grab a beer, then decide to get the Whiskey I have hidden under the sink instead. The one good thing is I haven't used alcohol as a crutch. The last thing I need is to be a guilty asshole alcoholic. But today I'll give myself a pass since I'm here alone and won't have to look at the hopeless stare Gwen has given for me the past few days.

WHEN THE DOORBELL rings, I'm a little dizzy, the bottle of Whiskey half empty from when I started. I might have overdone it . . . I make my way to the door, and when I open it, she's there. The light on the porch illuminates her face, calling attention to her bright, seductive eyes, her plump lips. She's like a tempting angel. She's breaking the rules. Rules that she made up the first night after we crossed the line and she said we should have rules to keep things from getting messy, from going bad. One of the rules was for her to never show up here for me, that we'd never be in my house alone. Maybe she doesn't know I'm here alone. But she has to know Chris isn't here, and Gwen's car is gone.

"Can I come in?" she asks. It's cold out, freezing. Her cheeks are red. She doesn't have a hat or scarf on, just a coat that really should be classified as a jacket but has fur around the hood.

A little voice in my head says, "Walk her to her car. Tell her you're sorry you ruined her life and she'll find someone who makes her feel the way she says she does with you and who can love her how she wants, how she deserves." But the other parts of me win out aided by the whiskey. I step aside and watch her pass. We stand in the kitchen.

"Is it just us?" she whispers.

I nod, and her lips turn upward but not into an actual smile. She begins to take off her coat, and I clear my throat. I see a flicker of anger in her eyes, but she doesn't stop. I stop my eyes from roving her body, reminding myself I know what's under her clothes.

"So you're just done with me now?" she asks quietly.

"Don't make it sound like that," I say in the same volume she uses.

"But that is what you want?" She looks at me with innocent eyes, her expression hurt.

"This isn't good for either of us. Tell me you're happy. You're not happy!" I say in a hushed whisper, my tone sharp. I hope she gets my point.

"You make me happy," she says, looking me in the eye.

"You were happy the last time I saw you?" I ask her sarcastically.

She squints at me. "You're drunk?"

I sigh. "I'm not drunk. I just had a few drinks."

But I think that's a lie because I'm fighting the urge to kiss her, to feel her, to do things I'd never think about doing in this house. It's off-limits, and I was supposed to be ending this. She runs her hand through her hair, gives me a seductive smile, and walks toward me. I swallow hard and step back until I bump into the refrigerator.

"I'm sorry," she says, running her hands up my chest.

"Lisa, not here." But my words are weak, and my body is even weaker. She looks up at me, and I feel my resolve deteriorating.

"I know you want me," she purrs. Her hands slide down and go inside my pants."I can feel how much."

She kisses me, and she does it with everything in her, all her passion, all her love, all her fear. She emotes, giving herself to me in each kiss, in each touch. She loves purely and selflessly, and she makes me feel how I used to with just a kiss. I get lost in her. When our bodies are connected, I forget how old she is, that she's my son's best friend, that I'm married to a wife I love.

Before long, I'm inside her, not thinking of anything but how good she feels, how good this feels. I forget that she's not supposed to scratch my back. I forget that I'm in my house, in our kitchen, with her pressed up against the wall I painted with my wife last summer. I forget that she's moaning my name loudly in the house I share with my family. I forget all of that until I hcar footsteps.

Before I can quiet her, I see my son, his face white, eyes wide and horrified, and I freeze, unable to move. Lisa notices and looks behind her, and she loses all color when she sees him. He's frozen, shocked, taking in what he's seeing. I think it takes him a minute to realize it's real. Time has slowed down.

"Chris," she shrieks, and her voice wakes us both.

I let her down, and his expression goes from shocked and horrified to angry and disgusted.

"What the fuck?" he screams.

"I-I—" I try to think of something to say.

Lisa grabs her pants and underwear off the floor, and I pull up my own.

"Son, it's not—" I can't even get the lie out of my mouth before he runs out of the house. I buckle my pants and chase him. "Chris!"

I hear Lisa behind me. She's crying and looks as terrified as I feel.

"Go home. Right now. I'll call you," I tell her, but she seems stuck. "Now, Lisa!"

She nods, snapping out of her trance, and she runs out the back door.

"Chris!" I yell.

He's off the front porch, and I run down the steps but stop when he reaches the bottom of the steps. Tears come from his eyes without stopping, and he's shaking, his face red.

"Stay the fuck away from me!" he shouts, and the look in his eyes stops me in my tracks.

"Chris, just let me explain. Please," I beg.

"Don't fucking talk to me. You stay the hell away from me!" he shouts, catching his breath, and I start to cry too. "All these years, all lies. Your moral code, your rules and lectures. You're a liar. A fucking hypocrite."

I can't say anything. What can I say? I open my mouth to tell him I'm sorry.

"I hate you," he growls.

"You don't mean that, son. You're angry. You're upset."

He turns away from me. By the time he looks back, he's different. In an instant, I see the change in him. He's gone from broken, hurt, and emotional to cold as ice and vicious. A smug grin replaces his devastation.

"I should thank you, *Dad*. You've just created the biggest problem of your life." He gives me a satisfied smirk, one that cuts through me, and I'm frozen.

He hops in his truck, and I wake up. I run toward it, but he pulls off and flips me off as he drives down the street. I go back in the house and splash cold water on my face, take a deep breath, and kick the refrigerator so hard all of the magnets fall off and the door pops open.

I try to think of a way to do damage control, but I can't think of one. My life is over. It's going to crumble around me. I don't have a life without my family, and it hits me like a ton of bricks. All this time, I've been searching for myself, what makes me happy, wanting to feel alive. Now I realize that I have no reason to be alive without my family. They're my everything, and it takes me being on the cusp of losing them to realize it.

The realization comes far too late.

I don't feel alive anymore. I'm dead.

lisa

MY HANDS TREMBLE each time the phone rings. My heart still feels as if it's pounding out of my chest. I feel as though I'm on the edge of a panic attack. The anxiety in my body won't let up and is going to make me explode. I wait and wait for a mob led by Chris and his mom with Deanna and Claire in tow to show up to my house *screaming homewrecker, slut, evil selfish bitch*. I've been pacing and crying since I got home. My best friend is going to hate me, everyone is going to hate me, which shouldn't matter since I hate myself right now. It's all my fault. I could tell he had been drinking a lot. If he hadn't, he never would have had sex with me there. I just wanted to make him feel better. I wanted to feel better, so I broke one of the most important rules.

Never in his house.

I bite my lip as I dial Amanda's number and wait for her to pick up. It's been about two hours since Chris walked in on us.

"Hey, Leese," she says happily, and just a flicker of my anxiety goes away. She hasn't heard yet.

"Hey. Uh, have you heard from Chris?"

"I talked to him about three or four hours ago. He was helping Shawn with his sister's party. I was thinking about heading over there if I'm bored. You want to come?"

Her world isn't falling around her.

"No, I gotta go. Talk to you later," I say, practically hanging up on her.

I wring my hands and continue to pace. I just wish I knew something. Not knowing is almost worse than knowing what's going on. I sit, but I can't keep still. When I hear the knock at the door, I jump to answer it but hesitate once I get there. There's hard knocking again, and I open the door.

It's not Will—it's Chris. I stand there slack-jawed. My blood's gone cold, and I wait for him to say something. To call me a whore, to ask how I could do such a thing. How could I let it happen, why did it happen and when? But when I allow myself to look at his face, I see he doesn't look upset at all. He looks indifferent. He is different.

"You going to let me in? I think that's the least you can do," he says in a voice that's colder than his normal tone.

I'm shocked. This isn't the reaction I'd expected. Chris is supposed to be hurt, mad, disgusted, not this. I step aside, and he walks in, flops on the couch, and stretches out his legs. His eyes fall on me, and I search them for anger and disgust, but I don't see either. I see something else that I can't put my finger on.

"Chris, I'm so sorry," I say, walking up to him.

I wait for him to flinch or lash out, but he doesn't. He just puts up his hands as if to tell me to stop talking. I'm sure I look shocked.

"Stop calling me that," he says sharply.

"What?" I ask, confused.

"That's not my name." His eyes are hard, and I start to see the anger he's hiding.

"A-are you high?" I ask nervously, searching his face.

He laughs in a way that scares me, because if I wasn't looking right at him, I would swear he isn't my best friend. It's as if he's someone else completely, and it scares me.

"No, I'm not high, but I hate that name, that name he called me," he says angrily, grabbing a pillow and squeezing it.

"W-what do you want to be called then?" I ask cautiously.

A mischievous grin spreads across his face. He walks toward me, and I feel stuck in place. I've never been bothered by Chris's height, but he's standing in front of me, our chests almost touching. He looks down at me, and I feel intimidated, and I know he can sense it.

He smirks and licks his lips. "I'm going to keep your secret for you."

I force myself to breathe.

"I'm not going to tell anyone. After this, it'll be like it never happened."

Is he serious? He has to be high on something. I want to believe what he's saying, but right now I'm more worried about him. Why he is acting like this, like he doesn't care—frankly, like he doesn't give a flying fuck?

"Are you okay, Chris?"

His expression hardens. "Don't fucking call me that!"

I flinch. He grabs my wrist, pulls me to him, and kisses me. I'm so caught off guard I don't know what to do. Is my best friend kissing me after seeing me having sex with his dad? Is this some twisted revenge? I gather up my strength to push him away, and he only laughs.

"What the hell is wrong with you?" I demand, my anger outweighing my guilt.

"That's the last kiss you'll ever get from a Scott," he says cockily. "I'll tell you this: if I ever catch you or even think that you're doing anything with my dad again, even looking at him in a way that you shouldn't, I'll make sure everyone in this town knows what a fucking cunt you are."

His words are like venom and his eyes like daggers. I'm going to vomit.

"Please," I respond, my lips quivering.

"There's nothing more to discuss. You stay the fuck away from my family. If I didn't think it would kill Gwen, I would broadcast around this whole fucking town what a whore you are."

I stay completely still, looking at this person who isn't my best friend. Did I do this? Did I break my friend? I'm shaking.

He only grins and walks to the door and opens it. "See you in school, Leese." Before he leaves, he leans back in with a smug grin. "Oh, and just so you know, I'm Cal." He winks before shutting the door.

I run toward it and lock it as my heart pounds in my ears. With that, I burst into tears and slide onto the floor.

I cry over losing the best friend I've ever had.

chapter twelve

gwen

"DO YOU LIKE it?" he asks.

I suppress my smile. He's beaming, his eyes hopeful, as he waits for me to answer. I look around the big colonial farmhouse he's just shown me. He's so excited about it—it's a property his uncle owned—and I know it makes him feel proud. He's imagining all the possibilities, and he sees himself here. It isn't his stepdad's—just his.

"What do you think?" he says, almost bursting at the seams.

"I love it," I finally reveal with a large smile.

He picks me up, kisses me, and spins me around. He sees himself here, and I see myself wherever he is.

"This is where our life starts," he says, holding me close.

We're definitely in need of a fresh start. It's been a tough year for us. After Gia kicked me out and told my mom about us, Mom called and spazzed out on Will and me. She said we were despicable and asked how we could do that to Gia. My mother concluded by saying that as long as I continued to see Will, I would never be welcome in her home.

It's been a year since then, and losing two people after my dad has been hard. It hurts, and every day it bothers me, but I can't imagine my life without William. I see myself growing old with him. We didn't do what we did out of lust or some silly infatuation. We're in love. I love him with every fiber of my being.

"I was hoping you'd say that," he says triumphantly. "There's one more thing I have to show you."

I look at him quizzically, but I love surprises. He takes my hand and leads me outside to the shed I saw when we first pulled up. He stands in front of the door and tells me to close my eyes. I giggle. I hear the door open then feel his hands cover my eyes as he ushers me into it.

"Your eyes are still closed?"

I nod. I feel his hands leave my eyes.

"Look up," he says.

When I do, my jaw drops. The shed is dark, but on the ceiling, *Will you marry me?* is spelled out in lights. My eyes begin to tear up, and my heart flutters. His voice has always given me comfort, joy, and peace. But today, his voice has been outdone by these tiny glittering lights, and I've fallen in love with him all over again.

"I'd never ask you to move in with me again and not be my wife. You're already my best friend, my confidant, my soul mate. I want to love you forever and never stop. It can be us, forever, against the world," he whispers.

I nod furiously. "Yes, a thousand times yes." I thank God that these are happy tears. I've cried too many tears of guilt, sorrow, and anger. These wash those away and create a new start. "I want to make a thousand babies with you."

"Well, we do have a farm."

I hug him and know that even in my worst mistake, being with Will is the best decision I've ever made.

lisa

"I CAN'T BELIEVE he broke up with me. He's acting like such a bastard," Amanda cries into my shoulder while I stroke her back.

Chris and Amanda are over.

"He kept saying that it made sense to end it now, that he was ditching this pathetic town soon and it'd be better to make a clean break before I got hurt." She sniffles. "And I'm like, 'What about prom?'" She cries harder.

"Prom is almost four months away. You're beautiful, Amanda. You'll find someone to take you," I say.

"B-but the craziest thing about it is, do you know what he said when I asked about prom? H-he said, 'Fuck prom.' What popular senior says, 'Fuck prom'? And he's quit the band, and h-he's just acting so crazy." She lets out another wail.

I hold her tight as tears well in my own eyes.

"I could see if he was one of those anti-anything-fun kids, but Chris isn't like that. He's captain of the football team, class treasurer, and now he doesn't even care about prom? I talked to his mom, and she said he'd come around, that she doesn't know what's wrong with him. He's being an asshole to her. What's wrong with him?" She sobs.

I hand her a Kleenex and feel multiple stabs of guilt. *I'm* the reason Chris is this way. Will and I, we destroyed him, and now he's turned into this badass rebel who doesn't care about anyone and who hurts people and is mean. But he isn't a liar, because he hasn't said a word to his mom or anyone about his dad and me. The sad part is I think him keeping it in is turning him into the devil.

I spend the night at Amanda's since she's so upset. I stay up all night staring at the ceiling, as I have every night. Granted, Amanda has a much better ceiling. I think about all that's happened, how badly I've screwed things up.

I talked to Will right after Chris left that night and told him what happened. The crazy thing is he seemed relieved that Chris wasn't going to say anything. Of course he'd be relieved, but he didn't seem to care much that his son was acting weird and possibly high.

But apparently he wasn't high on anything but his anger, his disappointment in his father, his disgust with his best friend. Other than talking to Will that night, I've kept my part of the deal by staying away from Will. Not that I have any reason not to. I get the distinct feeling that if Will never sees me again, it will be too soon for him, and that hurts. I block out the indescribable pain by knowing how much pain the truth could cause so many other people.

I finally lie on my stomach to try to get some sleep, and I scrunch up my nose. The pillow has some strange fragrance, and it turns my stomach. Literally. I jump out of Amanda's bed and head to her bathroom—thank God she has an ensuite. A couple more seconds and the pizza we ordered would have been all over the floor. I vomit until there's nothing left in my stomach, then I hear Amanda behind me.

"Oh God, was the pizza bad?" she asks, covering her nose and looking disgusted.

I sigh, catching my breath. She hands me a cup of water, and I rinse my mouth.

"I don't know," I say after flushing the toilet.

"I feel fine." She starts to play with her long blond braid.

"I think I have some weird stomach bug. I got sick after eating donuts at work this morning too." I wet my face at her sink, and when I turn toward Amanda, she's looking at me with her eyes bugged out. "What?"

She seems to gasp solely for dramatic effect, but that's classic Amanda, "A-are—do you think you're pregnant?"

I laugh. "No." I head back into her room and get under the covers.

She stands next to me with her arms crossed. "Are you sure? Who throws up donuts except pregnant women?"

I roll my eyes. "I'm on the pill." Thanks to Evie's reminders after Brett started to come over, I take them every day.

But Amanda doesn't look convinced. She walks across the room, pulls a box out of a drawer, and drops it in my lap.

"You keep pregnancy tests in your drawer?" I ask in disbelief.

She nods as if it's the most normal thing in the world.

"Wow," I say in disbelief.

I pick up the little test. I'll humor her. After all, with Aidan gone and Chris probably never talking to me again, she's the only friend I have left. I go in the bathroom, drink a little water, and wait a few minutes while Amanda chatters outside the door about her and Chris's first time together. That's still too weird for me to hear about, so I run the water to drown her out.

I pee on the stick and set it on the sink. I'm not worried at all. I know for sure there's no possibility I could be pregnant, so it's almost a waste of time and eight bucks. Will and I always used condoms—he made sure of that—so there's no possibility . . . Well, except that one time. I stare at the test. Things become blurry after I see those two pink lines.

I DIDN'T GET any sleep all night. I didn't even really get a chance to process the test. I stuffed it in my pajamas. When I opened the door and saw Amanda, I couldn't tell her. I lied—for the first time convincingly—and told her it was negative, that she was overreacting. She hugged me, saying she was so relieved and how messed up it would be if I was pregnant by Brett. God, at this moment, I'd kill for it to be Brett's. That would be a thousand times less complicated than whose baby it really is.

I'm having a baby. I'm pregnant with Will's baby. For the slightest moment, a tiny part of me was happy. I thought it could be a sign from the Fates giving us permission to be together. I thought that because if I had his baby, there's no way I could never see him again. It's the one thing that would require us to try to make things work.

I was delusional thinking about the fantasy of being a parent—Will and me living together. I'd get an apartment and go to school, and he'd come and sit on the couch and play with our cute little boy or girl, and after a little while, Will would realize he loved me and he'd be with me. In that fantasy, I didn't think of Chris or Gwen or any part of reality. Maybe it was Amanda's beautiful house with beautiful things and my stomach being empty and queasy that made me so delusional and stupid.

Because now, sitting on my bed and hearing Evie scream her head off at Jack while our roof leaks and my head hurts and I feel like I have to throw up, reality knocks the ever-living shit out of me.

I'm pregnant.

I'm a pregnant teenage girl who's still in high school.

No, it's worse. I'm a pregnant teenage girl who's still in high school with a crazy mom who's just barely taking care of me, and I'm pregnant by my best friend's married dad. I'm going to hyperventilate.

AS I SIT in front of their house, I realize I have no way to get in touch with Will. I'm afraid of calling and Chris answering. Will's cell phone is off. I have no other choice. I'm going crazy. I feel overwhelmed, and to be completely honest, I'm terrified. I take a deep breath and ring the doorbell and close my eyes. I hear footsteps approach.

"Please be Will. Please be Will," I say to myself. When the door opens, my stomach drops.

"Hi, Lisa," Mrs. Scott says in a cheerful tone.

"Hi, Mrs. Scott." I hold my breath to try to calm my nerves.

"It's so good to see you. It's been awhile," she says, opening the door for me to come in. "Is everything okay?" She looks concerned when I don't move.

"I-is Chris here?" I ask, and her smile softens a bit.

"No. No, he isn't." She sighs. "Come in, Lisa."

I nervously step inside. "It's just you?" I realize what an odd question that must be coming from me.

"Yes, well, technically," she says with a bright, wide smile.

I notice how pretty she looks. I've never really looked as Mrs. Scott, but she's beautiful, with long red hair, beautiful green eyes that smile at you, and she's glowing. I'm nervous just being around her. So much has changed since I was last around her, and I feel sick.

"I-I haven't told anyone."

I look at her curiously, then I realize she said technically she's the only one home.

"Is W—Mr. Scott here?" I hurry to correct myself.

She shakes her head, her hand covers her stomach, she rubs it and she practically beams at me. My stomach falls through the floor.

"You're—you're pregnant?" I'm afraid to hear her answer.

She nods enthusiastically. "Yes!" She's obviously ecstatic. "It's early, and the doctor said I should wait before telling everyone, so I'm keeping it to myself. Trying to anyway—it's really hard. But I haven't told any of my friends or family except for Will. He's so excited. We needed this." Her wide smile softens.

I feel dizzy. She's pregnant too. Oh my God. I'm going to pass out.

"A-are you okay?" she asks, and I nod.

"I-I've got to go, Mrs. Scott," I say, making my way to the door.

"Are you sure? You look a little peaked," she says.

At that second, Will walks in. I'm sure all the color has drained from my face, and he joins the club of looking as though he's just seen a ghost. The ghost of all his transgressions standing right in front of him. I feel anger and sadness, hurt and betrayal, coursing through me. How could he? He was sleeping with both of us. I thought he didn't sleep with her. God, I knew she had his heart, but I'd convinced myself I had his body. I suck in a deep breath.

"Hi, Lisa. How are you?" he asks, recovering quickly.

It takes everything in me to not yell at him or start crying. I want to blurt, "I'm pregnant with your baby, asshole," but I don't. Instead I swallow my tears.

"Congratulations, Mr. Scott. I heard the good news," I say with fake enthusiasm.

He looks at Gwen, who looks a little embarrassed but still ecstatic.

"I had to tell someone, honey," she says, staring at him with so much stupid love in her eyes.

"Since Chris isn't here, I'm going to get going. Don't tell him I stopped by. Please!" I say before leaving.

When I'm out of the house, I practically run to my car and throw up outside of it. I wait a few minutes to see if he's going to come out and talk to me, to explain what I just learned, to apologize for not calling me, for abandoning me with this secret, to tell me that he only slept with her once. But he doesn't, and that hurts more than anything. Will has his child, the one he's been waiting for, who will give him what he needs to be fulfilled, and he doesn't need me anymore. I drive down the road to park and sit in my car and cry harder than I've ever cried before.

My phone vibrates, and I know it's him. I look at his text.

I'm sorry for everything, Lisa. I never meant to hurt you. I hope you find the happiness you're looking for. I wish I could say this to you in person, but I think this way is best.

I squeeze the phone and scream. I roll down the window and throw it on the ground. At this moment, I hate him. I hate myself. I hate this thing growing inside me who will never live up to *their* perfect child. I cry, resting my head on the steering wheel, then I drive home. I run up the stairs and swing open the door.

Evie's on the couch, smoking a cigarette. "What's your problem?"

I thought she would be passed out. She worked a double today, and I saw her on her second beer before I left. I roll my eyes and storm past her into my room. I slam the door before throwing myself on the bed. Moments later, the door swings open.

"What the hell is your problem?" she shrieks.

I look at her, anger swirling around me. I want to make sure someone feels like I do. "You don't care what's wrong with me. You don't care about anyone but yourself and your stupid fucking husband!"

She looks caught off guard, then her face hardens. "You don't talk to me about what I care about. You're in my house, under my roof, and you will respect me!" She sounds like a parent who deserves respect—she must have picked that up from the TV she listens to when she's screwing or is passed out.

"I don't have to respect you. You're a terrible mother. I want to rip this parasite out of my stomach, and it would probably be for the best because I'll probably be a screwed up parent just like you and dad."

She slaps me so hard I fall onto the bed. I look at her, and the look in her eye makes me suppress the urge to slap her back. She's furious, and I edge away from her.

"How fucking stupid are you!" she yells.

I move farther away from her.

"Is it Will's kid or that college boy's?" she yells.

My eyes widen. How the hell does she know?

She cackles. "You think you're so smart and I'm so stupid. You're not, and Will is just as stupid as you. I've seen his car parked down the street, and Jack's noticed him sneaking out."

I feel as if I'm going to throw up.

"A married man, Lisa? And Will Scott of all people? He's never going to leave his wife. He loves her. You were just a hot piece of young ass. That man's going through a midlife crisis, sweetie. You don't mean anything to him, and that kid most likely won't either. Do you even know whose kid it is?"

I want to shout at her that she doesn't know anything, but instead I feel like a silly little girl. I nod. She doesn't question which man is the father. She most likely doesn't care.

"Have you told him?" she asks, and it sounds as though her anger is subsiding.

I shake my head.

She nods and lets out a long sigh. "Well, what do you want to do?"

"You mean I have a choice?" I ask with a small amount of sarcasm.

She nods. "Yeah, honey, you do. I won't have you putting a death on my hands, using me as a scapegoat."

I cringe.

"You've really screwed up though. Just like I did." She chews her lip and sits next to me on the bed. "You have a chance to go to school, make something of yourself." She shakes her head.

"It's not like I have the money to go anyway," I mutter.

"I don't have money, but your grandparents do. They've had your college fund set up since you were born," she says.

I frown at her. "What? Why didn't you ever say anything? I've been working my ass off at the stupid coffee shop to save money."

"There's nothing wrong with a little hard work," she counters. "They're not going to pay if you're knocked up though." She looks at my stomach as if it's an alien.

"So, so . . . you think I should get rid of it?" I ask.

"If you want to, that's up to you, or you could take a trip to your aunt Dani's," she says and stands.

"What do you mean?" I ask.

She looks back at me and shrugs. "It may be a win-win situation if that's something you'd want. Dani's been dying for a kid. She'd take anybody's." She laughs before leaving the room.

I lie back on my bed and rub my stomach while looking at the ceiling, and I think and think. Then let out a deep breath. I pick up the phone in my room. "Hey, Aunt Dani, I have something to tell you."

THE VERY NEXT day, my aunt Dani is back in Madison. We're transferring my school records. I say good-bye to Amanda, who thinks Evie and I got into a huge fight and she kicked me out. We cry, we laugh, and I promise to visit her in the summer before she leaves for school. As I walk to my aunt Dani's car, I see Chris in the distance, leaning against the school wall. I wave at him, and surprisingly, he waves back.

chapter thirteen

lisa

IN NINE MONTHS, no one knows that I had a baby. The secret of a fall that never should have happened.

And when I return to visit—with no baby—I'm surprised to find out that Gwen also has none.

after

chapter fourteen

gwen
present day

TIME HAS A way of making you see things differently. After so long, you convince yourself of your own truth even if things didn't happen exactly that way. Maybe it's the mind's way of helping you cope after you know you've really screwed up, when you've done so much wrong. I wonder if that's what Will's doing. If he's looking back on what happened and his mind is convincing him that what he did wasn't that bad, that he only acted out of goodness and love . . . or whatever he feels for her.

It's hard for me to even look at Gia after telling her everything and even harder to stomach after remembering everything Will and I did to her. I expect her to look happy or smug, to say I told you so or how could you think he'd be faithful and loyal to you when he wasn't to me. I expect to hear her say all those things, but it only comes from the voices in my head scolding myself.

She's the opposite—she cries with me. After everything, my sister cries with me.

"You didn't deserve what happened, Gwen. No one deserves to be hurt, to be betrayed," she says, holding my hands as tears trickle down my cheeks.

"I did it to you! We betrayed you and hurt you, and this is life's payback, my karma come round!" I cry into her shoulder and feel terrible for it. After everything I did, she forgave me. It took years, but she forgave us both, fully and completely and never ever threw it back in my face.

"Look at me," she says, holding my chin up so that I face her. "Love can make good people do bad things."

My heart hurts, falling into a thousand pieces, and I feel as if it's never ever going to be fixed. "How long—how long before the pain goes away? When will I wake up and not feel like I want to die?"

She looks away. "It will take as long as you make it. If you hold on to the hate and the anger, if you guard it, cherish it, and feed it, it will stay with you forever." She takes my hands. "Trust me, it isn't easy to forgive, and you never forget, but you have to try to let it go, or you'll be miserable for a very, very long time."

I hug her, but I don't know if I'm ready to let go of my pain. I need to hold on to it a little bit longer.

I STAY IN Illinois with Gia for three days to clear my mind, to think and think and cry and cry and try to understand. I try to understand what he was thinking, how it could have happened. After what happened with us, after Gia told me she hated me, I wished she could just understand, that she could know that deep down, I never meant to hurt her. I know now that it doesn't matter if the person meant to hurt you or not—what matters is the fact that they did.

But Gia forgave me. I'd never forget the day she showed up at our little farm, which was still half empty, in the process of coming together. I was reupholstering a chair while sitting on the porch, and I looked up at her getting out of her car with a beautifully wrapped silver box. My heart stopped as joy and fear coursed through me. Her hello was simple.

"I missed you so much, little sis, and I don't want to hate you anymore," she said.

She gave me back the necklace she had taken back from me that day she found out. Then I was ecstatic that she understood. She got it, and she forgave—me at least. She didn't stay long. Will was still on her shit list, but it was a start.

Today though, as I walk back into my own house where the betrayal took place, I wonder how she could do that. How could she put her hate aside and just welcome me back into her life with open arms? I realize for me, it starts with learning the truth. I know from experience that sometimes you imagine the monster under your bed to be a lot scarier than it actually is. The house is quiet. Chris and his family are back in Chicago.

I walk through the house and search for him. I notice the house is clean, immaculate. Not only cleaned but sanitized, the smell of lemon still in the air. I walk up the stairs and see him. My heart jumps when I see him scrubbing the walls. He stops and turns to look at me, his arms covered in soap. His eyes are tired and red, but when he sees me, they widen, and he smiles. He's called me a thousand times, and that was before I turned off my phone.

"What are you doing?" I ask, crossing my arms.

He sets the soapy sponge into the big white bucket beside him. "I wanted the house to be clean when you came back . . . if you came back."

I can tell he's nervous from the way he's fidgeting with his overalls, his eyes shifting. He's quiet, obviously watching his words, afraid of saying the wrong thing.

"I'd like to talk. I'll meet you at the dining room table when you're ready," I say quickly, turning away and heading down the steps.

I don't give him time to react, to say anything. I can't. I need to hear the things I have to know. Because along with this hatred I have, as tangible as it is, I still feel love, and that hurts more than anything.

I SIT AT the dining room table, trying to mask my emotions. I want to appear hard and indifferent, but I know the moment he walks in, he'll see it's a façade. So I decide to let him see me without the mask and see all my anger, pain, and even love. I hear him hesitate in the doorway, then he walks in and quickly sits across from me. He's cleaned himself up, though his eyes are still a shade of red, and bags are still under his eyes. He smiles at me, and I close my eyes and sigh. His smile is still the same, and it calls me to smile back. Then I wonder if he gave her that same smile, and I frown at him until his smile disappears.

"I've missed you so—"

I put up a finger to stop him. "There are some things I need to know."

He nods as if to let me know he's ready to tell me anything. If only I was ready to hear it.

"When did it start?" I ask.

He sighs and glues his gaze to the table. "A couple of months after I started tutoring her." His voice is pained and full of guilt, and I cringe.

I shake my head, remembering it was my bright idea to have him tutor her. She needed the help, and Will was a shell of himself going through a midlife crisis. I chuckle angrily. Pairing a hormonal, impressionable, beautiful teenage girl with a handsome older man who felt lost, old, and for some reason unwanted had to have been possibly the worst idea in the world. He looks at me, trying to gauge my reaction, and I let out a small breath.

"How long did it go on for?" I will my tone not to break.

"Only a few months," he says.

My eyes lock on his. "How long is a few months? How many?"

He shakes his head as if recalling it is difficult, as if he can't pinpoint it, and my fists clench underneath the table.

"Maybe six, seven at the most. It was so long ago," he says reluctantly.

I let out a deep sigh, feeling my eyes tear up. "Chris, he said he caught you in our house. How many times did it happen in our house?" My tone is incredibly weak from the burning in my throat.

He looks at me sorrowfully and with pity. I don't want his pity. I want his answers.

"Gwen, is this important?" he pleads.

"Don't you dare ask me what's important or not!" I yell.

"Twice, only twice. The time Chris caught us and one other time. It wasn't actual sex the first time," he says painfully, and I cringe not wanting to know what he's talking about.

I hear the frustration in his voice, and I resent him for it. Tears that I can't control are coming, and I want to get up and run. He doesn't deserve to see them, but I have to finish this.

"Why her, Will? Of all people, why a girl who grew up with our son, his best friend, a teenage girl?"

He covers his face in his hands. "I don't know, Gwen. It just happened."

I feel my face harden.

"And I don't mean to make it sound trivial or simple, but I don't know! It was just a terrible situation that I regret every day. I regretted it while it happened," he says and huffs.

"Not enough to stop it! If Chris hadn't caught you, would you have stopped?" I yell.

"Yes, I would have. I loved you. I know it was wrong. I just . . . I was weak. I was stupid. She made me feel alive. I felt dead! I don't know why. I can't explain, but she did," he says frantically.

I'm sobbing now, and it looks as though my wails cut though him.

"I'm so incredibly, unbelievably sorry," he says, tears pouring from his eyes.

"You didn't love her. At all," I say, looking into his eyes.

He squints at me. "No, it was never love. Not how I felt for you, how I feel for you."

"You cared about her at least!" I say in disbelief. I can't believe the man I loved, whom I'm still undeniably in love with, would do this to me and to a young girl without caring about her at all.

He looks at his hands. "Yes, I did care about her."

I'd thought hearing that would make me feel better, but it makes me feel worse. "How could you pretend that it didn't happen? After she moved back here, how did you both just act like what you did never happened?"

He grips his hands. "That night Chris found us, it was a wake-up call. I realized that what I had been searching for, I'd always had, and I was on the cusp of losing it all. My son, my wife." He sobs, and I close my eyes. "I knew at that moment that I was a fucking idiot! That I had to be crazy to do anything as foolish as I had. That I wouldn't make it without you and Chris. Without you, there was no point in living." He sounds so genuine it makes me sick.

"You had to sleep without our son's eighteen-year-old best friend to figure that out?" I ask in disbelief, and his face falls. I can't hear anymore. "Now you have another reason to exist—your love child. You don't need me anymore, Will." I stand from the table.

"Gwen, please!" He rushes over to me and pulls me close.

I push him away.

"This was eight years ago. I made a mistake, please," he cries, holding me. His whole body shakes as he cries, and I begin to cry too—a hard, ugly cry. "Please forgive me. I'll do anything you want. Please don't leave me. Hate me, hit me, treat me like shit, but please don't leave me. Give me a chance to make things right. I'll do counseling. I'll do whatever it takes." He looks up at me, his chin resting on my stomach.

"I don't know if I can," I tell him, hatred and love crashing against each other inside me when I stare into his sea-blue eyes.

"Try, please," he says, his grip loosening on my waist.

I slowly step away from him. "Have you seen your daughter yet?"

He glances at me guiltily. "I went there to confront Lisa about telling Chris. I saw her briefly. I don't know if I'm in a good state to be anyone's father right now." He holds his head.

I sigh. "Well, you should get there. You're a couple of years behind already, I think." With all the strength in me, I walk out the door.

lisa

present day

"LOLLI!" WILLA RUNS up the steps and squeezes the golden retriever sitting on my aunt Dani's porch. "I missed you so much!"

William's sudden appearance sent me into one of my patterns from so long ago. It used to be a lot easier to run away from my problems. Now it's like no matter where I run, I have to carry them with me.

"Willa bear," my aunt Dani says, stepping out on her porch, her brown hair peeking out from under her scarf. She's so much thinner than she was just a few weeks ago, and I do my absolute best not to give away how bad it hurts to see her like this.

"Mommy," Willa says, letting go of Lolli and jumping into Aunt Dani's arms.

It takes Dani a minute before she can lift her. "I missed you so much." Dani strokes her hair.

"I missed you too," she says, squeezing her tight.

I meet them at the top of the stairs.

"Are you having fun at Lisa's?" she asks.

"A little bit. There's not a lot to do there, and she keeps fighting with people," Willa says.

I sigh as Aunt Dani cuts her eyes to me.

"Your cousin's always been a fighter. Just like her daddy," she says, but the look in her eyes shows me she's not happy. "Why don't you go to your room and play with Lolli while I talk to your cousin, okay?"

"Come on, Lolli," Willa says, going into the house and heading up the stairs with her best friend in tow.

"Why don't you come in and catch me up on what's going on," Dani says, opening the door for me.

We sit down in the living room, and she makes sure to turn the TV on so Willa can't hear us.

"What on earth . . ." She pauses, obviously trying to calm herself but unable to hide her frustration. "You're fighting around Willa?"

"I told you I had a lot of things to work out," I say quietly, too embarrassed to meet her eyes. I hear her frustrated sigh.

"Lisa. You can't do those types of things around her. I thought you taking her this weekend would be a step in the right direction. For you to start preparing things for her," she says, exasperated.

"I told her father about her," I blurt out quickly.

"You. Did. What?" she says, her anger rising with each word.

"That was the best way for me to get things prepared for her," I say urgently.

She shakes her head then covers her face. "I can't believe you did that. That was not the right thing to do right now. Why did you do that?"

I'm caught off guard. I'd thought that me clearing up the past and attempting to build a relationship with her father would have gotten me a "you did the right thing" at least.

"I thought that was the right thing to do!" I say defensively.

She removes the scarf from her head and squeezes it in disbelief. "Sometimes you are just like your mother," she says with a bitter laugh.

"Wow. Okay, I'm going to go and try to figure this out. Since I obviously royally screwed up this parenting thing before I even started," I say, standing and heading to the door.

"Lisa, sit down!" she demands.

I stop but don't turn around to face her. I feel tears forming in my eyes, but I quickly wipe them away.

"Sit down please," she says sternly.

I let out a deep breath and sit on the sofa across from her.

"First things first. When you start this parenting thing full time, running away when things get rough is not something you're allowed to do. Got it?" she says, and I nod. "So I'm guessing the whole 'telling the truth' thing turned out to be a lot worse than you ever imagined?"

I fold my hands in my lap. "The bad part is I haven't even faced the worst of it yet."

She lets out a long sigh. "Do you want to tell me who her father is now?"

My stomach tightens. I can't . . . I can't have her look at me the same way everyone else looked at me after they found out. "Not right now. If that's okay."

She nods, though I can tell she's not happy about it.

"I was hoping I could stay here this week. I called in to work. I'm going to take a leave," I add.

"You should save some of that time for when Willa comes to live with you," she says.

"It's only a couple of days," I mutter.

She coughs. When she can catch her breath, she asks, "How was it with her this weekend before all hell broke loose?"

"Willa's great. You've done a good job with her," I say, sitting up straighter.

"Lisa, I've seen you with those kids you teach. They love you, and Willa would love you too if you gave her a chance."

"How can I give her a chance?" I ask, dumbfounded.

"She can tell you're keeping her at a distance. That warmness you exhibit with other children isn't there with her. You of all people should know that children have a sixth sense. They can be very perceptive, especially your daughter," she says, and my heart skips a beat. That's the first time she's referred to Willa as my daughter.

I start to feel hot, and the house seems a lot smaller than it was. I stand quickly. "I changed my mind. I'm going to go."

"Lisa, come on," she says, unable to hide the disgust in her voice.

"I just need time." I stop before exiting. "Tell Willa I said goodbye."

Before I get in the car, the little food I had this morning shoots up through my throat.

MY HEAD IS pounding. I open my eyes to see a blurry version of Aidan standing over me. He's holding a half-empty bottle of Jack Daniels and shaking his head disdainfully. He looks angry. I sure as hell don't want to deal with his shit and a pounding headache at the same time.

"Where's Willa?" he asks sharply.

I roll my eyes, still feeling a little drunk. "I took her back to my aunt's. I'm not ready yet." I roll over in the bed and pull the covers over my face.

He promptly rips them off me. "You're not ready yet?" he asks in a bitter, sarcastic tone.

"Just get out." I tug the covers from him, but he's so much stronger than me, and I fall back when he lets them go. "Why are you being such an asshole!" My voice quivers. "Don't you know what I'm going through right now?"

His eyes practically bug out of his head, and he laughs. "Are you fucking kidding?" His eyes have gone dark, and his nostrils flare. "What you're going through? Let's see. You ruined your best friend's life by fucking his dad, you had his kid, and the only mother that kid has ever known is dying. Let's not forget you've probably broken up Will's marriage over some eight-year-old bullshit. Not that you shouldn't have said anything, but come on, eight fucking years later? When things are finally going good for everyone? And after all of that, you're sitting here, crying and drunk, throwing a pity party and thinking about what *you're* going through?"

I stare at him looking like a fake Captain America. His blond hair's grown out from the buzz cut he came home with from his tour in the army. I can't believe he just said that to me. I open my mouth to defend myself, but I can't think of anything to say. So I jump off the bed, and I push him as hard as I can in his chest. He just pushes me back on the bed with one hand. I jump off again and swing at him, and he grabs my arm and twists it behind my back.

"Let go, Aidan!" I screech, but he forces me to walk toward my full-length mirror.

"If you want to be mad at someone, look. She's right there. That's who you should be pissed at, not me. If I were you, I'd suggest you be a little nicer to me because right now, I'm the only friend you've got," he says before letting my arm go.

The fact that Aidan's my only friend makes me want to burst into tears. I wish I was back in the fifth grade when I could actually kick his ass. The only good thing about him being here is that I won't let myself cry in front of him—I still have a single shred of pride left. I grab a pillow and scream into it.

I fucked up, which happens a lot, but I really fucked up this time. I can't believe I did this! Usually when Aidan and I fight, I call Chris . . . I was so estatic when I got back from school that he was talking to me again . . . I may never be able to call Chris again. I feel my emotions fighting to get out of me, but not here, not in front of him. Anger, frustration, and bitterness are what Aidan handles. Genuine sadness and regret are what Chr—

"I'm not ready for this." And I cry, as much as I don't want to.

He looks at me for the first time with sympathy. He sits beside me and pulls me into a hug.

"I'm not ready to raise a daughter, especially not by myself. She deserves better than where I am in my life. I don't want to be her Evie," I say. My phone starts to ring.

"Want me to look and see who it is?"

I nod.

"Aunt Dani," he says.

I laugh and shake my head. "I can't talk to her like this, not when I'm still half drunk and frantic."

He nods. "Y-you're a teacher though, Leese. Kids love you. You really don't think you'd be a good mom?"

I chuckle. "In some weird, twisted way, and don't hate me when I say this, I became a teacher because of Will. Kids love me, and I love kids, but to have one twenty-four-seven? To be responsible for what type of person they become?" I sigh and cover my face. "I think she'd probably be better off with my grandparents."

His face falls. "Aren't your grandparents, like, in their seventies?"

"Yeah."

My phone vibrates again. Aidan picks it up and sighs. He passes it to me. It's a text message from Will.

Can I see her?

I roll my eyes and turn off the phone. "I think I need to get away from here. From this town, these people, the memories." I quietly rub the back of my neck.

"Do you remember Brett?" I ask hesitantly, and he rolls his eyes.

"The guy you dated in high school?" he asks hesitantly.

"Yeah, he has his own real estate company in San Francisco. We've been talking, and I think it would be a good change of scenery," I say, and Aidan shakes his head. Brett was always a great guy, and San Francisco is an amazing place. It fits me better than where I am now, living in this awful fantasy life.

"What about Willa?" he asks, and I see the worry in his eyes.

"I'm not saying forever. Just for a while, just until I can get all of this out of the way and move on and be better for her," I say, trying to convince him that this is a good thing, trying to convince myself. He sighs and gets off the floor.

"I'll see you later, Lisa," he says with a small smile, and I nod, and when he leaves, I cry, feeling like I've just lost my last friend.

I'VE BEEN HOME alone for two days. No calls, not from Aunt Dani, Will, or Aidan. The days blend together, and I spend most of them drinking and watching bad daytime TV, searching for anyone who seems to have done worse things than me. I don't see anyone until I watch a daytime show titled "I'm Sleeping with My Stepbrother and My Stepdad."

My doorbell rings. I just ordered a pizza, but this would be record time for delivery. I grab my wallet off the table and swing the door open, and my hand becomes paralyzed when I see her standing there. My breath hitches. It's the first time I've seen her since she found out. My eyes won't leave her no matter how badly I want to look away. I swallow hard, trying to think of what to say. No words seem good enough. She doesn't look angry or sad or anything. Her expression is completely unreadable, and that's scarier than anything.

"Can I come in?" she asks quietly, as if it's the most normal thing in the world, as if she's here all the time and we're friends.

My mind scans through the Lifetime movies I've seen, and I wonder if she's here to kill me.

"Or you can come out. I'd just like to talk to you," she says, maybe reading my mind.

I realize I'm being ridiculous. If she wanted to kill me, I don't think it'd be in broad daylight with her car parked in front of my house. I nod because I'm literally unable to speak. I step back to allow her into my house, and I close the door behind her. She looks around briefly and sits on the couch. I stand nervously.

"You're probably wondering why I'm here," she says.

My stomach drops. "I think I have some idea why," I say carefully.

She nods.

"I know my words are worthless to you," I say hesitantly.

She looks at me, her eyes boring into mine, and I feel uncomfortable. But I know this won't be a comfortable experience—who would expect it to be?

"I just want to know why. I-I think that's why I'm here," she says as if even she's unsure of why she's here.

I sigh. That's a reasonable question. If I was in her shoes, I'd want to know why, but if I was her, I wouldn't want to hear the answer I have to give.

"It just happened," I say quietly, and I see her mouth tighten. I know it's a bullshit answer, but I'm afraid to say any more.

"Can you be a little more specific?" she says stoically.

I let out a deep breath. "I thought I was in love. I was young and stupid, and I thought he was the one for me."

"Even though he was married and Chris's dad?" she asks, her voice raised just slightly.

"Very, very stupid," I admit.

She nods and folds her hands in her lap. "Did he initiate it, or did you?"

This is when my stomach flips in on itself. I get it—she's here to ask the questions she can't bear to ask him, and I hate what I'm about to say.

"I did. I came on to him. I kissed him first, and I seduced him," I say, feeling my cheeks burn.

She looks at me in disbelief. "Why him?" Her voice breaks.

My throat burns from seeing the pain in her face, witnessing firsthand the damage I've caused.

"I thought . . . he made me feel different. Not like a stupid kid whose mom was a whore who lived on the wrong side of town. He looked at me like I was somebody, like I could be whoever I wanted, and it made me feel . . ." I try to think of a phrase that's respectful in some form.

"Alive," she answers with a bitter chuckle.

I nod. "If it helps, I feel like the worst person in the world. You may not believe this, but I looked up to you. I thought you were the greatest mom, that Chris was so lucky."

She raises her hand for me to stop, and tears slide down both our faces.

"Will said that you two had only been . . ." She sighs as if it pains her to continue. "*Seeing* each other for a couple of months."

I nod.

"And it stopped right after Chris saw you together."

I nod again.

She takes a deep breath and lets it out slowly. "Your daughter. She's how old?"

"She just turned seven," I say.

She smiles, biting her lip. She starts to say something but pauses. "There was a night. When you came over and"—she laughs bitterly—"I thought you were looking for Chris, and I told you I was expecting."

I know it's difficult for her to say these words, and I know my answer will be difficult for her to hear if she asks what I think she will.

"Were you pregnant then?" she says quickly and breathlessly.

I nod, and she does the same. She rests her face in her hands, and I hear her whimpering. She raises her face and wipes her tears.

"Do you have any idea how lucky you are, Lisa?" she says through her tears and whimpers. "I would have given anything for my child to be here. For my little girl or little boy to have made it into this world."

I can literally feel both our hearts breaking into a thousand pieces. She's trembling, and I know she's trying to gather her bearings.

"Where is your—where is your daughter?" she asks.

I feel like scum, embarrassed, worthless, and I choke up as well. "She's not here. I don't know if I'm ready for that right now."

She shakes her head and holds her hand to her chest, her expression pained. She stands and looks at me, and I can see the fury she's holding back, and I know it's not because Will—it's because of what I just said. She lets out one last breath and walks to the door. I follow her.

"Will made a mistake with me a long time ago. I know he loves you. A part of me hated you for it because even as good as I made him feel, he could never really be happy with me because of you," I say, and I hope it's some consolation.

"Good-bye, Lisa," she says quietly. Before she turns to go, she grabs my hand, and with tears in her eyes, she smiles. "I forgive you."

With that, she walks out the door. I watch her leave as tears spill down my cheeks.

chapter fifteen

will

IT'S BEEN THREE weeks since it all happened—when I looked into my wife's eyes and realized that she would never look at me the same way again, when my worst nightmare came true, when a truth so ugly that it had repercussions past my home was found out. I knew if Gwen ever found out, there would be no going back.

Living with her now is just that—we live together. We exist, but that's all. She has a wall around herself keeping me at a distance, but I take it because at least she's here. It could be a whole lot worse. She could be gone. I could be alone. My son could stop speaking to me again. Things aren't great, they aren't even good, but I thank God every day because I know they could be so much worse.

Still, it's hard to be in the same house with her and feel her anger, her disappointment, her hurt radiating off her. There are some moments when I can make her smile, when she forgets for a fragment of a second that she hates me, then she hates herself for it. The only time I get to see her not so weighed down and heavy is when she talks to the kids in Chicago. She's so happy when she does. Chris is renewing his vows. The date is set, and Gwen has thrown herself into those plans. They make her happy. I think they distract her and make her forget.

I'm in the yard pulling weeds when the car pulls up. It's Lisa's. I swallow my anger. I can't be mad at her anymore for not keeping our secret, for telling it when everything in my life was just making sense. But I am furious with her for after telling me I have a child, not answering my calls or answering the door when I went over there.

She climbs out of the car and walks toward me. She's still beautiful, but she's still as impulsive and immature as the day we started all those years ago. How could I not see that then?

"It's good to see you," I say sarcastically, standing.

She looks at me, and I see tears in her eyes. I sigh. Her eyes can still make me feel like a cruel jerk.

"I'm sorry I haven't been answering your calls. It was immature and stupid," she says.

I feel my expression soften. I look toward the house, hoping Gwen doesn't look out and see us and get the wrong idea.

"I won't be here long," she says quickly, "and I'm not here to purposely cause trouble."

I look at her a little skeptically. *Purposely.*

"My aunt Dani passed away last week," she says.

"I'm sorry, Lisa. She was a great person." Danielle was always a really cool girl when we were younger, and it seemed as though nothing had changed the last time I saw her.

"Uh, she's who Willa was living with. Dani's husband never really wanted kids, and my grandparents are too old, and Evie's completely out of the question," she says with a bitter laugh.

"What are you saying?" I ask.

"I can't do this, Will," she blurts, tears streaming from her eyes.

"Do what? Be a mother?" I ask, and she nods. "But you're a teacher."

She sighs and laughs. "Guess why I chose that profession."

I shake my head. "Lisa . . ."

She chuckles. "No worries, I turned out to be pretty good at it, but I'm taking a break. I'm going to stay with a friend in San Francisco and just find myself. The new me, the person I make—not Evie's daughter or the woman I chose to be for you."

"You're taking a seven-year-old with you to live with your roommate in San Francisco?" I ask, my anger about to choke me.

She huffs and smiles at me and shakes her head. She walks away, and I follow her.

"You can't be that selfish or self-absorbed. What the hell is wrong with you?" I say angrily.

She whips back around, and her eyes shoot daggers at me. "Can you just shut up and stand right here and try to look like the man I fell in love with instead of his pissed-off cousin?"

I'm floored. She walks to her car and opens the back door, revealing a beautiful little blond girl holding a pink teddy bear. The girl gets out, her eyes on her feet. Lisa squats in front of her.

"Remember the prince I told you about in all of those stories?" Lisa says in a sweet, quiet voice. "This is him—Prince William." Lisa smiles at me, her eyes full of tears.

"Hi," the girl says quietly, and my heart starts to beat out of my chest.

"Hi, beautiful." I feel my throat burn.

"This is who your mommy wants to take care of you," Lisa says, rubbing the girl's hair.

She looks at me, her eyes bright like her mother's, but they're my color. She has my nose, my dimples. She has Lisa's long white-blond hair.

"You knew my mommy?" she asks me shyly.

My eyes cut to Lisa, and she smiles tightly.

"Yeah, I did," I say, giving the girl a warm smile.

Lisa reaches into the car and pulls out a big purple duffle bag with stars on it, and she drops it near my feet. "I had so much fun growing up here. When I was here, it always felt like home. Remember all the stories I told you?" Lisa picks up the girl, and she nods. "Things are going to be so great."

The little girl smiles, and I have to stop tears from coming to my eyes.

"Will, this is Willa," Lisa says, putting the girl down and scooching her forward.

"You're going to call and come visit?" Willa asks.

"We'll see, princess," Lisa says, standing. Her eyes find mine.

I want to say so much to her. Why wouldn't she talk to me about this? Why didn't she give me any time to prepare? But then again, this is Lisa.

"I love you, Willa bear," she says before kissing her cheek and giving her a hug. Lisa walks over to me, and we stare into each other's eyes. She leans over to my ear. "I-I wish I could tell you her favorite food and bedtime story and color and all the things I should know, but I can't, and it will mean more if you find them out on your own anyway." She pulls back. "I hope she understands."

Then Lisa gets back in her car. This doesn't seem real. Is this really happening? When Lisa pulls away with a little wave and Willa starts to cry, I realize that it is.

"Hey, sweetheart, don't cry," I tell Willa. I want to hold her hand, but mine has dirt all over it. "Do you like animals?"

She nods.

"Oh well, you're in the right place. I have horses and pigs and chickens," I say.

"Really?" she asks, giving a heart-breaking smile.

"Yup. Are you hungry?" I ask, and she nods. "Well, let's get you something to eat, and then we can go see all of them, okay?"

She takes my hand, smudged dirt and all, and I wonder if this could be my happiness now.

gwen

I CAN'T BE here anymore. My heart hurts too much.

Today is the day I'm going to do it. I'm going to tell Will I can't do this anymore, can't be around him anymore. The only person I've been able talk to about this is Chris's wife, Lauren. She told me to keep the divorce papers for six months and if I still wanted to do it, to go ahead, but I can't wait any longer.

It all hurts too much. It hurts because I still love him, and I hate myself for that. I know I have to forgive, then things will be so much better for me, but it's hard. I feel slapped in the face all over again sometimes when I look at him. I hate myself for waking up and still wanting him. Each morning, I wake up in our bed and wish he was next to me. How can I still feel this way after everything he's done? Why? Last night I promised myself I'd stop loving him. Today I woke up and saw him and knew I'd lied. I'm tired of lying to myself.

I don't want to hate him, but it's killing me to still love him.

I walk in the front door, the papers in my purse and tears in my eyes. I hear laughter though, and it throws me off. I haven't heard him laugh like that in so long that it almost takes my breath away. I quickly head to the dining room, and my heart almost stops when I see him and a beautiful little girl with blond hair, blue eyes, and his smile. He looks at me, and his smile softens, but it's still there.

"Hi," the little girl says before she takes a bite of a cookie I baked earlier.

She's wearing a milk mustache, and she warms my heart. I know it's her because she looks just like him. I was always afraid that when I saw her, I'd hate her. It's crazy to think you can hate a child, and I never wanted to be that person, but I thought I would. The product of their love, their affair, his betrayal—but she's sitting there, and she's none of that. She's just a cute little girl who looks like the man I love, and I feel sick. I'm confused, and Will sees it.

He stands quickly. "Willa, you finish off these cookies and your pictures, and when I come back, we can go see the horses," he says in a voice reserved for children.

It's soft and kind, and I want to block it from my ears. He ushers me into the living room, and I pull away from him as soon as we're there.

"What is this? Is Lisa here? Are you working things out with her?

Why didn't you say anything?" I say frantically.

"Lisa's gone."

I look at him skeptically. "What do you mean gone? Like she's gone while you spend time with your daughter?"

"No, like gone and she's not coming back for her," he says, looking me in the eye.

I can only swallow hard. "That doesn't make sense."

He gets me to sit on the couch, and he explains that Lisa left for San Francisco, that she feels as though she can't be a mother. She left Willa's birth certificate, medical records, and a box of other documents.

"Is she serious?" I ask, rubbing my temples. This is so much at one time. I don't know how to process it.

"She also left you this," he says. He hands me an envelope that says "For Gwen." "Before you open it, I want you to know how much I love you. I want you to know how much I hope you'll forgive me, but I know this could be a lot, even for you, and I don't want to guilt you into doing anything you don't want to."

With tears in his eyes, he takes my hand and kisses me on the forehead before getting up and heading back into the kitchen. My head is pounding, and I hear blood coursing through my ears. My hands are shaking. I stare at the envelope for so long. I don't know how long exactly, but I know Will and Willa have finished their cookies and gone out to the barn by the time I let out a deep sigh and open the envelope. There're three pieces of paper, one of which says, "Read first." It's folded, so I open it and see that it's handwritten.

I know you said you've forgiven me. I wonder how that's possible after everything I did and all the pain I caused you and your family. You only ever treated me with kindness. It hurt to see in your eyes that you meant it, that it wasn't some bullshit you spouted to feel better about yourself but you really meant it. I was angry that day. I wished you did hate me. It would have made me feel that much better because in that moment, I realized the difference between a girl and a woman. As much as I liked to believe that I was this forward-thinking, beautiful, adventurous woman so many men desired, I realized I was still just my mother's little girl . . . You showed me how a real woman should be, how a good woman is, and I aspire to be that one day. Right now, I'm not, and I know me and Will have taken so much from you already. My selfishness, my needs always came first, and I'm going to do my best to work on that. I promise. But before I do, I have one last selfish request to ask of you. I ask that you don't hate my daughter, that you love her like you would have loved your own, that you give her what she needs to not become another me. That you help Will raise her, guide her, love her. She's the best of both of us, and I don't want either of us to ruin her. I hope that you consider this. If it's too much, I think that Lauren, Chris's wife, would be the next best thing, but you are my first choice.

With sorrow and a plea for forgiveness,

Lisa

I open the other stapled letter. My hear drops when I see it includes the adoption papers she's already signed. Next to the line marked Adoptee is not just Will's name but my own.

one year later

ONE YEAR AGO, I'd never thought I'd have my granddaughter asleep on my chest, my husband asleep by my side, and his daughter between us with her arm over me. I never thought I'd consider his daughter my own. A year ago, I hadn't even known he had a daughter. I hadn't known the pain I'd face. The betrayals I'd discover. Going through that pain was worse than anything I've ever faced.

Six months ago, I'd thought I'd be divorcing my husband as his daughter with my son's best friend was the flower girl in my son's vow renewal. Six months ago, I never thought Lisa, the woman my husband betrayed me with, would be in my prayers, that when she called and checked in briefly and infrequently, I'd smile when I heard her voice, that I'd be grateful for the gift she gave me.

I'd always imagined my house full of laughter and children, but I never imagined it'd happen this way. A year ago, I thought I was losing my son, that my dream of having children run around was lost. But today, with my little granddaughter Caylen; a daughter I call my own, Willa; and my son's wife, Lauren, expecting twins, I know that my dream, though nothing like I'd imagined, has come true.

Some people would never be able to see this as a happy ending. They'd think I was desperate and foolish to forgive. To them, I say that when you're hurt, you want to hold on to that pain as though it's a life jacket. You think that by letting go of that pain, you're saying its cause isn't important. What you don't realize is that pain weighs you down. The hurt suffocates you, wraps around everything good about you.

Animosity is a weapon, and it's not used against the person you can't forgive—it's used against yourself. Your bitterness doesn't hurt them. If they love you, it will hurt them for a while, but it doesn't stop them from living their life. Your anger doesn't make them carry their pain or their hurt any longer. I realized that when Gia told me she hated me and she'd never forgive me. It hurt like hell for a while, but each day it hurt less and less, and there were some days I never even thought about it.

I could have left my husband and been brokenhearted. I'm sure I could have found someone else to love. I don't know what could have happened if I'd chosen differently, but I realized you don't get to choose what happens to you. You do get to choose what happens after though, and the best thing to choose is whatever makes you happy, and I never thought in my wildest dreams happiness would be this way, but life has a way of surprising us all.

the end

Thank you for reading! If you enjoyed *What Happens After please tell a friend and when you get a chance, leave a review where you purchased. If you* would like to be kept up to date on other releases, promotions and give-aways from Portia Moore Books sign up for my newsletter.

Like Portia Moore on Facebook

www.facebook.com/portiamoorebooks or visit *portiamoore.com*

about the author

I'M OBSESSED WITH blowing kisses. I guess that makes me a romantic. I love books and cute boys and reading about cute boys in books. I'm infatuated with the glamour girls of the past: Audrey, Dorthy, Marilyn, Elizabeth.

I'm a self confessed girly girl, book nerd, food enthusiast, and comic book fan. Odd combination huh, you have no idea . . .

other books by portia moore

THE *IF I BREAK* SERIES

If I Break

Before I Break

Almost Broken

Beautifully Broken

acknowledgements

WHEN I FIRST hit the publish button on *If I Break* last year in June, I wasn't sure what would happen. All I knew was that I wanted to share my story with the world. Somewhere in me, I hoped I could write for a living, that I could do what I loved and provide for my family that way. I am so grateful to God that today I can say that it has happened. He blessed me with every one of you. I can't say thank you enough to every reader, blogger, and editor who has helped me bring my stories to life. I cannot express how grateful I am. There are a few people who stand out that I must recognize. Of course my family and friends who still love me even when I'm in crazy-writer mode and yell and become a complete B when I'm interrupted. The ladies over at Sizzling Pages who promoted my first book before anyone even knew I existed. Neda Armini at Ardent Prose who's a godsend. Amy Marxen Jennings who invited me to my very first signing and spread the word about my little series. Lashawnda Glover, my very first beta reader and the person who pushed me to take the chance on this self-publishing thing. Murphy Rae for such a beautiful cover. Cassie Cox and Chelsea Kuheul for taking this from rough draft to readable. ☺

Ivette Pacheco one of my most loyal and vocal street team members. The entire twisted party posse. Love you girls! My lovely sister Reanna who does all the real life and boring things for me that have to be done so I can write. I hope I'm not forgetting anyone. My best friend Sada who, even though she doesn't read, will fool you with the beautiful things she makes and events she plans for my books. All of you guys. I feel so incredibly blessed and, love my books or hate them, I still thank anyone who's spent time in their life making my stories come alive. God bless!

Xoxo
Portia

Made in the USA
Charleston, SC
01 December 2015